Tempt the Night

By Dixie Lee Brown

Tempt the Night
Whatever It Takes
If You Only Knew
When I Find You
All or Nothing

Pamela — So nice to "meet" you! Good luck with your future endeavours.

Tempt the Night

A TRUST NO ONE NOVEL

Dixie Lee Brown (signature)

DIXIE LEE BROWN

AVON IMPULSE
An Imprint of HarperCollinsPublishers

This is a work of fiction. Names, characters, places, and incidents are products of the author's imagination or are used fictitiously and are not to be construed as real. Any resemblance to actual events, locales, organizations, or persons, living or dead, is entirely coincidental.

Excerpt from *Various States of Undress: Georgia* copyright © 2014 by Laura Simcox.
Excerpt from *Make It Last* copyright © 2014 by Megan Erickson.
Excerpt from *Hero By Night* copyright © 2014 by Sara Jane Stone.
Excerpt from *Mayhem* copyright © 2014 by Jamie Shaw.
Excerpt from *Sinful Rewards 1* copyright © 2014 by Cynthia Sax.
Excerpt from *Forbidden* copyright © 2014 by Charlotte Stein.
Excerpt from *Her Highland Fling* copyright © 2014 by Jennifer McQuiston.

TEMPT THE NIGHT. Copyright © 2015 by Dixie Lee Brown. All rights reserved under International and Pan-American Copyright Conventions. By payment of the required fees, you have been granted the nonexclusive, nontransferable right to access and read the text of this e-book on screen. No part of this text may be reproduced, transmitted, downloaded, decompiled, reverse-engineered, or stored in or introduced into any information storage and retrieval system, in any form or by any means, whether electronic or mechanical, now known or hereafter invented, without the express written permission of HarperCollins e-books.

EPub Edition FEBRUARY 2015 ISBN: 9780062328328

Print Edition ISBN: 9780062328335

AM 10 9 8 7 6 5 4 3 2 1

*This book, the fifth in the Trust No One series,
is dedicated to the Blue Ridge Literary Agency.
To Dawn, our fearless leader, who gave me a
chance when a significant number of others passed,
thank you from the bottom of my heart.*

*When an author signs with BRLA, she doesn't just
become another name on the roster—she becomes a
member of the BRLA family. To those awesome and
talented agency writers who accepted me as an author
before I had a single book published, who answered
dumb questions, gave advice and offered friendship,
shared and tweeted until their fingers were blue—you
know who you are—I respect and admire you all.*

Chapter One

THE CRESCENT MOON disappeared slowly beneath a thin veil of clouds, and a shiver rushed through Mac, stopping her in midsentence. What her brother would have referred to as *the heebie-jeebies* raised goose bumps on both of her arms. She hugged herself, the balance of her words forgotten.

Get a grip, girl. There's nothing sinister about the moon. Inhaling a deep breath, she glanced sideways at the man behind the wheel, who studied her with an amused twinkle in his eyes.

She reached out to touch his arm. "Thanks for coercing me into this dumb ride-along tonight. It really was just what I needed."

A scornful laugh burst from him. "Telling you I wasn't going to cook for you ever again if you didn't come doesn't exactly qualify as coercion, Mac. But it's good to see you laugh for a change, even if I am the butt of most of your jokes."

2 DIXIE LEE BROWN

"Don't be a poor sport, Paddy." Indeed, Mac *had* laughed until her cheeks ached. No one could get her out of a funk like Paddy. Clearly, he was concerned about her after her breakup with Douglas, the most recent disaster in a long line of unfortunate relationships he'd suffered through with her. She suspected the real reason behind his invitation was to get her out of the house and back among the living.

"Now see, there's another thing. Do you think, while I'm on duty, you could refrain from calling me that?" He tried without success to hide his teasing smile.

Her gaze swept over him as he flipped on his blinker and turned onto Harbor Road. "I suppose you'd be wantin' me ta call ya Patrick, all proper, would ya?"

One of his eyebrows shot upward as her fake brogue intensified. She shouldn't taunt him, but then someone had to keep him from taking himself so seriously. Although, she had to admit he made a striking figure in his state trooper uniform, his badge displayed prominently on his shirtfront. It'd been his dream for as long as she could remember, and she'd been almost as proud as he was the day he graduated from the Police Academy.

"Actually, I was thinkin' you might call me Officer Callahan."

He hadn't gotten the name all the way out before she hooted and held her sides while she laughed helplessly. After a moment, and Paddy's exasperated sigh, she managed to contain her amusement.

"Maybe…if we hadn't been friends since we were both four years old…no, you'll always be Paddy Callahan—the blond-haired boy who played dress-up with me, who taught me how to cover second base, and who talked me into going skinny-dipping more times than I want to remember."

Best friends all of their lives, Mac knew Paddy better than he knew himself...and vice versa. She'd tagged him with his nickname back when she was too little to wrap her tongue around *Patrick*, and now he was stuck with it. Similarly, he'd rejected Samantha Anne McCallister as being way too long, and she'd been simply *Mac* from that day forward.

Her father had returned from Viet Nam with PTSD, which ruled out the possibility of him ever returning to the front lines. The Air Force, always quick to treat the symptoms instead of the cause, gave him a recruiting job, which he held until he retired two years ago. After Mac's mother quit her nursing position at the hospital, they'd sold out and moved to Anchorage. Now with Mac's brother stationed at Anderson Air Force Base in Guam, Paddy had become the one she leaned on...probably too much. Bless his heart—he never seemed to mind.

The radio crackled to life and they both automatically tuned in to the dispatcher. "Anyone in the vicinity of six thirty-three Lincoln Street, we have a ten-ninety."

Silent alarm in progress. Mac always got a little shot of adrenaline when a call went out sending one of the Alaska State Troopers into an unknown situation. Most nights, she'd have been the one to make that call; if not for this silly ride-along Paddy had talked her into. Eight years on the job gave her seniority among the small staff

4 DIXIE LEE BROWN

of dispatchers she shared her duties with, but she still chose the graveyard shift. Inevitably, the whack jobs and sickos came out after midnight.

Paddy scooped up the mike and held it to his mouth. "Copy that. Sierra Tango eighteen responding."

"Roger, Sierra Tango eighteen." Mac's friend, Lucas, was covering her shift tonight.

"That's just around the corner." Paddy returned the mike to its hanger beside the radio. "Okay, finally, something to do besides drive around and argue with you. We'll go in quiet and dark."

The radio chirped again. "Negative, Sierra Tango eighteen. Simpson and I are right out front. We've got this."

"Oh, hell." Paddy's disappointed sigh clearly indicated his level of boredom with the inactivity of the evening. He grabbed the radio. "Roger that. Sierra Tango eighteen out." He turned toward Mac with a grin. "Your buddy Gallagher…cutting in on my action."

Mac chuffed a contemptuous breath. "He's not *my* buddy."

"Well, you went to the homecoming dance with him our senior year."

"I can't believe you! That was eight years ago. Give me a break. Besides, that was before I found out how horny he was." She'd never told Paddy just how awful that night had been.

He snickered and reached toward her, pushing her long brunette waves behind her shoulder, his eyes asking forgiveness for bringing the whole thing up. Mac met his gaze, and memories of the two of them growing up

TEMPT THE NIGHT 5

next door to each other, inseparable all through school, filled her mind. He was the one person she could always count on—no matter what. She loved him like a brother and could never stay irritated with him for more than two seconds.

Paddy moved his hand back to the steering wheel, hit his blinker, and turned left onto Lincoln Street.

"What are you doing?" It was a foolish question, and she knew the answer. Except for her misguided decision to attend college in Anchorage, ended by a disastrously short career as an exotic dancer, she'd lived in Sitka all her life. The address the dispatcher had given was home to Wagner's Fish Packing Plant, and it occupied most of the next block.

Paddy grinned and winked. "Just a little drive-by—making sure they don't need backup." He slowed as they approached the intersection, then braked sharply. "What the hell?"

Mac followed his gaze. The packing plant was on the right, an Alaska State cruiser parked on the street, and three guys stood in front of the entry, illuminated by the streetlight on the corner. "Do you recognize them?" Sitka was a small town, but she'd never seen these men before.

Paddy shook his head slowly. "Those are automatic weapons they're packing." He killed the lights and made a quick left into a dark, sparsely populated lot, parked in the farthest corner, and grabbed the mike. "Dispatch, this is Sierra Tango eighteen. I'm at six thirty-three Lincoln Street. Be advised of a possible ten-thirty-two. Are you in contact with Gallagher and Simpson?"

6   DIXIE LEE BROWN

"Negative. No contact since they entered the building."

"Copy that, dispatch. We're going to need some more backup out here. I'll have a look around." Paddy placed the mike back on its hanger.

Lucas immediately put out the call for additional help, but Mac only heard bits and pieces of the thread. If she hadn't taken the night off, she'd be the one making that call, sending backup to Paddy's location. Man, it seemed so different—clinical—on that end. Out here it was just plain scary. Her heart pounded in her ears, and her stomach ached with dread. This wasn't what she'd anticipated when Paddy had convinced her to ride along with him. She was a complete coward. *Oh my God!* She couldn't breathe. She was hyperventilating.

Suddenly, he gripped her hand, and his quiet, calm voice broke through her panic. "Remember what I told you. Lock the door when I leave. Under no circumstances should you attempt to leave the car or follow me. Got it?"

She nodded. Questions tumbled over themselves, fighting to be asked. Why couldn't he wait for the backup? What did he plan to do? He was coming back safely, right? She clamped her lips closed. This was his job, and he was good at it, so she shut up and let him do it.

He laid her hand on her leg and gave it a pat as he smiled. Then he opened his door and stepped out. She followed his movements to the rear of the car, where he opened the trunk and closed it a few seconds later. When he appeared at her side window to point at the door lock, he carried his pump-action shotgun.

TEMPT THE NIGHT 7

Mac locked the doors and returned his wave just before he walked away. As he ducked into the alley leading to the rear of the plant, a chill shook her from head to toe and drew her eyes to the crescent moon that now hung brazenly in the night sky.

She fought down the dread that rose like bile in her throat and turned partway in the seat so she could more easily see the front of the plant. The three armed men had moved single-file through the entryway a few minutes ago. The sidewalk was empty now. She alternated between watching the door and looking up and down the street. Where was the backup Lucas had called? *Hurry up. Let me see those pretty blue lights.* The waiting was excruciating, and after a while, she had to physically stop herself from climbing out of the vehicle.

Her fingers twitched to grab the radio and ask Lucas what was taking so long, but that was too public. She scooped up her purse from the floor, rifled through it for her cell phone, and dialed the nonemergency number.

"Dispatch." It was six rings before Lucas answered. Must be a busy night in the district.

"Lucas, where's that backup? What's taking so long?" Mac strove to attain the same level of detachment she exhibited on the job but failed miserably.

"Mac? We've got a regular free-for-all out there tonight. A riot broke out over on Waterfront Street near the new strip club…thirteen hurt so far. Every uniformed man we've got is trying to get a handle on that. I'll get someone there as soon as I can." Lucas was in his

8 DIXIE LEE BROWN

early forties and had worked the radio most of his life. Nothing ever seemed to chip away at his calm.

That's right. She'd heard that call go out earlier. Paddy had been on the outskirts of town checking out a domestic disturbance at the time or he'd have responded to that location too. "I know you're doing the best you can, Lucas. It's just…it's way different from this perspective. This ride-along was a really dumb—"

A blast of automatic weapons fire ripped through the quiet street. Mac fumbled with the phone, and it disappeared between the seat and the console. She shoved her hand through the gap and felt for the device but went still as movement caught her eye. Her gaze shot toward the front of the packing plant in time to see Simpson and Gallagher exit the building and jog toward their cruiser.

Seconds after their car laid rubber and took off, the three men who'd walked in with rifles in their arms reappeared with them slung over their backs. They paused and peered around carefully. Mac ducked as they looked her way, even though it would have been nearly impossible to see her in the dark so far away, especially while they stood under a street light. It still unnerved her. She breathed a sigh of relief when they got into a vehicle a few doors down, started it, and drove away.

Thank God. It's over. Her gaze never left the alley as she waited anxiously for Paddy to come back.

But he didn't. Five minutes…ten minutes…fifteen minutes. Mac was kidding herself. Something was terribly wrong, and in spite of Paddy's orders, she couldn't sit there any longer. She should have gone to find him as soon as those men left. Truth was, she'd been too scared to move.

Now the only thing on her mind was getting in that building to look for Paddy. He could give her hell for leaving the car later. She opened the passenger door and slid out, then reached back inside to grab the flashlight off the dash and shine it beneath the seat until she located her phone. Pocketing it, she glanced around carefully, noticing how deathly quiet the street was. It was nearly three o'clock in the morning. Even the drunks would be sleeping it off by now.

Mac took a deep breath, hoping to bolster her confidence, and crossed the parking lot, keeping a sharp eye out for any sign of life before stepping into the street. She ended up in front of the entrance to the building way before she was ready to go inside.

The only thing that got her to move was the growing knowledge that Paddy had to be in trouble. She tried the door handle, relieved when it opened for her. After everything else she'd seen tonight, the fact that whoever those men were had left the door unlocked in the middle of the night wasn't even noteworthy. Just inside, she flipped on the flashlight and shone it into the darkness. The long room before her smelled slightly of fish and was filled with stainless steel tables, conveyor belts, machinery, and huge vats. On the far side was a set of wooden stairs leading to Cecil Wagner's windowed office, which overlooked the plant floor. It was stone quiet, to the point where she could hear herself breathing.

"Paddy?" Her whisper was shockingly loud in the silent room, but she'd have to call louder if she expected him to hear her. "Paddy, where are you?"

Thump.

Mac's gaze darted to the room at the top of the stairs. Had she really heard something? Or was it only her heart pounding in her ears?

Thump.

That was definitely something, although, if it was Paddy, why didn't he simply show himself? She hurried across to the stairs, took them at a jog, and stopped outside the small office with her hand resting on the doorknob. More afraid than she'd ever been in her life, she pushed it open.

Immediately, she heard a raspy, wheezing, gurgling sound that chilled her to the bone. She shone her light across the floor and almost dropped it when the spotlight landed on Paddy, lying on his back. One fisted hand raised and dropped, again making the noise she'd heard from downstairs. So much blood…everywhere.

Mac choked back a sob and rushed to him, the knees of her jeans soaking up his blood as she knelt beside him. *An ambulance.* Desperately, she fumbled for her phone.

Paddy was badly hurt. Two bullet wounds in his chest and one in his throat. There may have been more, but that was all she could see. The one in his throat was keeping him from talking, although it didn't stop him from trying. His eyes were open and locked on hers, desperation written there.

TEMPT THE NIGHT 11

Mac had to hold it together. She was all he had right now, and she wasn't doing him any good being on the verge of a crying jag.

Without taking her eyes off Paddy's, she dialed Lucas's number again. "Paddy's hurt. We need an ambulance."

"Mac? Are you still at Wagner's?" Lucas's voice rose for a second before his customary calm returned. "I'll call it in. Stay on the line, Mac."

"No...I can't. I have to help him. Tell them to hurry, Lucas." She dropped the phone and smiled at Paddy even though her heart was aching. "They'll be here in no time. Now, let's get this bleeding stopped." She glanced around and spotted a stack of towels near a sink. Jumping up, she grabbed several of them. As she knelt beside him again and began applying pressure to his wounds, he put his hand to his throat and formed words with his lips, but, except for his frustrated grunts, no sounds came out.

Mac placed her fingers on his lips and held his gaze until he quieted. "Tell me later, after they get you patched up." There were a thousand questions she wanted to ask, but now wasn't the time.

The fear that grew in his eyes almost did her in. Slowly, he slid his hand to his badge and pulled it free. He pressed it against her hand frantically, until she had to leave the towel and take it from him. Next he reached for his gun and became highly agitated when it wasn't in his holster.

"It's okay, Paddy. It's by the door. I saw it on my way in." What had happened to his shotgun?

If she had let him, he would have crawled over to retrieve it. After ordering him to lie still, she went and

12 DIXIE LEE BROWN

got the weapon. He was pulling a business card from his front shirt pocket when she knelt beside him again, and he shoved it at her along with the gun she tried to put in his holster. She had no idea why he wanted her to have those items, only that he was calmer when she gave in and held them in her hands.

Too calm. Paddy's eyes fell shut and his breathing reduced to a shallow inhale with no apparent exhale. *Where was that damn ambulance?* Didn't they know her best friend's life was leaking out through her fingers?

"Stay with me, Paddy. You hear? You're going to owe me big-time when you're back on your feet. I'm going to take you up on that trip to Hawaii you're always yammering about." She was only talking to give him something to hold on to, but hope sparked within her when a tiny trace of a smile flitted across his face.

Mac heard something downstairs and then voices. The backup Lucas had called for had finally arrived. She was about to scramble to her feet, go to the door, and holler for them when Paddy caught her wrist with more strength than he should have had. The gaze that met hers was clear and purposeful.

"Help has arrived." She tried to pull free, but he held her tightly and slowly wagged his head from side to side. Glancing toward the door again, she tensed. "Do you think the perps are coming back?"

Paddy nodded. Then, with deliberate intent, he motioned toward the other side of the room with his eyes, once...twice...three times, and mouthed a word she couldn't mistake.

Hide.

Her gaze turned in the direction he indicated. Like any other kids who'd grown up in Sitka and spent any time with old man Wagner in his fish packing plant, they were both intimately familiar with his office.

She faced Paddy again. "You want me to hide in the dumbwaiter?"

He nodded and swept his eyes that direction again, as though trying to hurry her.

"You're crazy if you think I'm going to leave you." She turned away as tears filled her eyes.

Still grasping her wrist, he pulled her down and toward his face until his lips hovered by her ear. "Do… it…for…me."

The words were nothing more than breaths exhaled one after another, but there was no mistaking his meaning. What shattered her into a million pieces, however, were the tears in his eyes when she raised her head and looked at him.

It was an impossible situation. How could she leave him? She wasn't strong enough to carry him, and she couldn't ignore the request that obviously meant so much to him. "Okay. I'll do what you say…but don't get used to it." With her heart ripping open inside her chest, she held his gaze until he released her, then she stumbled to her feet. With footsteps creaking on the stairs, Mac tried to give him his handgun, but he again shook his head and motioned toward the side wall. Finally she gave up, her vision blurring as she hurried toward the dumbwaiter.

14 DIXIE LEE BROWN

Mac threw open the miniature overhead door and curled herself into the small, dark space. Obviously, she'd been much younger the last time she'd played in here. She hadn't remembered it being such a tight fit. Hoping the old contraption would hold her weight, she shoved the door closed, placed Paddy's weapon and flashlight on her lap, and waited. One tiny Plexiglas window gave her a limited view of the room.

She jumped when the door across the room flew inward and banged against the wall. Two figures walked in, but without the aid of her flashlight, she couldn't tell who they were. One of them flipped on the overhead light, and a dim fluorescent glow pushed the shadows back. Gallagher and Simpson stood over Paddy, and Mac practically screamed her elation, until Gallagher's words stopped her cold.

"Where is she, Callahan? We know she called you an ambulance, so she must be here somewhere. Too bad you had to have her along tonight. It's really *your* fault she has to die." He turned toward his partner and smirked. "Callahan's not very talkative tonight."

Simpson moved alongside him. "We won't get anything from him. We'll have to find her on our own." He pulled his weapon and stood over Paddy. A second later, he fired one shot, point blank, into her best friend's chest.

Mac slammed both hands against the window, wanting to erase the image that was now seared on her retinas. "Noooo!" The wail escaped with the force of her sorrow behind it. When both troopers jerked their gazes toward her, she understood the magnitude of her foolish mistake.

TEMPT THE NIGHT 15

These men wanted to kill her.

And although the reason behind that escaped her, Paddy had known and had sacrificed his life to give her a chance. If she didn't get away, his death would be in vain.

Frantically, she searched for the button old man Wagner had installed on the inside of the makeshift elevator. As Simpson and Gallagher started toward her, she jabbed the switch, and the old apparatus began its descent. Her last view from the window was Paddy's still form and the flying feet of the two dirty cops as they scurried out the door, no doubt on their way to intercept her in the kitchen downstairs.

Luckily, Simpson wasn't from around here, and Gallagher hadn't chosen to hang out with her group of friends when they were kids, so neither of them knew Mr. Wagner's secret. They'd find the dumbwaiter in the kitchen all right, but she'd be long gone.

Cecil Wagner was a womanizing old fool, married to the toughest female logger Sitka ever knew—tough but apparently not that smart. Cecil came and went on his trysts via the dumbwaiter and a special stairwell he'd had built just for that purpose. Sadly, Mrs. Wagner had been the only one who didn't know. Cecil had made a game of his frequent disappearances—one that included the neighborhood kids who were used as lookouts and bribed well for their silence. In hindsight, Mac wasn't proud of helping lie to Mrs. Wagner, but at the moment, she was exceedingly glad to have the information that would get her safely away.

She pushed the button to stop the machine, shoved the door open, and stepped down into a small enclosure

16 DIXIE LEE BROWN

no bigger than a coat closet. Making sure she had Paddy's gun, his badge, and the business card he'd given her safely stuffed in her pockets, she closed the door and started the conveyance downward again. She'd love to see the looks on their faces when they opened her hiding place and found her gone, but she had to take advantage of the contraption's slow descent to make her escape.

Moving toward the opposite side of the small box she could just barely stand up in, she used the flashlight to find the lever. Mac pulled it, and a hidden door to the outside silently popped open. She peered out cautiously, pleased to see that the tall timber still circled the ladder built in the shape of a trellis that descended into the darkness. Carefully, she closed and secured the secret entrance before slipping quietly to the ground and moving deeper into the stand of trees.

She couldn't even think about Paddy. His death was a sorrow that would incapacitate her, and she couldn't give in to it now. Where could she go and be safe? It would be too dangerous to return home. Simpson and Gallagher would surely search for her there. Were there other dirty cops in on whatever had gone down tonight? How could she trust any of them after what she'd seen? The backup they'd requested had never arrived…or the ambulance. Did that make her friend and coworker, Lucas, suspect too? No…she'd never believe that, but whomever she went to for help she'd likely be putting in danger, as well.

On impulse, she pulled out the card Paddy had forced into her hand and shone her flashlight on the lettering. It was one of his business cards, but when she flipped it

TEMPT THE NIGHT 17

over, she saw neat handwriting that she didn't recognize was centered on the back.

Meeting Brady Friday, midnight, 110 Gardner Street.
Thanks for watching my back! M.

No clue what that meant, but if Paddy thought it important enough to hand her moments before he died, you'd better believe she was going to be at that meeting and find out why.

That didn't help her now, though. She shivered in her light fleece jacket. The dim glow of her watch revealed the time—three forty-five a.m. First light wasn't far off, but she had eighteen hours to kill before the midnight meeting. Considering the fact that she was covered with blood, people would be suspicious of her at best. At the worst, they'd call the cops, and with her luck, Gallagher and Simpson would respond. She had to get out of sight before someone spotted her.

Uncle Benji's fishing boat. It was docked at the marina, and he was in Anchorage for the month. No one would think to look for her there, but she needed to go back to Paddy's car for her purse. She'd eventually need money and her ID.

Mac made her way back to the shadow of the packing plant. Then she took a wide detour and approached Paddy's car from the opposite side. She searched both sides of the street and the parking area for Gallagher and Simpson's cruiser, but it was nowhere to be seen. They might double back to try and spot her, and she wasn't taking

18 DIXIE LEE BROWN

any chances. Quickly, she grabbed her purse and left the car behind.

The first gray hues of dawn were spreading on the eastern horizon as she hoofed it to the marina, staying in the shadows as much as possible. She found Uncle Benji's boat and climbed below deck. Then she slid to the floor, hugged her knees to her chest, and finally gave in to the waves of grief that rolled over her.

Chapter Two

THE WHITE LACE curtain at the upstairs window flicked open a fraction of an inch and, a heartbeat later, dropped back in place, confirming his suspicions. Jim Brady lowered his night-vision binoculars. His heart rate kicked up a notch as anticipation slowly woke those parts of his body that had gone to sleep in the last two hours. Finally—something out of the ordinary. But the ache in the pit of his stomach insistently warned that this new player was *not* the woman he'd chased halfway across the friggin' state—the one who was supposed to meet him here tonight.

For what had to be the hundredth time, he scanned the deserted street in front of him, searching the dark shadows and natural hiding places, and then inspected the field of vision in the rearview mirror of his rented car. He scraped his fingers through his close-cropped hair, and a frustrated sigh echoed loudly in the silence.

20 DIXIE LEE BROWN

Brady fingered his cell phone, undecided. He should call his boss and check in, but what new information could he give Joe Reynolds at this point in the game? Brady had a front row seat, and he still didn't have a fucking clue. Besides, the minute he touched a button on his iPhone, it would light up like a friggin' Christmas tree. Whoever was keeping watch from that window would spot him for sure, and Brady didn't need to be noticed until he determined who was skulking in the shadows.

Maria Alverez was the reason he'd been sitting in a cold car, watching a dark house while he slowly lost all the feeling in his ass. Her five-year-old son, Marco, rescued less than two weeks ago from a Mexican drug cartel by Joe's band of mercenaries, including Brady, was eager to go home to his mother. It was a desire Brady understood only too well. Having returned from Iraq with PTSD of a violent and unpredictable nature, he'd made the decision to protect his own family by staying away from them. Lucky for Marco, *his* wish would come true. Brady would make sure of it.

The simple-sounding mission had proved more difficult than he could have imagined, however. Brady had been looking for Marco's mother for the better part of a week but had yet to catch sight of the woman. Finally, a midnight call to Joe from a woman claiming to be Maria Alverez led Brady to the small town of Sitka. He'd arrived two nights ago and checked into a motel. The next morning, a note shoved under his door listed the address of a cottage on the Gulf, a time—midnight Friday—and the initial *M*.

TEMPT THE NIGHT   21

He was there—where the hell was she?

The hard truth was it could have been anyone who called Joe, and there was no guarantee the note was legitimate either. Even so, it was the only lead Brady had at the moment and was not one he was willing to pass up. Rescuing Marco from the Mexican cartel should have been the hard part of this operation, but it was starting to look easy compared to finding Maria. Of course, it didn't help that Brady had promised the kid he'd find his mother. He'd always been a damn sucker for the lost and defenseless.

The possibility that it was Maria lurking behind those curtains warred with Brady's instincts. Whatever her reasons, it appeared she was on the run. Everything about her disappearance had been cautious and careful. It was doubtful she would knowingly back herself into a corner where she'd have to fight her way out. He didn't know Maria well—had only met her once, but a woman as small as she was, with no obvious defensive skills, wouldn't stand a chance against…say…a man like himself who stood between her and the exit. His gut told him it wasn't her who waited covertly in that darkened room on the second floor, which could mean only one thing: someone else was waiting for her too—someone who no doubt believed he had all his bases covered, that he could handle himself well enough to come out on top in any confrontation.

He wouldn't be the first man Brady had met who thought that. Only time would tell if he was right.

It was ten after midnight. If Maria had set this meeting up, it looked like she wasn't planning to show.

22 DIXIE LEE BROWN

Maybe she'd already been here and knew there were too many people waiting for her. In any case, Brady had to clear that upstairs room and find out what the hell was going on.

He fished out his pocket knife and inserted the tip of the blade beneath one corner of the plastic dome light cover on the car's roof, wiggling it around the edge until the cover dropped into his lap. A quick wrench on the tiny bulb ensured the car would remain dark when he opened the door.

The curtain lay lifeless and undisturbed in the window directly above the front door. He did his visual check of the street one more time before easing his tall frame into the passenger seat, opening the door, and rolling onto the ground beside the car. He'd parked two blocks away on the opposite side of the street, but judging by the lack of activity he'd witnessed since he'd been there, any movement would likely be noticed, especially by the watcher in the upstairs window. If he gave a convincing enough performance, perhaps he'd look as though he belonged out on the street at zero dark hundred.

Brady pushed to his feet and ran—a just-home-from-the-office-and-knocking-down-some-stress run. But anyone really paying attention would notice he wasn't dressed for a jog, so the sooner he got out of sight the better. Two blocks down, he crossed the street and followed a wooden fence to the alley that would take him directly to the rear of the house with the white lace curtains.

He slowed as he approached, waiting and watching for any sign of activity inside or out. All appeared deserted, which made him wonder if he'd imagined the furtive movement in the upstairs window. Still, he knew better than to ignore his gut, and his gut said someone waited there.

Four concrete steps led to the back door and what appeared to be an enclosed porch. He kept to the shadows beside the steps and studied the knob, then removed a small metal container from his pocket and chose a pick. Apparently, security in Sitka was fairly lax. The lock might as well not have been there for all the time it took him to open the door and step into the dark interior.

Brady slid his handgun out of its holster and clicked off the safety. The enclosed porch opened into a tiny kitchen. The small living area beyond held the staircase on the south wall. He stopped to listen every few feet. No creaks, no footsteps, no voices. Moving without making a sound had been a necessary part of his training, but few had had the incentive or determination that he and his fellow SEALs did to make it part of who they were.

A nervous tic in Brady's eye interrupted his focus, and he blinked impatiently. He drew in a deep breath, held it for a few seconds, then let it escape slowly. At the foot of the stairs, he stopped again. This is where he'd be the most vulnerable. Once he started up the stairs, someone above could spot him without being seen. He'd be an easy target with nowhere to go but up or down.

His gun leveled straight ahead, he began his ascent, careful to stay as close to the wall as possible. He moved quickly and silently, raking his gaze over the shadows at the top of the stairs. The moon's feeble light shone

24   DIXIE LEE BROWN

through a skylight above the landing, creating a ghostly aura. An eerie silence lay like a thick fog over the house.

Two more steps and he'd reach the top. Once he made that last step, the room with the lace curtains would be behind him and he'd have to circle around the stairwell. No guarantee the intruder was still in that room, but it was as good a place to start as any.

His heightened senses were focused on detecting anything that breathed within these walls other than himself. As his foot came down on the second step from the top, the soft brush of feet on carpet above and behind him made his skin prickle. He crouched, half turned, and brought the weight of his right foot to rest beside his left.

Shit! The aged floorboards beneath him creaked and groaned with his unplanned movement. Brady dove for the landing and hit the floor facedown, then crab-crawled silently to the relative safety of the shadows just outside the room overlooking the street.

The barely discernible footsteps had come from inside that same room. Brady needed the intruder in good enough shape to answer questions—and he had a shitload of them. Unfortunately, he'd lost the element of surprise with one careless step. Now, the trick would be getting the trespasser to agree to talk without anyone getting hurt.

He pushed to his feet, gun in hand, and advanced toward the doorway, stopping outside the threshold to get the lay of the land. Straight across from him, the window where the watcher had stood now stared vacantly back at Brady. The moonlight threw slivers of illumination halfway across the floor. Dark drapes hung to each side of the lace curtains.

On his left was a closet, its door standing open, a bed, a chest of drawers with a large mirror. To his right, a wooden rocker and an antique armoire. The room was deathly quiet—too quiet. Not many places to hide, unless one was adept at hiding in plain sight.

The hair on his neck was standing on end, and his skin tingled with the certainty that his target was close. He remained still and swept his gaze slowly around the room. Lifting his head, he breathed in, sampling the air.

So unexpected was the aroma that teased his senses, it was a few seconds before the correct answer settled into place. A *woman* hid somewhere in the darkness, smelling subtly of vanilla and apple pie. Sweat tinged the air as well. She was afraid. And blood? Was she wounded?

Regret stole over him, and he frowned. His mama hadn't raised him to terrorize women, but he'd learned the hard way that the fairer sex could be far more dangerous than any man he'd ever tangled with.

A sound jerked his gaze toward the curtain. He remained immobile as he scrutinized the floor, the bed, and the shadows that constantly changed with the clouds passing in front of the moon. A lump of blackness caught his attention at the base of the heavy curtain. When next the moon's rays shone their fullness through the window, he confirmed his first impression.

The tips of a pair of lady's shoes peeked from beneath the heavy fabric. Whether the shoes held a pair of feet,

26 DIXIE LEE BROWN

he couldn't be sure, but the situation called for him to proceed as though they did.

Silently, Brady stole across the room until he stood directly in front of the shoes. He jerked the curtain aside, shoved behind it, and came up empty. The next instant, a gun barrel pressed against the small of his back. He froze, a grudging admiration forming for his opponent who'd managed to get within arm's length without alerting him.

"Looking for someone?" Her soft voice trembled slightly.

"I seem to have found someone." She was holding herself together in spite of the fact that she was afraid. Brady almost felt sorry for her, because it was going to get worse before it got better.

"Drop your weapon and kick it away." She nudged him with the gun.

Brady raised both hands to shoulder level, holding his handgun with two fingers in front of him. "Do you mind if I don't drop it? Just in case it was to go off accidentally. Don't want to attract attention, do we?" He knelt and placed the gun carefully on the floor and shoved it away from him.

She took a breath, and Brady could almost feel her relax even though it was way too optimistic to consider the battle over. She apparently didn't know that, but she was about to find out.

Starting to rise, he swung his arm back, grabbed one of her bare feet, and jerked it out from under her, flipping her ass over teakettle. She landed hard on her back, and all the breath whooshed from her lungs.

Brady was on her in an instant, straddling her, pinning her hands to the floor while he pried the gun from her fingers. She struggled with more fight than he'd expected. The fear in her light-colored eyes stabbed him through, and a rare bout of conscience bit him in the ass.

He had to give her credit—she didn't give up easily, but she eventually wore herself out and went still beneath him.

Immediately, he loosened his grip on her wrists. "Finished?"

Her gaze narrowed. "Let me go. I'm a state trooper." As though her body sought to negate her words, a tremor vibrated the length of her.

He studied her eyes, searching for the truth even as instinct told him she was lying. "Is that the story you want to stick with? You don't act like any cop I've ever met."

She tried to jerk her hands free again, and he tightened his hold, stretching her arms above her head. An impatient breath escaped her full, pink lips. "Tell me… what's a state trooper supposed to act like?"

"Well, for one, they don't usually hide in the dark and surprise people. The ones I've known prefer a more direct approach. And they always seem a little too cocky—arrogant even."

His gaze swept over her and homed in on her partially open mouth. Her breaths escaped in hot bursts, and the tip of her tongue appeared briefly and wet her bottom lip. Her heart-shaped face was framed by dark-colored hair. That's all he could tell by the light of the moon's muted rays, but he found himself wanting to reach out and touch the flowing curls that collected above her breasts. She was a pleasing mixture of firm softness where his ass met her midsection, and the feel of her between his legs elicited a distracting response from his lower regions.

Brady forced his gaze back to her eyes. "I'm afraid you'll have to prove it. Cops still carry ID, right?"

Her lips thinned. "Let go of my hands, and I'll get my badge for you."

He gave a short laugh. What was her game anyway? "That seems reckless. Tell me where it is, and *I'll* get it."

Her perfectly groomed eyebrows flew up toward her hairline. "You put one hand inside my clothes, and I'll have to kill you."

Brady chuckled. "That's better. You're catching on to that cocky, arrogant thing." He had to force what was undoubtedly a goofy grin into submission. If looks could have done the job, he'd have dropped dead on the spot.

He didn't need to search for her credentials. This girl was no more an Alaska State Trooper than he was. Now all he needed to know was why she was pretending to be one.

Brady tugged her wrists toward him and folded them on her stomach, circling them loosely with one hand.

She watched him with distrust and wariness evident in her frown, but she seemed to breathe a little easier.

"What's your name, sugar?"

"Well, it's not *sugar*, sweetheart." She hesitated a second, apparently weighing whether the truth or a lie would serve better. "Samantha McCallister."

"Nice to meet you, Sam." Brady pushed to his feet in one motion, pulling her with him. He tugged her toward the bed. "Have a seat while we sort this out."

TEMPT THE NIGHT 29

Her gaze darted to the open door. He hadn't expected anything less. One eye on her, he inspected the gun he'd taken from her. The safety was still on. Odd for a woman making the bold play she'd tried. He tucked the handgun in his belt.

"I'm not going to hurt you, Sam…unless you force me to. I just need some answers." Like why in the hell was she here when she was so obviously in over her head?

"Please don't call me that." She watched him guardedly as she moved to the edge of the bed and dropped down. Her hands came up to cover her face in a gesture of defeat.

Her moment of vulnerability poured ice water on his small victory, and compassion warred with his need to learn what she was doing here, hiding and waiting for Maria. Brady turned away to retrieve his weapon from the floor, put the safety on, and returned it to his holster beneath his jacket before he looked at her again.

The moon unfurled its full strength for a few seconds, catching her in its beam and allowing him his first glimpse of her bloodstained clothes. *Holy shit!* It was clear she'd been involved in something violent, and worry for Maria was nearly eclipsed by concern for this girl who hadn't even taken the safety off her weapon before engaging him.

He stepped in front of her and waited until she turned apprehensive eyes on him. "Okay, so don't call you Sam. What *would* you like me to call you?"

"Mac. Everyone calls me Mac." Her voice broke on the last part. She cleared her throat and glared at him in a clear attempt to prove how tough she was.

30 DIXIE LEE BROWN

Brady wasn't buying her act. He stared back until she dropped her gaze.

Disgusted with himself for purposefully intimidating her, he had the crazy impulse to reach out and lift her chin, which he rejected as not being in either of their best interests. On the other hand, they weren't going to get anywhere if this battle of wills didn't come to an end. Somebody needed to take the high road, and it looked like it would have to be him.

After another moment of silence, he knelt beside her and looked into eyes so tortured that he lost track of what he was going to say. She flinched away from him, and he let her, figuring he'd had that coming.

"Are you hurt?" He found his tongue but was blindsided by an unsettling protectiveness. Literally forcing himself to keep his hands off of her, he resisted the impulse to draw her into his arms and shield her from whatever demons chased her.

"What?" Obviously, that wasn't what she'd expected him to ask.

"You're covered with blood. I'm asking if you've been hurt."

She wagged her head slowly. "It's...not mine." Renewed anguish rolled across her expression, and she bit her lip.

"Mac, did you hurt someone?" He hoped to hell that wasn't the case.

"No, of course not." A spark of anger ignited in her eyes, and her gaze narrowed. "Who are you, anyway?" She dropped her head and raked both hands through her hair.

TEMPT THE NIGHT 31

There was no reason not to tell her. Maybe he could foster some trust by leveling with her. "Name's Jim Brady. I was supposed to meet—"

"Brady?" Her head snapped up. "Who were you meeting? Do you know anything about Officer Patrick Callahan?"

"Never heard of him. I was supposed to meet a woman."

She fished in her pants pocket, brought out a crumpled, bloodstained card, and shoved it toward him. "*M*? Are you here to meet *M*?"

Brady took the card and studied it. Then he reached for his wallet and produced a slip of paper that contained the same neat handwriting. He held it out to her. "Was that note for your friend, Officer Callahan?"

Mac nodded, still studying the paper he'd handed her.

"Want to explain why you're here and not Callahan?" Brady fought down a jolt of anger at the man who would let her walk into an unknown situation alone.

They both froze as someone rapped loudly on the door downstairs. "State troopers. Open up." The gruff command from below drove the curiosity from her eyes, replacing it with a level of anxiety quickly approaching panic. Her breathing became instantly erratic, and Brady could practically hear her heart pounding as she jumped to her feet. He placed one hand on her arm, held his finger to his lips, and strode silently to the window.

He barely flicked the curtain aside and saw the two uniforms standing on the steps at the front of the house. "It's okay. They really are troopers."

32 DIXIE LEE BROWN

"You don't understand. They'll kill me." Her eyes begged him to believe her.

So many unanswered questions tumbled in his head, yet in the split second he had to decide, he went with his gut. This woman had been involved in something devastating, yet still found the courage to search for the writer of the note she carried, taking Brady on in the process. Why that was so important to her was only part of the mystery. The bottom line was he believed her. Instinct said the fear and pain in her eyes were genuine. If he was wrong, eluding a cop would probably be the least of his worries.

He strode toward her. "Grab your shoes, and let's get out of here."

Chapter Three

ONLY MOMENTS AGO, desperation had brought the lie to her lips, even knowing no one in their right mind would believe Mac was a cop. Brady hadn't either, so what made her think he'd believe the state troopers downstairs were out to kill her?

That he *did* threw her for a moment. He had no reason to trust her, any more than she did him. They'd known each other for less than ten minutes—and *known* in this instance was highly exaggerated—yet he grabbed her arm and dragged her toward the landing, reaching behind him to remove his weapon from his belt.

Mac pulled back, bracing her feet, when it became clear he intended to descend the stairs and go right through the middle of Gallagher and Simpson. That would be crazy, especially with a perfectly good escape route on the second floor.

34 DIXIE LEE BROWN

She tugged on his arm until he turned. "Across the hall. There's a window in the other bedroom—that's how I got in."

Without hesitation, Brady switched direction and headed for the door to the right of the landing. She followed him inside, and he closed it behind them.

Not daring to relax for a moment until they'd put sufficient distance between themselves and the two downstairs, she rushed to the window and shoved it open. The roof sloped off steeply toward the sixty-foot white fir that grew near the edge of the overhang. Mac glanced over her shoulder to where Brady had been and found him right beside her. She tried to hide the gasp that escaped, but his apologetic grin clearly said she hadn't fooled anyone.

"It's a bit of a jump from the roof, but it's an easy climb to the ground. Can you make it?" Oh damn. Out of breath and talking nonsense to boot. His brief smile called her on it. He obviously couldn't believe she'd just asked that any more than she could. The man was fit, muscular, and rock solid. It was plain to see he probably worked out every day, and not just for a hobby either, but like his life depended on how far he could run, how fast he could climb, and whether or not he'd have the upper hand in a fight.

Mac looked into the most intent and determined eyes she'd ever seen. Surprise jolted her. She was about to put her life in the hands of this stranger whom she knew nothing about. Why should she care whether he made it to the ground? He could be the reason *M* wanted Paddy to watch her back, in which case Mac was probably already

TEMPT THE NIGHT 35

in over her head…but for some reason she couldn't put her finger on, she wanted to trust Brady.

She needed him for his connection to *M*, because she was sure the mysterious woman held the key to explaining why Paddy was murdered and bringing his killers to justice. Brady was clearly a dangerous man, yet he'd said he wouldn't hurt her, and she believed him. She'd be in big trouble if she was wrong about that, but for now she needed him in one piece.

Suddenly, a loud crash and the sounds of wood splintering carried up the stairs.

A dark scowl spread over Brady's face. "No time like the present to find out. Go. I'll do my best to stay right behind you."

With heavy footsteps invading the floor below, Mac didn't wait to be told twice. She threw her legs over the windowsill, dropped to the roof, and took small, careful steps toward the edge. Brady was closing the window silently when she glanced back, but as he started toward her, she faced the tree again, picked her spot, and jumped. One branch at a time, she lowered herself.

The tree shuddered under his weight when he landed on a branch above her head, but like everything else he did, there was no sound. She'd have thought a big man like him would have made some noise, kind of like a moose in dense forest, but he moved more like a lone wolf.

Once on the ground, Mac darted to a nearby spruce and knelt at the base. Brady dropped out of the tree into a crouch, pulled out his gun, and ducked behind the trunk just as lights illuminated the room they'd vacated. The murmur of angry voices floated on the breeze, but Mac wasn't able to make out their words. It was clear by the pattern of their speech, however, that they weren't happy.

Brady darted across the space that separated them and knelt behind her. His low voice so close to her ear sent a shiver from head to toe. "My car's on the street two blocks south." He straightened slightly and drew Paddy's weapon from his waistband. "Do you know anything about guns at all?"

Mac felt a flush of heat crawl up her neck as she shook her head. She'd been stupid to try getting the drop on him. Stupid…and desperate.

He reached around her and pressed the gun into her hands, his finger on a small tab to the left of the barrel. "This is the safety. It won't fire unless that's off. If the situation warrants, push it away from you and keep pulling the trigger until you either run out of bullets or there's no one left standing. Got it?"

She grasped the weapon and held it to her chest as she met his gaze over her shoulder. "Are you leaving me?" The prospect filled her with dread, and she told herself it was because she didn't want to lose her only contact with M.

His gaze bore into her, and he waited the space of a few heartbeats before he replied. "Sugar, if I was going to leave you, I'd have been smarter to do it before I shimmied down a tree and went on the run from the law."

A trace of anger flickered over his features for an instant, but Mac couldn't decide if he was mad at her or simply irritated in general. He probably hadn't expected

TEMPT THE NIGHT 37

to be saddled with a strange woman, running from the police, with only her word that they intended to do her harm. She barely believed it herself. How could she expect him to?

She drew in a deep breath. "You should go. This isn't your problem. The troopers don't have any reason to suspect that you even know me. You can get to your car and get out of here. I wouldn't blame you."

He gazed at her, searching her face, and for a moment it seemed like he'd take her suggestion. Then he gripped her elbow and pulled her with him as he stood. With long, silent strides, he followed the tree line through the backyard until they reached the graveled alley and turned right.

"No doubt I'd be a hell of a lot better off if I took your advice, but I wouldn't be able to live with myself. I'm kinda old-fashioned that way. If there are any more creeps like those two around, you may not make it through the night. So, you're stuck with me, at least until you explain *why* we're running from two of Alaska's finest." Brady's gaze searched hers as he clearly waited for said explanation.

"I wish I knew why they were trying to kill me...but I don't." Mac pressed her lips together and returned his gaze. She wasn't ready to talk about Paddy—not with this stranger. He was right, though. She was way out of her league. Just what had she planned to do if he'd left her? She had no place to go except back to her uncle's boat. How long could she stay there with no food or heat? Cold, hungry, and grieving, part of her didn't care if she

38 DIXIE LEE BROWN

survived, yet something deep inside still prodded her to get her ass moving.

That was exactly what Paddy would have said if he were there. She batted her eyelids against the tears that threatened. *Damn you, Paddy.*

Brady issued an exasperated sigh and grabbed her hand before he started walking again. As they traversed the alley, the terrain went from flat and open to a narrow lane rimmed by a three-story brick apartment building on one side and small businesses with back entrances on the other. They crossed two intersecting streets before Brady pulled her into the shadow of an overhang at the edge of Marine Drive.

He peered down both directions and seemed satisfied. "You'll be okay here. Stay back in the shadows…out of sight."

It was everything Mac could do to keep from grabbing the front of his jacket and begging him not to leave. "Couldn't I go with you?" The trembling of her voice no doubt gave away her fear.

"You're the one they're looking for, so for now you'll have to stay hidden. I'll bring the car and pick you up on the street. Don't come out until you know it's me. I'll blink the lights."

"What if the troopers see you?"

"They won't see me unless I want them to."

Was it arrogance that spurred his boast? Or hard-won abilities that gave him confidence in himself? Mac had a feeling Brady was capable of whatever he claimed and that he possessed sufficient-enough skills that he didn't

TEMPT THE NIGHT 39

have to invent ones that didn't exist. The man had already proved he could move from point A to point B without making a sound.

Still, worry cascaded over her. "What if you don't come back?"

Brady laid his hands on her shoulders and squeezed gently. "Breathe. Again. That's better." He smiled as he skimmed his hands down to the tips of her elbows and back up again.

The warmth of his touch sent a tingle shooting through her arms. "I'm not usually such a mess. I've just never had anyone trying to kill me before." Her laughter, bordering on hysterical, abruptly died, and she frowned. "Obviously, I don't know what I'm doing, and it scares the hell out of me." A shudder vibrated through her body.

Brady tilted her chin so she met his gaze. "No one knows what to do in this situation, Mac—especially not me. I just make it up as I go. Actually, I'm kind of glad to *know* this isn't a normal Friday night for you. My mama warned me about wild girls like that." A twinkle appeared, making his eyes come alive. "I'm going to get the car and come back for you. Then we'll figure out what our next move is. Can you handle it here alone for a few minutes?"

Mac answered his smile with one of her own in spite of the fact her insides still ached. "I think I'll be okay." Just his proximity inspired confidence and made her less afraid. Strange, considering he'd taken her gun away and sat on her less than an hour ago.

40   DIXIE LEE BROWN

He stepped away from her. "Don't forget what I told you about the gun." He turned to walk away. "And Mac? Try not to shoot yourself."

His parting advice made her smile, but her good humor didn't last. As soon as he disappeared, the darkness closed in. She had only just met Brady, and not under the best of circumstances, but his calm demeanor and obvious strength had given her a small amount of courage when she'd had none of her own. It seemed to leave with him, though, and she clutched the weapon tighter as she broke out in a cold sweat.

To her right, the recessed back door to one of the businesses offered some cover, and she glanced up and down the alley before backing into the farthest corner. She slid down against the wall and strained to hear any sounds.

She could see a narrow strip of alleyway. The street wasn't visible from where she hid, so after a few minutes, she crept out of the entryway and along the wall to the edge of the street, then peered around the corner. There was no activity. Mac leaned her head back against the wall, closed her eyes, and breathed deeply.

Was that a car? Her eyes popped open, and she leaned sideways far enough to see down the street to where the noise originated. Relief surged through her when she saw the car coming, still a block and a half away. Its lights flicked off and on twice. Holding the gun tucked close to her leg so it wouldn't be easily noticed if anyone was on the street, she stepped out of the alley onto the sidewalk.

"Hold it right there, Mac."

TEMPT THE NIGHT 41

Gallagher's voice came from the shadows to her left, and she faltered, her gaze darting toward Brady's car.

"I figured you had to come out of this alley sooner or later. I'm sorry you got involved in this, but you can see our problem, right? Can't have any witnesses. The man in charge wouldn't be happy. So we're going to get in that car across the street and find a quiet spot. You're lucky *I* found you instead of Simpson. I'll make it quick."

She was only listening to half of what he said as she watched Brady's car make a left turn and disappear. Where was he going? Was he leaving her after all?

As though he'd been waiting for the street to empty, Gallagher moved toward her. Mac's grip tightened around the weapon in her hand, her thumb pushing against the safety until she heard a soft click. Paddy's gun and a couple of hurried instructions from Brady were all she had between her and certain death. Brady had apparently deserted her, and she might be wasting her time, but she wasn't going down without a fight.

Turning partway, she kept the handgun pressed against her leg. The trooper was ten feet away, his gun trained on her. "What's this about, Gallagher?"

"It's business. You wouldn't understand." He held up a set of handcuffs and started to walk toward her. "Turn around, Mac."

No way was that going to happen. Mac raised her weapon with both hands.

Instantly, Gallagher stopped, his smirk fading to dead seriousness. An eerie calm came over Mac, and time slowed. She didn't want to take a life, but she would if he

42 DIXIE LEE BROWN

forced her hand. He hadn't been the one who shot Paddy, but Gallagher hadn't tried to stop Simpson either. That made him equally as guilty in her mind. Paddy must have known she would need his weapon, and he would expect her to defend herself. That's exactly what she was going to do.

The second Gallagher's finger curled around the trigger, she fired. Brady's words echoed around her as clearly as though he stood there with her—*keep pulling the trigger until there's no one left standing.*

At least one of the bullets she fired found its mark, and Gallagher jerked backward a step. He dropped to his knees, his weapon thudded to the sidewalk, and he collapsed like a spineless doll.

Mac lowered her weapon and stared. As blood pooled near his head, horror slammed into her. Throwing up seemed inevitable. She backed away slowly, struggling to push air into her lungs, and shook her head to rid herself of the ringing in her ears. Unable to gaze at the trooper's still form another minute, she whirled and ran aimlessly.

From the shadow of a parked car, someone lunged toward her and grabbed her hair, nearly jerking her off her feet. She dropped the gun, and it clattered to the sidewalk. A hand covered her mouth and an arm wound around her waist, pulling her roughly against a solid body.

"Gallagher always was an idiot. Too soft. Made him careless. You'll find I won't be so easily disposed of."

Simpson! Mac should have known that snake would be here somewhere. She struggled against him, fighting for her life, but he seemed to hold her effortlessly.

He swung her around and slammed her against the brick building, his hand still covering her mouth. "You've made enough noise for one night. Let's finish this quietly." He brandished a wicked-looking knife in front of her face.

Terror drained her remaining strength, and Mac sagged against the building. Her legs might have collapsed if he hadn't been pressing her into the wall. It was her worst nightmare coming true, but she refused to give up without a fight.

From deep down inside, her instinct for self-preservation awakened new resolve. She put every ounce of it into a right cross that probably hurt her more than it did him. The moment's surprise it afforded her, however, loosened his grip long enough for her to slip out of his grasp.

She made it two steps before he was on her again. He apparently wasn't going to give her another chance to escape and arced the knife toward her chest as he slammed her backward into the wall. *This was it.* She'd failed Paddy.

Mac squeezed her eyes closed, held her breath, and braced for the blow that would send pain and death ripping through her flesh.

It didn't come.

A strange rattle raised goose bumps on her arms, and she peeked through lowered lashes. Simpson was directly in front of her, a soundless scream twisting his mouth. She choked on a sudden influx of air, her eyes flew open the rest of the way, and she met Brady's angry glare from where he stood beside the trooper. He had gripped

44 DIXIE LEE BROWN

Simpson's knife hand with one of his, keeping the death blow from falling. His other hand grasped the hilt of what must've been his own blade, which he'd buried in Simpson's ribs.

Mac's world tilted and shimmered. She was floating. Brady was saying something, but his voice was warped and distorted. Her feet wouldn't move. Was she dreaming? Was she dead? Soundlessly, she thanked Brady for somehow making it painless. Strong arms caught her and wrapped her in warmth as darkness closed in around her.

Chapter Four

MAC'S EYES ROLLED back in her head, and Brady reached for her, catching her as she slid down the wall. He did a quick check for wounds and was relieved that the bastard at his feet hadn't touched her with the knife. The fury that had roared through his veins when he'd found that worthless son of a bitch holding a blade two inches from Mac's heart was worse than any PTSD episode he'd ever suffered.

Brady had barely gotten there in time to save her after seeing the initial attack go down. Betting they were too smart to kill her on a public street might have been an overestimation of their intelligence. Parking his car so they wouldn't see him coming, he'd raced the rest of the way on foot. He didn't want to think about the rampage he might have embarked on if he'd been too late.

Something about this girl awakened responses in him that had lain dormant for a long time by his own

46   DIXIE LEE BROWN

choosing. She was gorgeous with long, wavy, dark hair accentuating high cheekbones, wide, full lips, and light-colored eyes that seemed to draw him. But that wasn't what hooked him. Somehow she'd tripped his protective switch early in their association, and in spite of the fact that he'd known her for less than an hour, he couldn't walk away. She shouldn't have any effect on him at all, and why she did wasn't a topic he wanted to tackle at the moment.

It stunk that he hadn't arrived before she'd been forced to pull that trigger. His first kill as a Navy SEAL still haunted him at times. How bad would it be for Mac if the man she'd shot was dead?

Holding her against him with one arm, he jerked his Navy combat knife from the slain officer, wiping the blood from the six-inch blade onto the AST uniform that had already been sullied by the trooper's actions, then inserted it into the sheath at his waist. If he'd had any doubts about Mac's claim that the troopers intended her harm, they'd all been put to rest. These two were as dirty as they came. How many more were involved? Could he trust the local law enforcement at all? What the hell was going on?

Brady leaned to the right, slid his arm under Mac's knees, and swept her up, carrying her the few feet to the end of the alley before setting her gently against the wall. He peered up and down the street. It was still quiet and deserted, so he quickly pulled the other officer into the alley, being careful not to leave boot prints in the blood. This one wasn't dead, and judging by the wound where a bullet grazed his temple, he'd be fine aside from one hell of a headache. For a few seconds, he debated finishing what Mac had started. He'd probably regret not taking care of business, but he couldn't help thinking it would be easier for Mac if he could tell her the man she'd shot was alive and well. If Brady had the good fortune to come face-to-face with this guy again someday, there'd be no more second chances.

He wasn't looking forward to the phone call to Joe telling him he'd killed an Alaska State Trooper. Sometimes he wondered why Joe kept him around, but Brady was very grateful that he did. Joe's compound was the only home he had now. Anyway, Joe would know who to call to launch an investigation into what was happening here, not to mention report the carnage in the alley before some poor innocent stumbled across the scene.

He strode back to where Mac was slumped against the wall, lifted her to her feet, and threw her over his shoulder. Halfway to the car, he got his answer about how badly pulling that trigger would affect her.

She moaned and squirmed against him. "Oh God. Let me down."

"Keep still. It's me…Brady. We're almost to the car."

"Put me down if you don't want me to throw up all over you." Her voice was little more than a groan.

Brady stopped and let her slide down the front of him. The instant she landed, she stumbled a few feet and spewed up her guts. He barely got there in time to pull her hair back and steady her with a hand on her waist.

48 DIXIE LEE BROWN

Long after her stomach was empty, dry heaves racked her. Nothing made a man feel more helpless.

When she finally straightened, tears shimmered in her eyes and wet tracks lined her face. Brady's stomach clenched at the misery etched there as he handed her his handkerchief and then held out his arm in the only comfort he could offer.

She came into his embrace without hesitation, additional testimony to her despair and confusion. Her head rested just below his chin, and her cinnamon-vanilla aroma filled his senses.

"You did good, sugar. You did what you had to do to save your life, but don't be too hard on yourself. He's going to live." He lightly brushed his lips over her forehead.

She looked up at him, a question in her eyes. Maybe she found the answer she wanted because she seemed to relax in his arms.

"We should get off the street. Are you ready?" If not for the fact they were out in the open, exposed, and in imminent danger, Brady wouldn't be ready to let her go yet. Not by a long shot. That revelation scared the shit out of him.

She nodded. He quickly released her and stepped back, noticing the absence of her warmth immediately. He took her hand, and they walked the final block to where he'd left his car. After opening her door, she slid onto the seat, and he helped her buckle her seatbelt before he closed her in and went around to the other side.

What the hell was he thinking, holding her like that? Grudgingly, he admitted the immediate attraction that

TEMPT THE NIGHT 49

threw him off his game, but he better get over it…and quick. He couldn't be attracted to this woman. There were at least a hundred reasons why that was a lousy idea. The same reasons that had kept him from choosing to return to his hometown and his family after his last tour was over. The nightmares that prowled around in his brain and came out in the open at the least opportune moments. He was dangerous and unpredictable…and he wouldn't take a chance with people he cared about. So, he *never* let himself get too close.

Mac would be no different. Besides, he was only empathizing with her because she was in a whole lot of trouble, and that could be a cold and lonely place. They had a mission in common ahead of them—finding out if *M* was really Maria Alverez as he suspected. After that, he'd get Mac someplace safe, reunite her with friends and family, and she'd be fine…and he'd be back on track. He dropped into his seat, latched the seatbelt, and started the car.

"Where are we going?" Mac threaded her fingers together in her lap and stared at them.

"I thought we'd go to my motel room. You can get cleaned up—get some rest." He glanced at her. "Unless you have somewhere else where you'll be safe."

"No…I mean, just my uncle's boat. I stayed there last night, but I'd rather go with you if that's all right." She finally met his gaze.

The false bravado he saw in her eyes told him two things. First—the lady wasn't used to needing anyone else to take care of her, and it was tough for her to ask.

50 DIXIE LEE BROWN

Second—she was going to be okay. She'd get through this and be stronger for it—providing he could keep her alive.

"Good." He smiled in spite of himself. "We'll figure out what happens next after we get a good night's sleep." He eased out into the street and headed for the motel.

Brady drove around the block once, then eyed the parking lot carefully before pulling in and parking close to the lobby. Except for the *no vacancy* sign in the front window, everything was dark.

"Stay here for a second." He opened his door without waiting for a reply and went around back to the trunk. Inserting the key, he opened it and grabbed his rifle and the paper bag of groceries he'd placed there earlier. He closed the trunk silently and went to Mac's door, swung it open, and offered his hand. She took it and stepped out, hesitating slightly and blanching as she stared at his rifle.

"You okay?" He searched her eyes, but the moment had passed.

"Yeah." She smiled shakily. "You just…reminded me of something."

For now, he'd have to accept that, but if he was going to help her, she'd have to come clean. He rested his hand on her lower back and turned her toward his room. At the door, he handed her the paper bag, told her to wait again, and entered with gun drawn. When he was satisfied that no danger lurked within, he returned to the door and beckoned her into the room.

She stood awkwardly just inside, clutching the bag. He tugged her gently toward the bed and motioned for her to sit. "The bathroom's right there. Feel free to shower if

TEMPT THE NIGHT 51

you'd like. That always makes me feel better." He grabbed his duffel and rummaged inside, holding up a pair of exercise shorts. "These are probably too big for you, but maybe you can tie a knot or something." His shrug elicited a smile from her that almost stopped his heart as it sent bursts of longing straight to his groin.

Shit! She was beautiful. This was the first time he'd seen her in the light. Her brunette hair was tinged with auburn streaks. Blue-gray eyes were soft and, for the moment, unsure. Skintight jeans hugged shapely legs and well-rounded hips. Her breasts were not too big, and hell…just the way he liked them. He continued his slow perusal up the fine slope of her neck, across her delicate chin to her full, rounded lips—damn—most excellent lips.

"Are you through staring at me?"

Already too late to stop his burgeoning arousal, Brady wrenched his gaze from her lips and met her eyes. Eyes that now held streaks of lilac and looked like a thunderstorm was about to hit. "Sorry." He coughed and focused again on his duffel, holding up a gray T-shirt. "Will this work to sleep in? We'll figure something else out tomorrow."

"Thank you." She accepted the shirt, a self-conscious smile flitting across her features. "Do you have any shampoo?"

"In the bathroom. Oh…" He dug through his bag again and found the cardboard and plastic package he'd been looking for. "I always carry a spare…just in case." He held the unopened toothbrush out to her.

52   DIXIE LEE BROWN

"Wow! I could kiss you for that, but…" Pink tinged her smooth cheeks as her gaze rested on the bulge in the front of his jeans. Then she slowly raised her eyes to his.

Brady felt the heat of a rare blush working up his neck, but he couldn't control the cockeyed grin that tugged at his lips. So much for hoping she wouldn't notice.

Mac skirted around him and headed for the bathroom, something close to amusement in her half-closed eyes.

Huh. Of all the reactions she could have had, that one he hadn't expected. It was good that she had a sense of humor. He'd rather she laugh at him than be afraid. He usually had more self-control than that, and it was a reminder that he'd have to be careful. Strong emotional responses seemed to be the order of the day around her.

Disgusted with himself, he grabbed the paper bag she'd left on the bed, ripped it open from stem to stern, and spilled its contents all over the floor. Swearing under his breath, he bent stiffly to gather up the few groceries he'd bought. A can of soup, a loaf of bread, a jar of peanut butter, and one of jelly. The remnants of the bag still held the box of plastic utensils he'd grabbed at the last minute.

He opened the soup with the can opener he still carried on his key chain. His father had used it when he was stationed in Germany and had given it to Brady when he enlisted. As he traced the edges of the small utensil with his thumb, sadness swirled in the farthest recesses of his mind where he'd relegated the memories of his family. If his dad were alive today, would he be disappointed in his son? His father had been stronger than Brady. He'd

TEMPT THE NIGHT 53

gone away to war too, but he hadn't come home broken. Brady squeezed his fist around the can opener, forced the disturbing questions away, and shoved the key chain in his pocket again.

He poured the soup into two paper cups and set them side by side in the microwave. Stealing napkins from the motel's coffee and creamer packets, he spread them on the table and proceeded to assemble two PBJ sandwiches. Hopefully, Mac's stomach was settled enough that she'd be able to eat. It wasn't a gourmet meal by any means, but it would keep them from starving.

The shower turned off, and a few minutes later, the bathroom door cracked open. Brady glanced up, then did a double take. *Shit!* What was so damn sexy about a woman wearing his clothes? His T-shirt nearly swallowed her, falling to midthigh, all but covering his shorts that could have held at least two of her. Her wet hair hung straight behind her back. A self-conscious smile tipped one corner of her lips, and she crossed her arms over her chest.

As she stepped farther into the room, everything below his waist tightened. He was going to be in big trouble if he couldn't think of something else to concentrate on. He should have let it go...but hell, what was the fun in that? "Nice getup." He grinned and winked as his gaze slowly swept from her feet to her slightly pink face.

Mac sucked her lower lip into her mouth and bit it, ratcheting his lust up another notch.

Brady took a deep breath. "You may think you look silly in those things, but I guarantee you look better in them than I do."

54   DIXIE LEE BROWN

That got a laugh, and she walked slowly toward him. "What are you working on?"

"Dinner…or breakfast since it's Saturday morning…whichever you prefer." He stepped aside so she could see the sandwiches.

She shook her head, the smile disappearing. "I couldn't eat anything."

Brady pulled out a chair and motioned her into it. She hesitated, but then did as he requested. He set the timer on the microwave for two minutes and hit the start button.

"It's been a rough night." He leaned over her with one hand on the table and one on the back of her chair. "This isn't over. Not even close. I caught a little of those guys' conversation while I was climbing down that tree. They weren't only disappointed that you weren't there; they were pissed and damn worried about someone named Hernandez finding out you were still alive. Know anyone by that name?" Brady knelt down beside her, drawing her gaze with him.

"I've never heard of anyone around here by that name. Sitka is a small town. I'd know." Fear and hopelessness clouded her expression.

Damn. If only he had some hope to give her, but until they knew what was going on in this town and how it involved the lady *M*, who may or may not be Maria, they wouldn't know which way to duck. Brady reached for her hand. "We'll figure this out, but you need your strength, and that means you have to eat. After that, we'll talk."

TEMPT THE NIGHT 55

The microwave dinged, and he set the two cups of soup on the table, putting plastic spoons in each.

Mac made no move to eat, but then shrugged. "It does smell kind of good." She brought the spoon to her mouth tentatively and had to try a couple times to swallow, but she finally made it and flashed him a pathetic smile.

Brady chuckled and finished his soup before reaching for his sandwich. Questions flooded him. Who was she? Why had she really shown up at the house on Gardner? Most of all, why had two Alaska State Troopers tried to kill her? And who the hell was Hernandez?

"Are you a PBJ fan?"

Her question dragged him from his ponderings. "You could say that." She had finished her soup and was half-way through the sandwich herself. "You too?"

"My favorite." She took one final bite, wrapped the remains in her napkin, and pushed her chair back. "You cooked—I'll clean up." With a smile, she grabbed both cups and his napkin, tossed them in the garbage, and walked the rest of her sandwich to the refrigerator. She straightened and brushed the crumbs off her hands, then looked at him expectantly.

Brady shook his head. "I think I got the worst end of that deal." He studied her as she smiled. She was holding up damn well. Too well. She'd been through hell tonight, and heaven knows what had transpired the night before. The other shoe would fall. It was just a matter of when. For now, maybe she could answer a few of his questions. It was never that easy, though. The best way to get someone to open up was to answer their questions first. That wasn't always possible for Brady, since much of his work for Joe Reynolds was off the books, but he'd answer what he could.

He motioned toward her chair. "How about some question and answer time?"

Her expression instantly became wary, but she walked toward him and sat.

He waited until she began to fidget. "You first. Ask away."

Her gaze darted to his. "Uh...okay." Clearly she hadn't expected to be the one asking the questions. The crease in her forehead deepened, and she cleared her throat. "Who are you, and who is *M*?"

Brady leaned back in his chair and crossed his legs in front of him. "As I said earlier—my name's Jim Brady. I'm fairly certain *M* is Maria Alverez. Until just recently, she was a child-care provider and housekeeper to a former FBI agent living in Anchorage. Maria's five-year-old son, Marco, was kidnapped eight months ago and was being held by a drug lord in Nogales, Mexico. My boss got a team of men and women together, including myself, to go after him. We got him out without too much trouble, but now his mother has disappeared.

"I finally tracked her to Sitka, and the night I arrived, that note I showed you was shoved under my motel room door. You know the rest." Brady rubbed his hand across the back of his neck.

"That doesn't make any sense. Why wouldn't she want to step up and claim her son? Does she know that's why you're here?" Disbelief darkened Mac's eyes.

TEMPT THE NIGHT   57

"She was kept in the loop from the minute we found out where Marco was being held. When we left for Mexico to rescue him, she was so excited that we thought we might have to physically detain her to keep her from heading down there too. From the last conversation we had with her, she was all packed and ready to go back to Montana to get her son as soon as she got the call saying we'd been successful. But by the time we made that call, she was gone. Something happened that sent her on the run, and I don't have any idea what it was. I was hoping she might shed some light when I met her last night, but I found you instead." He raised an eyebrow. "Why were *you* there?"

For a moment, he didn't think she would answer. She straightened in her chair and folded her arms across her chest, nailing him with a calculating stare.

"Why should I trust you?" Her words held a plea. Undoubtedly, she wanted him to convince her she hadn't screwed up.

Holy shit! What else did he have to do to prove himself? Brady laughed mockingly. "Perhaps you should have asked yourself that question before you walked into my motel room."

She paled for an instant, but then indignation smoldered in her eyes. "Answer the question…if you can."

He'd miscalculated. His sarcasm had caused her to doubt. He'd have to be more careful. "All right. Let's recap the obvious. I think I'm the only guy you've run into tonight who hasn't tried to kill you. In fact, I saved you from a seriously painful death. I held your hair while you puked. That should be worth something. I cooked for you, and I let you wear some of my sexiest clothes." He counted the items off on his fingers, glancing up when a short laugh escaped her lips. Satisfaction coursed through him. It was working better than he'd hoped.

Brady watched her school her expression and pretend she hadn't found him amusing. That was all right as long as she listened to his final point. "The main reason you should know you can trust me and not be concerned that you walked in here is because you can walk out that door any time you want." He stood and stepped aside so she had a clear shot at the door. "I won't stop you if that's what you want to do."

She glanced at him, then the door, and back to him as though considering her options. He breathed easier when she leaned back in her chair and crossed her legs.

"Yesterday morning at about three a.m., my best friend was murdered. His name was Patrick Callahan. He was a state trooper. I was on a ride-along with him… and I saw him die." Her struggle for control was obvious, but her voice cracked and broke in spite of her efforts.

Brady returned to his chair. "Let me guess. Our two troopers?"

She nodded. "He was wounded…when I found him. Blood everywhere. Then Simpson and Gallagher came back, and Paddy sacrificed himself to give me a chance to get away." Tears rolled down her cheeks, and it was everything Brady could do to keep from pulling her onto his lap.

"He…um…made me take his gun, his badge, and the card with the information about the meeting with *M*. I

TEMPT THE NIGHT 59

figured if it was that important to Paddy, maybe this *M* would be able to tell me why he was killed and who was responsible." She swiped at her tears.

He practically had to bite his tongue not to scold her for irresponsibly putting herself in a dangerous situation. She was a smart girl, yet she'd chosen to hide in that upstairs room anyway, with a gun she had no business wielding. It sounded a lot like something he'd do, but he had the strength and the training to back it up. In any case, she'd had about all the lessons she could take for one day, so his lecture would have to wait. "Did your friend know Maria Alverez?"

"He never mentioned anyone by that name."

Brady silently mulled over the sparse information Mac supplied. For sure, they had more questions than they had answers. It was time to call in some backup. He'd fill Joe in at daybreak…which was only about three hours away.

He pushed his chair back, stood, and offered his hand to Mac. "Come on. Let's get a couple hours of sleep."

She rose fluidly and followed him to the bed, then stood back, apparently waiting to see what he would do.

He glanced at her, recognizing the obvious discomfort in her crossed arms, white knuckles, and the sexy way she chewed on her bottom lip. It wasn't hard to guess the cause. "You take under the covers. I'll sleep on top. There's a spare blanket in the closet." He unbuttoned his shirt and hung it on the back of a chair, then bent to remove his boots and socks. Sleeping in his jeans would likely be uncomfortable, especially considering the effect she seemed to have on him, but he'd go the extra mile in his bid to get her to trust him.

By the time he retrieved the spare blanket, she was lying stiffly beneath the covers, as close to the edge as possible. He spread the blanket over both sides of the bed and flopped down, reaching out to turn the bedside lamp off. Darkness filled the room, and the only sound was her quick, shallow breaths. Soon, his chest was rising and falling to the same erratic rhythm. At this rate, neither of them would get any sleep.

He rolled toward her and propped himself up on his arm. "Do you want to talk since we're both miles away from being able to sleep?" Brady could just make out the outline of her face as his eyes adjusted to the dark. He could practically feel her gaze sliding over him, as sure as if she stroked him with her hands. The resulting sensations did things to him that she probably wouldn't appreciate.

"No. Not really. Sorry if I'm keeping you awake." Mac shifted to roll away from him, and he reached for her.

She stiffened when his hand closed around her elbow and his thumb started slow strokes across the tender fold of her arm as he tried to reassure her.

"We don't have to talk about you. Ask me anything you'd like. Nothing's off limits."

She was quiet for a few seconds and then let her breath out slowly. "You believed me when I told you the troopers would kill me. You didn't laugh. You didn't ask me any questions. You didn't make me feel like I was crazy. Not that I don't appreciate it, but…why?"

TEMPT THE NIGHT 61

Brady squeezed her arm. "That's easy. I knew you were telling the truth."

She snorted. "How could you possibly know? I was a stranger, and I had just held a gun to your back. Why would you trust me?"

"That's true enough, and the first words out of your mouth were a lie. Remember? You tried to tell me you were a trooper. Why on earth did you do that, anyway?"

"I have no idea." She laughed, more relaxed than she'd been so far.

"Well, that lie gave away your tell."

"I have a tell?" Her voice held a suspicious tone.

"Everyone has a tell."

"Really? What's mine?" She leaned closer as though he needed to see her in order to remember.

Her sweet aroma filled his nostrils. He slid his hand up her arm, over her throat and chin, until his fingers gently outlined her lips, ignoring the tension that sprang back to life in her. "When you lie, the right side of your mouth tips up, and you won't look me in the eyes." He brushed his hand lightly across her forehead and down her cheek. Damn, she was so soft and silky.

She remained silent for a moment, apparently digesting that. Finally, she relaxed beside him. "What's yours?"

It was his turn to laugh. "I never lie."

Mac chuckled. "That was good. I almost believed you."

Her face was close to his, and he imagined her smiling as they shared the moment. Without realizing, he leaned toward her, brushing his rough and whiskered cheek over hers, breathing in her distracting aroma. An instantaneous stab of desire penetrated his defenses, and he hardened in response.

Her soft intake of breath jolted him back to reality. Still, it was tough getting his mind to stop dwelling on her soft skin and perfect proximity and wrapping it around how raw her emotions were and how much she needed his help. For damn sure, she didn't need him coming on to her when she had enough on her plate just trying to stay alive another day.

Brady had plenty that he should be focusing on too, and he couldn't afford to get close to anyone…ever. The danger of hurting someone—someone he cared about the most—would always exist. Even the slim chance the doctors had warned him about was unacceptable. He'd made his decision some time ago. Long-distance relationships with his mother, sisters, nieces, and nephews would have to do. As far as women went—he'd had his share, but he made sure he was never there in the morning.

"Oh sorry. Bad idea. Let's get some sleep." He laid his head back on the pillow. Was he losing his mind? She didn't strike him as a one-night stand kind of girl, even without all the drama in her life. But the last twenty-four hours she'd been through hell…so what's the first thing he does? Gets a fucking hard-on for her because they happen to be lying in the same bed and she smells so damn good. *Shit! Been an adult long?*

Mac didn't move for a few seconds but finally turned onto her back and pulled the covers over her arms. "Sleep—sure. Um…thanks for distracting me."

TEMPT THE NIGHT 63

Her voice was low…distant, the laughter of a few minutes ago gone. The silence settled between them like a thick fog. He'd crowded her…scared her. Undoubtedly, she was lying there trying to figure out the quickest way to get as far from him as possible, and he couldn't blame her. But, he couldn't allow her to leave either. She was in serious danger, and whether she knew it or not, he was the only chance she had.

Brady had to fix it, but he was more adept at midnight ambushes than polite conversation with beautiful women. Here's hoping he wouldn't make things worse just by opening his mouth.

"Mac?"

She rolled her head toward him. "Thought you were sleeping."

"I want you to know you're safe with me. Don't be afraid. I won't hurt you. I'm sorry if I scared you. It won't happen again."

She turned onto her side and braced her head on her arm. "You didn't scare me, Brady."

If he could see her face clearly, he'd bet the right side of her mouth would be tipping up, telling him she was lying, but he let it go this time. "We're good then? You can relax, go to sleep, and know I've got your back?"

Mac laid her fingers across his lips, keeping him from saying more. "Brady. Hold that thought." She leaned into him, stretching until her lips brushed the corner of his mouth.

Whether from shock or fear that he might wake up and lose the dream, Brady lay motionless as her lips moved to the opposite corner and kissed him sweetly. A groan vibrated through his chest as her soft mouth settled on his, and her tongue teased and licked, reawakening the desire that still lingered from the mere thought of her beside him.

Brady opened his mouth to allow her inside at the same moment his arm went around her lower back and pulled her close. He covered her lips and nipped playfully at her bottom one. He held back, returning her tentative kisses with gentle replies, not giving in to the desperation building within him, wishing it didn't have to end, but knowing it did. He'd made her a promise, and even if she *did* initiate the sexiest damn kiss he'd ever been a party to, it couldn't go any further.

Brady released her mouth and pressed his lips to her forehead. Leaning back as though he might see her eyes in the darkened room, he pulled her with him until she laid her head on his shoulder.

He kissed her forehead again. "Go to sleep, Mac."

"Oh God. I'm sorry. I shouldn't have done that." She tried to squirm away from him.

He tightened his arm around her shoulders. "Believe me when I say you have nothing to be sorry for."

"I guess I just wanted to feel something besides fear for a little while. I know this sounds ridiculous because I barely know you, but I'm safe here...with you."

"And don't forget that." The trust in her voice chipped away at his defenses. "I've been where you are more than once, and I understand how you feel, but let's not

TEMPT THE NIGHT 65

do something you'll regret in a couple hours." He spoke softly, his lips next to her forehead.

"What makes you think I'd regret it?" A tiny thread of humor laced her words.

Brady chuckled. "Just a hunch…but I'll tell you what—if you're not totally relieved that nothing happened when we wake up in two or three hours, we'll revisit the subject."

Mac laughed. "Deal." She was silent for a moment. "We're good then?"

Brady smiled as she repeated his question of a few minutes ago. "I think we're good."

She lay quietly for a while but obviously still couldn't sleep. "Where are you from, Brady?"

His breath was harsh as she moved beside him. "Kalispell, Montana. I live on a ranch of sorts with friends."

"Do you miss it?"

"Sure. Doesn't everyone miss home?"

"I don't know. I've lived here my entire life." There was a wistful edge to her voice.

"You've still got time to see the world."

"Paddy wanted to go to Hawaii in the worst way. He was always bugging me to go with him, but I thought we'd have plenty of time." The sadness that flowed from her ripped at his heart.

"You'll go for both of you now." It was a reflex action to hug her closer, offering something of himself to fill the hole in her life.

66 DIXIE LEE BROWN

She splayed the fingers of one hand on his chest. "Maybe I will...someday." She laid her head on his shoulder again, and the remaining tension left her on a sigh.

"Everyone should see Hawaii at least once." God, she felt good tucked against him, even if there was a ton of bedding between them. She'd cuddled up to his side and seemed totally relaxed. Would it bother her to know that, thanks to her, certain parts of him were fairly rigid?

A few minutes later, she was on the verge of restful sleep, and her breathing deepened and evened out. Again, her strength had surprised him. She was going to be all right—providing she survived. Brady would do everything humanly possible to make that happen.

The vow came from nowhere, sliding into his thought process like it was the most important thing in the world. In reality, it wasn't so different from what he'd been trained to do, although he had a nagging suspicion his motives were slightly out of whack. Just this once, maybe he wouldn't examine them too thoroughly.

For quite some time, he held her and listened to the rhythm of her breathing until he was dropping off himself.

A noise called him back to full wakefulness and left him lying tense and unmoving, listening for the source of the trouble. Suddenly, a vehicle squealed to a stop in front of the motel. Two car doors slammed, one after the other, and the unmistakable sound of a voice through a police radio blared just outside in the parking lot. Brady was on his feet in an instant, headed for the curtain to peer outside, when pounding sounded on the door.

"Alaska State Troopers. Open up."

Chapter Five

MAC JERKED AWAKE, and through the fog of deep sleep, it was a few seconds before she could separate her dreams from reality. When she did, it was worse than she thought. There really were troopers banging on their door.

In the near darkness, she could see Brady's silhouette as he moved away from the window, crossed the room on silent feet, and pulled her covers back, putting a finger to his lips in silent command. His eyes gleamed with steel-hardened determination that chilled her and started her chest aching.

"Put your shoes on."

She jumped to do as he whispered, sliding her feet into her bloodstained canvas sneakers. He draped his coat around her shoulders, then helped her slide her arms into the sleeves.

His calm manner frightened her more than anything. It was obvious that being startled awake in the early hours of the morning by police officers, or similar chaos, was something he took in stride.

She was grateful for his help, and she wanted to trust him, but she had to keep reminding herself that she didn't really know who he was. Was it only a coincidence that he'd appeared the same night that three strangers with automatic rifles had shown up in town? Would she be better off in the hands of the troopers than with Brady?

Mac didn't have the answer, and that was the problem. She needed Brady in order to find out who *M* was and what, if anything, she had to do with those men outside Wagner's plant. *M* was the only hope she had of finding out who was behind Paddy's murder and exacting justice for his death. She would accomplish that if it was the last thing she did.

Brady disappeared into the bathroom and returned with her clothes, stiff with dried blood, rolled into a bundle. He handed them to her and pulled her with him into the bathroom, where a small window leading outside was already open.

He was going to send her out there alone? Nausea swirled in her stomach as she faced the window, the prospect of leaving the only safety she'd felt in hours too impossible to comprehend in the few seconds she had. She almost leapt out of her skin when the banging came again.

"Give me a minute," Brady growled toward the door, just loud enough and sleepy enough to pass for someone disturbed from sleep in the middle of the night.

TEMPT THE NIGHT 69

He grabbed her shoulders and turned her so she faced him. "Wait in here. If they insist on coming inside, I'll make enough of a fuss that you'll have a few seconds to slip out. Toss those clothes in the first Dumpster you come to and head for your uncle's boat. Don't worry—I'll find you." He released her and turned to go.

"What if they arrest you?" Fear for him added to her terror.

"I'm not on their radar yet, but if they do, I won't be in long. You stay put at the boat and wait for me." He pointed at her and then winked, like it was all a big game to him.

Impossibly, it made her breathe easier. She crawled onto the counter and waited by the window as he disappeared, closing the door behind him.

The next sound she heard was the door in the other room opening. "What the hell? Can't a man get a decent night's sleep around here?"

"Sorry, sir. Can I see some ID please?" The trooper's voice was quiet, more conciliatory, which raised Mac's hopes a notch.

A moment of silence passed, and then his next words almost brought her to her knees.

"Thanks, Mr. Brady. We're looking for someone who might have been seen in this area. Do you recognize this woman?"

It was quiet while Brady no doubt studied a picture of her.

"No, Officer. I'd remember. She's a real looker. What did she do? Too many parking tickets?"

70 DIXIE LEE BROWN

God, he was good. Drawing the trooper in with his good-old-boy routine.

"No, sir. She killed two of our own—state troopers."

What? Mac slammed her hand over her mouth, not sure if her shocked response had slipped out aloud or not. *Two?* Brady had said Gallagher was alive—that he'd be okay. Only Simpson had died in that alley. Her breath whooshed out as the only possible answer coldcocked her in the chest. They were accusing her of killing Paddy. Revulsion and sorrow filled the pit of her stomach, and suddenly she wanted nothing more than to escape through that window and disappear. Brady's low whistle brought her back to the moment, anchoring her in his trust. It was only part of his act, but it reminded her that there was one person who believed her story even if his faith in her was only based on her *tell*.

"Holy shit! It's always the pretty ones you have to watch out for. Rest assured, if I see your cop-killer, you'll be the first to know."

"All right, sir. Sorry to have bothered you." A few seconds later, the officer knocked on the next door in line, announced himself, and began his spiel again.

Mac didn't hear the door in the other room close, but suddenly Brady burst into the bathroom. Dim light from the other room illuminated the concern scrawled across his face. He drew the window closed before turning and lifting her off the counter. His thumbs swiped at tears she didn't know she'd cried.

She dried the rest with the palms of her hands. "I swear to God I *never* cry." She followed that declaration with a big hiccup and smiled miserably.

TEMPT THE NIGHT 71

He held her gaze. "I figure you have good reason. Did you hear?"

"Oh my God. Why? Why would they say that? Paddy's parents will hear. *My* parents. It will kill them." Her voice broke again, to her disgust, and she buried her face in his chest—his bare, very solidly muscled chest. A light coating of hair tickled her cheek. Hyperaware of his masculinity, she raised her hands to push herself away, but they lingered of their own accord, exploring the ridges and planes of his abdomen.

Mac raised her head to look at him just as his hands circled her waist and tugged her against him. Green eyes, the color of crystal-clear ocean water, darkened as she stared, and a muscle twitched in a stubble-covered cheek. His arousal tented the front of his jeans and became more pronounced by the second, and still she gripped his sides, unable—or maybe unwilling—to turn away.

He stared at her lips, and she longed to feel him kiss her, but as he leaned in slowly, raising her up on her tiptoes to meet him, she remembered where she was and the reason she'd been about to flee for her life. She had one mission—bring Paddy's killer to justice. Getting cozy with a man she'd just met, though she had to admit this particular man intrigued her, wouldn't help to achieve her goal. Brady had cautioned against doing something they'd regret, yet they'd both been drawn as though by an irresistible force. Taking such a chance was not only foolish, but dangerous. If Paddy were here, he'd kick her butt. It's not like she was usually a risk-taker. She was the proverbial girl-next-door—not the kind of woman who

72 DIXIE LEE BROWN

frequented shabby motel rooms with dark and mysterious men.

"Brady…" She stepped back, and he let her go. Instantly, embarrassment washed over her. "I'm sorry. I'm…"

"Don't apologize. It's on me. I shouldn't have let that get out of hand. We've got bigger things to worry about." Brady passed through the doorway into the main room.

When Mac followed him a few seconds later, he was packing in the light of the bedside lamp. "Are you leaving?"

He didn't stop what he was doing. "*We're* leaving. That is, if you still trust me."

"Brady? Why are you helping me?"

He stopped and looked over his shoulder. A quick smile softened his rough features. "Damned if I know."

Mac smirked as she studied his naked back. He'd become her only lifeline in a few short hours. Paddy would have given her hell for trusting this stranger, and then he probably would have run his name through the computer at the precinct and told her in graphic detail why she shouldn't. She didn't have access to that insider information anymore. She had to trust her instinct. More than that…she had to trust *someone* if she was going to make it out of this alive.

He slipped into his shirt, stuck his weapon in the waistband of his jeans, and hurriedly donned his socks and boots while she stood there, clutching her bundle of clothes, not sure what to do next. She sensed he was still on high alert, which did little to settle her nervous stomach.

TEMPT THE NIGHT 73

Brady stood and faced her. "I'll need my jacket. I have to go out for about thirty minutes. You might as well try to get some sleep."

Mac almost laughed. *Sleep? Not likely.* She ducked out of his jacket as he reached for it. "Where are you going?"

He produced a small notebook from his jacket pocket. "What size do you wear?"

"Where do you think you'll find clothes this time of night?"

He stood ready with a pencil hovering above the paper. The muscle in his jaw twitched again. "If it's going to bother you, you probably shouldn't ask."

His icy green stare said he'd do what he had to whether she liked it or not, so Mac dropped her argument before she got started. "Um...size eight pants, medium shirts, size seven shoes...something slip-on if possible." She laughed at his exaggerated frown.

"Underwear?" He slowly raised his eyes to hers, and one of his brows shot up toward his hairline.

Mac rested one hand on her hip and met his gaze. "I think not. I can wear what I have."

"Think again. Your bra and panties are rolled up in that ball you're holding. If they didn't have blood on them before, they do now. Unless...you'd like to go without?" Amusement sparkled in his eyes.

"Oh good grief! You're enjoying this, aren't you? Six for panties...and thirty-four B. Happy?" Embarrassment sent a wave of heat cascading through her as she dropped her bundle of clothes on the floor.

74   DIXIE LEE BROWN

Brady hastily scrawled the numbers and headed for the door.

"And don't forget socks." If he was going to get underwear, he might as well get it all.

He snapped a quick salute, then stopped with one hand on the knob. "I almost forgot." Returning to his duffel beside the bed, he pulled out Paddy's handgun and held it out to her.

She froze. Images of shooting Gallagher flooded her—him jerking as one of the bullets she'd fired struck him—stirring the contents of her already nauseated stomach. Brady said Gallagher would live. The worst part was she couldn't decide if she was sorry.

Brady, apparently sensing her misery, laid the weapon on the nightstand. "You did what you had to do, Mac. I know it doesn't seem like it now, but you'll eventually come to terms with that." He turned and walked toward the door.

Dragging her eyes away from the gun, she focused on his retreating back. "Thank you, Brady."

"You're welcome." He stopped for a moment and glanced over his shoulder. "Mac? Try not to shoot yourself, okay?" The door opened and closed behind him silently.

Mac almost laughed at his repetition of the words he'd spoken in the alley. Did he really think she was a danger to herself? Or was he trying to take her mind off darker memories? Her money was on the latter, which meant Mr. Macho wasn't as gruff as he'd like to think.

Chilled without Brady's coat, Mac crawled under the covers and pulled them up to her chin. She'd just lay there and wait for Brady to return. A few minutes of

TEMPT THE NIGHT 75

undisturbed sleep had been hers while he held her earlier, but that wouldn't happen in her current state of turmoil. And after last night's experience on the boat, she wanted no part of sleeping alone.

Well, *sleep* might have been a misnomer for what had happened. At best, it could've been considered fitful bouts of losing consciousness only to be jarred awake by dreams of automatic weapons fire, a dumbwaiter falling to the bottom of a long, dark shaft, and Paddy's horror-stricken face. Now, though exhaustion pulled at her arms and legs, the thought of sleep, and the nightmares waiting there, scared her awake.

Mac groaned, turned on her side, and curled into a ball. Despair and uncertainty rolled over her in waves. She'd made the conscious decision to put her trust in Brady, but every time she turned around, she second-guessed herself. True, he'd saved her life in that alley. Simpson would have killed her in the most gruesome of ways if not for Brady. Her body quaked at the memory. She owed him big-time for that.

What if he didn't come back? The insidious idea wormed its way into her thoughts, and even though she tried to shut it out, it wouldn't be denied. He'd given her no reason to suspect he was leaving for good, but a glimmer of apprehension began to grow anyway. What if he decided a woman who stuck a gun in his back and was suspected of killing cops was too much of a liability? She wouldn't really blame him for that.

He was tall and solidly built, and his presence made her feel protected, something she'd gladly sell her soul for

76 DIXIE LEE BROWN

at this point. He was obviously capable of defending her as he'd proved in the alley, but that didn't mean he chose to. If Brady had gotten out while the getting was good, where did that leave her?

She rolled to her back and stared at the ceiling. Self-pity wasn't her thing, although the last twenty-four hours had been a test to her convictions. It was time to start taking care of herself again. She needed a plan, and getting out of Sitka seemed like a good start. If Brady really was gone for good, so was her opportunity to find *M*. There'd be no reason to stick around and wait for whoever was behind Paddy's murder to kill her too.

Paddy had been the only reason she'd stayed here this long, but now she'd be leaving for a whole new reason. She'd be running for her life, but eventually she'd have to stop. If it took her final breath, she'd find a way to prove her innocence and see the people behind Paddy's murder behind bars.

A barely discernible noise pulled her attention toward the door and brought her to a sitting position. She grabbed for Paddy's gun, held it in both hands, and pointed it none-too-steadily toward the door. Maybe Brady had come back after all...but what if it wasn't him? What if he'd found the state troopers and told them where she was? She fumbled with the weapon until she clicked the safety off just as the knob turned and the door opened with a quiet snap. Mac held her breath as she laid her finger on the trigger.

"Mac? It's me—Brady. Don't shoot." His whisper filled the room.

TEMPT THE NIGHT 77

Mac dropped the gun as she released the breath she'd been holding, flew off the bed, and flung her arms around his waist before he was all the way inside.

He pushed her backward a step until he could close the door and then leaned against it, one hand holding the handles of a small black bag while his other arm went around her back and cinched her snugly against him. "Not that I don't appreciate the warm welcome, sugar, but is everything all right in here?"

Between her relief at seeing him, her embarrassment for her outward display of…whatever the hell it was, and him calling her *sugar* again, Mac started to laugh. The look on his face that said he was sure she'd gone bonkers made no difference as Brady led her toward the bed and encouraged her to sit.

He grabbed a cup from the table, disappeared into the bathroom, and returned with water that he handed to her. She drank it down as a strange sense of calm steadied her nerves. Maybe she really was slipping off the edge of sanity. Fear that she was having a psychotic break fit in nicely with all the rest of her worries.

With no small effort, she took several deep breaths and succeeded in calming her wildly racing heart. She didn't realize she was shaking until Brady grabbed the blanket and wrapped it around her. Apparently Paddy's murder, the attempts on her life, shooting a man, and then hearing she'd been accused of killing two cops, one of them her best friend, had put her over the top. Imagine that. She'd always considered herself a strong person, but clearly she'd hit a wall, and the race was over unless

78 DIXIE LEE BROWN

she got her act together. Squeezing her eyes closed, she counted slowly backward from a hundred, sure she would wake up from this nightmare before she reached one.

Brady sat on the worn blanket beside her and spoke soothingly as he stroked her arms. She didn't have a clue what he was saying, but the sound of his voice was her salvation, pulling her back from the edge of an abyss that called to her with promises of never having to think of Paddy again. Part of her wanted that...to ease the sharp grief that sliced her to the bone, but the thought of forgetting him forever—no. She would never forget him. Her psychotic break would have to wait.

Gradually, her breathing slowed and the sharp ache in her chest dulled. Her eyes opened to meet Brady's clear green ones, filled with concern.

He handed her another cup of water. "Want to talk about it?"

Did he really need her to enumerate her insecurities? Well, too bad, because they didn't have nearly enough time for that. "I owe you an apology. I shouldn't have mauled you at the door when you returned. It's just that I really thought you'd left for good...as in *not coming back*." She gripped the cup and took a long drink of cold water.

He met her gaze with a hint of a smile. "So, you were happy to see me then?"

Mac felt the deep flush prickle along her skin and into her cheeks again.

Brady chuckled. "Look, you don't know me. I get that, but I'm not the kind of guy who deserts a lady in trouble, and sugar…you're in trouble. I said I'd be back; I said I'd be thirty minutes; I said I'd bring you a change of clothes." He held up the black bag that sat beside him on the bed. "I wish you'd trust me just a little bit, because I think you could use my help. And, just for the record, it's been a long time since anyone was so happy to see me, so *mauling* is definitely on the approved list." He winked and grinned.

Mac couldn't help but smile, albeit briefly and with embarrassment. Obviously, it would be a while before she lived down *that* enthusiastic greeting.

"Time to get dressed." He gestured toward the bathroom as he glanced at his watch. "And you can ease your conscience. I didn't steal them. I found a Goodwill store a couple blocks from here, and the back door was unlocked, so I helped myself…and left money on the counter."

She scoffed. "How convenient."

"It's not all that unusual. Not all of Goodwill's clientele shop during the day, so they've been known to leave a door open on occasion."

"And you know this how?"

His gaze darkened as he pinned her to the spot. "I spent a little time on the street before I found where I was supposed to be."

She weighed his explanation, and, deciding he didn't look like a man who wanted to elaborate, she let it go. "Are we leaving now?" It was nearly four thirty in the morning. Paddy had been dead for over twenty-four hours already. How was that possible? Mac pushed the thought away before the pain could take root.

80 DIXIE LEE BROWN

"I think that would be wise, don't you?" He pulled her to her feet and placed the bag in her hands. His gaze searched her face, a tiny frown furrowing his brow.

"Where are we going?" With her nerves on edge from his scrutiny, she lowered her gaze to his chest and found it impossible not to appreciate the stretch of his T-shirt across well-formed pecs. When he didn't answer, she raised her eyes to his, only to find he'd been watching her blatant inspection. A sensuous grin slowly eased his impatient expression, and he raised one brow as though waiting for her to take the next step.

The desire that instantly heated her blood took her by surprise. Turning hastily away, she retreated toward the bathroom. Suddenly, his hands slid around her arms and drew her back against the solid chest she'd been admiring.

"Wait. Don't go." His voice was gravelly, but he buried his face in the curve of her neck, and his warm lips on her sensitive throat were gentle.

Mac glanced toward him, and her breath caught. His eyes had gone a dark shade of green, and the intensity of his stare caused her heart to do a major flip-flop, sending an air of expectancy to the pit of her stomach. She tried to step away from the heat of his body pressed against the length of hers, but his lips brushed her neck again, ever so gently, as he held her immobile, igniting liquid fire just beneath her skin. She drew a sharp breath and leaned against him, giving him full access to the column of her throat in spite of the warning that raced round and round in her brain.

TEMPT THE NIGHT   81

He took his time, kissing a path upward to her jaw, then covered her ear, practically causing her knees to drop out from under her. Her swollen nipples ached for his touch, straining against the fabric of the T-shirt he'd loaned her. Suddenly, she was soaking wet between her legs.

Delicious sensations buffeted her and blocked out the voice of reason that echoed in her head, telling her this was a really bad idea. Mesmerized by his lips, his voice, and the warmth of his arms next to hers, she gave herself over to the raging need within.

Soft lips and the bristles of his five-o'clock shadow brushed the pulse point in her neck, the unexpected contrast sending another wave of desire through her. His mouth hovered above her ear. "We'd be good together, Mac."

Wait. Hearing him say the words suddenly shone a harsh light on the end results of their growing physical attraction. This was moving way too fast. Mac wasn't ready to be good, bad, or otherwise with anyone. She could certainly see how she'd given him the wrong idea though. Tensing, she tried to pull away, needing some space to examine the inconsistencies that had taken over her reason, but his hold on her didn't give an inch.

"Just making an observation, sugar. You don't agree?"

Mac wanted this whole topic of conversation to go away. It made her all kinds of uneasy…because now she couldn't help thinking the same thing. His chocolaty-smooth murmur made her lose track of the words she'd wanted to say.

82 DIXIE LEE BROWN

"I want you, Mac. I'm sure that's no big secret at this point. You should know that you have nothing to fear from me. Whatever happens will be strictly your choice. Out of respect for the loss of your friend, I won't try to push you or sway you in any way…yet. I'll just be my usual charming self, which I'm confident you won't be able to resist for long." Humor filled the last words, and his breathy laugh moved the hair by her ear, causing her to shiver.

She'd almost bought into this strange seduction, hanging on his every word…until he mentioned the loss of Paddy. At the abrupt reminder, Mac stiffened, and, seconds later, Brady released her. She fought back the worthless tears formed by guilt and misery. How could she have dishonored Paddy's memory before he was even buried? A moan slipped between her clenched teeth.

Brady didn't give her a chance to put any distance between them, threading his fingers through hers. His expression was clinical and serious. "In the interest of full disclosure, I'm going to give it to you straight." He reached out to push her hair behind her shoulder, almost apologetic. "I'm attracted to you, and it seems like it's mutual. I'd like to spend some time together…get to know each other better. I want to be clear, though. Due to some inconvenient baggage I brought home from the war, I can't do long-term or permanent. All I can offer you is *now*, for however long that lasts, and a promise that I'll treat you right. You might not give a damn about me or any of this, but I thought it only fair to lay it out on the table. Truth is, I don't have much to offer unless you're looking for a few nights of mind-blowing sex, in which

TEMPT THE NIGHT 83

case I'm your man." He paused, his eyes clearly inviting her to say something...anything.

When she didn't reply, he turned away, removed his gun from his belt, and laid it on the small bedside table. "If I've offended you, feel free to turn me down flat. I'll still guarantee my protection until we get you safely away from here."

Mac stared at him, stunned and speechless. Did he really just proposition her for sex with no promises and no strings attached? If he'd wanted to get her mind off Paddy, he couldn't have found a better way. Walking out seemed appropriate, but if she tried to move her legs, there was no doubt in her mind she'd trip over herself. They were wobbling like Jell-O at the moment.

Damn him for proving she was putty in his hands—for making her forget all about Paddy and the trouble she was in and showing her how much he could make her want him. If the heat in her throat and cheeks was any indication, she'd flushed crimson. With good reason. The way she'd responded to his touch—his kiss—no one had ever made her react like that before.

But humiliating her hadn't been enough. He'd made her empathize with him—have compassion for the man who'd come home from the war, forever changed. God, she was a sucker for a man who knew he wasn't perfect, but she had no intention of feeling sorry for him. Nor would she enable him to isolate himself from the one thing that made him human—love.

Jim Brady apparently carried some deep, dark secrets around with him. Secrets that made him afraid to get

84 DIXIE LEE BROWN

attached to another person. Was he worried he'd hurt someone if he got too close? The war he'd mentioned had no doubt ravaged him...distorted his image of the world and himself. Through her mother's eyes, she'd had some experience with that.

Dad had been a lieutenant in the Air Force, shot down behind enemy lines in Viet Nam. A POW for fifteen months, he'd returned a shell of the man he'd been. They'd awarded him a Purple Heart and the Medal of Valor for bravery, but the war continued to rage within him long after he'd been honorably discharged.

It was her mother's unwavering determination that had enabled her to stand by him through the nightmares, the cold sweats, and his consuming rage. By the time Mac and her brother came along, the worst was over, but their father continued to be ever watchful, overprotective, and leery of crowded spaces. Without her mother's faith in him, her father might not have survived those early years. Did Brady have anyone who believed in him that way?

If her father could heal and take his life back, there was hope for anyone—even Brady. He didn't know it yet, but he needed her help.

She swallowed, her mouth suddenly dry. "What branch of the service were you in?"

He turned toward her again. "Navy. SEALs."

Mac nodded. Her brother had followed their father's footsteps, enlisting in the Air Force, but from what she'd heard, the SEALs played by entirely different rules. What baggage had Brady brought home with him? Would he

TEMPT THE NIGHT 85

talk to her about it? She wouldn't push him. She'd let him talk when he was ready.

His troubled eyes met hers. "Thanks for telling me, Brady." She pivoted and headed toward the bathroom, more lighthearted than she'd been in a while.

Brady had said he wanted her…completely in the physical sense, of course. Yet he'd thought enough of her to warn her that it would only be an affair—short-term. There'd be no house with a white picket fence in their future. How did she feel about that? The attraction between them was electrifying. He turned her on simply by touching her. What would it be like to make love to him? A guilty smile broke free as she closed herself in the bathroom. It was definitely worth her consideration, but Brady had some decisions to make too. His protection, as well as his help to get out of Sitka, was a Godsend, but if he thought he was staying locked inside his Navy SEAL camouflage, he'd better think again.

Chapter Six

BRADY FOLLOWED MAC with his gaze as she turned on her heels and marched into the bathroom. Damn, she was sexy—and smart. He'd been prepared for her to turn down his proposition—most respectable women like her did—but she hadn't addressed that issue at all, skipping right to his military career. Touché, Samantha McCallister. They each had a topic that would lay them too bare, and they both knew better than to continue the conversation.

He'd do well not to underestimate her. Maybe *he* was the one in over his head. The bottom line was, it wasn't in his makeup to abandon women in trouble, but maybe he'd be better off if he did just that. It wasn't like he didn't already have his hands full with trying to locate Marco's mother.

Aw, hell. Who was he kidding? He couldn't do it. Mac had gotten under his skin, and he wasn't willing to walk away just yet. He jerked his cell phone from his belt and dialed. Time to check in with Joe and let his boss know how fucked up the game plan was.

In spite of the early hour, Joe picked up on the first ring. "I was beginning to wonder. Did you locate Maria?"

Brady scrubbed a hand through his hair, frustrated that he didn't have better news. "No, and…it gets worse."

A flurry of movements filtered through the phone. "You're on speaker, Jim. Walker and Ty are here too. What's happening?"

Brady could imagine his fellow team members straddling chairs, leaning close to hear. "I still haven't confirmed that the note came from Maria, but whoever set up that meeting didn't show. Someone else was there waiting for the illusive *M* too. A woman—Samantha McCallister. Once I determined she wasn't a threat, I… sort of helped her evade a couple of state troopers." Brady closed his eyes and rushed on. "I killed the one that was about to slice her up."

Complete silence on the other end. This was the first time he'd ever left Joe speechless, and he couldn't imagine that was a good thing. Brady could almost see the looks that were flying around Joe's study.

"Damn. I knew I should have gone with you." Walker broke the stunned silence.

Brady grinned at his friend's disappointed tone. "It's not as bad as it could have been. Mac got the other one before I could reach her, and he's only wounded."

Joe's sigh was audible. "And where is this *Mac* now?"

"She's in my bathroom getting dressed."

88 DIXIE LEE BROWN

A truncated laugh erupted from Walker.

"Let's start from the beginning, Jim," Joe said. The sound of a chair sliding across the floor screeched in Brady's ears.

"Long story short—we've got some dirty cops that killed another trooper who happened to be a friend of Mac's. She saw it go down, and they were going to silence her. One of the dirty cops is dead now, and the other has a non-life-threatening wound, but we don't know how many more there are. She also saw three strangers carrying automatic weapons, and there's somebody named Hernandez who's apparently mad as hell that she's still alive. To top it off, local law enforcement is calling her a cop-killer. If she goes to the police for help, they'll lock her up and probably not look very hard for the real killer."

Joe exhaled as though he'd been holding his breath. "I suppose *you* want to help her?"

"I...can't walk away on this one, Joe."

"So we've got Hernandez...and what's her friend's name—the trooper who was murdered?" Ty's voice echoed from farther away in the room.

"Patrick Callahan." Brady felt some of the weight lift off his chest. Joe and the rest of the team might not appreciate the circumstances, but they'd help, just like they always did.

Joe and Walker were former Marines, Special Forces. When Joe's last hitch was over, he did a stint with the Secret Service, where he met a lot of people in high places, many of whom had jobs that required Joe's training along

TEMPT THE NIGHT 89

with the ability to be very, very discreet. He bought the ranch in Montana, started a training facility for special ops and law enforcement, and began collecting capable men to help him. Walker had joined up after Joe led a team that rescued him from a North Korean prison; Ty used to be a cop and required a place to lay low for a while; and Brady was starting over because he couldn't go home to the family he loved. Fucking misfits all, but it worked for them.

"Got it. I'll check it out and also see what the scuttlebutt is in the Division of AST. Maybe I'll pick up on something. Do you want me to check out the girl?" From the sound of his voice getting farther and farther away, Ty was already on the move.

"Good idea. Thanks."

"What else do you need us to do?" It was Joe's standard response in any situation and only one of the reasons Brady respected the man and would do anything for him.

"I need a safe house somewhere outside of Sitka, and as soon as I find Maria, I'll need a quick extraction."

"Okay. I've got a couple possibilities. I'll get back to you with an address and try to locate you a friendly pilot. Any leads on Maria?"

"Nothing, but assuming it was her who left the note, Callahan had a business card with her handwriting and the same initial she signed on the slip of paper she left for me. I'm afraid she's mixed up in this somehow, which means I need to find her before she ends up dead like Callahan—if it's not already too late." The bathroom

90 DIXIE LEE BROWN

door opened, and Brady turned, letting his gaze trail appreciatively over Mac as the light bathed her from behind.

"I'll see what I can do from this end. I know someone in the governor's mansion who'd be very interested in this story." Joe's voice jerked his thoughts back to the problem at hand. "I'll text you as soon as I have something. Check in again…say eighteen hundred hours."

"You got it. Thanks, Joe. I owe you."

"The hell you do. Watch your back, Brady." The next instant Joe was gone.

Brady clenched his fist around his phone, still studying Mac. Her secondhand clothes looked like a million bucks on her. The jeans encased her hips like a second skin, and the long-sleeved, sunflower yellow top he'd chosen looked beautiful against the auburn tones of her hair. He should have picked something more neutral in color for blending in, but when he'd seen that yellow, he'd known he had to get it for her. Hopefully, she liked the pale yellow lace bra and panties he'd found new and hanging on a rack by the checkout stands.

She blushed as though he'd said it out loud, and a warm smile drew him in. "I couldn't help overhearing. Who were you talking to?"

"Friends who'll help us get out of here when we're ready." He slid his cell phone onto his belt and sat on the bed, leaning back against his elbows. "You look great."

"Thanks. Everything fits perfectly."

Brady patted the bed beside him. "Come here and sit for a minute. I want to talk to you."

Wariness sprang to her eyes, but she moved slowly toward him.

When she stood in front of him questioningly, he motioned to the bed again. "I want to make sure we understand each other." He eyed her patiently, almost feeling bad about her discomfort. Clearly, she expected his topic to be his offer of sex and companionship. He'd let that one settle for a while. They'd be spending a lot of time alone together. If she was interested, he'd know... and she'd know what the parameters were.

She finally flopped down beside him.

"I know you want to find out why Callahan was killed, and you think Maria might know something." He rushed on, holding his hand up to forestall her interruption. "I want to help you. Maria will help too. I don't know her very well—only that she's a good person. But I need you to do something for me."

"What?" Mac slanted a glance at him.

"Let me do what I think is best to keep you and Maria alive."

She dropped her gaze. "This safe house you asked your friends to find—are we going there?"

He nodded. "You and I will stay there until I hear from Maria. Then we'll meet up with her and get out of Dodge." He cocked his head. "We're all going together, Mac. You have to trust me."

"I do...it's just...faith in my fellow man has taken a beating recently." She threw him a crooked grin.

"Been there—done that. It makes a comeback eventually."

92 DIXIE LEE BROWN

A smile sparkled in her eyes. "You're...different. I've never met anyone like you before."

Brady snorted a laugh. "Uh-oh. Good different or bad different?"

"I feel safe with you, so that must be good, right?" She shifted sideways to face him. "Very few of the men around here are secure enough to laugh at themselves, and respect for women can sometimes be in short supply."

"Well, the men around here obviously didn't have my mother because she would have thumped them upside the head for even *thinking* disrespectfully about women."

Full, honest laughter spilled from Mac, and it made Brady smile.

"It's a man's world up here. More than a few are running from something—the law or ex-wives. For others, drinking is the favorite pastime, and fighting. I can say that because it's quite likely I've dated every loser in town. Don't get me wrong. There are some good ones, of course." Sadness crept into her voice. "Paddy used to tease me about being a magnet for narcissistic alpha males, and he was right. I gave up on men and the whole dating scene after Douglas, my last unfortunate choice."

"Seriously? That sounds a little rash." And that was something he probably should have known before he offered her a no-strings-attached tour of his bed a few minutes ago. "Ever thought of moving to the lower forty-eight?" Apparently, Callahan had been just a friend as she'd claimed. Had he been involved with someone else? Or gay? If he was available and the great guy she professed him to be, why hadn't she gone for him?

TEMPT THE NIGHT 93

Why did it matter? Brady pushed the thought away.

"Since Paddy died, that's all I've thought of, but I have to take care of something first."

"Revenge?"

She didn't answer.

"You're not a killer, Mac. You're not equipped for it. You asked for my help, and I'm happy to give it, but we're going to do it my way."

"I know. Your first priority has to be finding Maria. That's why you're here, and there's a good chance she may be in some kind of trouble too. Believe me...I want you to find her just as badly. Everything depends on it."

Brady felt the weight of her despair and had to shove his hands in his pockets to keep from taking her in his arms. It was the only way he knew how to comfort her, but words would have to do until she gave any indication that something more would be welcomed. "I'll find her. There's no option on that one. I gave my word to a five-year-old kid, and I won't go back on that promise. As soon as I locate her, we're getting the hell out of here. I know a place where you'll be safe, where I can teach you whatever you'd like to learn. I've got connections that can help us find out what the hell went down with your friend Callahan." When she was ready, they'd come back and clear her name, but not until they knew what they'd be walking into, and they wouldn't come alone. Brady held his breath, half expecting her to tell him she didn't need one more alpha male in her life.

It was a long time before she said anything. "Why would you do that? I stuck a gun in your back yesterday."

94   DIXIE LEE BROWN

He laughed. "I haven't forgotten." Brady shrugged one shoulder. "You've set a course for yourself that I'm afraid will get you killed if you're not prepared, and I don't want to see that happen."

Again, there was an extended silence before she spoke. "I don't know how to thank you."

"We'll think of something, I'm sure." Brady winked and chuckled when her eyes narrowed. "But right now, we have to go."

He held out his hand to pull her to her feet, and she returned to the bathroom. A few minutes later, she reappeared in a pair of leather hiking boots and a brown canvas jacket, carrying the black bag with the clothes she'd slept in peeking out from the top.

"We may have to do some walking, so I opted for more sturdy footwear. Hope you don't mind." Brady liked the way her muscled calves flexed when she walked.

"You're right. These are much more practical. I'll pay you back for the clothes when I can."

"Forget it. You don't owe me anything." Brady grabbed his duffel and held out his hand. "Ready?"

She handed him her bag, and he led her to the door. When he was satisfied the parking lot was deserted and all was quiet, he slipped outside and rushed her to his car. He opened her door and waited until she slid inside to close it behind her. Quickly, he circled the car, threw the bags in the back, and dropped into the driver's seat.

"Stay down until we make sure no one follows us." He pulled out onto the street.

TEMPT THE NIGHT 95

Mac laid her head on the console, and Brady was tempted to fist his hands in her silky hair. He reached for the rearview mirror instead, adjusting it to get a better angle on the road behind them.

Shit! Here we go. A jacked-up, black truck eased away from the curb and matched their speed.

"Hang on, Mac." Brady accelerated to twenty miles per hour over the speed limit and slid sideways around the next corner. A few seconds later, the black truck did the same.

"Somebody wants to play." His gaze darted between the rearview mirror and the front windshield as he accelerated again.

"What is it?" Fear strained her voice.

Brady gripped her shoulder and squeezed gently. "Nothing to worry about. We just picked up a tail. You can sit up, but stay low."

"Who are they, and how did they find us?" Mac peered over the back seat and through the rear window.

"That's a good question. What d'ya say we find out?" He stomped on the gas pedal, and the car lurched forward. Apparently caught by surprise, the other driver took a few seconds to increase his speed and catch up.

Brady floored it again and careened onto the highway leading out of town. The turnoff he wanted was about a mile from the city-limits sign. He'd stumbled on it yesterday afternoon while killing time before the meeting. He found it with no problem now, and the familiar one-lane dirt road wound through the densely treed park, following the base of a rocky hill around a tight turn where the edge of the road dropped off dangerously on the passenger side. Brady threw the car in reverse, hit the gas, and spun the wheel. The tires tried for traction but couldn't get any in the loose sand, and the car slid at a ninety-degree angle until it sat sideways, blocking the road. The rear of the car sunk in the soft sand as Brady slammed on the brakes. He threw open the door, stepped out, and took cover behind it, his .357 lying over the top, leveled at the spot where the strange truck would appear.

Mac, apparently afraid of heights, peeked from behind her hands, which she'd thrown up to cover her eyes when he'd gotten a little too close to the drop-off. She scrambled over the console and driver's seat, followed him out and pushed against him until she had enough room to crouch beside him, her friend's state-issued semiautomatic pistol braced atop the window next to his.

He glanced at her, his brows raised in question.

Her lips curled fleetingly. "What? I've got *your* back this time."

A smile stirred, and he turned away so she wouldn't get the mistaken impression he found her loyalty humorous. Nothing could be further from the truth. Something moved within him—possessiveness…protectiveness…pride—maybe all three. The one thing he did know for sure was that Mac's gesture of complete trust had touched him deep down inside where no one had been for a very long time.

He was just about to slide his arm around her waist when the truck raced around the curve, and the driver hit

TEMPT THE NIGHT 97

the brakes, sending the vehicle sliding toward the side of the road. It came to a stop with two tires on the dirt lane and two buried partway in sand and shale.

Brady couldn't have planned it any better. The driver of the big truck could spin his wheels and try to jockey himself out of there all day. All he'd do is bury his front end deeper. The poor sap was stuck, unable to go anywhere without a tow, and that wasn't happening unless Brady said it was.

"Stay here." He lowered his sidearm and stepped around the open door.

"Brady? What are you doing? You can't go out there." Her eyes pleaded with him.

He stopped. Again, pleasure in being valued stole over him, and he couldn't hold back a smile. "We have to find out who it is. I'll be fine, Mac. You've got my back. Remember?"

"But I'm no—"

Brady waited, curious to know what argument she'd use this time, but her gaze flew toward the black truck. He whipped around in time to see the driver's door swing open and someone drop nimbly from the cab of the jacked-up vehicle.

Chapter Seven

MAC'S GAZE SNAPPED from Brady's reassuring grin to the open door of the black truck that leaned awkwardly off the edge of the road a few feet away. Whoever had followed them from the motel apparently wasn't hiding any longer.

Her mouth fell open as the slender, petite form emerged and dropped to the ground. Long, black hair, drawn back in a ponytail, bounced from side to side as the figure swung toward them. *A woman?* Mac hadn't been expecting that.

Brady swore quietly and incredulously. Apparently, this wasn't who he'd expected either. He shoved his weapon in his waistband, and with a frown furrowing his brow, he stomped toward the woman.

She was pretty, dark skinned, and exotic looking. Fashionable black slacks, a light blue sweater, and knee-high

TEMPT THE NIGHT 99

black leather boots that matched her jacket drew attention to the fact she wasn't from around here. Brady obviously knew her. Was she a friend? A girlfriend who hadn't followed his rules about not getting involved? There's a shocker…with someone who looked like Brady. In any case, Mac wasn't going to miss this. She wedged Paddy's handgun in her bag and hurried to catch up.

"What the hell, Maria?" Brady stalked to within two feet of her.

Mac stumbled over something unseen in her path as her gaze darted to the pretty woman's calm face. "Maria?"

Both of them glanced Mac's way, and exasperation was written all over Brady's fatigued features. "I thought I told you to stay at the car."

Mac jammed her hands on her hips. "Does everyone do what you say all the time?"

Brady rubbed his brow with the fingers of one hand. "Hell no. You'd have been the first."

A snicker escaped before Mac caught it. The scowl he leveled on her said it all—there was nothing funny in his corner of the world. To be fair, she could understand his frustration. He had done everything possible to find Maria, and she had tailed them from the motel as though playing a game.

Maria's eyes sparkled as she bit her bottom lip, apparently schooling her expression to something more serious. A slight nod acknowledged Mac as Maria turned and retrieved a bag and her purse from the floor of the truck, then looked toward Brady.

"Come on. Let's get the hell out of here. You can explain this stunt later, right after you give me a good reason for standing me up last night." Brady took the bag from her and motioned toward the car.

Maria skirted around him and headed straight toward Mac. "I'm Maria Alverez." She offered her hand and smiled. Her Hispanic accent was thick and melodic, but her English was perfectly understandable.

"Samantha McCallister. Everyone calls me Mac." Did she imagine that Maria caught her breath and searched her eyes for a second too long? Maybe, but Mac didn't think so. She'd be willing to bet that Maria had recognized her name.

"Let's go. We can get acquainted later." Brady hurried them toward the car, opened the front and back doors, and let them situate themselves while he tossed Maria's bag in the trunk and jumped behind the wheel.

Mac resisted the urge to cover her eyes this time as he jockeyed the car back and forth and managed to get it pointed back in the direction they'd come. He visibly relaxed once they left the park behind.

He was clearly still annoyed with Maria, however, if his testy mood was any indication. "Where the hell *were* you last night? Do you realize your son is already afraid you've forgotten him?"

A soft gasp came from the backseat, and Mac turned in time to see Maria wipe away a tear. What was Brady doing? Maria didn't deserve that.

Without thinking, she glared at him until she caught his eye. "That's enough, Brady. Did that make you feel like a big man?" Anger flared within her, and she wasn't about to remain still and let him use Maria's son to punish her further.

Brady flinched as though he'd received a blow. His gaze swept slowly over Maria's face in the rearview mirror, and his expression revealed regret. "Aw, hell. I'm sorry, Maria. Don't pay any attention to me. I'm an asshole. If you don't believe me, just ask Mac."

"No, you're right to be angry. I was late getting to the house on Gardner. A friend was supposed to drive me and then watch the street so no one surprised us. He didn't show up, and by the time I made arrangements to borrow that truck and got to the house, there were state troopers at the front door. I wasn't sure who I could trust, so I tried to stay out of sight—quite a feat in that huge truck. I still don't understand why the troopers were there. I used to work with the man who owns the house, and he assured me it was a safe, private place to meet. I'm sorry to have caused you trouble."

"Distrust of the police around here seems to be an epidemic." Brady glanced sideways at Mac curiously.

Maria continued as though she hadn't heard his quiet words. "I didn't see you leave. When the officers finally pulled out, I drove around for a while trying to figure out what to do. But I knew I had to make contact with you to be reunited with Marco. I had no choice. I'd been to your motel once already after talking with Joe…and left you the note. So I parked on the street and followed you when you left." Maria shrugged.

102 DIXIE LEE BROWN

Mac fisted her hands in her lap, still considering the mention of Maria's *friend*. It had to be Paddy, but a giant lump in her throat kept her from asking. She sensed Brady's gaze on the side of her face but didn't trust herself to look at him.

"Who are you running from? Who were you afraid was going to show up at the house? Why were you avoiding the law?" Brady's cell phone chirped, and he reached beneath his jacket to unhook it from his belt. He glanced at the display briefly and set it on the seat beside him.

"A man I used to know in Mexico City. After almost four years, he found me in Anchorage. I still have friends in Mexico who were able to warn me that he'd learned where I was, and I slipped away just in time. That meant I also had to give up on meeting you at Señora Bree's house as we'd planned, so I called Joe, hoping you would follow me. Now, I'm afraid I've put both of you in danger. This man will stop at nothing to find me again."

"Does this man have a name?" Brady glanced over his shoulder.

"*Sí*. Raul Hernandez."

The breath caught in Mac's throat, momentarily choking her, and Brady reached to touch her leg in obvious reassurance. Hernandez was looking for Maria? Why? The only connection Mac and Maria shared had been Paddy. What was Maria's relationship with Mac's best friend? Why wouldn't he have told Mac about this woman? She knew all of his other friends. They were her friends too. The questions piled up on her tongue, leaving a bad taste in her mouth, but Mac wasn't ready to share Paddy yet.

Brady glanced her way again. This time she met his questioning gaze and gave a slight shake of her head. He frowned, but let it go. Paddy was *her* friend, and Mac would tell Maria about his death when she was ready.

He picked up his cell, swiped his finger across the screen, and read aloud. "Reservations confirmed. GPS coordinates attached. Shouldn't be far—you are on an island after all. Keys are under the flower pot. Oh yeah... walking is involved. Joe."

He touched the screen a few more times, probably downloading the attachment and opening his navigation software. "Sorry. My boss's idea of humor. It means he's found us a safe house." He pulled over and did a U-turn. "Sounds like you might get some use out of those hiking boots yet." He smiled and winked, then held her gaze for a second or two as though assuring himself that she'd forgiven him for his callous words to Maria.

The concern she imagined he was feeling sent a surge of warmth through her, and she smiled back. What was it about a guy who winked? It was a totally arrogant gesture...and totally sexy...and it looked especially good on Brady. *Careful, girl. You've been warned. Don't fall for this guy. He's not available.*

Saturday morning had dawned with a trace of fog and a heavy bank of clouds on the horizon. With any luck, they'd reach their destination without the intermittent drizzle that had dampened the last several days. It was seven fifteen when they reached the end of a very questionable road, but Brady's GPS said they still had three miles to go, up the side of a mountain, apparently. The rutted lane stopped where the wooded hillside began. A barely discernible path went straight up for about forty feet before it zigged to the left and disappeared in the dense underbrush.

"Looks like we walk from here." Brady stepped out and went to the trunk.

"Are there bears out here?" Maria had been quiet for the last several miles, but now her face was drawn with concern.

"We don't usually see them this close to town during the summer." It was a lie, but maybe God would forgive Mac if it was for a good reason. She grabbed her purse, pulled herself to her feet, and followed Brady to the back of the car.

He handed her the black bag. "Keep your weapon where you can get to it...just in case."

She nodded, and her hands shook a little as she took Paddy's gun from her purse and tried to find a place to carry it that would be comfortable. As she stood there, undecided, Brady came up behind her. He reached for the handgun, pulled her jacket and shirt up, and slid it into her waistband.

Mac took a few tentative steps, balancing the weight against her back. "That feels okay. Thank you."

"Anytime, sugar." He clearly had more to say, but Maria stepped around the rear of the car at that moment and reached for her bag. Brady gave Mac another devastatingly sexy wink as he busied himself with a deadly looking rifle and spotter scope. The trunk also yielded a backpack into which he stuffed extra clips, high-caliber rounds for the rifle, his knife, and what looked like military-issue binoculars.

Mac swallowed hard. This guy meant business. She was aligned with him now, like it or not. Should she be happy he was so obviously a dangerous man with skills that could save her life, or should she be scared to death?

"I'll come back and get rid of the car, but for now, make sure you don't leave anything that could identify you." He closed the trunk, shrugged into the backpack, slung the rifle over his shoulder, and hefted his duffel in his left hand. "Okay. If you're ready, let's go."

Mac brought up the rear, wanting Maria in between her and Brady, at least until she determined how well Maria would keep up. Mac needn't have worried. Brady set a brisk pace, and except for Maria's smooth-soled boots sliding on loose rock, it appeared she was more than ready for the challenge.

Still, it was nearly an hour of hard walking before they crested a ridge and saw the house in a narrow valley on the other side. Mac stopped to catch her breath, awestruck at the beauty of the setting. A large one-story log cabin sat in the eastern-most corner with snow-peaked mountains at its back and a creek meandering by the front. Like one of those charmingly rustic paintings she'd seen. All that was missing was smoke curling from the chimney.

A couple of neat, well-kept outbuildings lay behind the house, and beyond them a bare patch of ground with markings of some sort painted white in the center.

"*Yes!* Thank you, Joe." Brady broke into a grin as he turned toward Mac and Maria. "We have a chopper pad."

Another fifteen minutes got them to the house. Brady found the key where the text message had said it would be, and he unlocked the door.

Mac stopped on the large porch, feeling a tiny bit apprehensive. "Are you sure there's no one else here?"

"I'll have a look around, but Joe wouldn't have set this up if there was supposed to be anyone else here." He glanced behind her to Maria. "You're safe for now, and we'll probably be out of here by tomorrow."

Mac heard the warning in his tone and realized too late that voicing her uneasiness could cause Maria's current level of anxiety to skyrocket. Apparently, the woman wasn't the outdoorsy type so commonly found in Alaska. The hike through the woods had left her tense and jumpy. Mac hadn't intended to make it worse. All she'd have had to do was assure Maria that all was well and that they'd soon be someplace where that creep Hernandez wouldn't find them. Simple enough. But Mac had to start believing it first.

"Go on in. Find a room and make yourself at home." Brady stood aside and motioned Maria through the door. When Mac stepped toward the threshold, he gripped her elbow. "Can we talk for a minute?"

Brady looked every bit as tired and stressed as she was. Unexpected humor lifted her spirits as a smile claimed her lips. There was every possibility the poor man had decided that taking on the care and feeding of *two* women was over his pay grade. She nodded, taking a couple of steps away from the house, and waited for him to close the door. When she raised her gaze to his rugged face, green eyes filled with compassion threw her for a moment.

"You didn't tell her about Callahan."

She stiffened, crossed her arms in front of her, and wagged her head slowly. "No…and you didn't ask why Hernandez was after her."

His eyes narrowed. "Talking about Callahan and how he died is going to be hard. No doubt about it. Your grief is still too close to the surface. Trust me, I know. It would be easier simply to bury your feelings and go on, but are you being fair to Maria? If she and Callahan were friends, she deserves to know what happened to him and why he stood her up." Brady's voice took on a gentle, quiet tone, and he stepped closer. "I know it won't be easy, Mac, but you can handle it."

The sensation of butterflies swirled in her stomach for a moment, so unforeseen was the pride and encouragement in his words. Instead of demanding he take care of his own business and never mind hers, she melted under his kindness. And, damn it, he was right.

Brady swiped her hair behind her ear, and his hand lingered there, but as she leaned toward him, he stepped back. "I know you'll do the right thing." He lifted his duffel and backpack and carried them just inside the door, where he dropped them on the floor.

Mac followed him inside. "How long will we be here?"

"Not long. I'll let Joe know we've found Maria, and he'll send a chopper. A day, maybe two." He stopped in

108 DIXIE LEE BROWN

front of her. "I'm going back to hide the car as soon as I have a look around outside. I might be two or three hours. Don't go far from the house."

"I know—bears." Mac whispered the word in case Maria was listening.

Brady grinned. "I'm sure there's food of some kind in the kitchen. Help yourself. And Mac? Keep your gun handy."

She rolled her eyes. "God, I'm getting tired of you telling me what to do, Brady." She tried not to smile, but his grin was too contagious.

He traced a finger down the side of her throat. "You could tell *me* what to do later…if you'd like."

"Sounds good, but do you even know how to cook or do dishes?" She bit her lip, trying to keep a straight face.

Brady laughed again, winked, and strode through the doorway.

Mac closed the door and leaned against it. This big, strange house, without Brady's larger-than-life presence, was intimidating. The room she stood in was one big living area. The whole place was immaculate and surprisingly well cared for. The entry to the kitchen was on the left. To the back and right, closed doors probably hid a bathroom and bedrooms. She might as well get settled. Mac gripped her bag and started for the closest door just as Maria swung it open and stepped out.

Mac smiled. "Brady went to dispose of the car. He said to help ourselves to food. Are you hungry?"

TEMPT THE NIGHT 109

"Yes, a little. It's been a while since I've eaten." Maria fidgeted with her hands and finally looked away.

"Why don't you see what you can find for breakfast? If we feel like it, we could make something to warm up for Brady's lunch when he returns. I'll be right there after I claim a room and wash off some of this dirt. Then maybe we could talk?" Mac's heart lay as heavy as a brick at the mere thought of the conversation ahead of her. Remembering Paddy's death and relating the horror of that night to Maria would be like living it all over again. The only way she'd maintained her composure last night and today was by putting the nightmare completely out of her mind. Brady was right though—Maria deserved to know.

"Take your time." Maria strode toward the kitchen.

Mac proceeded to the room next to Maria's and found a cozy space with a comfortable bed, a chest of drawers, a rocking chair, and a large closet. She dropped her bag on the bed and went in search of a bathroom.

A short hallway led her to the facilities she sought as well as a small mudroom with washer, dryer, and an outside exit. The bathroom was furnished in rustic elegance with a long, granite countertop and a large glass-enclosed shower. Brightly colored towels hung in a row and enticed her with their plush softness. She couldn't help but be curious about who lived here and how Brady's boss was able to get permission for them to pop in unannounced.

After running the water until the steam billowed from the sink, she soaked a washcloth and scrubbed her face and arms, removing the dirt and sweat from their long hike. Later, she'd return and make good use of that decadent shower.

Feeling only slightly cleaner, she retraced her steps to the front entrance and grabbed Brady's bags. She carried them to the last room at the back of the house and swung the door open on a spacious master bedroom. Stepping on thick, soft carpeting, she gazed longingly at the king-sized bed, private bathroom, fireplace, and sliding glass door that opened onto a deck with a view of snow-capped mountains that looked close enough to touch. Too bad she didn't discover this room for herself, but fair was fair. She placed his bags on the bed and turned to leave. The room was fitting for the man who was saving their lives. How do you adequately compensate someone for standing in harm's way for the life of another? No reward would be enough for what he'd done for her...and there was every chance he wasn't finished yet.

When Mac walked into the kitchen a few minutes later, Maria motioned her to the table where a bowl, a box of cereal, and a gallon of milk waited. Apparently already finished with her breakfast, Maria was busy cooking.

"I decided on meatloaf for later. Is that all right?" Maria took a package of meat from the microwave and crumbled it into a bowl.

"Sounds great." Mac poured cereal and milk in the bowl, sat, and started to eat. "As soon as I'm finished here, I'll give you a hand."

TEMPT THE NIGHT   111

"There are potatoes and carrots in the pantry if you don't mind peeling and cutting them up."

"Say no more. That I can handle." Mac would be happy to have something to do. Anything to keep from talking about Paddy. A few minutes later, she rinsed her bowl in the sink, put the cereal box and milk away, and with a colander in her hand, headed in the direction Maria had pointed. Before long, potatoes and carrots were washed, peeled, and ready to be cooked.

Maria slid the meatloaf into the oven alongside the potatoes, and the carrots waited atop the stove to be steamed at the appropriate time. Mac poured them each a glass of apple juice she'd discovered in the pantry, and they pulled out chairs at the table.

"Smells pretty good in here." Mac took a swallow from her glass.

"Thanks for your help, Mac."

"Thank you. You did most of the work. Anyway, I figure we're in this together from now on." Silence descended over them for a moment.

"May I ask you something?" The weight of Maria's question seemed to linger on her pale face.

Mac was sure she knew the topic Maria had in mind, and in spite of trying to psych herself up for it, she wasn't ready. Clearly, she never would be. She let out a sigh. "Of course. Anything."

"Patrick told me all about you. He never mentioned me to you, did he?"

His name ripped the breath from Mac's lungs. She had to concentrate to keep from breaking into a million

112   DIXIE LEE BROWN

pieces. No sound came when she tried to force the answer out, so she shook her head slowly instead.

Maria sat straighter. "He's dead...isn't he?"

Oh God. Don't cry. Mac nodded, swallowing hard. She was a complete coward compared to the steadfast acceptance she saw on Maria's face.

"I thought as much. He would have come to me as he promised if he could have." She reached across the table and patted Mac's wrist. "I'm so sorry for your loss. He'd still be alive if I hadn't come here to Sitka."

"How did you meet him?"

"We met several years ago in Anchorage. I worked for a former FBI agent who consulted on a case Patrick was involved in. It was just a chance meeting, and I knew nothing could come of it. To get involved with someone would also endanger him. But Patrick wouldn't take no for an answer, and he called me whenever he was in town on business. We didn't mean for it to happen, but we fell in love. Patrick wanted to get married, and I had to tell him about Hernandez so that he would understand why I couldn't. When Hernandez learned I was in Anchorage, Patrick begged me to come here so he could protect me." Maria stood, paced to the window over the sink, and gazed outside.

"Why did he keep it from me? He was my best friend." Sadness swirled in Mac's stomach. Had she really known him at all?

Maria turned toward her again. "He wanted to, but he was afraid that the knowledge would put you in greater danger. He hated keeping it from you."

TEMPT THE NIGHT 113

Mac blinked back the threat of tears. "It was Paddy, then, who was supposed to meet you and watch your back last night?"

"Yes." She smiled sadly as though remembering something bittersweet. "How did he die?"

"I was on a ride-along with him when he saw three armed men outside a business near the harbor. He went in to check it out, and someone shot him." Mac stopped short of sharing the bullet wounds, the blood, the pain, and the anguish of Paddy's death. Maria didn't need to carry that image with her the rest of her life. It was bad enough that Mac would.

"Do you know who it was?"

"I know who fired the final shot—a state trooper. He's dead now. Brady killed him before he could stab me." She shuddered as the icy memory clawed at the corners of her mind. "Brady overheard two troopers talking about Hernandez. Apparently, he wants me dead too, but I don't even know who the man is."

"Perhaps he was there and believes you saw something."

"I suppose he could have been one of the three armed men, but I really didn't get a good look at them." This wasn't the first time Mac regretted the panic attack that had kept her from paying closer attention, and it certainly wouldn't be the last.

Maria stood and wobbled slightly. Her sorrow had chiseled deep lines in her face, taking its toll on her stoic composure. "Would you mind taking care of the meatloaf? I think I need to be alone for a while. I'd like to lie down." Maria paused beside her and touched her shoulder. "Patrick hated not telling you. I'm sorry we had to meet like this."

"As long as you were happy together, that's all I care about. I'm glad you found each other, even if it was cut short." Mac almost blurted out how sorry she was that she'd left him lying on the floor of the fish packing plant. She'd saved herself and let him die. If the lump in her throat got any bigger, she was going to choke, and if she couldn't find a way to release this heartache soon, she would shatter.

Maria murmured something and hurried from the room, obviously on the verge of a crying jag. Mac couldn't comfort her. She couldn't even console herself.

Brady should be back soon. She rose to check on the meatloaf and potatoes and turned the burner on under the carrots. Suddenly, needing something stronger than apple juice, she rifled through the cupboards until she found a bottle of Merlot, grabbed a corkscrew and a glass, and returned to the table. She opened the bottle, poured herself a little, and tried to relax as she sampled the wine.

After three swallows, she gave up on it, carried her glass to the sink, and dumped it out. She turned the oven down to warm, flipped the stove off, and poured the carrots into a glass bowl, which she set on the top shelf of the oven. Wiping her hands, she folded the towel as she stood in front of the window. Although she was staring through the glass, the images in her mind weren't nearly as scenic or peaceful—blood, violence, fear, and death soured her stomach. She swayed and would have fallen if she hadn't grabbed the sink and braced her arms against the countertop.

Dropping her chin to her chest, she closed her eyes and hung on. Sobs rose from deep within and crashed against the delicate barrier she'd erected to keep her all-consuming grief from swallowing her whole.

Chapter Eight

BRADY TURNED THE key in the lock and pushed inside, hoping Mac wouldn't be too hard to find. She'd been on his mind all the way to the car and back. He couldn't pinpoint what it was about her that made him want to keep her next to him or even when his ill-advised fascination had begun. Sure...she was attractive, and sexy, and not afraid to stand up to him. Surprisingly, even the latter was a huge turn-on.

But she was also intelligent, compassionate, and courageous all in one drop-dead gorgeous package. What she wasn't was a cheap, easy, barfly who slept with men she barely knew and then moved on to the next. Brady regretted suggesting that she might be comfortable in that role. He couldn't begin to guess at the magnitude of his blunder. If only he hadn't kissed her—and if only she hadn't responded by pressing against him in all the right places and driving him to the edge of delirium with her

TEMPT THE NIGHT 117

tongue in his mouth. How in the hell was he supposed to resist her?

The smell of something meaty and delicious met him just inside the door and drew him toward the kitchen. When had he eaten last? His stomach growled, indicating it was about damn time.

He stopped abruptly when he saw Mac, her back to him, leaning heavily against the counter in front of the sink. He started to greet her so she wouldn't be startled by his sudden appearance, but the way she stood, hunched over as though protecting something fragile, kept him quiet. What was she doing? Reading a recipe? Praying? As though in answer to his questions, she rocked forward, bowing her head, and her shoulders quaked with an unseen force. She buried her head in her hands, bracing herself on her elbows, and then the sobs came, her body shuddering with the weight of her sorrow.

Brady took a step backward, ready to retreat before Mac realized he was there. She'd probably get all bent out of shape if she knew he'd seen her cry. Where she got the idea that emotions equaled weakness was a mystery, but it surely did piss him off. Her grief, however, was a very personal and private thing, and he should respect that. Besides, when had he ever wanted to hold a woman while she cried? Surely that broke about a dozen of his self-imposed rules.

Maybe...but it didn't change the fact that he longed to hold *this* woman any way she'd let him. If that meant comforting her and drying her tears, so be it, which was all the more reason he should leave. Damn. He was turning into a friggin' wuss.

With no conscious effort, Brady took a step toward her. Suddenly, her legs gave out, and she tried to catch herself without success. She whacked her jaw against the countertop on the way down, and a low moan reverberated in the small space.

Brady raced to catch her before she sprawled on the floor and lifted her into his arms. Immediately she tensed and pushed against him, but thanks to a jaw that had to be throbbing like hell, she apparently wasn't in an argumentative mood. He took full advantage, hauling her ass out of the kitchen and through the living area.

"Which one of these rooms is yours?"

Mac made a pathetic picture as she held a hand to her jaw and pointed to one of the doors with her other arm. Tear tracks crisscrossed her cheeks.

Brady suppressed the sudden urge to dry her tears with his lips. "Where's Maria?"

Mac pointed again.

He switched directions, striding away from her room toward the one at the rear of the house. "Then this one must be mine."

"What do you think you're doing?" Mac's speech was impeded by the fact she apparently couldn't, or wouldn't, open her mouth all the way. She wiggled and twisted in his arms. "Either put me down or take me to *my* room." Her words sounded funny, but at least her jaw didn't appear to be broken.

TEMPT THE NIGHT   119

He swung the door open and set Mac on her feet. She tried to dodge around him and escape, but he closed the door and placed his body between her and the exit. Mac stared at him distrustfully, her hiccups and tear-stained face tugging at his conscience.

He sighed, raising his hands in surrender. "Mac, I just want to help. Damn it. I can't stand the thought of you all alone and in pain. Just let me be there for you. I won't say a word unless you want me to."

She crossed her arms and tapped a foot. "That's what this was all about? You could have said that instead of doing your caveman routine."

Yeah…she could be right. Wouldn't be the first time he'd gone overboard trying to make a point. But Mac's anger appeared to be mostly an act. In fact, she was trying to hide a little smile that pulled at the corners of her sexy lips.

She ran her hand through her hair. "Look, Brady. That's sweet—sort of, and I don't want to argue with you right now."

"Me either…but you're not leaving yet."

Disbelief and then amusement flashed in her eyes. "You really think you can make me stay here?"

Brady nodded. "Yeah, I think I can, but I'd rather you agree with me and stay because you want to—because it's the smart thing to do." He stepped toward her until he was close enough to take her hand in his. "You won't let yourself break down in front of anyone. You and I both know if you go to your room alone, your grief will ambush you. I'm merely suggesting you let that happen here, where I can monitor you and you'll have someone to talk it out with."

Mac snorted a laugh and slapped her hands on her hips. "Okay, Mr. Monitor. Are you ready to talk out *your* problems too? Because I might stay to see *that*."

"What problems?"

"I think you called it *baggage from the war*."

Brady held her blue-gray gaze for a second. He was usually a better judge of character than that. He hadn't expected Mac to throw his confession back in his face. Bitterness settled over him. "Trust me...you don't want any part of that." He yanked the door open and stood aside, waiting for her to get the hint.

A myriad of emotions streamed over her face. Regret, understanding, curiosity, but mostly acceptance. She stood there watching him, her mouth set in a determined line. "I get it. It's okay for you to help me through the death of a friend, but if I want you to talk through something a hundred times worse...that's not okay? You can't have it both ways, Brady."

Mac brushed by him, grabbed the knob from his hand, and held his gaze as she gently returned the door to its closed position. Then she closed the distance between them and stood toe to toe in front of him. "I don't like to cry in front of people. So sue me. But you—you're a master at hiding *your* true feelings, aren't you?

Brady grabbed her around the waist and jerked her against him, then got right in her face. Wide-eyed, she tried to squirm away from him, but all she managed to do was give him a raging hard-on.

TEMPT THE NIGHT 121

His lips hovered over hers, teasing, testing. "Yeah, I'm damn good at it…except where you're concerned." He pulled her harder against his erection, and when her eyes sought his, equal parts anger and desire smoldered behind half-closed eyelids.

His name escaped her lips on a heated breath, and Brady lost the last shred of his control. His mouth covered hers. It wasn't a tender kiss, but rather comprised all the desire and longing she'd ignited in him, along with a healthy dose of frustration. He was hungry in a way he hadn't thought possible, and his lips devoured hers, branding her as his and his alone.

Something about that thought broke through his haze of desire. This was wrong on so many levels. She couldn't be his. Not forever. Common sense warred with feelings that wouldn't be denied. He should walk out that door—but damn it, it was way too late now.

He raised his head and brushed the hair back behind her ears, trying to read her face. After running his fingers lightly over the bruise on her jaw, turning purple and swelling, he kissed it ever so gently.

She leaned her forehead against his chest and let her breath out slowly. "I'm not that woman you're looking for, Brady. I wish I was." Mac lifted her head and looked at him with sadness pooling around the edges of her eyes. "Sex isn't just a biological function to me. I get attached. You've been completely honest with me, and I respect you for that. I want you to know where I stand too. I've had more than my share of broken hearts. I don't need another one."

Well, hell. Brady had expected her rejection, yet the sense of loss and disappointment was almost too much. Familiar rage at the atrocities of war, which made it impossible for him to lead a normal life without putting those he held dear in jeopardy, dropped like a bitter pill in his stomach. He'd come too close to the unthinkable once—barely stopping before killing a woman who'd invited him into her bed—and he wouldn't go down that road again. Not ever. As a result, he'd walked away from his parents, his sisters, and his hometown because he wasn't prepared to take the chance of losing his cool and hurting someone else.

He'd have to walk away from Mac too—although he didn't like it one damn bit. The problem was she needed his help to stay alive at the moment. He wouldn't leave her until she was safely away from here. Then he'd place her in Joe's capable hands to figure out what was going on in Sitka and clear her name. Funny—he trusted Joe with his life, but the idea of leaving this woman in his care made Brady squirm.

There was no future for them, only today, and she'd had the final say on that type of short-term, meaningless connection. Of course she was right, but the thought of her moving on, disappearing for good, taking all of the might-have-beens with her, sent his world spiraling downward.

He stepped away to give them both some breathing room and held his hands up. "I totally understand, and I know you're not *that woman*. That was just my wishful thinking, but hey, I knew you were a smart lady, and

TEMPT THE NIGHT 123

you've made a wise decision. Not that I wouldn't have liked this to go the other way." He grinned, hoping to relieve her discomfort.

It seemed to have the opposite effect. Mac glanced away, then strode to the bed and perched on the edge. Fatigue lined her face, and she reminded him of a lost child for a few seconds before she breathed deeply and put on her game face.

"I don't feel particularly smart or wise right now." Mac fingered her bruised jaw and grinned minutely.

Brady followed and knelt in front of her. "Eventually, you'll see that you did the right thing, but we've got some unfinished business to take care of. We'll be spending a lot of time together until this is over." When it came down to it, Brady wasn't ready to give her up, even if it meant denying his burgeoning feelings. "What do ya say we try to be friends?"

"Friends?" Mac sounded distinctly skeptical.

Brady laughed. "Yes—friends. No benefits. Just watching out for each other."

"Do you have any other friends who are women?"

"As a matter of fact, I do. My best friend is a woman. Her name is Alex Morgan. She lives in Portland, Oregon, now, but up until just recently, she lived in Montana. I'm going to miss her like crazy, so I'll need a friend." He winked, and Mac smiled, a slight blush giving her some color.

Then a shadow of loss clouded her expression. "In a strange coincidence, I'm short one best friend too." She studied him for quite a while, then nodded. "I guess we could try this friend thing."

124 DIXIE LEE BROWN

Brady reached for her hand, but stopped short, letting his fingers trail down her leg instead. He stood, offered her a hand, and dragged her to her feet. "Good. I'm going to shower, and then I'll meet you in the kitchen. That *was* something good to eat I smelled when I came in, right?"

"Uh-huh. Maria made meatloaf, and I baked potatoes and steamed carrots."

"Where is Maria?" Brady whipped his sweaty shirt off over his head and dug in his duffel for clean clothes.

"She wasn't feeling well, so she went to lie down. I... told her about Paddy."

Brady stopped, a pair of jeans folded in his hands, and met her gaze. "Good girl. Are you all right?"

Mac shrugged. "Take your shower. I'll tell you about it while you're eating." She strode toward the door.

"Mac?"

A sweet smile greeted him as she glanced back.

"Thank you." Brady wasn't sure she'd understand. He barely understood himself. All he knew was that he'd almost lost her, and for some reason not completely clear to him yet, that was unacceptable. That she'd agreed to be friends after the shabby way he'd treated her filled him with gratitude.

Her smile graduated to her eyes, and a moment of understanding passed between them. "You too, Brady."

"So, we're okay then?"

"We're good. See you in the kitchen." She gave him one last searching glance before she exited his room.

Brady dropped onto the bed and ran his hands over the rough stubble that decorated his face. He didn't have a fucking clue what he was trying to do. Why it had suddenly become of paramount importance to maintain some sort of connection with Samantha McCallister was the question of the hour. The answer was best left hidden. Jumping at the chance to keep her as a friend when all else failed was surely the desperate act of a mad man, and yes—that description fit him to a tee.

Nevertheless, he wasn't sorry, and he would try to live within the constraints of their newfound relationship.

Brady rose, strode to the bathroom, and turned on the shower. He shed the rest of his clothes and entered the stream of water. Five minutes later, he was lathered, rinsed, and towel dried. He slipped into a pair of well-worn, comfortable jeans and a blue sweatshirt with *Navy* emblazoned across the front. Barefooted, he left his room, headed for the kitchen and food.

Mac was just lifting the meatloaf from the oven when he entered the small cooking area, and the enticing aroma sent his stomach into hyper-drive. "Can I help?"

She nodded toward the rest of the meal sitting on the counter near the stove, along with three plates, silverware, and glasses. "Grab a plate and dish up. What would you like to drink?" Mac squeezed by him on her way to the refrigerator. "There's apple juice, red wine, something that may or may not be Kool-Aid, and beer."

"Bingo," Brady said. "Why would anyone even have that other stuff in their refrigerator?"

Mac laughed. "I'm sure there must be a reason, but it escapes me at the moment too." She turned away from the refrigerator with two beers in her hands and set them

126 DIXIE LEE BROWN

on opposite sides of the table. Pushing behind him again, the soft brush of her body making contact with his, she grabbed the glasses and some napkins and carried them to the table too.

Brady followed her with his loaded plate, sat, and waited for her.

In short order, Mac joined him, her plate not even half as full as his. "You didn't have to wait for me. Eat, before it gets cold."

"Oh, you don't know my mother. Somehow she'd know if I didn't show proper respect, and I'd hear about it the next time I call." Brady enjoyed her cute little giggle.

"Your mother is big on respect, huh?"

"You could say that." He raised an eyebrow. "How'd she do?"

Amusement sparkled in her eyes. "If I were you, I wouldn't ever leave your mother and me alone in the same room."

Brady chuckled as he forked a big chunk of meatloaf. "I think that's sage advice."

Mac was barely eating, mostly moving her food from one side of her plate to another.

He watched her curiously for a few seconds. "This is delicious. Kudos to you and Maria."

She set her fork down and pushed her plate away. "It's good. I'm not very hungry I guess. Actually, I'm a little worried about Maria."

"Did she take the news hard?"

Mac concentrated on her plate. "They were in love. I had no idea. If I'd known, I could have softened it somehow. He was my best friend. He dated a lot, but he never said a word to me about finding someone special." She raised her eyes and looked directly at Brady. "Is that the kind of friends you and I are going to be?"

He choked on a mouthful of potatoes, and it was a moment before he could speak. "Well, that got back around to me pretty quickly." He tried a teasing smile, but she wasn't about to be distracted. "Did she say why he kept it from you?"

"Apparently, Paddy knew she was hiding from someone and felt I might be in danger if I knew about them. Obviously, keeping it from me didn't work either. Someone is still trying to kill me."

"True. Did you ask her why Hernandez was after her?"

"That's your job, remember? I did *my* part. Now, answer my question." She stared into his eyes.

"You mean the one about whether I'm going to be the kind of friend who keeps things from you?"

She continued to stare without responding. Time for some honesty. "There's a lot of shit in my past that's still classified. I can't talk about any of that. If I learned something that I thought would endanger you if you knew… I'd probably do exactly the same thing your friend Callahan did. I'd err on the side of caution and hope it would keep you alive. But anything else you want to know—I'm an open book."

Mac looked like she was going to cry for a minute, her eyes brimming with moisture, but she held it together. "Thanks. I'm going to hold you to that."

128   DIXIE LEE BROWN

Son of a bitch! What the hell was wrong with him? He was itching to pull her into his arms and assure her she'd know everything there was to know about him, but how could he put her through that? His life was the stuff of nightmares.

Chapter Nine

THE COMFORTABLE BED was wasted on Mac. She rolled and tossed and fought the covers until she was utterly exhausted—but not sleepy. Checking the bedside clock for the umpteenth time, she groaned: one fifteen a.m. Sunday morning. Her life had taken a nosedive into the bizarre, and she couldn't keep up. God, she missed Paddy and the hometown wisdom he'd distributed on a regular basis. What would he say about all of this?

He damn sure should start with an apology for keeping the single most important thing in his life a secret from her. Was pushing Maria's note into her hand as he lay dying his way of asking Mac to help her? Of course, Mac would do that without being asked. What would Paddy have to say about Brady? One minute, the former Navy SEAL was shutting her out. The next, he went into full-on seduction. Then he changed gears completely and wanted to be her friend. Mac couldn't figure him

130 DIXIE LEE BROWN

out. Normally, she'd gladly walk away from the drama, but the problem was, she was drawn to the tall, hard-bodied warrior who could turn her knees to rubber with one kiss.

Mac groaned again, pummeled her pillow into submission one more time, and flopped face down. Thirty seconds later, she flounced onto her back and kicked the covers off. It was too damn hot in here.

The house was almost creepy quiet. Earlier she'd heard a wolf howl, the eerie sound amplifying the loneliness in her heart. Was Maria lying awake as well, hurting? Mac should have insisted she have something to eat instead of staying in her room with the door closed all day. Brady and Mac had fixed meatloaf sandwiches for dinner about six o'clock, and still no Maria. They'd fixed her a plate, covered it with plastic wrap, and left it in the refrigerator in case she got up in the night. So far, Mac hadn't heard anything from the room next door.

Hopefully, tomorrow they would catch a ride out of here, away from Hernandez and the little town she'd called home all her life. Her parents would be worried sick if the news about Paddy and Mac's supposed guilt had reached them in Anchorage. She'd contact them as soon as it was safe. The last thing she wanted to do was call Hernandez's attention to them. Her brother, Ray, had joined the Air Force a year and a half ago and was now stationed in Guam. They'd never been all that close. She had a few good friends she got together with once in a while. She could just see them on the evening news saying: *Samantha was always kind of a loner, but we never thought she'd kill someone.* Her short list of ex-boy-friends would probably think her name sounded vaguely familiar.

Other than that, she had no one but Paddy. She'd stayed in Sitka primarily because of him, and now that he was gone, perhaps moving on was the right thing for her. People started over all the time. Mac could manage too.

It was a darn shame Jim Brady couldn't be in her plan for a do-over. A smirk teased her lips. Did he even realize how incredibly sexy he was with his firm muscles, ruggedly handsome face, and those smoldering eyes?

She yawned and brought up a hand to cover her mouth. If only that meant she was ready to fall asleep. Closing her eyes, she concentrated on breathing as though sleep were actually possible. It couldn't hurt, right? *In slowly... out slowly... in—*

Her eyes popped open and she lay absolutely still, sampling the air again. There was something—

Smoke!

Mac leapt from the bed, her heart pounding, and rushed to the door. Remembering her fire safety classes from school, she placed the palm of her hand on the wood. No abnormal heat. She jerked it open...and stepped into hell.

Fire consumed the small kitchen, floor to ceiling. The table where she and Brady had eaten and talked while they ate their dinner sat cockeyed, two of its legs burned away and the other two soon to follow. The walls on both sides of the front entrance were ablaze, making escape in that direction impossible. Flames licked hungrily on

132   DIXIE LEE BROWN

the far edge of Maria's room, blackening everything in its path as the fire crawled ever closer.

Mac raced through the other woman's doorway. *"Maria! Maria!"*

Maria squinted at her from the bed. In the spreading light of the fire, Mac could read the alarm in Maria's expression the instant she comprehended the meaning of the red glow from the other room and the ever-thickening smoke in the air. Her eyes grew wide, and she clawed to the edge of the bed.

"Grab your shoes and your bag." Mac started toward the door.

"Did he find us?" Maria quickly slipped her boots on and followed.

Mac didn't need to be told who Maria was referring to—Hernandez—but it hadn't occurred to Mac that this was anything but a tragic house fire. "I don't think so, but we have to get out of here."

Staying low, the two women darted toward Mac's room. Brady almost bowled them over as he exited with her bag and her hiking boots in his hands at the same time Mac tried to enter. Relief flashed briefly in his eyes when she met his gaze.

"Let's get out of here." Brady didn't give them time to think about the situation. His two bags and the rifle were piled in the hallway leading to the mudroom and the back door. He grabbed his things and went ahead of them as they hurried through the smoke toward their only escape.

When they were all inside the mudroom, Brady closed the door. "Get dressed. It's cold out there."

TEMPT THE NIGHT 133

Mac looked down, only then realizing she was wearing the T-shirt he'd loaned her to sleep in the night before. It covered her bottom, but not much else. Oh well. The house was burning down around their ears. That automatically made this an acceptable place to walk around half naked, and Brady could just deal with it.

As he turned his attention to inspecting the rifle, or whatever military types did with guns, she quickly covered herself and slipped into her boots, lacing them up. Maria was donning her jacket when Mac walked toward the door and peered out the window into the darkness.

"Mac! Get down!"

Startled, she swung around. Brady had already dropped the rifle and was sprinting the ten feet that separated them. He tackled her, his sudden weight forcing the air from her lungs as he brought her down, sandwiched between the wall and his equally unyielding body. As she sucked in a breath to demand he get off of her, the crack of a high-caliber weapon echoed from somewhere close at hand. The window she'd been gazing out of seconds ago exploded inward, spewing shattered pieces of glass across them and the floor halfway to where Maria crouched, covering her ears.

"Oh my God!" Mac instinctively raised her arms to protect her head only to find that Brady was already shielding her. She was only too happy to let him since her entire body had gone weak with fear. Fury radiated from him in waves, and his heart pounded hard but steady against her breast.

"Shit, Mac." There was a slight tremble in his voice.

134 DIXIE LEE BROWN

On impulse, she reached out and caressed his rough cheek, but drew back quickly when he flinched away.

Brady leapt to his feet and brought Mac up beside him, backing her against the wall. "I think it's safe to say the shooter is the same person who torched the house. There's probably more than one of them, and sooner or later they'll come to check on their handiwork."

"Torched...someone set the house on fire? On purpose?" Her thoughts swirled as her mind rejected the idea that another human being had started a fire to kill them. Yet there was no question whoever had pulled the trigger and blown out the double-paned window two feet from her had meant to take a life. "How did you know there was someone out there?" She searched his face.

"A hunch. If it were me, I'd have at least two shooters outside." Brady glanced away and stepped back. "Mac, I need you to get down low and scoot back with Maria. Whatever happens, I want you to stay there until I give you the all-clear. Understand?"

"What are you going to do?"

A muscle flexed near his jaw. "I won't let anyone hurt either of you. Trust me on that."

Did she have any choice at this particular moment in time? She nodded, trying to school her expression so he wouldn't know she was scared out of her mind.

"Go." He jerked his head toward Maria.

Mac bent at the waist, ducked her head, and ran to the opposite side of the room. She knelt down beside a shaking Maria and gave her the instructions Brady had issued. Smoke was filtering under the door now, and it wouldn't be long before they'd be forced to go outside even if someone *was* waiting out there to shoot them like fish in a pond.

Mac's gaze darted toward the broken window. Had she just heard something out there? Brady put his finger to his lips and pressed himself between the wall and a storage cabinet to the right of the door. He'd evidently heard it too.

They waited, not moving, barely breathing. Just when she was willing to admit there was no one there, the door splintered and flew open. A stranger with a hunting rifle stepped slowly into the room. His hard, dark eyes drilled straight through Mac.

"Found 'em." He spoke into something on his wrist as a smirk announced his satisfaction with how things were going. Suddenly, he seemed to remember that he was one short and swept his gaze around the room.

He was too slow, and Brady moved like a panther— quickly, silently, and deadly. He made absolutely no sound as he covered the distance between them, approaching the man from behind. Wrapping one arm around the gunman's throat and jerking him off balance, Brady reached around him with his other hand, grabbed the back of his head, and twisted. A sickening snap and the way the man dropped like a fallen tree told Mac his neck was broken.

She couldn't help staring at the body, and when her gaze rose to Brady, he was watching her. No emotion glimmered in his eyes. Mac attempted to stand, more

136   DIXIE LEE BROWN

than ready to see the last of this place, but Brady pointed at her and Maria, and his message was clear. They weren't done here yet.

They didn't have long to wait. Only a few minutes had passed when another man, who apparently moved as quietly as Brady, appeared in the doorway. His cold gaze took in his dead partner before coming to rest on Mac and Maria.

He snorted a laugh. "Well, lookie here. Did you two sweet little things surprise my friend? Or did you have some help? Don't worry. I'll have a look around after I'm through here." His leering gaze shifted to Maria. "You— come with me. Somebody wants you alive." He shifted his weight slightly and stared through Mac. "Too bad you had to stick your nose in this. The party's over for you. A damn shame as far as I can see."

Mac tensed as he raised his handgun, pointing the large barrel at her face. She resisted the almost over-whelming urge to cower. She wouldn't give him the sat-isfaction. Her black bag sat on the floor behind Maria. With thoughts of Paddy streaming through her mind, she pulled out his Glock, released the safety, and leveled it at the man behind the rifle.

The stranger's dark eyes registered a heartbeat of sur-prise, but otherwise he didn't even flinch. It made no difference. She aimed and fired, and then fired again, intending to keep pulling the trigger until no one was left standing…just like Brady said.

Her first shot hit his gun, knocking it sideways and throwing him partially off balance. A complete fluke evidently, since her next two shots sailed harmlessly by him. At the same time, Brady slipped from hiding and let fly with his vicious-looking blade.

The man jerked, dropped to his knees, and his weapon clattered to the floor. He toppled onto his face with Brady's knife sticking from his back. Mac stared in revulsion as Brady strode to the man, wrenched his knife free, and cleaned it on the gunman's shirt before seating it back in its sheath.

He searched the men for identification but found nothing. "Let's go." He grabbed his bags and the rifle and turned toward them expectantly.

Maria had climbed to her feet and hefted her bag, but Mac's legs were apparently made entirely of rubber. She hadn't been able to quiet her breathing, and any minute she was sure she'd be sick. Brady's look of sympathy did nothing to ease her discomfort.

He approached her, took the gun, put the safety on, then placed it back in her bag. "We can rest a couple minutes. In the meantime, hand over your cell phones. I should have done this a long time ago." He took the phones they handed him.

"Should have done what?" Maria released hers reluctantly.

"Gotten rid of them. Phones have a GPS system that can be used to track a person. I should have realized we had a problem when the bad guys kept showing up at the same places we were." Brady left the devices lying on the dryer. "Let's get out of here. Smoke's getting heavier." He bent toward Mac and helped her up.

138   DIXIE LEE BROWN

"What about your phone?" Mac lifted her bag and clutched it in front of her.

"It's different. No one finds me unless I want them to." Brady put his hand on her back, and they followed Maria onto the deck. He stopped and slipped his backpack on while he studied Mac. "You up to this?"

She smiled fleetingly, suffering every minute of the sleep she hadn't gotten. "Is there another option?" The concern in his gaze succeeded in making her feel like a whiner. She straightened and took a deep breath, vowing that she wouldn't be the one who couldn't keep up. Yes—she felt tired and queasy, and a little like her world had imploded, but she was still alive and there had to be a reason she'd been spared. *So just keep on goin', girl.*

Brady grinned like he was inside her head reading her thoughts, and it brought out a previously unseen dimple in his left cheek. He sobered and glanced toward the tree line, a dark shadow in the moonlight. "Stick close—both of you." With the fast pace he set, they left the burning house behind and were soon trudging through the wilderness area that had briefly been their backyard. After several hundred feet, they stopped on a slope facing back the way they'd come.

From there, they caught glimpses of the flames shooting into the air, devouring the rustic log cabin that was supposed to be their safe house. A growing anger burned in Mac's veins. How much more life and property would be lost? Was nothing safe from these tyrants?

When Brady started walking again, Mac used her rage to force one foot in front of the other. Fatigue and hopelessness would *not* get the best of her. Not while Paddy's

TEMPT THE NIGHT   139

death cried for justice, and not while she and Maria were being stalked and threatened.

For the second time in less than twenty-four hours, she'd come face-to-face with someone who would have killed her without thinking twice. Both times Brady had saved her life. He'd killed three men, all with their sights on her, in the short time she'd known him. What did that make him? Assassin? Or savior?

She nearly ran into the back of Maria when the woman stopped abruptly. Mac had been so wrapped up in her thoughts she wasn't sure which direction they'd gone or how far they'd walked.

Brady had removed his backpack, set the rest of his possessions next to a tree, and slid his knife from its sheath. "We've got a couple hours until daylight. You should try to get some sleep."

Maria snorted and mumbled something about bears before she folded her arms and turned her back.

Mac covered her mouth to keep from laughing aloud at the poor woman's obvious fear. She met Brady's gaze and saw the same amusement there. He winked, and a strangely warm and comfortable feeling stole over her. *Definitely savior.*

He began hacking pine boughs from several small trees and arranging them in mats for sleeping. More boughs were piled close to each mat, which Mac assumed were for covering them. As soon as he finished that task, he cleared a spot nearby, circled it with rocks, and started a fire. Soon the heat radiated out several feet, warming Mac and making her sleepy.

140   DIXIE LEE BROWN

"Is it a good idea to start a fire? What if there are more of them?" She watched him throw another armload of dry limbs into the pit.

He moved over to stand beside her. "I don't think there's anyone within radio distance. Those men both wore transmitters and receivers. The first one let the second one know he'd found us. The second one didn't try to send a message. I'm pretty sure we're alone for now."

"Thank goodness. I've never been so scared in my life. Will this ever be over?" Mac looked sideways at him.

"I talked to Joe when I went to the car earlier. He's sending a friend with a helicopter to pick us up about nine in the morning. He'll get us close to an airport in Canada where we can catch a ride to Montana. Once we get on that chopper, we'll be home free. You don't ever have to come back if you don't want to."

"That would mean Paddy's murderer would get away with it." She stared into the fire, the flames mesmerizing her.

Maria stepped toward one of the pine mats. "Can't hold my eyes open any longer. I'm going to get some sleep." She lay down and drew two boughs over herself. Before long, her even breaths indicated she was sleeping soundly.

Brady took a walk through the nearby trees, scavenging for dry wood, and returned with a huge armload, which he piled close to the campfire. He threw two more pieces on the dwindling flames and then retraced his steps to Mac's side.

TEMPT THE NIGHT 141

The quiet was only broken by the crackling of the flames as sparks spewed toward the sky. Mac felt the warmth of his gaze on her cheek and turned to see him appraising her. As soon as their eyes met, something dark and painful flashed in his for the space of a breath, and that muscle in his jaw ticked.

"I'm sorry you had to go through that back there. You were…brave as hell."

"Right. Bravely scared out of my mind." Mac laughed.

He smiled, but it faded quickly. "Couldn't tell it from where I stood. Most people don't run toward the fire, but you did to get Maria out, and you're getting the hang of that Glock…we're a good team." Looking away, he shoved his hands in the front pockets of his jeans. "I'm proud of you."

She studied the side of his face since he refused to meet her gaze. Surprise turned slowly to satisfaction. The man had just made a stab at opening up to her—a small first step—and she was grateful for every ounce of the privilege he'd accorded her. A little chink formed in her armor, and before she could stop herself, she reached out and touched his face, turning him to look at her.

God, she couldn't help herself. Her body reacted to his husky voice, her nipples pebbling, and an ache of anticipation settled low in her stomach. She was drawn to kiss him, not caring at the moment that it would be a mistake. She took a step toward him.

He slid his hands from his pockets and reached for her, but before he made contact, he stopped, fisted his hands, and dropped them to his sides. A wistful smile

142 DIXIE LEE BROWN

surfaced. "Hold that thought, would ya, sugar? I'm gonna come back to it as soon as we get out of bear country."

Heat rushed through Mac, and she was sure she turned three shades of red under his possessive stare. She cleared her throat and tried to reclaim a piece of her self-control. "Have you seen any bears?"

"Not yet, but Maria will have my hide if any get into camp on my watch." He winked.

She laughed, but she was fairly sure they'd all agree with Maria on that subject.

Brady clasped her hand in his and stroked his thumb across her knuckles. "You should try to sleep…before I change my mind and…"

Mac raised a brow and slanted a glance toward him. She had a pretty good idea what the *and* was. What would it take to make him veer from his course? Probably best not to go there. She pulled her hand back. "I'm a little tired. I could use some sleep. You'll be here, right?" The idea of him leaving them out here alone sent a jagged edge of fear knifing through her.

"Don't worry. I'm not going anywhere, and the fire will keep the animals away. You're safe, Mac."

The truth was, wild animals probably represented much less danger than man—at least the ones they'd been running into lately. Her gaze lingered on Brady's virile, strong chest and arms before her eyes rose to meet his. She owed him more than she'd ever be able to repay. "Thanks for what you did back there. I wouldn't be here—"

"Don't go there, Mac. It's counterproductive to dwell on what could have happened. That trap keeps you from

TEMPT THE NIGHT 143

appreciating the good things in life. I'm speaking from experience here, in case you were wondering." He leaned close and brushed his lips over her earlobe. "If you need something to keep that pretty little head occupied, think about everything I'd like to do to you once we get back to civilization."

As her breath caught, Mac pulled away but couldn't keep the smile from her lips, nor the lust from every fiber of her being. He knew it too, and the sexy grin he answered with made her knees weak.

So much for the *friend* experiment. Did Brady even realize he'd veered directions again? Why didn't his renewed efforts at seduction bother her? She'd never acted so recklessly in her life. That wasn't something she did... ever. Until now, anyway. This train definitely needed to slow down—maybe even back up. The fact that she was more attracted to this man than anyone else she'd ever known wasn't going to make that easy.

She skirted around him and stepped to the mat of pine boughs alongside Maria. Lying on her back, she scrunched and fidgeted until she'd made a comfortable trough in the makeshift pad. "This isn't bad." She whispered so as not to wake the woman next to her.

Brady folded his legs and dropped to the sleeping mat next to hers. "It'll do in a pinch. I've slept on my share of these, but I'm not ashamed to admit I prefer a nice comfy bed."

The silence settled around them, and the sudden hoot of an owl startled Mac. Brady chuckled, and she cast a glare his way. She was leaving Alaska with this man tomorrow. They barely knew each other, yet she was letting him call the shots. Not that he hadn't already proved he was worthy of her trust. What was bothering her then?

Certainly, running for her life wasn't the thrill ride the movies made it out to be. Leaving her home of twenty-six years with nothing but a bag of secondhand clothes was a little like dropping into a black hole. But that wasn't what turned her stomach inside out and set her on the edge of a killer headache.

It was leaving Paddy.

Feeling like she failed him in every way possible was a crushing stone on her chest, preventing her from getting a full breath. The prickling of tears behind her eyelids was the last straw. She gulped air with a pathetic sound as she turned on her side, away from Brady.

"Mac?"

There was no way she could trust her voice to answer him.

"Damn it, Mac." The swish of pine boughs heralded his movement, and the next thing she knew, he was behind her. "Scoot over."

She did as she was told, more to get away from him than to give him room, but he stretched out behind her, slid his arm around her waist, and twined one of his legs with hers.

He kissed her neck gently, and she shivered. "It's going to be all right. Tomorrow we'll be in the safest place on earth. No one will touch you there. Not even me…unless you want me to."

TEMPT THE NIGHT 145

Mac leaned back into his warmth as his mantle of protection fell over her. It was quite possible she'd lost her mind, but she couldn't escape the certainty that this was where she belonged. A short time later, with eyelids drooping and her body finally relaxed against the solid wall of Brady's chest, gently moving as he breathed, she whispered the words that had been tumbling over and over in her mind.

"I *do* want you to touch me."

Chapter Ten

THE SWEET SMELL of Mac filled his senses, and Brady stirred, waking slowly with what was surely a contented grin. Starting a new day with a smile on his face was a rarity—one that he wouldn't mind repeating in the very near future.

Mac lay on her side in front of him, and he spooned around her. His arm enfolded her tightly against him, and one of his legs sprawled across her soft thigh, tangling with hers. It'd been a long time since he'd wanted to laze in bed with a woman, but damn if that wasn't top on his list this morning—in spite of the fact that they weren't really in a *bed* and their present situation definitely wasn't conducive to lazing.

Not willing to break the contact just yet, he continued to lie next to her, breathing her in, until something began to niggle at the back of his mind. A sound? A change in the air? A subtle sensation that all wasn't right. Frowning,

TEMPT THE NIGHT 147

he concentrated on the missing piece of the puzzle—and then it came to him.

The barely noticeable vibration detached itself from the tree branches and the forest floor and became the steadily beating blades of a helicopter. Brady disentangled himself and leapt to his feet, swiveling until he determined the chopper's heading. It came at them from the mountain, in a straight line toward where the house had been.

He studied the craft as it flew low over the canopy of tree tops that veiled them. It was an older Huey, designed for inserting small numbers of troops in strategic locations during the Viet Nam War. Machine gun armaments were clearly visible, unusual once a chopper had been retired and sold. The FAA and DHS didn't much care for private citizens flying around in armed ex-military gunships.

Brady frowned. What kind of a hotshot had Joe hired to pull them out of here? And why was it bothering Brady so much? He slid his jacket sleeve up slightly so he could make out the time on his watch. Could it be he was edgy because it was barely six a.m.?

Mac rolled toward him. "Is that our ride?"

He didn't answer, his gaze following the path of the chopper instead. Clearly, the pilot knew where he was going and was headed directly for the helipad behind the house. Two minutes later, the whirling blades began to slow until they could no longer be heard.

Maria was already on her feet, her bag scrunched tightly in her arms, picking her way through the brush in

148   DIXIE LEE BROWN

the general direction of the house. "Thank God. Now we can get off this mountain."

Brady's hunch was practically burning a hole in his chest, and he'd learned a long time ago not to ignore the feeling that he was about to make a colossal mistake. Now—how the hell was he going to explain that to two women who just wanted to get out of here and someplace safe?

"No!" Explanations would have to wait. Brady kicked dirt onto the dying embers of the fire, then swung the rifle over his shoulder. "We need to put some distance between them and us. Let's go. Now."

Maria pivoted and stared as though he'd just sprouted another head. "What are you talking about? You *said* a helicopter would pick us up." She jabbed her finger toward the house. "*That's* a helicopter—and my son is waiting for me."

Brady met Mac's curious gaze as he pulled her to her feet, hoping for a small sign of support. It would be good if he didn't have to fight them both. "There's something hinky about this setup, and until I know what it is, we need to get moving—that way." He gestured toward the slope of the mountain, the opposite direction from the house.

He snatched Mac's bag from the ground and pressed it against her stomach until she wrapped her arm around it, and he started her walking with a gentle nudge. When he turned to hurry Maria along, the woman stood stiffly, arms akimbo, her eyes stony with rebellion.

He strove to adopt his most reasonable tone even though the SEAL in him was inclined to come down

TEMPT THE NIGHT 149

hard for insubordination. Clenching his jaw tightly, he managed to shut down his natural reaction. "Maria, we're going up a little higher where we can keep an eye on the new arrivals and see what happens when *our* chopper flies over at nine hundred hours. Give me that long—three hours—to make sure we're not walking into a trap." He motioned her to follow Mac, almost losing it at the defiant toss of her head.

Maria's gaze darted toward the chopper, then back at him. "This is ridiculous. You expect us to trudge around out there with the bears and God knows what else, when we could be on our way to my son?"

Brady's temper flared, and he took a step toward her. "Enough already with the fucking bears, Maria." Unseen, Mac had moved up behind him, and her low voice hissed through the trees. "Can't you see he's trying to keep you alive so you'll see your son again? What would Paddy want you to do?"

Mac's lips thinned, and Brady picked up on the warning in her eyes. Maria might want to think twice before answering that question any way other than the one that would keep her safe.

Maria glared at Mac until her eyes misted over, then dropped her gaze. With one last look toward the chopper, she rejoined them as Mac moved out toward the slope ahead.

Brady brought up the rear of their small procession. The ground sloped upward gently, and the trees began to thin. Going beyond the cover of the forest, where an aircraft on reconnaissance could spot them, was no

150 DIXIE LEE BROWN

good. He had his eye on a rock face about two hundred feet up the side of the mountain. With a low overhang, the formation was shaped like a miniature amphitheater. Would there be room to get inside and stay out of sight? If he had time, he'd leave the women and scout it out to be sure, but he couldn't take that chance right now. A short, steep climb would give them their best opportunity to stay hidden in a spot high enough to yield what he needed most—cell phone service.

They'd only covered a half mile through the dense brush and fallen trees when Mac stopped, clearly exhausted, and let her bag fall to her feet, dropping to her knees on its somewhat softer-than-the-ground surface. Maria blew out a breath and plopped on a downed log, burying her face in the bag on her lap. Brady rifled through his duffel for water and produced two bottles. He continued up the slope, handing one to Maria, then stopped in front of Mac and passed her the last bottle, kneeling close by.

"Thank you." Mac took a long drink and handed it back.

He accepted the bottle and sipped slowly as he appraised her. "I should be thanking you…for trusting me." He tipped his head toward Maria.

She glanced at the woman resting a few feet down the slope and then shifted her gaze back to him, searching his face as though there might be something new there since the last time she checked. "Don't read too much into that, Brady. It was nothing more than a gut feeling. I trust you on some things, but I don't really know you, do I? I'd like

TEMPT THE NIGHT 151

to, but I see you close up every time our conversation turns in a direction you're not willing to go. Apparently, you don't let anyone get too close, so I won't take it personally." A slight smile softened her curt observation.

Damn. Her brunette hair, mussed from her night on the ground, curled and bounced as she tossed a few strands out of her face. There was only one way he was going to get to know her better, and that was by opening up to her. The prospect of that scared the shit out of him, but so did the idea of her walking away before he was ready to let her go. He leaned back on his arms, and his gaze dropped to her lips. "And what if I did… let you in? Would you find me so hideous that you'd run screaming?"

She shook her head, warmth stealing into her eyes. "There's always that possibility, I suppose, but I doubt it."

The absolute sincerity of her words blew him away, and a deep longing for nothing more than her touch on his life made him feel empty without it. He snorted a laugh and gave her a wink. "Be careful what you wish for, sugar. It might come true."

He stood and pulled her up, reveling in the softness of her hand against his calloused one. "Let's get going," he said before she could reply. "I'll take the lead from here."

Brady walked away, sensing her still staring at his back. Was he seriously considering telling her the horror stories that made him not even trust himself? Of all the women he'd ever met, she was the only one who seemed concerned with who he really was and why. Could she handle it? Even if she could, it wouldn't make a difference one way or the other if his violent nature decided to put in an appearance. And that was the real fucking problem, wasn't it?

After another twenty minutes, they reached the relative safety of the rock overhang. It was better than Brady had hoped, with the inside sloping off toward the back wall, giving them a cave-like effect. The women crawled as far back in the shadows as they could. Brady lay stretched out facedown at the lip of the rock, a pair of binocs trained on the helipad, the charred remains of the log house, and the outbuildings. He counted eight men, all armed and dressed in fatigues. They seemed to be searching for something, and it didn't take a genius to figure out what that something was. Once again, his instincts had proved trustworthy. Now all they had to do was keep their heads down for a couple more hours until their rescue craft arrived. First though, he needed to talk to Joe and hopefully give their pilot a heads-up on what he'd be flying into.

He whistled to get Mac's attention and motioned for them to stay put. Crab-crawling to the edge of the over-hang, he reached what appeared to be a wildlife trail that circled around and came out on top of the rock face. The signal strength had been weak and spotty since they left the house. Once at the top, it alternated between two and three bars. That would have to be enough. He pressed in Joe's number.

The phone rang once before Joe picked up. "Been waiting for your call, Jim. I assume you made it to the safe house all right?"

"My signal's not too strong, so let me get the important stuff out first. Someone torched the safe house, and we had to evacuate. We're on the side of the mountain. There's a chopper here now—I counted eight men—looking for us. Your evac guy may need to do some evasive flying when he gets here."

"Shit. It's never boring with you, is it? How are Maria and our new friend holding up?" A chair scraped the floor, and he could imagine Joe rising from his desk to pace.

"They're doing remarkably well. The sooner we get out of here, the better, though."

"I might be able to do something about that. I'll give the pilot, Nick Taylor, a call and see if he can move up the timetable. Send me your GPS coordinates."

"Is your guy good enough to pluck us off the face of a rock?" Brady pushed the button that sent the coordinates off.

"Walker put him through his paces—what do you think?" Joe chuckled, and the call disconnected.

Brady grinned. Walker had been with Joe longer than any of them. Others thought he was crazy, but Brady had learned early on that it was a rumor Walker perpetuated himself for reasons of his own. He was one hell of a warrior who never hesitated to push the envelope, and he demanded the same from those he deigned to work with. If the flyboy had Walker's stamp of approval, he could probably walk on water too.

Brady waited a few minutes, taking advantage of the higher elevation to scout out their position before heading back down. The area around the helipad was too damn quiet. What were they waiting for? They should have moved on shortly after their unsuccessful search. Instead, all eight of them were holed up somewhere out of sight. None of the reasons he could come up with for that made him particularly happy.

Mac and Maria were conversing amiably as he approached, and surprisingly, that sparked a certain amount of contentment in him. It was good that the women were able to get past the angry words that had been spoken in the heat of the moment. Truth was, for having someone on their trail trying to kill them, they were doing all right. Hell, they were friggin' rock stars. He certainly couldn't blame Maria for wanting to get to her son. It'd been over eight months since she'd seen him. That had to be pure hell.

Their conversation lagged as he got closer, so he veered toward the outer ledge and pulled his binocs from his backpack. He sat cross-legged and peered through the lenses for a few seconds before he sensed the presence beside him.

"Maria, have a seat so you don't make such a good target." He lowered the binoculars and turned his head as she hastened to copy his position.

"I'm sorry, Brady. I shouldn't have argued with your decision. I don't blame you for being angry." Maria leaned her hands on her folded legs and appeared to brace for his wrath.

"Apology accepted...and I'm not mad."

She blinked, and then blinked again, as a smile slowly eased the tension on her face. She leaned toward him. "The little tigress isn't angry anymore either. We were

TEMPT THE NIGHT 155

discussing what we would fix for breakfast…if we had any food." A quiet laugh bubbled free.

"Little tigress, huh? I like that. I may have to borrow it sometime, if that's all right?" He delved into his backpack, sorting through the contents.

"Of course, although she may not be pleased." Maria grinned mischievously.

"Well, that's the idea." Brady joined her in a conspiratorial laugh, then handed her two protein bars he'd found in his bag. "One for the *little tigress* too."

Thank you, but I think you should take it to her." She pressed it into his hand.

He cocked an eyebrow. "You sure?"

"She would like that. I'll keep watch on the helicopter while you go." She made little *shooing* motions with her hands.

For a couple of minutes, he would indulge her…and himself. He handed her the binoculars and pushed to his feet. Mac sat leaning against the back of the grotto, her legs drawn to her chest and her cheek lying against her knees. She lifted her head as he approached and squinted against the sunlight. A slight smile moved her lips.

Brady dropped down beside her and held out the protein bar. "Maria seemed to think you might be hungry."

Her stomach growled loudly, and she slapped her hands over the offender, wide eyes preceding a red flush on her smooth cheeks. Then delighted laughter fell like music to his ears, and he couldn't help joining in.

"It's a wonder I was ever able to sneak up on you night before last." She shook her head.

He pushed the bar toward her hand again. "Just don't try it when you're hungry."

Humor shimmered in her beautiful blue-gray eyes, and Brady couldn't look away. She finally took the protein bar and ripped it open, then held it out to him. "The only way I'm going to eat this is if you share it with me." A grin crinkled her cute little nose. "Don't think too long, since I'm obviously so close to starvation."

Brady grabbed the bar, ripped the paper down, and took a big bite, trying not to chuckle at her surprise while he chewed.

She wiped her hand on her pants. "Wow. You could have let me get my fingers out of the way first."

Brady choked on his guffaw this time, and Mac ended up whacking him on the back while he coughed and tears ran down his face. Apparently, she thought it was damn funny because, although she tried not to laugh, her mirth spilled out around the hand she held to her mouth.

When he could talk again, he bumped shoulders with her. "You did that on purpose."

She swallowed her bite of protein bar and handed the rest to him. "Been paranoid long?"

He chuffed a laugh and passed the bar back. "Yeah." His gaze held hers. "That's only one of the things you're going to learn about me...unless you chicken out."

"I never chicken out...but why do I get the feeling *you* might?"

Brady grabbed her arm, ignoring her squeak as he jerked her across him until he cradled her against his chest. "Let's just see who cries uncle first, shall we?"

TEMPT THE NIGHT 157

Mac slid her arms around his neck, and her try-me grin went straight to his groin. He nuzzled her neck and found the spot where her pulse hammered, echoing her increased heart rate. Damn, she felt good—

"Brady! Brady!" Maria slid down next to him. "The helicopter is taking off."

"Don't panic. That's probably good news." He lifted Mac off of his lap, grabbed the binoculars from Maria, and started toward the ledge. Before he was halfway there, he caught sight of the chopper in the air and—*shit!*—coming straight for them.

Motioning for the women to get back as far as they could, Brady crouched where he was, still under cover of the overhang. Maybe the occupants of that bird just happened to be going this way and would fly right on by.

His gut told him that was wishful thinking.

How? That chopper must be equipped with a heat seeking device of some kind. Who the hell were these guys? Whoever they were, they meant business.

Suddenly a barrage of machine gun fire slammed into the rocks above him. Small bits and pieces of stone cascaded to the ground. He slid deeper into the fissure created by the overhang and caught Mac's eye long enough to mouth *stay down.* She frowned but did as he said.

Okay. Time to go on the offensive. He crawled to where his rifle lay across his bag, threw it over his shoulder, and grabbed some extra ammunition. Then he ducked and sprinted to the edge farthest from where Mac and Maria hid as the chopper crew strafed the rock formation again.

As soon as the lead stopped flying, Brady peeled away from the small indentation in the overhang and brought his Colt AR-15 to his shoulder. He pulled the trigger and kept firing. The best way to bring down a hovering chopper was to kill the pilot, but with seven other people on board, chances were good someone else would take the controls. So Brady aimed for the tail rotor, the most vulnerable spot and necessary for the stability of the craft. Unfortunately, it was also the smallest target, and though his bullets peppered all along the tail, none found their mark.

The pilot was apparently concerned enough by his actions, however, to circle around and hang back a few yards for their next machine gun blast. That was better than nothing, but at this rate, his two thirty-round magazines weren't going to last long.

Brady glanced toward Mac, relieved to see both women tucked back in the cave, heads down, barely visible. He had to get them out of here. Unless Walker's pilot had machine guns on board and someone to man them, he'd be crazy to get involved in this fight. They might take him out just for being in the same airspace. Best not to count on help from that contingent.

If Brady could hold the gunmen off until dark, Mac and Maria might have a chance to escape, but who was he kidding? He'd be out of ammo inside of five minutes. It wasn't looking good, but a SEAL didn't give up.

Leaping from cover, he laid down several more shots, falling back only when the chopper turned and lined up to spray his position with lead. One of his bullets might

TEMPT THE NIGHT 159

have gotten a little taste of the rotor that time. The chopper seemed to lean toward the left and vibrated, but as they pummeled the rocks with bullets, it was obvious it hadn't been enough. He was out of rounds in the AR-15, and that left his .357. He at least had a couple extra clips for his handgun, but it wasn't nearly as accurate as the rifle at long distances.

This time he waited for the chopper to turn in its circle before he stepped out and squeezed the trigger, aiming at the tail rotor, which was now the closest part of the bird. His first shot was so close a tiny piece of the fiberglass blade broke off. He just needed one more in the right spot. Concentrating so hard on his target, the first clue that he'd missed something important was the loud report of an AK-47.

His gaze darted toward the sound, and he saw the gunman leaning out from the cargo bay. Simultaneously, a sharp pain lashed his gun hand, and the .357 sailed out of his reach. He ducked and rolled to go after the weapon, but when he came up balanced for firing, the cargo bay looked like a pin cushion with rifles poking out all over.

One of the men laughed scornfully as the chopper drew closer to the rocks. His mouth moved—something about messing up his plans—but Brady couldn't hear it all over the beating of the rotors.

The bullet had only grazed him, but his hand was bleeding and stung like a son of a bitch. He let his weapon fall. He'd need it in a minute, but for right now, it was more important to make the gunmen believe he'd given up. He'd promised Mac he wouldn't let anything happen to her or Maria. He had one last chance to keep that promise. It appeared the pilot was moving in as close as possible to the rock ledge, probably so his crew could leap to solid ground and make sure Brady didn't have any information they needed before they disposed of him and rounded up the women.

Brady's timing had to be perfect. He couldn't let them jump off the chopper. A movement caught his eye, and his gaze swept slowly to his left. *Aw hell! Mac!* She crept out from under the rock overhang until she stood in full view of the men in the chopper, and she held that state-issued Glock that Callahan had given her. Was she nuts? They'd see her.

Brady dove for his gun, but before he regained his feet, the Glock recoiled in her hand, the chopper window shattered, the pilot slumped over in his seat, and the craft veered sharply to the right, away from the ledge. The damn fool woman had taken his shot...and made it.

Panic was written on the faces of the crew, except for the one who had apparently recognized the source of their trouble and was drawing a bead on Mac. Brady aimed and fired. The gunman, a neat hole in his forehead, dropped his rifle and pitched out the open door.

The others weren't so lucky. Some overconfident crew member apparently grabbed the controls and overcorrected, sending the rotor blades whipping into the side of the mountain just below the ledge. By the time Brady reached the edge and peered over, the ruined craft was rolling down the slope. Finally, it exploded and came to rest at the foot of a rock pile.

TEMPT THE NIGHT 161

Brady swung around in time to stop Mac as she barreled toward the edge, keeping her from seeing the devastation. She gasped and her face went pale when she spotted the angry gash on his hand and the blood flowing freely.

With one arm over Mac's shoulders, he gave in to her gentle persuasion. The women insisted he sit and elevate his hand above his heart while they cleaned and wrapped it in strips from one of his shirts, force-feeding him Advil from Maria's purse for the pain and swelling. He let them fuss over him because it took their minds off what had just happened...and because—hell—it felt damn good.

Maria kissed him on the cheek. "I will never doubt you again, Mr. Brady."

He chuckled. "I'm glad to hear it, but easy on the *Mr.*, okay?"

She laughed and went to retrieve the water bottles from the back of the rock cave.

Mac stayed by his side but had yet to look him in the eyes. "I'm so sorry...so sorry."

Confused, Brady turned her chin with his good hand until she looked at him. "This is nothing, Mac, and besides, it wasn't your fault. You have nothing to be sorry for."

She wrenched her chin from his fingers. "I should have done something sooner. I'm such a pathetic coward. First Paddy...now you."

Brady sighed. He'd convince her that wasn't true if it was the last thing he did. "Are you serious? You looked damn brave from where I was standing. I can't believe

162   DIXIE LEE BROWN

you made that shot. That was supposed to be my shot, you know?"

"They were all watching you. They would have killed you as soon as you picked up the gun. Even as petrified as I was, I had to do something. I counted on being able to sneak up on them while all the attention was on you." She looked down at her hands folded in her lap.

He was speechless. She'd made that gutsy move to save *his* worthless life, and still she called herself a coward. Damn it. What would it take to persuade her? *Quid pro quo?* Perhaps sharing his insecurities with her would help her deal with her own. He'd have to give that some thought.

Maria returned and laid a water bottle in his lap. "May I use your binoculars? I'd like to make sure they didn't leave anyone at the house."

Brady lifted the strap over his head and handed her the binocs. "Good idea." This new, more cautious Maria would no doubt live longer.

Mac started to get up, but he caught her elbow, pulled her against his chest, and slid his arm around her shoulders. He kissed the top of her head and laid his cheek on her silky hair. "A hero does what needs doing in spite of being afraid. Fear does its job—gets the adrenaline going. The old fight-or-flight response. The choice is ours, and the answer is different for every individual and each situation. Different…but not *wrong.*"

She squirmed as though she was preparing to run right now, but Brady held her firmly until she quieted. "I don't know how you could think back over the last

TEMPT THE NIGHT 163

forty-eight hours and see yourself as a coward, but you must have your reasons. Maybe someday you'll share them with me."

Mac didn't say a word—just settled her head against his chest and snaked her arm across his stomach. He hugged her tighter. She was so damn soft, yet strong and capable. He trusted her with his life. How many women had he ever been able to say that about? *None.* Yep…he was getting in over his head, but right at the moment, he didn't give a rat's ass.

BRADY HADN'T INTENDED to doze off, but when he opened his eyes, the sun was nearly midway to its zenith. The picture Mac presented, still sound asleep on his chest, sent a jolt of possessiveness through him. For a moment, he just watched her, savoring the image. Then, unbidden, another memory surfaced. Another woman who'd been soft and willing, until he'd awoken from his special brand of nightmare with his hands around her throat, squeezing the life from her.

Aw hell! This was going to be a fucking train wreck. He should do the right thing before they both got hurt. Get out while he could. Right…except every indication pointed to the fact it was already too late. He'd just have to be more careful and follow the rules: never spend the night, don't get attached.

The sound of a helicopter came in on a breeze, and Brady smiled. Blackhawk. He'd recognize it anywhere. Maria must have heard it too, because she turned and trained the binocs on the approaching craft. Apparently satisfied, she glanced toward him, and he waved his acknowledgement.

He ran his fingers down Mac's ribs as his lips lingered against her forehead. Too bad he wasn't waking her under different circumstances.

And, just like that, he'd apparently already forgotten the rules.

Her eyes popped open, and she stretched, a sleepy grin making his manhood react to his sudden and urgent need for her.

"Our chopper's arriving shortly. We should head down. Ready?"

She climbed to her feet. "How long were we asleep?"

"Half an hour. Maybe a little more." He leaned forward to scramble up but had to stop and let the dizziness pass.

"Are you all right, Brady?" Concern crinkled her forehead. She held out her hand to help him stand.

He didn't know how to answer her question, hoping his gut feeling was wrong for a change. He forced a smile and pushed the conversation in a different direction. "I guess I can't tease you about shooting yourself anymore." He accepted her proffered hand and rose in one controlled movement.

She brightened. "That's right. Except...I think it was kind of an accident."

Brady chuckled.

"I was hoping maybe you'd teach me to shoot." Mac cocked her head and grinned with mock superiority. "I'm good...but I'm sure there's room for improvement."

TEMPT THE NIGHT 165

She leaned over to grab their two bags, and Brady didn't hesitate to admire her shapely ass.

When she stood facing him again, he cleared his throat. "Anything you want, sugar." He leaned closer. "But if you improve yourself *very* much, I'm going to blow my mind." He winked as he hoisted the rifle onto his shoulder, looked for his backpack and found it hanging off Maria's arm, then turned to lead the way back to the helipad.

Chapter Eleven

"Name's Nick Taylor." The sandy-haired stranger pushed back a black cowboy hat and removed a pair of aviator sunglasses, revealing deep blue eyes that took in each of them before he swept his gaze back to Brady. "Nice to see you're almost all in one piece. Thought the worst when I saw that helo smolderin'. Decided to take a little walk while I was waitin' and see what was what."

Mac had always been a sucker for a cowboy with a little Texas drawl. This guy had the hat, the boots, the black leather vest, and a pair of Wranglers that drew her gaze below the belt. It didn't hurt that he was tall, and tan, and easy to look at either. If all of that wasn't enough to put him toward the top on her list of favorite people, his chopper sitting on the helipad had to be the best sight she'd ever seen. She hung back to listen to him talk while the man introduced himself.

TEMPT THE NIGHT 167

"They're all dead, in case you were wonderin'." Nick gripped Brady's hand and pumped it twice, then stepped back and tipped one corner of his hat in her direction. "Ladies."

"Jim Brady. Glad you could make it ahead of schedule. We had a few complications." Brady shrugged the sling off his shoulder and leaned the rifle against a tree, then slid down alongside it.

Mac took one step toward him before she stopped. He was definitely moving slower. Their walk down the slope had been hard on him, although they'd gone at a moderate pace and stopped frequently to rest. His hand must be hurting, but the wound didn't appear bad enough to cause his sheen of sweat and loss of energy. She wanted to help, but there wasn't much else she could do, and he would probably resent her hovering over him.

"No worries. Your boss said there was some urgency, so I put the spurs to her all the way." Nick turned toward Mac and Maria. "Nick Taylor," he said again.

Mac smiled. "Nice to meet you, Nick. This is Maria Alverez...and I'm Samantha McCallister. Everyone calls me Mac."

He nodded briefly at Maria before offering his hand to Mac. "It's not often a man finds two beautiful women in the wilds of Alaska. A shame you'll be leavin' now that we've finally met."

His gaze lingered on her face, sparkling with good humor and distinctly inappropriate suggestions. Under other circumstances, she might have been flattered—at

168 DIXIE LEE BROWN

least interested—but out here in the middle of nowhere with people trying to kill her…all she cared about was a shower, a soft bed, and a door with a good dead bolt.

Mac tactfully slipped her hand from his grip. Not even listening to his good-old-boy drawl was balm enough to take the stone-cold dread from her chest.

She skirted around him and knelt beside Brady. "Hey. How's your hand?"

"It'll be fine as soon as we get you and Maria out of here." He clenched his teeth and winced when he tried to move his arm.

"That good, huh? Wish we had some ice."

He reached out with his good hand and ran a finger across her brow. "No frowning, sugar. This is as close as we've been to home-free in a couple days. I want to see a smile on that pretty face."

Just him calling her pretty made a grin tug at her lips, but it was a lie. How could she smile when his injury was all her fault? Never again would she hide while someone else fought her battles for her. First Paddy and now Brady—the cost had been too high.

"That was a pathetic smile." He chuckled. "You need practice." He glanced toward the chopper as Nick climbed aboard and started the engine. "There *is* something you could do that might make me feel better."

"What?"

His eyes danced with mischief as he pointed to the corner of his mouth. "A kiss?"

"Seriously?" Mac shook her head and scoffed.

TEMPT THE NIGHT 169

"You bet. A kiss has been known to possess incredible medicinal properties." He leaned closer. "And, if we do it right, Flyboy might get off your case."

A full-blown laugh burst from her. "You noticed? It wasn't just my imagination?"

Brady shook his head. "I'd have shut him down for you, but I didn't know how you'd feel about that. Some girls really go for the cowboys."

Mac smiled self-consciously. She fit that description to a tee. Did Brady know that she'd hung on Nick's every word when he talked and ogled his ass in those tight Wranglers? That was as far as her obsession would go, however. Physical attributes were nice, but they didn't make the man.

"I'm turning over a new leaf. It's nice guys for me from now on." She hadn't expected the sorrow that flitted over his features for a second. Was it something she'd said? Or a memory of something lost? There were many things about this man she'd like to know, but more than any-thing, she wanted to remove that sadness from his face.

Impetuously, she leaned toward him. "Still interested in that kiss?"

"Thought you'd never ask."

She inched closer until her shoulder brushed his chest, then raised her lips to meet his in what she intended to be a warm, but brief, closed-mouth kiss. He apparently had other ideas. His hand wound through her hair, holding her head so she couldn't retreat. His tongue swept the edges of her mouth and gently coaxed her lips open, slipping through tentatively at first, then pulling back, letting her get used to him. With tender ministrations, he caressed her with his tongue and lips, until she was sure her soul lay bare before him. No one had ever kissed her like that. No one had ever possessed her this completely…and she didn't want it to end.

But it would. There'd be no long-term relationship between them. He'd said it plainly. But not even that was enough to make her walk away. She was an adult. She understood the rules. If she chose to play this game, it would be up to her to safeguard her heart.

A glimmer of caution caused her to pull back slightly, but he caught her waist and deepened the kiss until Mac melted against him. He pushed her hair back, a luscious grin taking her breath away just before he kissed her one more time.

He caressed her throat as his gaze met hers, the bit of sadness turning his expression serious. "I'm not the *nice guy* you're looking for, Mac."

She drew back, and her gaze narrowed on him. There it was—just in case she didn't hear him right the first time. *I want you, Mac. We'd be good together, Mac. Just don't expect forever, Mac.*

She should have been angry, but she didn't have the energy. It was easier to blame herself for stepping off a cliff when she'd already known how far it was to the bottom. Didn't she just decide she was an adult? That she knew the rules? What a load of sentimental crap! And what was wrong with her anyway—falling for a guy she'd known for all of two days?

TEMPT THE NIGHT   171

Mac inhaled deeply and smiled, echoing his sadness. "I think you're wrong about that, Brady...but I understood you the first time around."

His brow furrowed, and uncertainty clouded his eyes. "Mac—"

Nick hurried toward them. "If you two are done gettin' better acquainted, we're about to have some company." He nodded toward the sky to the north and stepped over Mac's legs to grab their bags.

Brady scrambled to his feet. Mac shaded her eyes and squinted, trying to locate the source of the men's concern as Brady pulled her to her feet. That's when she saw it. A small jet approaching, just above the treetops and in a big hurry. She stumbled as Brady gripped her arm and pulled her toward one of the outbuildings. Beside the chopper, Nick was trying to convince Maria to leave the cargo bay and follow him. She was shaking her head, her hands planted firmly on her hips. As Mac and Brady reached the shed and pushed inside, Nick grabbed Maria's legs, draped her over his shoulder, and dashed after them.

They took cover in the shed as the jet flew over, low and fast.

"Put me down, you big jerk." Red-faced and livid, Maria landed on her feet, stumbled, and glared at Nick. "Don't ever...how dare you—" She threw her hands in the air. "Oh, what's the use? *No se puede esperar modales de un hombre de las cavernas!*"

If her high school Spanish was any good, Mac agreed with Maria's sentiment. Nick *had* acted like a caveman... but it was for a good reason, and she would try to convince

172 DIXIE LEE BROWN

her of that as soon as Mac figured out what the heck was going on.

She ducked involuntarily as the jet flew over again. Brady peered through a small window in the door, and when the noise of the plane's engines faded once more, he turned toward Nick, and the two men exchanged a nod.

"Okay...talk! What the hell's going on?" Mac looked back and forth between the men.

"We're getting out of here." Brady stood by the door, ready to jerk it open.

"But...they'll be back." Mac stood where she was. She wasn't going a step farther unless they let her in on the plan.

A warning flashed in Brady's eyes, and for a moment, Mac could see him picking her up and carrying her, kicking and screaming, to the helicopter.

An instant later, he seemed to relax, and amusement stole slowly across his features. "Can we at least move out while we're talking?"

For a heartbeat, everyone stood still, waiting for her answer.

Brady broke the impasse by opening the door. "The occupants of that plane can't hurt us. They can't land anywhere around here. The only thing they can do is call in another chopper or a ground assault team. Hopefully, we'll be out of here before they arrive." He leaned his head against the door.

Nick and Maria pushed through the doorway and jogged toward the helicopter.

TEMPT THE NIGHT 173

Mac watched until they were out of sight, then strode to within a foot of Brady. "So, we're just going to take off? Just like that? What if they shoot us down?"

Brady grinned smugly. "They can't."

"How could you possibly know that?"

"They just made two passes over a Blackhawk with its engines running, ready to take off, and they didn't fire a shot." He reached for her hand.

"And that's proof that they can't?"

He closed his hand over hers and tugged her closer. "It is where I come from, sugar."

Well, that was simply ridiculous, but somehow, with his warm hand around hers and his sea green eyes holding her gaze confidently, it was a foregone conclusion— she was putting her life in his hands...again.

She snorted and stepped through the opening ahead of him. As they ran side by side toward the helicopter, Mac stopped suddenly.

He paused a couple strides ahead and turned to peruse her curiously.

"What's to stop them from following us?"

Brady's crooked grin drew her in. "That's the best part. If they want to play, we've got the toys." He pointed at the Blackhawk. "Machine gun mounted in the cargo bay. I think we can discourage them, but if not...I'll do whatever it takes." When she didn't respond, he turned and continued to the helicopter.

Mac watched him walk away. Was he willing to kill again to keep her and Maria safe? Or was he simply *a killer*? Is that what he was trying to warn her about? The

174 DIXIE LEE BROWN

panic growing in the pit of her stomach wasn't about him. How many people had *she* killed since this nightmare began? Aside from a few twinges of guilt and horror after wounding the trooper in the alley, she hadn't had any big attacks of conscience. Eight men died in that chopper, and she hadn't given them a second thought. *My God. Am I as cold and jaded as Brady?*

"Mac." He motioned to her from the helipad, concern drawing his brows together.

She hurried toward him, and he helped her into the cargo bay. Maria already sat, her back to the cockpit. Mac took a seat beside her. Nick exchanged a few words with Brady before returning to the controls.

Brady pulled himself into the cargo bay, wincing and swearing when his wounded hand slipped off the bay door and collided with a metal ammunition box. His face paled, and he clutched a nearby seatback as the Blackhawk lifted off and turned south. After a few minutes, he slid into the movable seat attached to the machine gun assembly that appeared to hang in midair, protruding out the open door. He was quiet, tense, and that muscle flexed in his jaw. Was that a *tell*? Did that give away how much pain Brady was in? She was seconds away from going to him when the jet appeared from nowhere and raced by less than thirty feet off the port side, jostling the chopper in its jet wash.

Brady retrieved a pair of headphones that were hanging on the machine gun armament, pulled them over his ears, and positioned an attached speaker near the corner of his mouth. He inserted himself into the seat behind

TEMPT THE NIGHT 175

the weapon with his legs braced on either side. To Mac, it appeared that the only thing holding him in the craft was his braced legs and his grip on the gun. She swallowed a giant lump in her throat.

"Okay, Nick. Red-con-one. Let's get some. Line up the hostiles for me." Practically yelling into the speaker to be heard above the noise of the craft, Brady seemed at home in this environment—confident and ready. He glanced at her and winked.

Warmth filled Mac at his stupid gesture. A heartbeat later, Nick must have cracked a joke laced with testosterone because rough and bawdy laughter erupted from Brady.

Her white knuckles stared back at her from the armrests of her chair, which her hands clenched so tightly her fingers ached. She nearly jumped out of her skin when Maria gripped her wrist. "Don't worry, Mac. I think these two know what they're doing…even if they are idiots."

Mac snorted a laugh and squeezed Maria's hand. She liked this woman more and more. It was clear why Paddy had been attracted to her. She was beautiful, for one, but also caring and loyal. Mac had to grit her teeth to keep the grief for what they'd all lost from sucking her down.

The helicopter veered abruptly to starboard and slowed until it hovered in place. Suddenly, the jet was visible again, rushing straight at the open cargo bay from a couple hundred feet away. Evidently, the pilot got a good look at the big barrel of the machine gun staring him in the face because in the next instant, he also turned sharply to starboard.

176 DIXIE LEE BROWN

"We're goin' hot." Brady held the gun with both hands and peered through the scope at eye level. "Got a little precision-guided whoop-ass for ya, boys!" He opened fire, and the spray of lead drew a perfect line across the port side of the jet plane.

They turned sharply until all Mac could see was their tail section as they faded in the distance, leaving a trail of smoke that hadn't been there before. Only time would tell if that would be enough to convince them that pursuing the Blackhawk wasn't advisable, but Brady smiled at her like the victor he was.

As though his sparkling eyes and the seldom-seen dimple in his cheek were only for her, Mac's heart beat an erratic pattern that left her short of breath. She stood and slowly made her way across the bay to where he was extricating himself from the gunner's seat. When he turned to her, she slid her arms around his waist and leaned back to look in his face.

But one glimpse of his eyes and there was no mistaking the fact that something was wrong. She'd erroneously judged the glaze there to be a sparkle, and the *dimple* apparently emerged because he was clenching his jaw so tightly. Whether due to pain or something else, Mac couldn't ascertain, but she didn't like the thin sheen of sweat that coated his face.

She rose on her tiptoes to brush his lips with hers and stepped back with something that felt like a rock on her chest. He was burning up.

"Brady, what's wrong?" She tried to use her dispatcher's voice, but even then, it was heavily laced with concern.

TEMPT THE NIGHT   177

"We sent them home with their tails between their legs. The jet sustained severe enough damage to require their immediate landing, but they'll be okay if they don't dawdle. You're safe. Whatever the hell that was, your part in it is over. What could be wrong?" He feathered the hair back from her temple.

"You know that's not what I meant. You've got a fever. Are you sick?"

He glanced over her head toward Maria, then met Mac's gaze again. "Don't panic." Gripping her hand in his, he backed toward a row of seats aft. "My body's just fighting an infection." He sat and drew her down beside him.

"Infection? You mean your hand? It can't be infected already."

"Yes—it can. I've seen wicked infections set in within two or three hours. Granted, that was mostly in steamy, bug-infested jungles, but you have to trust me on this."

She opened her mouth to argue, but he squeezed her fingers and claimed her attention.

"I've had some experience with this before, Mac. I know my body. I just need to rest, push fluids…and take antibiotics as soon as Nick gets us to a hospital."

She tried to pull her hand from his, the need to help foremost in her mind. "Hospital? I'll tell Nick. There's one in Ketchikan."

"Whoa. Hold on. I already talked to Nick before we lifted off. We're way past Ketchikan. We're in British Columbia, heading for Prince George."

"That's over five hundred miles away."

178 DIXIE LEE BROWN

"Three and a half hours. Piece of cake. Now stop worrying...although I think I could get used to you worryin' about me, sugar." A crooked grin settled into place, but he leaned back in the seat and closed his eyes.

Mac tried to calm her nerves as she settled into the seat beside his. Thoughts were swirling at Mach nine in her head, and she tapped one foot, annoyed with herself for not paying closer attention. In hindsight, the signs of his ailment were glaring. He hadn't been the same silent, sure-footed SEAL coming off the slope as he'd been the first night they'd met. His skin had been damp with perspiration by the time they reached the helipad. She'd chalked it up to being in a hurry to make contact with the chopper pilot before he took off without them, but in reality, they'd taken half as long coming down the slope as they had going up. Add in the extra burden of his wound, and she hadn't considered it out of the ordinary. Why? Was she so focused on herself and what she was going through?

It was hard to even remember the person she'd been two days ago when Paddy was still alive, but she'd never considered herself shallow or selfish. For sure, Paddy would have told her if she was. He would never have put up with her copping an attitude...and she wasn't going to start now.

"I'll get you some water. Do you need more Advil? Are you hungry?"

A low chuckle rumbled in his chest. "Water would be good, thank you...yes, please, on the Advil...and no, thank you. I couldn't eat a bite."

TEMPT THE NIGHT 179

She started to stand, but he caught her arm. "Maria doesn't need to know."

Mac stared at his closed eyes. "She's stronger than you think."

"I know how strong she is, but she's got enough to worry about right now."

She was glad his eyes were closed and he couldn't see the embarrassment that surely flooded her cheeks. Even sick and in pain, his concern was for those around him. He was so different from any man she'd ever known, and damned if she didn't want to know what made him tick.

"I'll be right back." She scooted from the seat and crossed the open cargo bay, beginning to get a feel for the movement and vibration of the chopper. Brady's duffel yielded one last bottle of water. Maria, apparently anticipating Brady's need, had the pills ready to go.

"He's sick, isn't he?" Maria stared at Mac, and there was no way she could lie to her.

"He thinks the wound's infected."

Maria nodded her head like she'd expected as much. "There's a trunk in the back—it says FIRST AID. Maybe you'll find something useful. Do you want me to help?"

Mac touched her shoulder. "Thanks, Maria, but I've got it." She spoke with way more confidence than she felt.

She took the water and Advil to Brady, then headed to the trunk. Inside was more water—good to know—blankets, a portable defibrillator, bandages of all sizes and shapes, and antibiotic cream. Mac grabbed a blanket and a tube of cream and closed the lid.

Returning to sit beside him, she shook the folds from the blanket. "Maybe you should stretch out on the floor. I'll find something to use for a pillow." His eyes were still closed, and for a moment she was afraid she'd awakened him.

His eyelids opened slowly, and he ran both hands over his face, heaving a long breath. "The floor's not a bad idea." He hoisted himself from the seat and knelt, his uninjured hand gripping her knee. "Stay with me?"

He was so totally serious that, for an awkward moment, Mac could almost imagine he was asking for something more long-term than sitting with him until he fell asleep. Of course, that was utterly ridiculous, and she quickly shook off the sense of finally coming home that threatened to waylay her.

She couldn't meet his gaze, allowing hers to linger only on his wonderfully soft and talented lips. "Did you take your pills?"

He nodded, then leaned forward, bracing his weight on his strong arms until he lowered his body to the floor with ease and control. Mac covered him with the blanket, then hastened back to the trunk for another that would have to suffice for a pillow. She rolled the blanket and tucked it under his raised head.

"I found antibiotic cream too. Shall we put some on?"

He held up his hand and studied it. An amused wink caught her off guard. "Tempting offer, sugar, but it feels okay right now. It's wrapped up all pretty, thanks to you. Can we do it later?" Brady reminded her of a small boy trying to wheedle his way out of bedtime.

TEMPT THE NIGHT 181

"Later it is." She had trouble keeping a straight face.

"Now, will you answer my question?" His brow shot up.

"I…uh…I'll stay until you fall asleep."

"Well, what good is that? I can take care of myself while I'm awake. It's after I'm asleep that I need someone to watch my back." His sleepy smile was subdued, but clearly he enjoyed teasing her.

Her eyebrows raised in mock outrage. Then she shrugged. "How about if I sit with you after you fall asleep as long as you don't snore?"

"Perfect. SEALs don't snore."

He uttered the words so solemnly, Mac choked on the laughter that rose in her throat. "That's impossible. How could they train you not to snore?"

"I don't know. Might have been hypnosis. Might have just been plain old necessity. However they did it, they probably saved my life a hundred times over."

Mac narrowed her gaze. His claim sounded an awful lot like bullshit, but the seriousness of his expression had her second-guessing herself. Finally, she abandoned her quest for the truth and rolled her eyes. "Just go to sleep, already."

He reached for her hand and gave it a quick kiss. "One more question. Can we go…on a date…after all of this?" He was clearly struggling to keep his eyes open.

Mac snorted a laugh. He was so darn cute, asking for a date like they were going to the prom. How many girls had fallen for his boy-next-door routine? Would it be one date or two before he decided she was getting too close?

182 DIXIE LEE BROWN

"A date? That's what people do when they want to get to know each other better, right?"

Brady frowned. "That's what I want…to get to know you." He brought her hand to his chest and closed his eyes.

"And will I be accorded the same?"

He peeked from one eye as humor curled his lips. "I already told you that you'd learn more about me than you wanted to know. Weren't you listening, or did you decide to ignore me?"

"Did you say something?"

"Yeah…that's what I thought." A contented smile remained for a few minutes before his perspiration-covered face relaxed in sleep.

Chapter Twelve

BRADY'S RECOLLECTION OF the chopper landing and him jumping off to help Nick refuel two hours into their flight was hazy at best, but Mac, dogging his every step, would stand out in his mind forever. By the time they were finished, every ounce of his strength was gone, and he was only too happy to have her tuck him back under the blanket and sit leaning against him until he drifted off again.

Actually, he may have passed out at that point, because that was his last distinct memory before he woke up here—wherever here was. Mac had been in the room the first time he woke, sleeping in a chair beside the bed with her head on his arm. Whatever he'd said to her must have been gibberish, because she patted his hand and, with sleepy eyes, whispered as though she were talking to herself. "Wherever you are."

Did she think he was dead? Brady didn't argue with her.

184 DIXIE LEE BROWN

The next time he woke, she was gone. A solemn, unshaven, black-haired hardass was plopped in her chair instead. A pang of loneliness caught Brady off guard.

"Where's Mac?" His voice was as rough as his throat was dry.

Walker picked his head up from the magazine his nose had been buried in, and a smile transformed his rough features. "It's about fucking time you woke up."

"Is Joe here too?"

"He's currently trying to find an official who can keep your name off the report of people admitted with gunshot wounds." Walker tossed the magazine aside.

"Shit." Brady rolled his eyes toward the ceiling.

"Aw, hell. He needed something to do anyway."

"How long have I been out?"

"About fifteen hours." Walker leaned forward and braced his elbows on his knees. "So, doc said blood poisoning. That's the third time in four years, isn't it? What's up with that?"

Brady considered not answering for a moment, until he caught the familiar bulldog glint in Walker's eyes. He sighed. "You know how it is. One of your missions doesn't go quite the way it was supposed to, and you come out of it a little…different." He glanced toward the door.

Walker followed his gaze. "We're alone, and it won't leave this room. If that girl you hooked up with hadn't pushed to bring you to the hospital before we boarded Joe's plane, it could have been damn serious. You can't keep us in the dark on this and expect us to pick up the pieces. Level with me, Jim."

TEMPT THE NIGHT 185

If the determination in his eyes was any indication, Walker wasn't letting this go. Brady had never talked to another soul, except the Navy shrinks, but if anyone on the planet would understand, it was Walker. Marine Special Forces, Walker had been detained in a shithole in North Korea for months. *Detained* was the PC word for what went down there. Brady had only heard bits and pieces of his story, but enough to lead to a bond of friendship between the two of them. Maybe it *was* time.

He exhaled, long and slow, searching for the right words. "Somalia. Six years ago. The Navy inserted my team into Iskushuban. The target was a group of pirates who'd kidnapped a high-profile American couple from a beach resort in Kenya. Intel was good. We took the pirates out on the first sweep, and the rescue went off without a hitch. Then everything went to hell. The attack came from behind, and my sergeant and I fell back to hold them off until the rest of the unit and the kidnap victims reached the choppers and lifted off." Brady was clenching his fists so hard his wounded hand throbbed.

"We thought more pirates. We weren't expecting a full-on military type ambush from a well-armed rebel contingent. They eventually overran our position, and it was clear they wanted us alive. By the second day, we knew why. They started on my sergeant, shooting him full of shit, asking fucked-up questions...like how many American merchant ships would sail into the Gulf of Aden in the next year? Which crews would the US come after, and which ones would they leave to rot in captivity? For some reason, they thought we should be able to

186 DIXIE LEE BROWN

give names, dates, and cargo. When they found out we couldn't, or wouldn't as they believed, they OD'd the Sarge right in front of me, and there wasn't a fucking thing I could do about it." Six years since he'd watched his friend and fellow SEAL die in agony, choking on his own vomit, yet Brady remembered every excruciating detail. Even here in a hospital room with Walker sitting across from him, his fists curled as rage gripped him, cloaking him in a blood-red haze.

It was in the past. There was nothing he could do about it. He repeated that mantra to himself several times as he struggled to control his breathing and tamp down the crushing need to kill someone with his bare hands, conscious of Walker's steady perusal. A moment later, he cleared his throat and looked up.

"Then they started on me, only they experimented with different drugs and combinations of drugs. Some of them made me so sick, I prayed for death. I don't remember much of anything after that, except the day my men came for us. When they found out the Sarge was dead…they didn't quit until every rebel soldier was dead."

Walker nodded. "But it wasn't over for you, was it?"

Brady's heart rate quickened as he shook his head. "Four months I was in that hellhole before my unit came to get me, but the real prison was inside my head, and I couldn't shake it no matter where I went. I came out of there a dope addict with anger management issues. That wasn't the worst of it though. Every time I got sick or cut myself shaving, my body went into hyper drive, fighting

TEMPT THE NIGHT   187

something that attacked from the inside—something those bastards infected me with."

"No cure?" Walker's eyes revealed his anger.

"None so far. It's better than it was. It doesn't happen every time now. Meanwhile, I was asked to leave three different hospitals because I would fly into a rage for no reason, and they were afraid I'd hurt someone. The VA hospital in Richmond, Virginia, locked me up and treated my drug addiction with more drugs. Fucking idiots." He'd be dead by now if he'd stayed there.

"One day out of the blue, the rest of my unit came by. They sneaked in a general's uniform, and I walked out of there with them. I didn't realize what I was in for though. They wanted me *right,* and they didn't care what they had to do. If I thought BUD/S was tough, it was nothing compared to this." Eight weeks of basic conditioning leading up to hell week at the Naval Special Warfare Training Center had been ten times harder than he'd imagined. Pushing him to the limit for five and a half days with a total of four hours of sleep, BUD/S had taught him exactly how much more he could take…after he'd reached the end of his endurance.

A grin cracked Walker's somber expression.

"Those men never left me alone for a minute. We ate together, trained together, lived together. The only place I could get some alone time was in the shower. I spent a lot of time there." Brady chuckled. "Gradually, I got better… or so I thought. The guys were shipping out, and I was heading home to Eureka Springs, Arkansas. I'd met a girl at a bar down the road, and that last night in Richmond

188 DIXIE LEE BROWN

she took me home with her. In the middle of the night, I woke up with my hands wrapped around her throat, yelling in her face about filthy pirates and accusing her of being a spy. I remember the rage as clearly as though it were yesterday. Wanting to kill her. *Needing* to squeeze the life out of her."

"What stopped you?"

He'd almost forgotten Walker was there in the thirty seconds it took the memory to overwhelm him, and he shook his head. "Hell if I know. But I couldn't go home and take the chance of hurting my family. I couldn't allow anyone to get close, so I started moving around, taking odd jobs. When I'd get too attached, I'd move on. I was doing a stint as a bouncer in a club in Portland when I met Joe. He gave me his card and said I had a job anytime I wanted. That was the turning point for me."

Walker's piercing gaze bored into him. One thing he could be sure about—his friend wouldn't judge. Still, Brady was curious to know what was going on in his head.

"You've never been home?" Walker sat back in his chair, making it sound less like a question and more like a challenge.

"No…but it gets worse."

Walker quirked an eyebrow.

"I've gotten attached…to Mac."

Again, Walker's thorough perusal swept over Brady. "I've never even seen you get mad. How long's it been since you lost your cool?"

"Four years, eight months, and sixteen days."

TEMPT THE NIGHT 189

Walker snorted. "Just a rough estimate, huh? Did you ever hurt anyone else in one of your episodes?"

"Not yet." Dread hung on each word.

"Maybe it's over…your brain's had time to recoup."

"How can I take that chance?" Brady glanced toward the door again.

"Mac, huh? I practically had to push her out of here so she'd go get something to eat. Seems she may be *attached* as well…and she's a good-looking woman. How can you afford *not* to take a chance?"

"How long do you think she'll be interested once she hears *this* story?" Brady studied his wounded hand, bandaged, nestled in a white plastic splint, and held together with an Ace wrap.

Walker shrugged, and a grin creased his stubble-covered face. "Well, I listened…and I didn't run away. But you know her—what makes you think she'll bolt?"

"Damn it. That's the point. I haven't had time to get to know her, but I wouldn't mind finding out what kind of a girl she is…among other things." He grinned at Walker's smug look.

"Then go for it. You'll have nothing *but* time at the ranch. Of course you'll also have Darcy, Cara, Rayna, and probably even Irene playing matchmaker for you."

Brady groaned. "Might as well add Maria to that list."

"You don't stand a chance, my friend." Walker chuckled as he stood, but the humor quickly faded. "Remember, Jim, your unit might not be around right now, but you've still got friends. A few of us will be watching your back." Walker met his gaze just long enough to telegraph the dead seriousness of his statement. "Now, are you feeling good enough to get out of here yet?"

Brady yanked the tape off his IV and pulled the needle from his good hand. "Fucking A!"

"Okay then. I'll see what I can do about getting you released." Walker strode toward the door. "Don't run off."

Brady leaned back against the pillows, exhausted from the weight of what he'd shared. He felt lighter though, like the act had unburdened him. For a moment, he allowed thoughts of his mother and two sisters to enfold him in a world with dense forests, intense humidity, and the smell of his mama's apple pies cooling on the porch. His mother had tried to be strong, but it was no secret that it had devastated her when he didn't come home. He tried to keep in touch by phone and e-mail, but sometimes he could tell it wasn't enough.

A growl rumbled in his throat as he tossed the blankets aside angrily. All this speculation that he might have finally beaten his greatest fear was just that—speculation. He wasn't going to make his family…or Mac…guinea pigs.

Brady swung his legs off the bed and stood, fighting against the light-headedness from rising too quickly. Other than that, he felt pretty damn good. His hand no longer hurt excruciatingly, although that could be because of something in the IV he just detached, but it was welcome nonetheless.

"Hey, what are you doing out of bed?" Mac's voice was music to his ears and instantly banished his irritation.

He turned and smiled, until he saw her red-rimmed eyes with dark circles beneath and the tremble of her jaw

TEMPT THE NIGHT 191

as she met his gaze. Even in the same jeans and yellow top he'd bought her at Goodwill and with her hair tangled and tousled, she was the most beautiful woman he'd ever seen. "Might have known you'd catch me in my fancy hospital gown."

A second of laughter brought a sparkle to her eyes as she looked him up and down, but it faded as quickly as it had appeared. "You could be the poster boy for hospital gowns."

"I bet you say that to all the guys." He held out his arm, inviting her closer, but she only stepped to the foot of the bed and sat, her back to him.

"No...I can't say I've ever said that before."

He walked around the end of the bed and sat next to her. "Sorry if I scared you, Mac." Something was definitely wrong. She was nervous, jumpy, and it was plain to see she'd been crying. The anger that welled up in him, knowing that someone had made her cry, was reminiscent of the old rage that he couldn't control. "Do you want to tell me what's wrong?"

"Nothing, now that I know you're okay." Her smile was a bit thin, but the right side of her mouth didn't lift, and she held his gaze without blinking. In the absence of her *tell,* he had to believe her.

She was no doubt exhausted and overwhelmed with everything that had happened in the last two days. In addition, she was grieving for her friend. God knew that was enough. Brady would make sure she got the rest she needed once they reached Montana. Still, heaviness gathered in his chest.

192   DIXIE LEE BROWN

Voices in the hall warned him ten seconds before Walker and Joe came through the doorway. Walker went straight for the white cabinet beside the bed and pulled out his clothes and boots. He tossed the clothes on the bed and slapped an envelope down on the table. "Got your walkin' papers, Jim. Need some help gettin' dressed?"

"I think I can manage, but thanks. Mac...this wild-looking character is Walker. Don't worry, he's harmless most of the time." Brady sensed her tension and swiveled his head to study her as she glanced toward Walker.

"We've met." She sent a fleeting look toward Brady. "He uh...sat with you for a bit while I went to get a bite."

"Right. She'd been here so long, I was afraid she'd pass out from hunger." Walker suddenly seemed on edge... wary.

As Brady watched him for a clue to what was making him so uptight, Walker's gaze went cold for the space of a heartbeat in what could only be considered a warning. To Mac? What the hell?

"Yeah, she was pretty worried about your sorry ass." Joe stepped forward and gripped Brady's shoulder. "Glad you got her here safe and sound. We'll do everything we can to make sure she and Maria stay that way."

"I can't thank you enough for helping. I've got a little money saved. I can pay you the rest over time, if you're okay with that." Mac seemed much more comfortable with Joe.

Joe's gaze swept to Brady and back. "This one's on us." He stepped back. "First order of business is getting you and Maria out of here and someplace where we can protect you."

TEMPT THE NIGHT 193

"Where is Maria?" Brady felt guilty for not asking before now.

"She's with Nick. He's taking good care of her. Oh, by the way, I offered him a job, so he's coming home with us to check it out." Joe turned to go. "I know for a fact you don't need my help getting dressed, so I'll meet you downstairs."

Walker was close on his heels. Mac grinned and got up to leave also.

Brady grabbed her hand. "Everything all right? Anything I should know about?"

"Everything's great." Her smile looked forced.

He could tell by the way her expression closed up that she wasn't being totally honest. "I wish you'd level with me, Mac." He reached to toy with a lock of hair that had fallen forward over her shoulder.

She jerked away, and a spark of irritation flashed in her eyes. He was sure she was going to let him have it for something he'd done or said, but she stopped and got to her feet.

In a way, he was sorry. He wanted whatever was bothering her out in the open. Mostly, he wanted her to trust him. But it was okay for now. He had time…and he wasn't giving up. "Will you wait while I dress? We can walk down together."

She brushed her hair off her forehead and gave him a weak smile. "Walk? I happen to know your wheelchair is already waiting in the hallway."

He snickered, reaching out to ruffle her hair. "Fine, then. You can push."

194 DIXIE LEE BROWN

"I can do that, but don't call me if you need help getting your pants on." Mac strode slowly toward the door. Halfway there, she glanced over her shoulder and must have seen his lewd smile. She turned with hands on hips. "What now?"

"Just thinking how much fun it would be to have your help getting them *off*." He kept a straight face while his gaze dared her to look away.

She didn't, and her angelic smile projected a challenge of her own. He was proud of her. Her expression went from shocked to amused in only a few seconds. Then she turned and started walking again, and her sweet voice drifted back. "Get your ass dressed, Brady."

Chapter Thirteen

No points for good intentions.

For at least the hundredth time since pausing outside Brady's room on her way back from the cafeteria, Mac berated herself for not simply walking away. Instead, her attention had been riveted on the tale of Somali pirates and kidnapping victims, related softly in Brady's low voice. Intrigued and curious, she'd stepped closer to listen, enthralled...and then stunned.

Frozen in place, tears rimming over and rolling down her cheeks, she'd slapped her hand over her mouth to keep her outrage at what had been done to him from escaping in groans of protest. Finally, she'd forced her feet to move, backing away until the voices receded, then glancing around to determine the best escape route.

She hadn't been quick enough. Walker had burst from the room with long strides and collided with her, his size

196 DIXIE LEE BROWN

and weight nearly sending her sprawling if he hadn't reached out at the last second and steadied her.

Clearly, he'd known immediately that she'd overheard at least part of their conversation. His obvious scorn and cold distrust had sent a shiver coursing down her spine. It had been an extremely personal confession from one friend to another...not intended for her ears. She understood that, and he wasn't the only one who'd wished she hadn't overheard. Still, his distrust had seemed excessive in the face of her minor indiscretion, and she'd been happy to stay as far from him as possible on the final leg of their trip.

It went without saying that hiding behind a door outside Brady's room wasn't how she'd envisioned learning about his private hell. She'd wanted him to trust her enough to look her in the eyes and share that part of his life. This way it meant nothing...except an extra layer of guilt to carry around. She grappled with the likelihood that Walker would tell Brady she'd been eavesdropping. He'd no doubt be hurt, maybe angry—feel betrayed. No way was she coming out of *this* with a gold star.

There was only one thing she could do. She had to tell Brady before Walker did.

Finding a moment for a private conversation was easier said than done during a whirlwind trip on Joe's private jet with six people, including one Nick Taylor making sure there was never any down time. Or in the black Hummer that met them at Joe's secluded airfield, adding a driver by the name of Ty Whitlock to the roster. And now, sitting between Walker and Brady in the second row of seats, she was about to enter the grounds of Joe's ranch, a few miles outside of Kalispell, Montana.

It was dusk. The sun had disappeared beneath the horizon, leaving a pink and reddish glow in the predark sky. Silhouettes of trees and mountains stood watch in the distance. A chain link fence, topped with a strand of razor wire, stretched as far as Mac could see in both directions. Even though the gate stood open, she didn't get a cozy, welcoming vibe as they drove through. When the gate closed behind them with a metallic clank, she jumped and probably would have had a panic attack right there if Brady hadn't calmly laced his fingers with hers.

"It's a good place, Mac. You'll like it. The house is big and comfortable, with lots of room. Most of the hired help stays there so there's always people coming and going. Joe also trains certain government employees in basic survival skills, among other things, so there are usually a few students hanging around. Everyone eats at the house, but the students stay in the bunker out back." He leaned closer, and his whispered words were for her ears only. "Relax, sugar. It's going to be all right."

Whether his pep talk had made her less apprehensive was doubtful, but she smiled into his eyes in silent appreciation for the effort.

"The gate keeps unauthorized people out. Doesn't mean you can't go into town or for a walk around the lake." Joe, looking back from the front seat, picked up the running narrative where Brady left off, making an obvious effort to include Maria, sitting in the third row of seats with Nick. "Tomorrow, Brady will give you the access code and explain the buddy system we'll use until we're sure you're both out of danger."

"All I care about is seeing my son." Anticipation rang in Maria's words.

Joe nodded. "That's what this was all about. You're welcome to stay here as long as you want, so you'll have to tell *me* when you're ready to figure out the next step." Joe's phone chirped, and he fished it from his shirt pocket. He studied the lighted screen for a few seconds, then typed in a return message.

Dropping the phone back in his pocket, he swiveled in the seat, and it was clear he now spoke to Walker, Brady, Nick, and Ty. "Change of plans. We've got company. An acquaintance of mine—Guy Hanford—special agent with the State Department. I've worked with him before. Rayna said he called right after Ty left to pick us up and wanted to talk. She told him we were a ways out yet, but he said it was urgent, and he wanted to come out and wait."

Walker snorted sarcastically. "If it's so urgent, why didn't he call you directly?"

Mac could tell by the silent confirmation that passed between the two men that Joe was equally suspicious. The way he avoided her eyes when his gaze swept to Brady made her wonder if there wasn't more to his concern— something to do with her and Maria.

"Turns out he wasn't alone. He brought three body-guards trying to pass as civil servants and a Mexican diplomat of some sort."

At the gasp from the back of the vehicle, Joe and everyone in the second row turned to stare at Maria.

TEMPT THE NIGHT 199

"Does that mean something to you?" That tick in Brady's jaw was making itself known.

The Hummer turned the final corner, giving Mac a view of a lovely three-story house surrounded by expanses of well-kept green grass and beds of wildflowers. It would have been enough to take her breath away if she hadn't been so focused on the black SUV with government plates parked in front.

The fear in Maria's eyes was unmistakable. Did she know who this diplomat was? A shiver of apprehension ran through Mac. Could it be only a coincidence that Hernandez, the man who was looking for them, was Mexican and there was an ambassador of Mexican descent waiting in Joe's house? Common sense said no. There was every possibility that the man waiting for them was responsible for Paddy's murder. Mac stared at the seat in front of her but saw only the upstairs room at the fish packing plant and her best friend barely clinging to life.

Brady squeezed her hand, searching her eyes with concern in his, and brought her back to the present.

She met the other woman's gaze, speaking softly. "They want to help, Maria. You can't let them walk in there blind. You have to answer their questions."

Maria was breathing erratically, clearly anxious. "Raul Hernandez is the Mexican Ambassador to the United States...but how would he know where to find us?"

"I think the question is...why has he gone to so much trouble to find us?" Brady turned toward the front.

Ty pulled up beside the SUV and parked. No one made a move to get out.

Joe stared toward the house. "Okay, Maria has left a few holes in her story, but we know enough not to trust him. I want him and his goons out of my house for now. Maria can enlighten us later. Here's how this'll go down." He swiveled his head, and his gaze swept over Mac. "Brady will take the women in the back door and upstairs. Rayna sent Sanchez up to hang out with Marco out of an abundance of caution. He's in the room next to mine."

His gaze locked on Brady. "We'll give 'em a few more minutes to stew until you get back downstairs, then go in together. Nick...this is what you came to see, so you might as well tag along."

"Wouldn't have it any other way," Nick said.

"Let's do it." Walker opened his door, a grin lighting his eyes as he stepped out, turning to pull his seatback forward, allowing Maria and Nick to exit. On Mac's other side, Brady jerked the door handle with his right hand and turned to look at her. Joe and Ty stepped out, leaving her and Brady alone in the vehicle.

"Mac?" Brady slid his arm around her shoulders. "He's not going to hurt you. We're going to take care of this. Come with me, and I won't leave your side until you feel safe."

She tried, but she couldn't move. A sea of anger roiled within her, and caution was apparently the first thing to be tossed overboard. If the person responsible for the plot to kill Paddy was in that house, she *had* to see him. More accurately, *he* had to see that she wasn't afraid. Ridiculous, of course, because her knees were shaking even now, but this was something she had to do for Paddy.

TEMPT THE NIGHT 201

"No!" Mac struggled to get the word out. As a result, it was louder and more desperate than she'd anticipated.

Brady's other arm came around her, enveloping her in his warmth. Joe, Walker, and the rest turned to stare.

Brady laid his forehead against hers. "Talk to me, Mac. What's going on?" His voice was calm and patient, as though they had all the time in the world to debate her sanity.

Mac leaned into him. He probably didn't know how his kindness grounded her. Someday maybe she'd tell him. "I have to see him, Brady. I need to look Hernandez in the face and make him understand he's not going to get away with killing my best friend."

"It's not a good idea, Mac. We don't know what they've got in mind or how far they're willing to go to finish what they started. It could be dangerous. I don't want you anywhere near him."

His protectiveness and concern went straight to her heart, starting a strange ache. She appreciated the way he always seemed to put her safety first—like she was important. Maybe she was…in his short-term world, but it didn't stop the burning in her gut. She raised her gaze to his. "I know…I know you're right, but I can't…I have to see the bastard."

Brady frowned and looked through the windshield to where Joe waited.

"Let her come." Walker peered through the door on her right, his expression unreadable.

A shiver vibrated through Mac, and she briefly pondered his motives, but surely his animosity didn't extend

202 DIXIE LEE BROWN

to hoping she'd get herself killed. She met Joe's gaze through the window.

"Up to you, Jim. You've managed to keep her alive so far." Joe turned toward the house.

Mac swept her gaze back to Brady. She straightened her spine and raised her head. "I can do this."

The muscle worked in his jaw—a habit she was starting to associate with concern. She hated worrying him, yet it warmed her insides to think he cared.

"I have to, Brady."

He shook his head and exhaled slowly. "*Don't* leave my side." He barked out the words.

Was he irritated with her? "I won't. I need you beside me." Mac looked away but still felt his piercing stare. After a couple of seconds, he released her and offered his hand. She placed hers firmly in his, and together they stepped out of the vehicle.

Joe had everyone gathered close to the house. "Ty took Maria upstairs. He'll be back as soon as he delivers her to Sanchez." As Joe finished speaking, Ty appeared around the corner of the house.

"All right. Everybody ready?" Joe looked directly at Mac.

She nodded, afraid her voice would quaver if she spoke.

"Stay with me." Brady brushed his arm against hers.

Nick stepped forward as soon as the door opened, following Joe and Walker into the house. Mac and Brady went next, and Ty brought up the rear.

Inside, they were met by a beautiful blonde woman dressed in a black tank top and camouflage shorts. She

TEMPT THE NIGHT   203

spoke quietly with Joe for a few seconds before falling in beside him as he strode down a hallway to the right and threw open the first door on the left. Mac could see a desk, stacked with papers and ringed by chairs, toward the back of the room. Five men turned simultaneously and stared.

Joe pushed forward, going directly to a stocky man of medium height in his midforties, with a full and unruly head of black hair. "Hanford, I'm confused. You know me, and you know how I work. Yet you brought strangers into my house without my okay?" Joe stopped three feet away, and his gaze flickered over the man's entourage.

A head shorter than Joe and clearly nervous, the man he'd addressed as Hanford looked as though he couldn't find the right place for his hands and a lot like he'd be happy to crawl into a hole if the opportunity presented itself. Mac almost laughed at the way Joe's words made him squirm.

Then her gaze landed on the man who could be none other than the *diplomat*. Five-ten or eleven, well-muscled build, brown skin, wavy black hair, and dark, piercing eyes that stared at her with such intensity she shuddered. His three creepy associates were positioned close beside him.

Hanford finally found his voice. "Joe, I'd like you to meet Raul Hernandez, the Mexican Ambassador to the United States."

Joe barely glanced toward the man who stood a couple of feet away.

"Ambassador Hernandez is here on a matter of some urgency, and under the circumstances, I thought you'd

204 DIXIE LEE BROWN

want to speak to him without delay." Hanford recovered his confidence and even managed a smirk.

Walker and Rayna fanned out to the right, parallel to the wall. Ty and Nick followed suit on the left. Mac and Brady stood together, front and center, and Hernandez still stared brazenly across the room at her. Beside her, Brady evidently noticed. He tensed, and a growl vibrated low in his chest.

Hernandez abruptly dropped his gaze, turned, and strode toward Joe. "Mr. Reynolds, please don't hold Special Agent Hanford responsible. I convinced him to help me gain an audience with you." He offered his hand.

Joe ignored the overture, his gaze traveling from the man's outstretched hand upward to his face. "By all means, let's hear what you have to say, Ambassador."

Hernandez beamed as though he'd just been paid the highest compliment. "I knew you were a reasonable man who would help me if you can. First, I wish to give you some information that could save lives." He swung his arm toward Mac. "You have a cold-blooded murderer in your midst." His voice boomed.

Mac stumbled backward a step, shocked at his public attack, and might have lost her balance if Brady hadn't caught her around the waist.

He leaned close. "Easy, Mac. Look him in the eye. Don't back down." His words were only a breath at her ear.

Right. Easier said than done once she'd already failed the test, but she stood tall, fisted her hands at her sides, and met Hernandez's gaze. Tension rolled off the occupants of the room, and Brady was no exception.

TEMPT THE NIGHT 205

Joe's voice was hard-edged and cold. "Worming your way in here and making allegations about one of my *invited* guests is two strikes against you. Make it three, and you're out. If I were you, I'd think long and hard about whatever you were going to say next."

Hernandez folded his hands behind his back and studied his shoes. "My apologies, Mr. Reynolds. It was not my intention to accuse anyone. Only to point out that your *guest* bears a remarkable likeness to someone the Alaska State Troopers have launched an extensive manhunt for."

Mac was livid. With each sophisticated-sounding word, she wanted to pummel Hernandez's superior expression. When she leaned forward, preparing to take the first of many steps to do just that, Brady's fingers shoved inside the back waistband of her jeans and kept her from moving.

"I suppose you're going to tell me what this person did to deserve all of this attention?" Joe's gaze shifted to the three uneasy bodyguards and then back to Hernandez.

The ambassador smirked. "Since you asked, I'd be derelict in my responsibilities if I didn't. According to the official police report, this…person laid waiting in the dark and killed two state troopers."

Joe's brow rose. "No shit? That would be quite a feat… for someone the size and strength of my guest."

"On the contrary. It takes no particular strength to stab one of them in the back and shoot the other, especially if the killer knew her victims and was able to get close to them without raising their suspicions."

206 DIXIE LEE BROWN

A moan of protest escaped Mac, drawing a sharp warning glance from Joe, and Brady rubbed her lower back, reminding her he was still close beside her.

"Thanks for the personal notice." Walker stared them down as Hernandez and his men swiveled and appraised the new speaker. "We'll be on the lookout for anything suspicious. If that's all, I'm happy to show you and your goons out now."

"If you'll allow me a few more minutes of your time, there is something else." Hernandez swung toward Joe.

Raising his hands partway, Joe shrugged.

"Two years ago, my wife abducted my son. Today, they took refuge with you."

Brady tensed beside Mac, and energy practically sizzled from his coiled muscles. She shared his shock and disbelief. Was he really Marco's father? If so, Maria must have had a good reason for taking off with her son. Hernandez was a liar and a murderer. What more did they need to know? Maria was obviously terrified of the man.

"Are you telling me that Maria Alverez is your wife?" Joe was apparently surprised too.

"That's not the name she went by back then, but we can go with that if you wish. Yes, Maria is my wife, and Marco is my son. I only ask to be allowed to speak with her…alone."

"No!" Mac's outburst startled even herself. She sensed everyone's gaze on her and rejected the urge to lean into Brady.

His hand on her back flexed ever so faintly, as though he could infuse her with his strength. "Tell him, Mac."

The trust in his eyes warmed her everywhere his glance fell.

Her breath trembled even though she despised herself for it. "This is the creep Maria's afraid of. She won't let him near her son. Hernandez is a liar. We already know that, but that's not the worst of it. He's responsible for Officer Patrick Callahan's murder." Mac started out looking at Brady—talking to him—but before she finished, she was staring straight into the cold, scornful eyes of Ambassador Hernandez.

"That's quite an accusation coming from you, Ms. McCallister." His lips twisted in a snarl.

"You haven't seen anything yet. I won't stop until you're behind bars." Mac smiled icily. He was just a bully—nothing more.

"I'm afraid your efforts will be wasted. I'm sure you've heard of diplomatic immunity." He threw his head back and laughed.

Mac inhaled sharply. Of course, she'd heard of it. She just hadn't thought of it in this context. Surely it couldn't be possible that this evil man would get away with murder. Her gaze flew to Brady.

His touch on her back reassured her as he stared soberly at the ambassador. "That's a fucking riot, Hernandez. Still, you might want to show a little more respect for Ms. McCallister."

Hernandez snorted scornfully. "And why is that?"

"Simple. She's the only one here who voted for putting you in jail, but she may come over to the dark side yet. There's only one cure for diplomatic immunity." Brady

208 DIXIE LEE BROWN

paused. "Go ahead and stick around town if you want to, but I wouldn't suggest it."

Surely anyone who heard the stone-cold hardness of Brady's tone would know how dead serious he was. Mac stared at his profile, overcome by the promise in his words. How far would he go? How far did she want him to go? Suddenly, an eye for an eye seemed far preferable to no justice at all.

"Is that a threat, Mr. Brady?" Hernandez took a step toward him.

Brady shoved Mac behind him and strode forward to meet Hernandez. The three bodyguards swarmed toward the action, hands going for something unseen under their jackets, but everyone hesitated at the sound of a pump-action shotgun chambering a round. Mac's gaze flew to Walker.

He stepped in front of Brady, stopping him six paces from Hernandez. "That wasn't a threat, *Ambassador*. That was a warning—the only one you're going to get."

Hernandez's eyes bulged with the rage that twisted his face into a sneer. "We're leaving, but this isn't over. You have my wife and child, and you have no right to keep them from me." He turned to glare at Mac. "As for aiding and abetting a wanted criminal, we'll see what the State Department has to say."

Hernandez tried to push Walker out of the way, but when he found that Walker couldn't be moved, he skirted around him instead. The bodyguards fell in behind. Walker, Ty, and Nick followed, probably to make sure they got through the gate without getting sidetracked.

TEMPT THE NIGHT 209

Hanford stopped beside Joe. "Son of a bitch. I had no idea, Joe. Don't blame you for being pissed, but I'll see what I can find out about the wife and kid and the murders he's talking about. I'll be in touch."

"Thanks, Guy. I'd appreciate that." Joe and Rayna walked him out.

Mac almost felt sorry for Special Agent Hanford, but he deserved to be stuck in a vehicle with the furious Ambassador Hernandez after bringing him here with no advance notice. Still, it was sure to be an unpleasant drive. She could barely breathe just being in a room he recently vacated.

Turning on her heels, she started for the door. "I need some air."

Chapter Fourteen

BRADY FOLLOWED MAC as she pushed by Joe and Rayna at the front door and was momentarily illuminated in the yard light. The ambassador paced near the car with barely restrained rage, his henchmen huddled close by, and Ty, Nick, and Walker stood watch over them. Mac gave no indication she even saw them as she jogged across the grass, turned the corner, and disappeared in the dark shadow of the house.

Joe dropped his hand on Brady's shoulder, stopping him. "I'd like you and Mac to be there when I talk to Maria. I think she'll be more comfortable if she has friends in the room."

Brady nodded. "Give Mac a few minutes to get her head on straight."

"Take as long as you need." Joe turned his attention back to the car.

Hanford slid behind the wheel and started the engine. The others hurried to climb in, clearly not good with the idea of being left behind. Brady would have liked to show them out himself, but no doubt Walker would leave a lasting enough impression. Anyway, Brady had more important things to do at the moment.

When he rounded the corner of the house, Mac was nowhere to be seen. Brady slowed and then stopped. Where in the hell had she gotten to so quickly? He listened. No footsteps. No faint breaths. Lifting his head, he drew in the night aromas. Pine trees, a fishy smell off the lake, the residual odor of gunpowder from the firing range…and there it was. Whatever scent she exuded reminded him of his mother's apple pies—sugar and spice.

He closed his eyes and concentrated, swinging in a slow circle. After a few seconds, he stopped, opened his eyes, and smiled. The dog kennels were a hundred and fifty feet north of the house. Dillon, Joe's shepherd, and Ribs, Rayna's pit bull, hadn't been turned out for the night yet. How had Mac managed to get anywhere close without them sounding the alarm?

As he approached, Ribs stood and gave a halfhearted woof. "Sure, now you bark…you sorry sack of—"

"I told them not to." Mac rose from her position kneeling against the wooden shed beside the kennels.

Brady halted, trying to make out her familiar curves in the moonlight. "Are you telling me you're a dog whisperer now?"

212 DIXIE LEE BROWN

"Don't be ridiculous. I didn't whisper." Her voice was thin and tired. Shoulders slumped as she turned away and braced her arms against the wall.

He strode to her. Reaching out to draw her against him, he hesitated. He wanted nothing more than to hold her, feel her softness against him. No, that wasn't entirely true. He also wanted her beneath him...his manhood deep inside her...thrusting hard and fast until his need for her was sated once and for all. His dick responded with a twitch.

He pivoted, leaning his back against the wall, so close to her his arm brushed her side.

Mac folded her arms above her head, leaning her body against the wooden structure. She turned her head and stared at him. "Can he really get away with it?"

Brady met her gaze. "Not if we don't let him."

"So what you're saying is that in order to stop him, we have to become as bad as he is."

"That's not what I said. Every day good people make decisions to stop men just like Hernandez. Navy SEALs, Marines, every division of the military. Men like your friend Callahan. Women too. Not everyone is equipped. Most shouldn't try, but my friends and I are uniquely qualified. I can guarantee you that Hernandez won't go unpunished."

Mac raised her head and studied him. "Why would you do that?"

"You mean aside from the fact that it *needs* to be done?" He paused and threw her a grin. "I'd do it for you...so you'd have closure, and most importantly, so you don't have to look over your shoulder for the rest of your life wondering when that SOB was coming for you."

Mac's chest heaved once…twice…as though she was having trouble breathing. Suddenly, she pushed away from the wall and stepped in front of him. "It's not fair."

Her angry eyes shone with unshed tears, and once again he had to redirect his thoughts to keep from pulling her into his arms. "Shit's never fair." His life was a testament to that.

She pursed her lips and studied him. "That's deep, Brady." A crooked grin gradually appeared, erasing the worry wrinkles in her forehead. Then, without any encouragement from him, Mac took a step closer and leaned into his chest, sliding her arms around his waist.

He hesitated only a second before wrapping her in his arms and pulling her close. A groan escaped him.

She shifted her head to glance up. "Do you mind?"

A soft chuckle vibrated through him. "Sugar, I'll hold you anytime—anywhere."

Mac snuggled closer, and he tipped her head with his fingers, slowly covering her mouth with his, giving her plenty of time to change his mind. When she didn't, he drank of her sweetness like a man dying of thirst. Again and again he kissed her, his tongue pushing into her mouth, swirling and dancing with hers. He couldn't get enough of her full, soft lips, her sweet taste, and the bold way she pressed against him.

Brady couldn't say which of the day's events was responsible for her change in temperature where he was concerned, but it wasn't important. They were taking

214 DIXIE LEE BROWN

steps in the right direction, and he wasn't going to do anything to screw that up. He wanted her warm and willing in his hands, but he also wanted her there for the right reasons. The decision was hers to make.

When he lifted his head, there were tears on her eyelashes, but her smile made his heart grab an extra beat. He let his fingers trail across the satin skin of her cheek as he kissed her neck tenderly and breathed in her sweet scent.

"God, you smell good." He kissed each of her closed eyes, then leaned his forehead on hers and took a deep breath. "I'd love for this to go on all night. Unfortunately, Joe wants us to meet with Maria." He steadied her as she straightened and took a step back.

Mac's gaze was uncertain. "We could meet later...if you want to..."

"Aw, sugar. If *I* want to? That's like asking if I want to keep breathing." He threaded his fingers in her hair and brushed his lips over hers. "I've wanted you since the first time you lied to me." Brady chuckled as her eyes lit up.

She punched his chest with a fisted hand. "Hey! That was the only time I lied, and I had a darn good reason. Some big galoot knocks me down, pounces on me, and then expects me to be truthful. Huh-uh. I don't think so." Her eyes sparkled with challenge.

"*Galoot*, huh? No more John Wayne movies for you, sugar."

She sucked in a big breath, and he could tell by the mischief in her eyes she was getting ready to let him have it. He touched his fingers to her lips to silence her. "Let

TEMPT THE NIGHT 215

me say this, okay? There's a good chance we'll go in and meet with Maria, and sometime before, after, or during you'll think about us—about me—and decide we're not a good idea. I want you to know two things. First…it's the best idea I've had in a long time. Second…if you decide it's a mistake or that you're not ready to get any closer, that's okay. No pressure."

He stepped back and gave her some room. It struck him that he'd just lied to her. What he said would have been true for any other woman he'd ever known, but he damn sure wasn't going to give up on Mac that easily.

A grin made the sparkle in her eyes dance as she slipped her hand in his. "Obviously, you're confusing me with some other woman, because I don't usually change my mind once it's made up, and I'm a big girl, so you can stop worrying that your charm, good looks, and sex appeal will bowl me over. As for thinking about you—yeah." She stepped closer and lowered her voice to a silky whisper. "You might cross my mind once or twice…so let's get this meeting over with."

"You got it, sugar." Brady couldn't remember when he'd been so contented—or when he'd ever used that word to describe himself before. Whether or not tonight ended with him in bed with this amazingly beautiful and brave woman didn't really matter. The last few minutes had made it clear that his interest in her went way beyond just the prospect of sex. He wanted everything she had to give. *Shit!* She'd turned him upside down and inside out until he doubted his own ability to walk away…or even if he wanted to.

216   DIXIE LEE BROWN

The dogs jumped up and paced their kennels as Brady and Mac skirted their enclosures on their way to the house. Mac paused to poke a finger through the wire and stroke one of their muzzles. "What are their names?"

Brady came alongside her and laced his fingers with hers. "Okay, Ms. I'm-not-a-dog-whisperer—the shepherd is Dillon. He doesn't like people much, except for Joe and his wife, Cara…and you, apparently. The pit bull belongs to Rayna. His name is Ribs, due to the fact he was mostly ribs when she found him. He's a cream puff…unless you're trying to hurt Rayna."

"Is she the pretty blonde who met us inside when we arrived?"

"Yes. Sorry there wasn't time for introductions. Tomorrow, I'll show you around, introduce you to everyone, and if you still want me to teach you to shoot, we can start whenever you're ready." Brady slid his arm around her waist and turned her toward the house.

As they approached the front door, he saw the women sitting on the porch. He should have known that now that the visitors were gone, these four wouldn't wait another minute to meet the new arrivals.

He sensed the tension in Mac. "Don't worry. You'll love them, and they'll love you." He removed his arm and grabbed her hand. "Just don't believe everything they say about me." He winked, warmed by the smile he received in return.

Irene was the first to rise and come toward them. She put her arm around Mac's shoulders and deftly pried her loose from Brady.

He started to protest and then just shook his head. "Uh...Mac, this is Irene. She manages the house and, well, pretty much everything else." He shoved his hands in his pockets and trailed along behind.

"Hi, Mac. Forgive me for butting right into your conversation, but I get so excited when we get a female visitor. We don't get very many of those, as you might imagine—although it's better than it used to be." Irene beamed at the three ladies still seated on the porch.

"Irene, Mac and I have to meet Joe. We're probably already late." Brady stepped toward the front door.

"And we're entertaining Marco while you have your meeting with Joe and Maria. It'll just take a minute to introduce Mac to the girls." Irene dismissed Brady with a wave of her hand.

One by one, she introduced Mac to Joe's wife, Cara; Walker's fiancée, Darcy; and Ty's girlfriend, Rayna. As Brady knew they would, the women welcomed Mac with open arms and a healthy dose of chatter. It was good to see her relax and smile, responding to the complete acceptance the others offered. Finally, though, he began to tap his foot and then cleared his throat.

Cara glanced toward him and stopped in the middle of her sentence. "Oh...we should let you go. We can gab tomorrow." She threw Brady an apologetic smile.

Irene patted Mac's hand. "Sorry, dear. It was really only supposed to take a minute." Laughter followed her comment. "I had your bag taken up to your room on the third floor. It's none of my business, honey, but there's not much in there."

218 DIXIE LEE BROWN

Mac's cheeks reddened. "I'd have less than that if Brady hadn't bought me some things." She stretched out the bottom of the yellow top she wore.

Irene glanced at him with appreciation in her eyes, then back at the women. "Ladies, I see a shopping trip in our future."

There were a couple of hoots and a shrill whistle. Mac smiled, and for the first time since he'd met her, she seemed to let her guard down. This—sitting on the porch with her new women friends—would be good medicine. He could already feel his jaw tighten as the thought of sharing her wound him up. Where the hell did that come from? First of all, she wasn't his to share. Second, even if she was, he couldn't keep her.

Nodding as the women included him in their goodbyes, he held the door open for Mac and followed her through.

Ty approached and jabbed his head toward the open study door. "Maria will be down in a minute." He walked on by them and entered the room.

Mac's apprehensive gaze met Brady's. "Joe won't be angry with her for not being honest about her connection to Hernandez, will he?"

"Naw. That's not the way he operates." They both turned as they heard Maria and Marco descending the stairs.

Marco waved toward Brady, his face glowing with a brilliant smile. His happiness, although understandable, was bittersweet for Mac. Paddy should have been in this picture too.

TEMPT THE NIGHT 219

Maria gripped Marco's hand and turned him to face her as she knelt in front of him, buttoning his small jacket. "You must be good for Señora Irene. I won't be long, and I'll come to get you as soon as I can." She caressed his cheek as his smile faded. "Don't worry, my son. We have nothing to fear in this place."

"I know, Mama, but you only just got here, and I wanted to show you around."

Maria rose and tugged him toward the door where the women waited. "And I want to see everything and meet all your friends. We'll have lots of time, Marco." The obvious love in Maria's voice made Mac's eyes sting for a moment before the enormity of the night's events diverted her thoughts.

As mother and son disappeared outside, Brady and Mac headed toward the office. Joe, Ty, and Walker, conferring quietly in front of the big oak desk that was the focal point of the room, all turned when they entered.

Joe nodded, and his gaze swept to Mac. "Thanks for coming. I want Maria to know she's not alone—that she has a friend. As that friend, feel free to call me on anything you don't like the sound of. You too, Jim. By the time this is over, hopefully she'll know we're all her friends. Sound fair?"

"More than fair."

Brady was still trying to find a reason for the thirty seconds of distrust that had been plastered on Walker's face when Mac had walked into the room. What the hell was going on in his head?

220 DIXIE LEE BROWN

But as quickly as it had appeared, Walker swept it away and resumed his gruff and good-natured manner. "Way to get in that creep's face, Mac. Interesting that when you accused him of killing your friend he didn't deny it. Just pulled the old diplomatic immunity card. If we didn't know he was guilty before, we do now."

Maria entered the room, and Mac went to her immediately. "How is your son, Maria? Was it a good reunion? I'm so sorry I missed it."

A proud smile warred with the concern on Maria's face for a moment. "I would like for you to meet him when we have more time. Marco is a good boy. We have much to catch up on." She turned toward Joe. "Thank you for finding him and bringing him here. I tried so hard to keep him safe, but now it appears I've brought danger to *your* doorstep."

Joe swept a hand toward a black leather chair in front of the desk. "Have a seat. Let's talk about some of the things you left out of the story the first time."

Mac's gaze jerked toward Joe, and she skewered him with a warning glare. Joe got it immediately, and in the split second before he turned his back, his eyes sparkled in a way that made Brady wonder if he'd been testing her.

Maria seated herself, and Mac took the matching chair a couple of feet away. Joe circled the desk and sat, bracing his elbows on the surface. Ty and Walker leaned their shoulders against a bookshelf on the wall, while Brady stood behind Mac's chair. Everyone's eyes were on Maria.

TEMPT THE NIGHT   221

"Why didn't you tell us he's your husband?" Joe's favorite technique when interrogating—start out with a bang and catch the subject off guard.

He obviously accomplished his objective. Maria inhaled sharply, paled as though she'd seen a ghost, and shook her head firmly. "*No!* He's *not* my husband, and I wish to God he never had been."

"You're divorced? When?" Joe cast a glance at Ty, who was already digging a small notebook and pencil from his shirt pocket.

"Three years ago."

"Marco *is* his son, then?"

"*No!*" Maria spat out the word. "Marco is not his, and Raul will never touch him again."

Mac reached across and covered Maria's hand with hers. "They're trying to help you keep Marco safe, Maria. Please tell them why Hernandez is searching for you if you're no longer married and Marco isn't his child."

Maria searched Mac's eyes and then nodded. Wiping tears from her face, she sat up straighter. "Several years ago, I was in love with a man I'd known all my life and planned to marry. My parents were very poor and old-fashioned. Behind my back, they arranged a marriage between me and Raul. He had promised to make the loan payment on my parents' farm. Without his intervention, they would have lost it, and it was all they had."

Brady clenched his fists as anger boiled to the surface. This woman's life had been stolen from her, just like his. Yanked away from all that was familiar, she'd been forced into an arranged marriage. No wonder she was bitter and

222 DIXIE LEE BROWN

distrustful. Hadn't he suffered the same at the hands of ruthless men? He'd been left scarred inside and out. Maria was obviously still dealing with her demons.

"So we were married the next month. I didn't tell him I was already pregnant, and he never asked why the baby came two months early…for two and a half years. Then one night he came home a little drunker than usual and wanted to know why Marco looked nothing like him.

"He was furious when I told him. He guessed who the father was. Our friendship had been no secret in our region. I didn't know he would go so far just to punish me, though." Tears rolled from closed eyes. "My life was hell, but the worst was watching him be cruel to Marco. There was nothing I could do to protect my son. Then one day, Marco's real father was found…dead. He'd been hanged, his hands sawed off while he was still alive. The next day, I found one of them in Marco's bed." Maria stopped to catch her breath.

Everyone else was fighting to keep their rage in check. Brady could see it in each of his friend's eyes. Mac sat stiff and still. That was probably more than she'd signed on for, too.

"I knew he was *loco*…that Marco and I would be next if I didn't get him away from there. So I packed a bag, and we snuck out in the middle of the night, and we've been running ever since. I never told my parents. No one. When I first went to work for Bree and Mr. Sean, taking care of their daughter, they helped me file divorce papers in Texas so Raul wouldn't trace us to Alaska, but he eventually did anyway. That's when Mr. Sean offered

TEMPT THE NIGHT   223

to hide Marco somewhere safe. I didn't know what to do. Mr. Sean worked for the FBI, and Bree still had some friends at the bureau. I trusted them. I thought it was the only chance to save Marco, so I let him take my son from me—and he gave Marco to a drug lord. If Joe and the rest of you hadn't rescued him, he might be dead now." Maria dropped her face into her hands, and sobs racked her shoulders.

Mac knelt in front of her chair and pulled Maria into a hug. "Shhh…shhh…no one will ever take Marco from you again."

She looked into Brady's eyes with the promise on her lips, and he knew without being told that she'd made her decision regarding Hernandez. Knowing that she stood with him in what had to be done stirred his possessiveness.

Joe exchanged glances with Walker and Ty. His chair creaked as he leaned back. "How long can you stay, Maria?" He waited patiently through the silence until she found her voice.

"A few days, I guess. He knows we're here so I have to move on…find work and a place to live."

Mac got to her feet and moved over next to Brady, her face strained with emotions that required crying, but tears would evidently have to wait.

"Did you meet Irene when we arrived?" Joe seemed to be drawing circles on a pad in front of him.

"Yes. She showed me to my room." Maria sounded wary, obviously finding his question strange in the present context.

224 DIXIE LEE BROWN

Mac glanced toward Brady, her brows furrowed. Brady winked, having a pretty good idea what was coming.

"She's a great lady, but she can be pushy as hell, and for the last three months she's been on me about needing more help. So here's the deal. I think you and Marco should stay indefinitely and work for me. You'll have room and board, and we'll settle on a fair wage. Marco has charmed everyone here, so you won't have any trouble lining up people to keep him company while you're working." Joe glanced up from his doodling.

"Darcy will be on the top of that list." Walker stepped toward the desk. "My fiancée loves the little ones, and presently she doesn't have any of her own."

Mac rested her hand on Maria's shoulder. "Even though Hernandez knows where you are, you and Marco will be safer here than on your own somewhere. Joe, Brady, and the rest of these guys will do everything they can to protect you. You won't have to run anymore."

Maria smiled through new tears. "It's an unbelievable offer. May I think about it overnight?"

Joe tossed his pencil down. "Absolutely. Just don't think too long because Irene is going to kill me if I let you get away."

As the laughter died down, Maria placed her hand over Mac's where it still rested on her shoulder. "What about you? Will you stay too?"

Mac dropped her gaze, refusing to look at Brady or anyone else. Her body language said she was clearly self-conscious and uncomfortable with the question. To make

TEMPT THE NIGHT 225

matters worse, the whole room had fallen silent, awaiting her answer.

Walker leaned against the corner of the desk and crossed his arms. "I'd like to hear the answer to that myself, Ms. McCallister. Will you stay...or run?" His voice was quiet, almost friendly, but Brady recognized the thread of steel that accompanied his words. For some reason that Brady couldn't fathom, Walker had just thrown down a gauntlet in front of Mac. Brady scowled. What the hell was Walker trying to do?

For a moment, it seemed Mac would accept the challenge and unleash the anger that cast shades of lilac through her blue-gray eyes. Instead, she took a deep breath, squared her shoulders, and smiled fondly at Maria.

"My situation is different. I'm wanted for murder. The only way I'll be safe anywhere is if I can clear my name. I'll stay for a few days until I figure out what to do next. That way I can check up on you and make sure you're getting settled."

"I'll be sorry to see you go, Mac. It won't be easy for you out there. Patrick would have been proud of you." Maria's voice broke.

The name clearly hit Mac hard, knocking the air from her lungs. She inhaled a shaky breath as wild eyes located the exit. Her gaze swept over each of them, lingering the longest on Walker and ending with Brady, who couldn't think of one damn thing to say that would make a difference.

226 DIXIE LEE BROWN

She smiled then, as though they were the only two in the room. "I'm exhausted. Please excuse me. I'm going to get some sleep."

He nodded slightly, resisting the urge to catch her around the waist and keep her beside him where she was so obviously ill at ease. The hurt in her eyes as her gaze slid away from his caused a corresponding ache in his soul.

Quiet conversation resumed between Joe and Ty as soon as Mac strode from the room. Brady raised his eyes to study Walker, who stared at the door long after Mac was gone. A frown creased his face, and he paced restlessly. What had happened to cause the animosity between Walker and Mac? Walker surely wouldn't appreciate Brady asking, and it probably wouldn't be pretty, but he intended to get an answer.

Maria said goodnight and left. Walker and Ty followed a few seconds later. Brady turned to go, planning to catch Walker for a private chat, but Joe motioned for him to stick around.

"Ty will do some checking on the situation in Alaska— see if we can find a connection between Hernandez and the two troopers who tried to kill Mac. I have a buddy up there who's a PI. If he can get through security to question the wounded trooper, maybe the guy will be willing to talk, given the right incentive." Joe was making notes as he talked. "Anything else you can think of?"

"Hernandez is obviously well connected. He knew where we'd be every step of the way. Hell, he got *here* before we did."

TEMPT THE NIGHT 227

"Good point. I'll have someone check out his known associates...although I might be the culprit this time. I talked to half the state government to find someone who'd convince your doctor to look the other way rather than report your gunshot wound. If Hernandez has friends in high places, he could have heard my name through the grapevine. It wouldn't have been hard to find me, especially if he could coerce a member of the State Department into driving him to my doorstep." Joe shoved his chair back and stood.

Brady dragged a hand across the back of his neck. "We'll never find out anything in time to keep Mac from going back and getting herself killed."

Joe studied him, a trace of humor relieving his serious expression. "That's where you come in. You have to make her decide to stay a while longer."

Brady huffed a laugh. "Right. And just how am I supposed to do that?"

"From where I stand, it looks like she already *has* a reason to stay. All you have to do is convince her it's not one-sided."

Damn Joe's smug grin. "Whoa, slow down. I'll admit I'm attracted to her, but that's as far as it goes. There *can't* be anything else. You know that, Joe."

"I know that's what you believe. People change, Jim... even you. You've gotten stronger in a lot of ways since you came here. You're a different man. In any other situation, you'd put yourself to the test. Why not this one?" Joe strode toward the door.

228 DIXIE LEE BROWN

Irrational anger started to build in Brady. It was easy enough for Joe to suggest a course of action. He wouldn't be around when it all went south. Mac was the one who would suffer if Brady didn't pass the test. And yet he wanted to believe that Joe was right.

He pivoted toward the door. "People change, huh? Like Walker? What the hell's eatin' him anyway?"

"Don't know. Have you asked him?"

Brady stopped and watched Joe disappear through the doorway. *That's the next thing on my list.*

Chapter Fifteen

MAC HELD HER head high and refused to give in to the panic attack that had every nerve in her body tied in a knot. She needed a private place to have her meltdown, where no one would see how weak and cowardly she was. Just a few more steps, and she slipped into the darkened kitchen. Struggling to breathe in and out with a semblance of normalcy, she paused to look around the unfamiliar room. The moonlight cascaded through the windows, confirming that she was alone. Residual smells of pot roast or maybe steak still permeated the air. She rushed across the tiled floor and braced her arms against the sink, sweating, and gasping, and praying she wouldn't throw up.

A few minutes later, as luck would have it, that's how Walker found her. "What the hell are you doing?" he growled.

Mac chose to ignore him, groaning her misery instead, but the next thing she knew, his shoulder brushed hers as

230 DIXIE LEE BROWN

he peered in the sink, no doubt trying to determine what she was looking at.

She couldn't help it—she started laughing.

He straightened and jammed his hands on his hips. "What's so goddamn funny?"

The scowl on his face sent her into another fit of laughter. "You...you're what's funny." She turned to face him, leaning her hip against the counter and crossing her arms over her chest.

He evidently wasn't impressed. "What the fuck are you doing in here in the dark?"

"Not that it's any of your business, but I was planning to splash cold water on my face to keep from being sick." Impossibly, she imagined his cold features warmed a degree. "It's my turn to ask *you* a question. What the *fuck* is your problem?"

His gray eyes went practically black. "*My* problem? You're the one with trouble dogging your every step." His voiced raised, and he jabbed his finger toward her.

"You call that trouble? Honey, where I come from we call that a bad day." She stopped abruptly and snorted a self-conscious laugh. What was she trying to prove? Out of nowhere, she'd started trading barbs with this black-haired wall of a man who seldom smiled unless it came with a growl...like she used to do with Paddy. But Paddy had understood that she was only blowing off steam and would give her a raft right back. Walker, however, didn't look like the understanding type.

She looked down, cleared her throat, and slowly raised her eyes to his. "You're right...I might be wading through

TEMPT THE NIGHT   231

a few problems at the moment." Mac shrugged, bit her lip, and cocked her head to the side, a small smile refusing to be dismissed as she waited for his next move.

Walker grunted, and his gaze traveled over her face for what seemed like a full minute before a one-sided grin appeared. "*Right*. Sister, you're up to your neck in trouble. It seems you have a knack for understatement."

"Well, everyone has to be good at something."

That earned her a more sincere, although brief, smile. He glanced at the sink. "Are you feeling better now? Do you want to get some air?"

"I'm much better, thanks. What I'd really like is to talk about what I did to piss you off so bad."

"You want a beer?" He stepped around her toward the refrigerator, pulled the door open, and came out with two bottles. He twisted the cap off one and handed it to Mac.

"Thanks. Do I need to sit for this?" She made a joke of it, but her stomach was beginning to roll again.

He pulled a chair out for her at the table and sat in the one next to hers. After taking a long drink, he set his beer on the table. "At the hospital, how much of Jim's story did you overhear?"

Heat rushed to Mac's face. Of course, she'd known—his beef with her had to have started there outside Brady's room—but still she wasn't prepared for the shame that flooded her at the mention of her trespass.

She forced herself to meet his gaze. "I didn't mean to listen at all. I've always had a lot of respect for the men and women who serve this country. Brady told me

232 DIXIE LEE BROWN

he'd been a Navy SEAL, but he never confided anything that happened. When I heard him talking to you in that room…it was exciting and heroic at first. Then it was… horrific. As badly as I wanted to, I couldn't move. It was wrong to eavesdrop, and it wasn't fair to Brady. I'll never repeat anything I heard, if that's what you're concerned about."

"It's not. He likes you. You know that, right?" His unwavering gaze held her in place. "When I saw that rabbit-in-the-headlight look on your face outside his room, I thought you'd bolt right then. He's a friend of mine, and real friends are hard to come by. I've never seen him care about a woman before. You heard him. It wasn't easy for him to tell me about the woman he nearly choked to death after making love to her. Did that scare you? Make you want to run? Or will you stick around and give him a chance to prove he's changed?"

Mac set her beer on the table and brought the palms of her hands down on her knees with a resounding slap. "*That's* what you're so cranky about?" She sat back in her chair and looked away from his intense stare for a moment. "I'm glad Brady has such a good friend, so I'm going to tell you something that would otherwise be none of your business." She cocked her head, and Walker saluted her with his beer bottle.

"My father was a POW in Viet Nam. That was before I was born, but he still suffers from PTSD today. My mother is his lifeline, and it wasn't always easy, but I couldn't have had a better example of unconditional love." She reached for her beer, picked at the label for a

TEMPT THE NIGHT 233

second, and then turned to him. "I'm not afraid of Brady. There's nothing he could do that would make me run—except tell me he doesn't want me around. But, as you pointed out, I'm in a heap of trouble. My priority has to be clearing my name. Right now my parents and Paddy's parents are being told I killed my best friend and another officer. They'll be devastated, and that breaks my heart." She stopped as her voice cracked.

Walker leaned toward her, plucked her untouched beer from her hand, and deposited it on the table. "Yeah, that has to be addressed, but Jim's not going to let you go off by yourself and get killed. Joe's already got some feelers out. He knows enough G-men to dig up everything there is to know about Hernandez."

"Jim won't *let* me? Tell me you didn't really say that." Snatching her beer back, she took a big swallow. She should be indignant about a demeaning remark like that—would have been livid two days ago—but she had to admit she was feeling pretty safe and protected by the raft of alpha males swarming around her. If that meant she'd turned into a helpless female…so be it. Maybe tomorrow she'd feel like carrying her shield and swinging her mace again.

The question was, could they pull off clearing her name and exact judgment on Ambassador Hernandez? Studying the confidence on Walker's face, she could almost believe it. Maybe, at the very least, she could give them the chance.

"Okay. I didn't really say that." Walker's grin made her smile.

"All right, funny man. Can we stop sniping at each other now?" She took another sip of beer and gazed at him over the top.

"Sure, about this anyway. I'll see what else I can come up with by tomorrow." He shot her a teasing glance, and then his gaze flickered to the doorway.

"I've been looking all over hell for you, Walker, but I didn't expect to find the two of you having a beer together." Brady's voice was oddly strained.

Startled, Mac swung her head around toward the entryway. He stood just inside, leaning against the door frame. She couldn't make out his face in the shadows, but the rest of him looked good enough to bring a smile to her face. "Hey, it's about time you got here. Come and join us."

Brady pushed away from the wall and walked slowly toward the table. When he came up behind her, he laid his hand possessively on her shoulder. "You okay, Mac?"

Walker scooted his chair back, screeching across the tiles, and stood. "Some reason you think she wouldn't be okay, Jim?"

Mac glanced between the two of them as they faced off.

"You've had a burr up your ass ever since you saw her. If there's a reason for that, I want to hear it. If not, it stops here." Brady's tension was obvious by the strength of his grip on her shoulder.

It was just like him to stand up to his friend in defense of her. Problem was, now Walker was going to spill his guts and tell Brady she'd eavesdropped on his most private conversation. Surely that wouldn't be good.

TEMPT THE NIGHT 235

"Everything's fine, Brady. Walker's just having a bad day." Mac bent her neck sideways to look up at his face, but he didn't take his gaze off his friend.

Walker took a step closer. "Well, we have a consensus. Seems everybody thinks I was being an ass, but she was the only one who had the balls to call me on it. We had a beer and talked it out. We're good now, right, Mac?"

She nodded. "Just a misunderstanding." Walker hadn't given her away. Maybe she'd still get to pick her own time and place for confession.

"Right." Brady's voice was flat and emotionless, which made it difficult to tell if he was agreeing or being scornful. Mac chose to believe it was the former.

Walker stepped to a large pantry and placed his empty beer bottle on a shelf inside, then strode to within three feet of Brady. "We were talkin', Jim. Mostly about you. If the lady wants to go into detail, that's up to her. Otherwise, let it go."

The two men stared at each other for a few seconds, as neither apparently wanted to back down first. Tightness gripped Mac's stomach, and the skin on the back of her neck tingled. She'd witnessed guys doing their chest-thumping routines before, but never between two such strong and dangerous men.

She was about to stand and insert herself between them when Brady's gaze slid to hers. He might have recognized the anxiety in her face or felt her shiver of apprehension. Whatever the cause, he blinked and his lips curved, although barely, but that was good enough. She smiled back in relief, expelling the breath she'd been holding.

236   DIXIE LEE BROWN

Walker wisely picked that moment to make his exit. "Darcy's waitin' for me. We can pick this up tomorrow… if you think it's necessary. 'Night, Mac."

"Goodnight, Walker." After he left, Mac got to her feet and turned toward Brady. "Are you going to make a habit of coming to my rescue?" That's all he'd been doing since she ran into him, and short of that, she didn't want to contemplate what her circumstances would be. With that in mind, it was impossible to be angry with him.

"Probably." Brady ran his hand through his hair and groaned. "I made a mess of that, didn't I?"

"You'll fix it. You can apologize tomorrow. Or go have a beer. Whatever guys do at times like this. Walker is your friend. He won't hold it against you." She wanted to put her arms around him and comfort him, but the words she knew she had to speak made her stay where she was.

His crooked grin appeared briefly. "And what about you? Are you going to tell me what you and my friend were talking about?"

Mac crossed her arms and dropped her gaze, casting about for the right way to explain. Her nervous laugh sounded strained. "I'm sorry. There's no easy way to say this."

"It's just you and me, Mac." He smiled and tucked her hair behind her ears.

A deep breath did little to calm her, but she forced herself to start talking. "At the hospital…I accidentally overheard you talking to Walker. I didn't mean to eavesdrop, but, when I realized what you were talking about, I couldn't make myself leave. Walker came out of the room

TEMPT THE NIGHT 237

and caught me listening. That's why he was suspicious of me at first. He was concerned that my reaction to the things I'd heard would somehow hurt you." Mac raised her eyes from the floor, and her gaze swept his face. "He was worried about you. He's a good friend, Brady. Please don't hold the things he said against him."

Brady cocked his head, and confusion lent him a blank expression. "What *did* you hear?" The sharp edge of caution in his voice made her flinch.

"You don't remember?"

He wagged his head as he rubbed the back of his neck. "The hospital stay was kind of a blur. Too much damn medication." Brady studied her guardedly. "Tell me what you heard."

"Um...you were taken prisoner in Somalia. They killed your friend, tortured and experimented on you. You escaped, but you had trouble adjusting to civilian life." She held his gaze, but his expression had gone cold, and she wasn't sure he was even seeing her anymore.

He jerked away from her and paced from one side of the room to the other, his one good hand balled into a fist. Stopping in front of her on his next pass, he seized her shoulders in a strong grip. "I remember telling Walker... but you left out the best part—the part where I almost killed a woman in a fit of rage because I mistook her for the enemy. Her only sin was to sleep with me. That should scare the shit out of you, Mac." He gave her a shake.

"I'm not afraid of you, Brady."

He pushed her back a step. "Well, you *should* be. Hell, I'm afraid *for* you. *I'm* afraid to go home to my family

238   DIXIE LEE BROWN

because I can't control the rage that comes from inside my own damn head. That's why I don't let people get close. Do you get it now?" Haunted eyes told of his deep-seated despair before he turned away from her.

Mac watched him silently for a moment. He'd shared a part of him that he was clearly very ashamed of, first to Walker and then to her. Anger stirred in Mac—not at Brady, but at the war, the government, the veterans' hospital, and public opinion—everything that had conspired to damage the beautiful minds of servicemen and women and then make it seem like they'd done something wrong.

Mac choked back a sob as she put one foot in front of the other. She wouldn't let him see her cry. Show no weakness—that's what her mother had said practically every day of her life, and now Mac understood why. Brady needed her understanding, her steadfastness, but mostly he needed her strength. He just didn't know it yet.

She stopped behind him and reached out to touch his arm. Apparently surprised by her closeness, he swung around and took a step back, his eyes searching her face. Mac stepped into him until their bodies touched and slid her arms around his neck. "I *do* get it, Brady, but I won't let it dictate my life."

She rose on her toes, sliding against him until their lips met, gently at first. Finally, with a groan, Brady wrapped his muscular arms around her like he couldn't get close enough, and their kisses turned urgent, demanding, until he pulled back and looked in her eyes. "Last warning,

TEMPT THE NIGHT 239

McCallister. This is a bad idea. You sure you know what you're doing?"

Mac bit his lower lip and then ran her tongue around the rim of his mouth, holding his gaze. "I know I'd sleep better if you were holding me. Your room or mine?"

An is-she-serious expression flitted across his face, erasing the dark shadows in his eyes. "Um…well, you're on the third floor. You might be the only occupant right now. It would be quiet and private—unless you don't want complete privacy…in which case…um…I could hold you in my room…"

"You wouldn't happen to know where my room is, would you?" She watched him through lowered lashes, biting her bottom lip.

A wisp of a smile transformed his features, and he kissed her hard on the lips. "As a matter of fact, I do." His one good hand gripped her waist as he nuzzled her neck, feathering soft kisses along her jaw to the corner of her mouth. The masculine scent of him clung to his skin, and she breathed him in. Then he took her hand and led the way up two flights of stairs to the first room on the right.

"Your room, milady." He released her hand.

Mac turned her back to the door and faced Brady. His concern for her was mirrored in the gentle brush of his fingers on her cheek. Although she fully understood the implications of his training and experience as a Navy SEAL, it was difficult to imagine him hurting an innocent woman. Lying in her bed, his large hands wrapped around her throat, choking her. An involuntary shudder convulsed her, and immediately wariness settled over his strong face.

Reaching for his hand, she turned the doorknob behind her and swung the door open. "Do you still want to come in?" She backed away, holding his gaze, and he followed until they were both inside her room.

Closing the door dropped them instantly into darkness. That and the unfamiliarity of her surroundings had her searching the wall for the light switch in a state quickly approaching panic. Light suddenly flooded the room, and she swung around to see Brady with one finger still on the switch beside her head. She could tell by the concern on his face that her alarm had been etched in her expression. With an embarrassed sigh, she leaned against the wall and drew in a slow breath.

"You okay?"

"I'm fine," she said a little too sharply, regretting it immediately. She smiled, hoping it would act like the undo button on her computer. "I just need a minute." Without waiting for a reply, she strode across the room to an open door that she hoped was the bathroom.

Locating the light switch before she closed the door, she stood for a moment in front of the mirror. The woman who looked back at her was pale and dirty, with black circles under her eyes and hair so matted she'd probably never get a comb through it again. What could Brady possibly see in her?

Her self-confidence had taken a beating, and that was the polite way to put it. Her best friend was dead. She'd been accused of his murder. Her parents and Paddy's

TEMPT THE NIGHT   241

would have heard the lies by now, and they'd be shocked and disbelieving right up until they started to wonder if it was really true.

She didn't have a clue what to do next or how to help herself. Without Brady's intervention, she'd likely be dead already. Her situation had gone downhill drastically, but the person she used to be should still be in there somewhere. She'd have to find her now if she was going to help Brady overcome the trauma he'd suffered.

Mac bathed her face with cold water, and as she stepped toward the towel rack, she saw a small black duffel bag sitting on the floor. Strange. Her bag waited on the bed. She'd noticed it on her way to the bathroom. So whose was this one?

Quickly, she dried her face and hands, then knelt and unzipped the bag. Men's clothes. Jeans, a gray T-shirt, underwear, and a small shaving kit. *Dirty* clothes. Did Brady bring her to the wrong room? *Her* bag was in the bedroom. *This* had to be his. The scoundrel. He'd showered and changed in her room? He must have come here before he found her talking to Walker in the kitchen. Had he been so sure of her that he thought he'd settle in without her approval? Wrong move. A grin lightened her mood as she closed and zipped the bag.

She opened the door and stepped out. Brady still stood in nearly the same spot she'd left him, his hands shoved in his front pockets, a question in his transparent green eyes.

Mac held his gaze for several seconds. "Are you sure this is my room?"

242 DIXIE LEE BROWN

"It's not what—"

"Why are your clothes in my bathroom?" She crossed her arms. "It seems a little like you were planning to stay here all along. Was my agreement just a formality?"

He started toward her but stopped when she raised her hand. "Of course not, Mac. When I couldn't find you or Walker earlier, I came up here to wait for you. But I couldn't stand my own stench, so I grabbed a change of clothes, planning to shower while I waited. I was worried about you, and when you still hadn't shown up by the time I was finished, I went looking for you and forgot to take my bag. It had nothing to do with whether or not I stay with you tonight, but for the record, you saying yes was no formality—it meant everything."

Shoot! Earnest and sincere eyes, a killer body evidenced by the way his clean white T-shirt stretched across his pecs and biceps, and he apparently, unerringly, knew the right thing to say to bust right through her defenses. How was she supposed to resist his little-boy charm? Or his fully matured sex appeal? She was so screwed.

She glanced at the queen-sized bed with its country-style quilt and white lace pillow shams. "Why don't you make yourself comfortable? I'm going to hit the shower too. Oh…except I don't have any clean clothes."

Brady strode toward the walk-in closet next to the bathroom. "I'd be surprised if Irene didn't put a few things in here for you to use until we can get you some of your own." He pushed the door wide so she could see inside. He moved to the dresser and pulled open the top

TEMPT THE NIGHT 243

drawer. "More in here." He winked at her. "Want me to help you pick something to sleep in?"

Mac was overcome with emotions. The kindness of Irene and the rest of these people she'd only met today totally blew her away. Tears tickled the back of her eyelids, and she had to walk away so he wouldn't see her cry—again.

The next instant, he was there behind her with his strong arms around her, drawing her backward into his chest. "I was only kidding, Mac." He rested his chin on her head.

She snorted a laugh. "I know. It's just...everything. You and everyone here...you're turning your lives upside down for me. What if I go to prison? How will I ever repay all of you?"

Brady pressed a kiss to her ear. "You're not going to prison, so get that thought out of your head. Secondly, no one here is looking for repayment, especially Irene. This is what she does—thinks of ways she can make life easier for all of us. And she wouldn't have it any other way."

Regardless of what he said, she'd figure out a way to let Irene know her thoughtfulness had been deeply appreciated. And Brady? How would she thank him? Well, she had a couple of ideas about that, but she wasn't at all sure if she had the nerve to see them through.

"You better help me pick something to wear. Otherwise, as tired as I am, I'll be sleeping in a towel." She ducked out from under his arms and returned to the dresser.

"Aw hell! Is it too late to vote on the towel thing?" He followed her, brushing against her arm.

244 DIXIE LEE BROWN

She whacked him in the stomach just hard enough to learn how firm and toned his abdominal muscles were. He bent slightly and grabbed his stomach as through it were actually possible for her to hurt him. *Yeah, he was cute.*

With Brady's wholehearted approval, she settled on black bikini panties and silk pajamas with shorts and a sleeveless top. Mac hurried into the bathroom with her new treasures and turned the water to as hot as she could stand. Taking a long, leisurely shower wasn't an option tonight. She was too tired. Besides, Brady was in the other room, and she would sleep like a baby in his arms. If by some quirk of fate, anything more than that happened, she'd take full responsibility. Desire flared to life as she thought of what it would be like.

Towel-dried and dressed in her new duds, she did a cursory job with the blow dryer—obviously provided by Irene also—but only good enough to keep her pillow from being soaked. Satisfied, she opened the door to a dimly lit room. Brady had switched off the overhead light and turned on the bedside lamp. He lay under the sheet, facing away from her side of the bed. His arms and a significant portion of his back and chest were uncovered. Was he sleeping?

She padded to the empty side of the bed and sat, bouncing a little to get his attention. Nothing. "Goodnight, Brady." Still nothing. Mac swung her legs onto the bed, lifting the blankets to slide under, taking note that he was sleeping in his jeans. Sheesh! He really *had been* prepared to just hold her, but apparently now she wasn't even getting the benefit of his arms around her.

TEMPT THE NIGHT 245

Who knew she'd be so disappointed? A wry grin tugged at her lips.

Oh well. If he'd managed to fall asleep without the warmth of her proximity, then she'd have to do the honors tonight. Just having him close would provide the good night's sleep she craved. She rolled toward him until she met the heat of his back, slid her arm across his rib cage, and settled her hand on his abs.

Good Lord! The man was pure muscle. A heartbeat of apprehension stole over her as the image returned of the woman in bed, Brady's hands around her throat. He was so strong, there'd be no way she could survive an attack.

Get hold of yourself, girl. He was no longer that angry, scarred, and war-weary man who'd lost control in a moment of confusion. Mac forced the gruesome picture from her mind. Brady was kind and considerate, and he wouldn't hurt her. He'd proved that on their first meeting, when she'd held a gun against his back; he'd had every right to retaliate with violence, but didn't.

Maybe he was beginning to trust himself more as well. Why else would he be sleeping peacefully in her bed? Now that she knew about the PTSD that caused him to keep everyone at arm's length, would he relax his rules? He'd made no mention of it, so maybe his condition wasn't the only reason he didn't allow attachments. Besides, she was in no position to form lasting relationships either.

It was too bad, really. She'd finally found an attractive, sexy man who didn't mind cuddling—and she couldn't keep him.

Chapter Sixteen

BRADY'S EYES POPPED open, and he came fully awake, staring at a spot on the wall across the room while the events of the last two days fast-forwarded in his brain. Dawn's reddish light stole through the windows and revealed where Mac's delicate hand rested on his sternum, but that wasn't what woke him.

The warmth of her body pressed against his back, her breasts moving ever so slightly as she quietly inhaled and exhaled, her right leg twined between his. She smelled faintly of Ivory soap and coconut oil. Combined with her naturally sweet smell, it wasn't an unpleasant aroma, but he missed her scent of apple pie.

Enticing? Yes. Tempting? Damn straight…but that wasn't what had woken him either.

The killer hard-on straining to burst through the zipper of his jeans was the culprit. He carefully eased one leg slightly forward in a useless attempt to lessen his

TEMPT THE NIGHT 247

discomfort. Lying as quietly as possible so as not to wake her, he held his breath and concentrated on less pleasant images. Walker kicking his ass. A skunk he'd encountered by accident while camping as a kid. Hernandez walking into this house and threatening Mac.

Well, hell. That didn't help. Now he was aroused *and* angry—a dangerous combination. A run. That's what he needed. Brady tossed the covers back and slipped out from under her arm, then crawled stealthily toward the edge of the bed. As he was about to swing his legs over the side, her cool fingers gripped the waistband of his jeans and rested against his back.

Mac tugged on his pants, applying additional pressure to the initial problem. Brady drew a deep breath, prayed for control, and met her gaze over his shoulder.

Sensuous lips formed into a pout as heavy eyelids shielded her beautiful blue-gray eyes, now so shaded with lilac that they resembled storm-filled skies. The effect was stunning, and Brady instantly forgot what he'd meant to say.

"You're not leaving yet, are you?" Mac braced her head on her elbow and tugged on his waistband again.

Brady choked. "I didn't mean to wake you, sugar. I thought I'd go for a run before we decide what to do today."

"Oh. Well, if that's what you want to do." She released him and slid her hand across his ribs to his abdomen and then down.

He caught her hand before it skimmed beneath the front of his jeans. In one fluid motion, he rolled over and

248 DIXIE LEE BROWN

pulled her tightly against him. "Shit, Mac. Now's not a good time to tease. If you're not as serious as I am, you better let me get out of here for a while." He ground his rigid member against her stomach, and her eyes widened.

Her soft lips opened in a sexy smile. "Oh…I'm pretty serious."

Brady studied her sparkling eyes. He ached for need of her and still he hesitated. This would change everything between them. She'd made it clear she wasn't a one-night stand. He didn't want that either, but somehow he'd have to be absolutely certain he wouldn't hurt her. How would that ever be possible?

Mac drew his head down to meet her lips, and her gentle touch shoved his doubts aside. He threaded his fingers through her hair, then grabbed a fistful and pulled her head back so he could sample the delicate softness of her throat.

"Prove it," he whispered against her skin.

She cocked her head and frowned. "Prove what?"

"How serious you are." He lifted his head and dared her with a grin.

Her laugh rang with surprising joy and echoed in the quiet room. She reached for the button on his jeans, but he grabbed her hand again, flipped her onto her back, and settled on top of her. He pressed his lips to each finger as he held her gaze. "One touch of these nimble digits and it'll be all over, sugar. You'll have to think of something else."

Eyeing him suspiciously, she went still except for one hand that tapped out a rhythm on her jaw as her forehead

TEMPT THE NIGHT   249

scrunched in thought. Several seconds later, an impish gleam spread to her eyes. "What would *you* have me do?"

He hesitated, wondering what she was up to, but then suspicion gave way to speculation about what he might be able to convince her to do, and the latter won out.

He rolled onto his back beside her and held up his wounded hand. "Well, I was thinkin'—damn this bandage anyway. My hand is worse than useless with it on. I'm going to take it off." He jerked on the bandage and got one wrap loose before she pounced on him and batted at his good hand. Hiding his amusement was easy when he caught the sincere concern in her eyes.

"You're doing no such thing. Tell me what you need… and I'll do it." She paused midway, seeming to suddenly realize the intimate tasks he might request.

He almost felt bad for his subterfuge, but then…not bad enough. He slid his hand behind her neck and drew her closer. Covering her mouth with his, he greedily consumed her honeyed lips until she was breathless, and he wasn't far behind. He had no intention of letting her catch her breath when he released her either.

"Prove you're serious. Undress for me, Samantha McCallister." For a moment, he thought he'd gone too far. Her eyes widened, then narrowed warily. It was a full thirty seconds before she pulled away from him and found her voice.

"Pardon me?"

Brady raised his bandaged paw again and shrugged. "I was going to need some help anyway. This way we can kill two birds." The rising color in her cheeks tugged at

250 DIXIE LEE BROWN

his heart, and he was about to tell her he was only kidding when a full-throated laugh burst from her, and she pushed to her feet in the center of the bed, whooping loudly.

He laughed and reached for her hand, pulling her down alongside him. "Shhh! These walls are fairly well soundproofed, but keep that up and someone will burst through that door thinking you're in danger."

"I just might be, Mr. Brady. You really are quite clever, aren't you?" Her smile tantalized him and made him want to taste her lips again, but apparently she wasn't finished. "Here's the deal. I do something for you—undress—and I get to ask something of you that you can't refuse."

He was intrigued by the guilt in her eyes. She obviously had something in mind. A preference in bed that made her tremble with desire? Something that those morons she'd been dating didn't have time for? Why else would she think he'd refuse? He hardened even more as he became obsessed with the mystery. Whatever it was, she needn't worry. There was nothing he wouldn't do to please her.

"Is it a deal?" Mac snaked her hand out and undid the button on his jeans.

Shit! As though he needed any more persuasion. "You have my word, sugar."

She rolled her eyes. "Why do you insist on calling me that?"

"Because you're about the sweetest thing I've ever tasted." He drew her lips to his and they melded together as though he'd been starving for her all of his life.

TEMPT THE NIGHT 251

She pulled away before he was ready. "Okay, tell me how you want this. I don't think we have any music… unless you want to sing. No pole, but I could use a chair. It's been a while, but I think I can remember how to do this. You want me in the center of the room or here by the bed?"

"A pole?" Brady's mouth had just gone dry with that picture.

"Didn't I tell you? I picked up a little extra cash in college working as an exotic dancer. My stage name was Bam Bam." She laughed, a throaty kind of laugh that went straight to his groin.

"I…um…Jesus, Mac. You're killin' me." Something had to give. He opened his zipper and the fullness of his rigid shaft tented his briefs, pushing through the opening of his jeans.

Smoldering eyes met his, and she reached for the waistband at his sides. "Rise up. Let's get you out of these."

Brady did as she instructed, and with much giggling and struggling, she dragged the pants, inside out, over his feet and tossed them on the floor. He caught her around the waist and pressed his engorged manhood against her. "I don't think we have time for the whole show right now, but I want a rain check. I'll even install a pole." He grinned and winked. "For now, just get out of the damn clothes." He kissed her roughly and pushed her away.

Mac stood in the middle of the bed, gazing down at Brady. Infuriatingly slow, she undid each button of her shirt. When it hung open down her front, she turned her back to him, and let the shirt slide off her arms and land

252   DIXIE LEE BROWN

on his lap. She whipped around to face him, her hair flipping over her right shoulder and landing on her breast.

Brady groaned as he stared at the woman before him. "You're just as beautiful as I imagined you'd be." He reached for her, but she slipped from his grasp. Damn her. He'd get even for all this taunting.

Mac hooked her thumbs in the top of her silk shorts and strutted in a small circle. When Brady thought he'd have to jump up and jerk them off himself, she turned her back again, bent over, and whipped the shorts down, presenting her bikini-clad ass just long enough for another groan to rise from his throat. She dragged her hands slowly up her calves and thighs as she straightened, stepped out of the shorts, and kicked them off the edge of the bed.

Long tanned legs led directly to the black bikini panties with her thumb hitching one corner down over her hip. That was all Brady could take. He reached for her, pulling her down beside him.

"I'll take it from here." His mouth came down on hers, hard and demanding, and he pushed his tongue between her lips to taste her—to own her completely.

He gripped her hips and pulled her against him, smoothing his fingertips across her satin skin from her panties, over her flat and firm stomach, to just below her breasts. With one finger, he stroked over her nipple and chuckled when she jerked in response. He swiped over the taut peak several times in quick succession, until her breath stuttered with small gasps. Wrapping his hand around the fullness of her breast, he lifted it and felt its

TEMPT THE NIGHT 253

weight. He dipped his head and drew a circle around the nipple with his tongue, then licked the aroused nub.

Mac jumped and uttered a small cry before she clamped a hand over her mouth.

He smiled and nuzzled her throat. Sliding his tongue in and out of her ear, his breath made her tremble in his arms. "Tell me what it is you want me to do, sugar. Anything you want. It's yours."

"Not yet."

"I can't hold out much longer. I need to be inside you." He alternately kissed her and nipped her bottom lip, then drew it between his lips and licked away the hurt.

"Yes. Do that. Inside." She tried to pull him closer while arching her body into his.

He stopped playing with her lips to look in her eyes. "Are you sure about this, Mac?" Sadness swept across her face for a split second, and Brady frowned.

The next instant, she smiled angelically. "I'm sure, already. Condom?"

"My wallet…in my pants." He rolled toward the side.

"Stay there. I'll get it." Mac hopped off the bed, grabbed his jeans, and turned back holding his wallet.

He took it from her and flipped it open with one hand, spilling part of the contents on the bed, including four plastic-wrapped condoms.

Mac snorted. "Four?" She continued to chuckle as she helped him pick up business cards and stray scraps of paper and shove them back in the wallet.

He loved to see her laugh, and that alone put a grin on his face. "Better too many than not enough…but don't

254 DIXIE LEE BROWN

make up your mind prematurely." His gaze dropped to her breasts, and he reached to trail his fingers from the base of her throat down over her responsive nipple and smirked when she inhaled sharply. "Come here." He crooked his index finger.

With humor dancing in her eyes, she crawled on hands and knees until she knelt beside him.

"Time for these to go." He skimmed her stomach and the top of her panties, then hooked his fingers over the elastic waist and tugged them down around her knees. Pulling her across his chest, he slid them to her ankles where she could kick her feet free. He held the scrap of fabric for a moment, smiling, before he tossed them onto the floor.

Mac reached for his briefs. "Your turn."

"We'll get to that." He tightened his arm around her, bringing his leg up between hers. As he claimed her lips in a heated kiss, he slid his hand down over her ass, and pressed her soft warmth into his erection.

She brought her thighs together around him and moved just enough to drive him faster toward the edge. He wasn't going to last long if he didn't slow this down. Rolling her over until he leaned above her, he rested on the elbow of his bandaged side. He dropped his other hand on the soft, curly triangle of hair that covered her mound and pushed between her legs, through her wet, slick folds, until two fingers explored the heat of her sheath.

She moaned with every stroke, and he swallowed any sound she might have made. He began a rhythmic massage with his fingers while the heel of his hand rubbed

TEMPT THE NIGHT   255

hard against the hub of her arousal. With each pass across the sensitive spot she convulsed against him, her fingernails scraping down his sides.

A small cry marked her climax as her entire body tightened around his hand. He raised his head and watched her face as passion glazed her eyes. Again and again, the spasms claimed her until finally she lay still and spent.

He sat up and reached for a condom, ripping the package open with his teeth. When he realized he wouldn't be able to put it on himself with one hand bandaged, he turned to her. Her sensuous smile caused his engorged shaft to twitch.

Mac held her hand out, and he placed the latex in her palm. "You could demand a heavy price about now." He grinned, then shimmied awkwardly out of his briefs.

She rose to kneel beside him with lust, or some equally raw emotion, turning her eyes a deep blue. "You already gave me everything I could have asked for." Her voice quavered slightly. She reached out, sliding her hand the length of him while her gaze locked on his.

As she caressed his throbbing erection, Brady clenched his jaw tightly, sure he would lose his battle for control. She leaned toward him and pressed her lips to his, boldly exploring the inside of his mouth with her tongue. Pulling back, she regarded him with a mysterious half smile before getting down to business and rolling the condom in place.

Expelling a deep breath, he tipped her onto her back again, spread her legs, and positioned himself at her

256 DIXIE LEE BROWN

opening. Drawing her gaze to his with her name on a whisper, he shoved inside.

She gasped as he filled her. He gave her a few seconds to adjust to his size before he pulled almost all the way out and shoved forward again. This time she squeaked and threw her legs around his hips, urging him deeper.

He smiled as he brushed the hair from the sides of her face. "God, Mac. You're incredible. So fucking incredible." Her sleepy, adoring gaze sparkled with pleasure and made him feel ten feet tall. He kissed her, gently at first, but then lust took over and he ground his mouth on hers, branding her as his and his alone.

Again, he pulled out and shoved home. Over and over. Faster and faster, until he lost himself in the burning need of his groin and the intense pleasure their union created. When he came, fire exploded behind his eyes... jet engines, bombs, and rockets screamed across a dark sky. He stiffened and ducked as he squeezed his eyes closed. *Shit! I'm in a fucking war zone! How the hell...*

"Brady?"

The voice of an angel called his name. It must be a lie. There were no angels in war.

"Brady?"

It had to be a trick.

Strong hands grasped his face, and he opened his eyes, ready to kick some ass.

Mac!

The gentle concern in her eyes called to the place within him that housed reality. He felt every inch of her warm body beneath his, and it grounded him. She was

TEMPT THE NIGHT 257

real—not the bombs or the rockets. There was no enemy here, except the one in his head. Apparently, only Mac had the power to keep that one at bay.

"I thought you left me there for a minute." Mac smiled serenely as though this kind of thing happened all the time in her world.

Overcome with gratitude, he couldn't talk for a moment. He pulled her closer instead and pressed his lips to her throat. "Better get used to me, sugar. I'm not going anywhere."

A short time later, he rolled off of her, pulling her with him until her head rested on his chest. The peace that invaded his soul was of her making, and he could no more let her go than he could jump off of a thirty-story building. She was part of him now, whether she wanted to be or not. He'd find a way to convince her to stay.

Her breathing was quiet and even, but he sensed she wasn't asleep. He'd give a small fortune to know what thoughts were going through her head right now.

He kissed the top of her head tenderly. "So, Bam Bam, how long did you work as a dancer?"

"Two whole weeks." She laughed derisively.

"Not exactly a career choice then, huh?"

"It was only intended to get me through college. It lasted until some guy got fresh, and I kneed him in the balls. Turns out he was the boss's son, and if I'd wanted to apologize to the creep alone in his penthouse the next night, I could have kept my job." She shrugged, and the flash of her eyes let him know she was still angered by the incident.

258 DIXIE LEE BROWN

"I take it there was no apology?"

"The job wasn't worth my self-respect. I moved back home, went to a junior college, and got a job as a dispatcher with the State of Alaska."

Brady hugged her tighter, half pissed off at some slimeball he'd never laid eyes on and half proud as hell of this woman he was more attracted to than ever. "Do me a favor, would you?"

Mac raised her head and looked at him curiously.

"Don't dance for anyone but me from now on?" She just stared at him, wary again. He lifted her so he could reach her mouth and sipped her heady brew until the first stirrings of desire awakened in him.

"Hey, you never asked me for anything. We had a deal, sugar. I was looking forward to fulfilling your every wish." He gently pushed the hair back that had fallen into her face.

She dropped her gaze and crossed her arms over her stomach, effectively distancing herself from him. "I've given you the wrong idea. It's not at all what you think."

He kicked himself for bringing it up, but now that the subject was on the table, it was fair game. "It doesn't matter what it is. Tell me. Please?" He guided her chin around and forced her to look at him.

Her bottom lip trembled, and she ducked away from his hand. "I was going to ask a favor."

"What is it, sugar? I can't refuse, remember? That's the deal." He smiled encouragingly, hoping to bring back the playful mood they'd shared moments ago. By now, he'd recognized that whatever she wanted wasn't a sexual

TEMPT THE NIGHT   259

favor, but he had no less desire to fulfill his end of the bargain. In fact, the need to see Mac safe and happy consumed him, regardless of what that entailed.

A loud knock made them both jump. Brady's gaze darted toward the door, and he swore under his breath when he picked up a smattering of women's voices and laughter.

"Mac? Are you up?" Cara, apparently the ringleader, yelled through the door, but Brady would bet Darcy and Rayna were out in the hallway with her.

Mac grabbed for the sheet to cover herself, a look of total disbelief on her face. She swept her gaze over Brady, naked as a jaybird, and groaned. It was all he could do to stifle the grin that tried to escape.

She rose to her knees. "I'm up. I just got out of the shower, and I'm not dressed."

"Well, hurry up, girl. We're going shopping, and we'll need your help." Darcy this time, followed by more laughter.

Shopping? How the hell was that a good idea? Brady sat up and paid closer attention.

Mac glanced at Brady, raising her eyebrows. "I'll meet you downstairs in a few, then…I guess."

"We want Jim to tag along with you, but we haven't seen him. You wouldn't happen to know where he is, would you?"

Hell, yeah. If she was going anywhere, you could bet he was going along to make sure nothing happened to her.

Mac wagged her head as her mouth dropped open, and she rolled her eyes heavenward. "No…no…haven't

260 DIXIE LEE BROWN

seen him since last night." She slapped her hand over her mouth, and a stricken expression accompanied her slumped shoulders.

"We'll find him. Come down as soon as you're dressed, and we'll talk. We're going to eat something before we go."

That had to be Rayna, always the one to interject details into any plan. She was a damn good soldier and a friend he'd trust watching his back. If there was no way to talk them out of this insanity, then he and Rayna would keep Mac safe. As the giddy laughter and voices receded, Mac flopped on the bed, hiding her face in the sheet.

Brady scrutinized her. Red splotches on her neck clearly said she was mortified. Apparently, almost being caught in a compromising situation with him wasn't on her bucket list. He could understand, but her obvious shame didn't bode well for him. He sat up and reached for her, drawing her closer until he could loop his good arm around her waist.

"You want to tell me why you're so upset?"

"They...we..." She threw her hand in the air. "I shouldn't have lied to them. I was just so embarrassed—I said the first thing that came to mind. Arrived yesterday and jumped right in the sack with the first man I saw. Jeez, Brady. What will they think?" She burrowed her face into his chest, and a muffled groan punctuated her humiliation.

A chuckle escaped as he tightened his hold. "You're worried about what those ladies will think of you?"

Mac nodded her head against his chest.

TEMPT THE NIGHT 261

Brady gripped her arms and pushed her away far enough to study her face. "For a second, I thought you were sorry you'd jumped in the sack with me. And that would be bad because I already made plans to spend tonight with you, and the night after that, and every night until you're not here anymore."

Her eyes widened as she stared.

"Is that all right with you?" He wasn't sure what he'd do if she said no.

She nodded her head again, a sparkle returning to her eyes.

Brady smiled. "Okay. That's good." *Who was he kidding? That was great.* "One thing though—those smart ladies," he said, motioning toward the door, "will figure it out in short order. You'll probably want to come clean. They're not going to judge either of us. Guaranteed."

Mac wrapped her arms around his neck, pressing her bare breasts against his side, and stretched to plant a kiss on his mouth. "I have to get ready," she said as she scrambled for the side of the bed. She rummaged in the closet, selected two or three articles, and rushed to the bathroom.

Brady debated whether the smile he couldn't rid himself of was permanent or not. It didn't feel like it was going away any time soon. He stood, pulling on his jeans and T-shirt, preparing to leave, track down Joe, and get to the bottom of this shopping madness. He was halfway down the stairs before it occurred to him that Mac had never told him what the favor she wanted was.

Chapter Seventeen

MAC CAST ONE more glance at the rumpled bed sheets and bit her lip as she stepped from the room, closing the door. Now, if only she could purge herself of the images in her mind so easily. At least half the time, she could feel the phantom touch of Brady's hands caressing her, his lips moving over hers. Molten heat coursed through her veins, and unquenchable desire raged throughout for no apparent reason.

None except Jim Brady. The memory of his green eyes going dark with lust made her heart beat like she'd just run a four-minute mile. It had proved hard to breathe as he'd settled her against his rock-hard chest, so sure of what he wanted and not afraid to take, yet equally willing to give. The control he exhibited over himself while he slowly and purposefully brought her to heights she hadn't known existed was the single most romantic gift she'd ever received. Desire pooled low in her stomach as

TEMPT THE NIGHT 263

she remembered him braced over her on one arm while he made love to her until he was the center of her whole world.

She'd chosen to trust Brady and push aside the possibility of his violence. When his past drew him, she'd been able to call him back to her. Would that always be the case, or would she eventually lose this tug-of-war?

Mac jogged down the stairs and followed the aroma of bacon and eggs to the dining area. Friendly conversation and the clinking of utensils on plates came from within. The noise stopped abruptly as she stepped to the doorway and scanned the room. Three sets of unfamiliar eyes turned toward her. She raised a hand in a cheerful greeting. "Good morning. Just looking for Cara."

A nice-looking forty-something man pointed with his fork while he finished chewing the food he'd just shoved in his mouth. "They're in Joe's office."

Mac waved again and continued toward the rear of the house. The door to the room where they'd met with Hernandez stood slightly open, and Mac increased her pace. She stopped outside as the first words reached her.

"Hernandez and his hoodlums are staying in town. Based on activity near his home in Mexico City, he may have sent for reinforcements—and weapons." It was Ty's voice, but he spoke as though he were reading from something.

"Hanford sent that late last night. He'll let me know if anything changes." Joe paused, and for a moment, no one spoke. "It's fair to say we're the only game in town that the ambassador would be interested in. We're ready, but

264 DIXIE LEE BROWN

I'd like to beef up security. Ty, get the word out. See how many hands we can get on deck for a few days."

"Damn, Joe. Under the circumstances, it's not a good idea to let the women take Mac shopping. Hernandez probably has us under surveillance." Brady was apparently in the room too, and his concern tugged at Mac's heart.

There was another brief silence. "I hope he does. I want him to see that the odds are changing. However, I don't recall signing off on a shopping trip for Mac. I'm afraid I have to agree with Jim."

"Jumping to conclusions doesn't become you, Joe." Cara's voice rose in reproach.

Suddenly, someone gripped Mac's shoulders from behind, and Walker's whiskered face leaned close. "This is getting to be a habit with you." He grinned and tipped his head toward the door. "Let's go in and join the conversation, shall we?"

He didn't give her a choice as he walked forward. She preceded him, his hands still resting lightly on her shoulders, guiding her steps. Walker rapped on the door with his knuckles and swung it open.

Brady's head came up, and he scowled. If Walker noticed, he didn't give any sign. He walked her to Brady's side and then veered off to slouch in one of the black leather chairs near Nick.

"Sorry I'm late," Walker drawled. "Mac was lost so I had to rescue her. Keep going though. We'll catch up."

Cara walked toward Joe, her hands on her hips. "This isn't my first rodeo. I understand the danger to Mac." She glanced at Darcy, whose eyes flashed with indignation as her red hair flounced around her shoulders. "We never intended for Mac to leave the safety of the compound. We've got it all worked out with Ty."

Rayna's blonde ponytail swung as she slapped Ty's arm in jest. "Don't you people ever communicate?"

Mac's gaze darted between the three women and Ty in confusion. It had certainly sounded to her like she was going shopping. From the perplexity on Brady's face, it was clear he'd believed so as well.

"Give me a break. I've been a little busy this morning." The affectionate smile Ty favored Rayna with belied his gruff words. He turned toward Joe. "We came up with a way that Mac can get the things she needs, have a hand in the decisions, and never leave the place." Ty help up the iPad that had been lying on the desk behind him, moving it in an arc so everyone could see.

"FaceTime." Rayna, Darcy, and Cara chimed in at the same time.

"Irene already provided a few things for Mac, so it's not like it will take very long. If Mac will give us a list, we can pick some things, and I can try them on. We're really close to the same height and size. What do you think, Mac?" Cara swung toward her.

"Um…that works, I guess…but you're going to an awful lot of trouble. I won't need but a couple things." She hesitated to announce to the group that it was mostly underthings she lacked. "And I don't have much cash. All I have is a credit card."

"Don't worry about money. I'll make sure you have enough." In spite of Brady's generous words, his tone was gruff.

Mac started to object, but something in his gaze stilled her tongue.

Joe looked pointedly at Cara. "I assume you've arranged for a couple of men to accompany you? With Hernandez in the area, I don't want to take any chances."

"It's all arranged. Sanchez and Walker agreed to go," replied Cara. "Irene offered to show Maria around this morning, so we just need someone to keep an eye on Marco for a few hours...and I was hoping you'd have time to watch your daughter."

Brady's arm flexed at Mac's waist, and his expression softened as she turned toward him. "We can take Marco, right?"

"Of course."

Walker turned toward the man in the cowboy hat. "How about you, Nick? Want to take a drive into town?"

Nick's gaze darted to Walker as though he hadn't been paying attention until he heard his name. "I think I'll hang around here, if that's okay with everyone." He glanced toward Joe, who nodded slightly and turned away.

"Okay. It's settled then. Sanchez, Walker, and I will go to town." Joe raised a hand to forestall Cara's argument. "I can take care of Lea just as well in town as I can here. Mac and Jim can do whatever the hell they want to while they're entertaining Marco. That leaves Steve and a half dozen special-ops guys, plus Jim to keep an eye on things

TEMPT THE NIGHT 267

here. Nick can look over the operation, and it looks like Ty is the only one who'll get any work done today." Joe slapped him on the back.

"So…just like any other day then?" Ty chortled to accompanying groans from Joe and Walker.

Mac had to admit she'd been looking forward to the female camaraderie, not to mention enough time away from Brady to clear her head, but with that lunatic, Hernandez, running around the countryside, staying here seemed like the smartest plan.

She huddled for a few minutes with Cara, Rayna, and Darcy, giving them sizes and styles for underwear selections, adding a toothbrush and her favorite shampoo to the list. Learning that Irene had also given them a request for a few groceries lessened Mac's guilt somewhat.

Brady suddenly appeared beside her. "Ladies. Do you have everything you need from Mac?"

"Got it. We'll be ready to go as soon as we find Maria and see if there's anything she needs." Rayna handed the iPad to Mac. "Hang on to this just in case we have any questions. If you're not familiar, Ty will get you started."

"Thanks. I have one just like this—or *had* one, I guess. Maria decided to stay then?"

"She told Joe this morning. Isn't it wonderful?"

Mac nodded. She felt sure Maria would be safe and happy here, but a moment of sadness gripped her as Paddy's absence in their lives squeezed the joy from the occasion.

Brady fished his wallet from his back pocket, opened it, and slid out a plastic card. Mac prayed that his extra

268 DIXIE LEE BROWN

condoms weren't lying on top for everyone to see. She breathed a sigh of relief when she saw it was all neatly organized again.

"My debit card. PIN's on the back."

Mac snorted.

"What?" He turned and grinned. "No one's gotten it away from me yet. No one will guess it either. I bet if I went through your trash or spent ten minutes on your Facebook page, I'd know *your* PIN and half of your passwords." He raised a brow, clearly daring her to scoff.

The way his smoldering eyes pinned her in place sent a tremor through her. Shoot! All he'd have to do is ask, and she'd *tell* him the damn passwords.

Cara broke the spell between them. "We'll ring in if we have something to show you. Don't be surprised if we pick a few things you didn't ask for. It would be more fun if you could go, Mac, but this'll all be over soon."

"Don't worry about me…and don't go crazy, okay?"

Joe and Walker had headed out a few minutes earlier, and Nick followed not too long after. Rayna, Darcy, and Cara went in search of Maria, leaving only Brady, Ty, and Mac in the study.

Ty grimaced. "They just want to help, Mac."

"Is it that obvious?" She couldn't help the humiliation that heated her skin. Having taken care of herself for a long time, she wasn't used to the idea of others shopping for her basic necessities. It rankled her, but the real kicker was the willingness with which these people jumped in to help. Almost like a family.

TEMPT THE NIGHT 269

"Only because every one of us has been in your position. It's not easy accepting help the first few times. Ask Jim about that sometime. Point is, if you stay around here very long…well, you might as well get used to people always on the edge of your business." Ty picked up his phone and grinned. "You two go have some fun today. We'll be inundated with new people by this time tomorrow."

Brady pressed his warm hand on her back and nudged her toward the door. "Let's go find Marco. He always has something he wants to do. Not all of them are things *you'll* want to do, unless you're into catching snakes."

A shudder rolled over her. Apparently feeling it through his hand on her back, Brady chuckled. As a young boy, Paddy had taunted her mercilessly with the mere threat of finding a snake. It had taken a couple of years before she'd learned that snakes in Alaska were extremely rare. She'd been so hurt by his teasing that she'd saved her allowance for three months and bought a corn snake. Somehow he'd known it was she who'd put it in his bed, and he'd never mentioned snakes again.

Mac glanced at Brady and smiled. "Nope. Not really into snakes."

Chapter Eighteen

"I KNOW! LET'S go to the...plat...toe! Marco accompanied his suggestion with a series of hops that effectively announced his enthusiasm.

Mac laughed and shook her head. Brady had been right about Marco. His first choice was going to the lake, but when Brady explained that they couldn't leave the compound today, Marco wasted no time in picking his second favorite. She glanced toward Brady for an interpretation.

"The northeastern perimeter encloses a stand of timber, a mountainside, and a flat rock formation we call the Plateau."

"Yeah! It's a long ways. We should take a lunch and lots of water." Marco was beyond excited.

Brady fixed Mac with a hopeful grin, and she smiled. "Why do I get the feeling I'm outnumbered here? I haven't forgotten the last hike you took me on, you know. How far is this plateau?"

TEMPT THE NIGHT 271

"We'll take a Gator to the edge of the timber and walk from there. It's probably a thirty-minute hike." With a smirk, he tipped his head toward the boy who hadn't taken his deep brown eyes off of her face. "Go ahead. Tell the little guy we can't go."

"You're incorrigible," she murmured so only he could hear. Then she turned to Marco. "I think that's a great idea. What would you like to take for lunch?"

"A turkey samwich, some 'tatoe chips, and some of Señora Irene's yummy cookies."

Mac leaned over and swiped the boy's curly hair off his forehead. "Got to appreciate a man who knows what he wants."

Brady came up behind her and trailed his fingers slowly down her arm. "I hope so." He moved away before the shiver had died out. "Come on, Marco. Let's go gas up the Gator and get some water and a backpack from the shed. Sounds like Mac will see to our lunches, and we'll all meet back here in twenty or so." His gaze shifted to Mac.

The heck with the cute five-year-old. It was Brady she couldn't bring herself to refuse anything. There was heartbreak in her future. She was as sure about that as she was that she'd already fallen in love with this man in spite of the dark past that made him so dangerous. If it was wrong, how come it made her feel alive?

"Twenty minutes ought to do it, but don't leave without me, okay?" She ruffled Marco's hair as he giggled and nodded his agreement.

The picture he made, walking beside Brady, trying to match his stride and keep up, was nothing short of

272   DIXIE LEE BROWN

adorable. He could have been walking with Paddy. He and Maria might have had a life together that included raising that little boy—if not for Hernandez. Tears prickled Mac's eyes. God, would it never stop hurting?

She turned away and hurried toward the kitchen. Her footsteps echoed in the nearly empty house. The shoppers had left fifteen minutes ago. Mac had heard the Hummer start up and drive away. Brady had mentioned there were other men and students on the ranch, but so far she hadn't seen anyone outside of the dining area this morning.

Irene and Maria were having a cup of coffee when she burst in on them. Irene popped up before Mac could stop her and poured another cup.

"Thanks, but I've got less than twenty minutes to make lunches for Brady, Marco, and me...if that's all right."

Maria stood. "I'll help. Marco is behaving, I hope."

"Your son is amazing, Maria. You're lucky to have him." Mac didn't miss the frown on her face, but it was the anger emanating from Irene that proved there was something amiss.

Irene opened the refrigerator and grabbed a loaf of bread. "What kind of sandwiches would you like?"

"I have a very specific request from Marco. Turkey sandwiches, potato chips, and Señora Irene's yummy cookies." They all laughed together.

"I've gotten pretty attached to that boy. I can't tell you how happy I am you're staying, Maria." Irene placed turkey cold cuts, mayo, and mustard on the counter by the bread.

TEMPT THE NIGHT 273

Mac and Maria stepped up beside Irene, and they all started putting sandwiches together. After a moment of silence, Mac couldn't stay quiet. "Is somebody going to let me in on what's wrong?"

If it was possible, the room got even quieter…until Irene, dropping her knife on the counter, made them all jump. "Tell her, Maria. This isn't something you can keep to yourself. There are other people involved."

Maria had finished her first sandwich, placing it carefully in a plastic bag, and quickly laid out bread and meat for another one. When she was finished, she sighed, wiping her hands on her apron. "Hernandez called the house this morning to speak with me. He said that if I returned to him of my own free will, he wouldn't try to take Marco. My son could have a life here or somewhere safe. But if I don't go back, he'll take Marco and raise him as his son." Maria delivered her news looking at the floor, clearly defeated.

Anger flared, and Mac's jaw clenched in response. "He's got a lot of nerve after being run out of here last night."

Irene finished the two sandwiches she was working on and cut them in half angrily. "He was the last person I expected when I answered the phone, and he surprised me so much I wasn't thinking. I should have transferred the call to Joe, but…" She took a deep breath.

Mac met Irene's gaze. "Don't blame yourself. Hernandez is the one at fault here." She turned to Maria. "You have to tell Joe as soon as he gets back. Ty needs to know, and Brady. Maria, for Marco's sake you can't keep something like this a secret."

274 DIXIE LEE BROWN

"I should just do as he says—go back to him. Marco would be safe. You'd be safe."

"You can't, Maria. That man has no conscience. He's already killed to get to you. He'll kill you too, and he won't care that he promised Marco would be safe. That promise is worthless." Mac shoved the two sandwiches she'd made into baggies, then paced in a short circle. "Damn it! Irene, where are the chips?"

Irene huffed. "You keep talking. I'll get the chips and the cookies." She opened a large pantry on the back wall.

Mac put her arm around Maria's shoulders. "I'm sorry. I don't mean to make it sound like this is easy or that I know what you should do, but I'm not going to let you sacrifice yourself. Paddy would never forgive either of us. This right here," she swung her arms wide, "is the best shot we've got."

"That's right, and if you won't tell Joe, I will." Irene slapped the chips down on the counter so hard Mac envisioned eating very small pieces later. "In fact, I'm going to call him right now. Do you want to talk to him, or should I?"

Mac hid a smile. Apparently, when Irene got fired up, there was no stopping her.

She stuffed the food in a large tote and shoved it toward Mac. "You go. Take care of Marco. I'll take care of Maria."

Mac gave the slight Mexican woman another hug, received a halfhearted smile through a haze of tears, and strode from the room.

Outside the dogs were loose, and Marco was delightedly throwing sticks for them to retrieve while Brady watched from the driver's seat of the Gator. Nick and one of the men Mac had seen in the dining area this morning stood beside the vehicle, talking and laughing with Brady.

This place—these people—seemed good for him. He laughed easier and was more relaxed. Maybe he *had* changed since he'd been here. Maybe this life was just the one he needed to keep him sane. She envied the peace on his face as he chuckled at Marco's antics.

The dogs made a beeline for her when they smelled the food. They must have remembered her from last night, because after a cursory smell, they raced back to Marco.

Brady hopped from the Gator, took the bag from her, and placed it in the back of the vehicle beside a case of bottled water. "Nick is bored. Do you mind if he comes along?"

Mac tried to hide her disappointment. "The more, the merrier. We have plenty of sandwiches. Hope you like turkey, Nick."

"I'm not the least bit fussy." He climbed into the back.

"Mac, meet Steve Logan." Brady directed her attention to the stranger.

She extended her hand, and his grip was firm and warm. "Nice to meet you, Steve."

"Same here. Nice day for a picnic."

"You're welcome to come too." Mac liked him right away. His smile was kind and sincere. Somewhere around midforties with dark brown hair graying at the temples, he was still a very attractive man.

"Thanks, but I've got work to do, unlike this yahoo." He grinned as he jabbed his thumb toward Brady.

276 DIXIE LEE BROWN

Brady chuckled. "It's about time you did some work around here. While you're at it, would you keep an eye on the house?"

Steve snickered and cocked his head toward Mac. "He'd be lost without me."

She laughed. "Obviously."

"Hey! Stop encouraging him, and get in the Gator. Marco, time to go." Brady winked at her.

Mac skirted around the front and climbed in the passenger seat. Brady lifted Marco over the sidewalls with one hand. Mac and Marco waved as Brady put the vehicle in gear, gave it some gas, and peeled out. Marco was talking Nick's ear off in the back, and Dillon and Ribs ran ahead of them, searching out the best smells, obviously excited to be included on the adventure.

It was warm for October. The breeze in her face cooled her, and she closed her eyes, enjoying the warmth of the sun and the smell of pine trees. At peace for the first time in days, she put off telling Brady about Hernandez's call, needing a few minutes to pretend that life was normal again. She wasn't ready to go back to reality when Brady parked the Gator next to a slope covered with evergreens.

Marco whooped and jumped to the ground. Nick followed him, snagging the backpack and slipping it over his shoulders.

"You sure, man? I can get that." Brady strode to the back of the vehicle.

"You've got enough on your hands." He smirked and glanced toward Marco, already heading up the slope.

TEMPT THE NIGHT 277

"Thanks." Brady grabbed four bottles of water and the bag containing their lunch and stuffed everything inside the backpack, then helped Nick cinch it down so it would be comfortable to carry.

"Marco, wait up," Mac called after the boy, hurrying to catch up as the dogs raced for the Plateau that loomed up ahead, their noses to the ground. She wasn't an expert with children by any means, but she'd feel better on this steep slope, with its thick brush and downed trees, if someone was close to Marco. Apparently, she was that someone for now.

"Mac? Do you know why the plat…toe is my favorite place?" Marco fixed her with a serious stare.

"No. Why?"

He pointed up the mountainside. "Because no one can sneak up on me up there." The sadness in his voice took her breath for a moment.

Brady had told her of the tragedy in Marco's life but hadn't shared the name of the kidnapper. Who would hurt this little boy? Hernandez? Someone else? She reached out to touch his shoulder. Not today—no one would hurt him today.

They kept moving, climbing steadily upward. Brady and Nick soon caught up, and they veered toward the right, where Mac could see the flat-topped rock formation ahead. Another fifteen minutes, and they scrambled onto the Plateau.

She stood at the edge and swung in a three-hundred-and-sixty-degree circle. The view was to die for. She could see the compound, the beautiful crystal-clear lake

278 DIXIE LEE BROWN

beyond, and snow-capped mountains in every direction shining brilliantly in the sun's rays. Brady appeared silently behind her and hugged her to his chest.

"It's gorgeous. Thanks for bringing me here." Mac turned her face so she could press her lips to his jaw.

He held her gaze. "It's never been quite this beautiful before." He kissed her cheek. "I'm sorry we couldn't spend the day alone."

"Me too." A different sadness gripped her, along with the sense of time running out.

Nick approached, holding out the iPad. "It's for you, Mac."

She took the device and instantly recognized Darcy, Cara, and Rayna surrounded by racks of clothing on hangers.

"Okay, Mac. See anything you like?" Cara panned her tablet to zero in on a selection of sweaters.

Brady kissed her ear. "I'll be over there with Marco if you need me."

Mac stared longingly after him as he and Nick walked away. She'd much rather spend the day with him than trying to convince these women to stick to the list she'd given them. Not only didn't she need anything else, but she wasn't in the right state of mind for shopping. By the sound of the giggling and chattering coming from the iPad, however, Cara, Darcy, and Rayna were in fine form. Unwilling to dampen their excitement, she forced herself to take a deep breath and relax, sat with her legs dangling over the side of the flat rock, and resigned herself to the task at hand.

TEMPT THE NIGHT   279

In the end, she'd had a blast, laughing until her cheeks ached like she used to with Paddy. She'd relented on a few items of apparel simply because her new friends were having such a good time she couldn't bear to let them think she didn't appreciate their efforts. She could always return them as soon as the whole Hernandez thing was resolved—especially the dress.

They'd gotten it in their heads that she needed a dress—for what she wasn't sure—and they'd apparently asked Brady's opinion on color before leaving. The dress they chose was sleeveless, yellow—the same color as the pullover Brady had bought for her at Goodwill—with a skirt that flared at the waist. Cara looked terrific in it for whatever that was worth. Darcy accessorized with an off-white knit sweater that fit loosely and hung open in front.

By the time they'd picked out running shoes, black flats, and yellow heels, the battery in the iPad was running low. Already feeling guilty and overindulged, Mac was more than ready to quit, but Rayna had one more purchase in mind.

"You need a jacket, Mac. The weather in Montana can turn cold anytime. And boots too. Snow gets deep."

"No, really. I won't be here that long, and anyway, I live in Alaska. I've got plenty of winter apparel at home. You've done enough."

"Are you blind, girl? Have you seen the way Jim looks at you? As long as I've known him, he's never shown more than a passing interest in a woman. He's in love

280 DIXIE LEE BROWN

with you, Mac. Look at him. How can you even think about leaving?" Rayna threw her hands in the air, clearly exasperated.

Mac glanced over her shoulder to where Brady, Nick, and Marco were searching for something on the ground, while the dogs lay nearby, still panting from their run. As though he sensed her gaze on him, Brady looked up, smiled, and winked. Aside from the fact that he wouldn't allow himself to get attached to her, he was probably the kindest, the best-looking, and the most desirable man she'd ever met. Too bad about that first item on the list, because it definitely made all the rest meaningless.

She forced herself to return his smile, then swung back to the iPad and Rayna's face. "Brady's great. I could probably get used to having him underfoot if I let myself, but I've got things to take care of in Alaska first. Clearing my name and making sure that sleazeball, Hernandez, never sees the light of day again take priority. I owe Paddy at least that much." She shrugged and blinked rapidly, unwilling to cry in front of these three. They had the uncanny ability to see right through her, and they'd probably know that Brady was part of the reason tears came so easily.

"Okay…look around a…what we can…"

One second Darcy was talking, and the next the screen in front of Mac went blank. The battery must have died. Probably the only way she could have won that argument. Mac sat still for a moment, just breathing and willing the tingling in her eyes to go away. When she was

TEMPT THE NIGHT   281

sure she had herself under control, she stood and walked toward the others.

No sooner had she gotten to her feet than Brady was beside her. He looked at his watch. "Wow. Two hours. Does that qualify as marathon shopping?" A teasing sparkle shone from his eyes.

Mac gasped. "No! Two hours? Really? Did you eat lunch? Marco must be starving."

Brady stepped into her, his arms drawing her against him. "If we were hungry, we would have eaten. Marco wanted to wait for you…and me too. It looked like you were enjoying yourself. Did you get everything you'll need?"

A short laugh burst from her. "*More* than I need. Those ladies wouldn't take no for an answer. I'll probably return most of the things. Hope you had plenty of money in your bank account." She forced a smile, but it soon faded. Spending his money on her just seemed wrong. "I don't care what you say, Brady, I'm going to pay you back."

He slid his hand behind her head, holding her still while he brought his lips down on hers in a scalding kiss. When he finished, she was breathless.

"The clothes are a gift, Mac. You're *not* going to pay me back. My job pays extremely well. All my living expenses are covered. I've missed having someone to spend money on, so please don't take that away from me. In fact, I think we should do it more often." Before she could argue, he took her hand and tugged her toward a grassy spot where the backpack waited. A few feet away, Nick and Marco

282 DIXIE LEE BROWN

reclined on their backs, pointing at the clouds while the two dogs rested nearby.

"Hey, are you two hungry?" Brady pulled out the sack with their lunch and started emptying the bag.

Marco rolled over and hopped to his feet with a huge grin. "Señorita Mac, you talked for a *long* time."

Mac caught him as he launched himself at her. "I know. I'm sorry, Marco." She hugged him close for a moment, savoring the feel of his small, warm body cuddled next to hers.

Soon, he began squirming, pulled loose, and accepted his lunch from Brady. Instead of dropping down to unwrap the food and start eating, Marco handed the items to her.

Touched, words failed her. She smiled at Marco and glanced over his head at Brady. He grinned and winked, and Mac felt sure he'd coached Marco. It was a thoughtful gesture, and Marco had benefited by having a father figure for a day. Brady was always surprising her.

She dropped her gaze to Marco. "Thank you. What a nice thing to do. You're such a gentleman, Marco."

He beamed and glanced at Brady, who motioned slightly with a water bottle. "Sit, señorita. I'll bring you water."

Mac walked a few steps and dropped down near Nick, who was already munching on his sandwich. Marco stopped at her elbow and handed her the bottle, then sat beside her and opened his lunch.

"Thanks," she said again, ruffling his hair.

"Cute kid," Nick said from her other side.

TEMPT THE NIGHT 283

She sensed Brady's presence behind her before he spoke. "With what that kid's been through, he's not only cute—he's friggin' amazing."

Nick shrugged and went back to eating. Mac smiled to herself. Did Brady realize he was getting attached to the boy? Maybe his self-imposed rule wasn't as hard and fast as he'd like to believe.

Chapter Nineteen

BRADY GLANCED SIDEWAYS at Mac as she held Marco across her lap while he slept. The boy had worn himself out running, jumping, and searching every crevice for arrowheads. He'd found a few too, and his excitement had been contagious. Everyone should get to be a boy at some point in life. That time was overdue for Marco.

Clearly Mac was sleepy too, and the midafternoon sun wasn't helping. She blinked her eyes slowly, and her lengthy lashes stayed down longer each time. Strands of dark hair whipped around her face as they raced toward home at the Gator's top speed.

In the back, Nick was alert and watchful. Brady couldn't help wondering about the man. What was his story? He'd been quiet, keeping to himself, since he'd arrived here, and today was no different. Nothing wrong with quiet...unless it was a method to hide something.

TEMPT THE NIGHT 285

Joe obviously trusted him, though, and Joe was seldom wrong about a man's character.

Brady applied the brake and slowed the vehicle as they approached the shed where it was kept. The dogs had arrived ahead of them and were lying in front of their kennels, panting.

Mac stirred and smiled sleepily over Marco's head, which was resting on her breast. "Thank you."

He smiled back, confused. "For what?"

"I haven't thought about Paddy since we left the house earlier. You make me believe I might heal someday."

"Not only heal—you'll be better and stronger, sugar. It's the natural order of things." Brady would have taken his right hand off of the steering wheel and reached for her if the uselessness of his bandaged left hand hadn't made it impossible to maintain control of the Gator at the same time.

Her gaze homed in on his with a speculative gleam. "Good to know. That's true for you too, right?"

Shit! He should have seen that coming. Obviously, she wanted to fix him, but she didn't know how sick he was. "Don't, Mac. What's broke on me won't heal. I've seen it on the battlefield too many times. The best I can do is learn my limitations." Brady guided the Gator through the open doorway and parked it beside two others.

He turned off the key and looked at her, so close to telling her that she'd brought hope into his life for the first time in years, but the words stuck in his throat. What if he was wrong?

Nick leaned forward suddenly, resting his arms on the seatback between them. "I'm goin' back to Alaska in a few days. Got me a job ferryin' a brand spankin' new jet up for a friend. I know you've got unfinished business up there, Mac, so if you're ready, you're welcome to go with me."

"She's not ready." Brady hammered each word home as he studied Nick's expressionless gaze. Was he simply offering a favor, a free ride? Or did he have an agenda that involved a double cross? Slowly, he became aware of Mac glaring at him, anger flashing in her storm-filled eyes.

"Where I go…and when…is my decision, Brady. You said there was nothing long-term here for me, and that's fine, but when I go, it'll be because *I'm* ready."

She turned to Nick. "Actually, I am interested. I want to see my parents and explain…if that's even possible. I don't want them going any longer than necessary thinking their daughter is a murderer. Thanks for the offer, Nick."

Brady clenched the steering wheel so hard his knuckles turned white. With no small effort, he managed to keep his mouth shut, preferring to save what he had to say until he and Mac were alone.

Nick glanced guardedly between Brady and Mac, then shrugged. "No problem, I'll let you know when I'll be leaving." He stood, jumped over the sidewalls, and sauntered across the compound toward the house.

Mac started to clamber off the seat with Marco, and Brady stopped her before she'd taken two steps.

He held out his arms. "Give him to me."

TEMPT THE NIGHT 287

"I've got him." She tried to skirt around him with her burden.

Brady blocked her path and then swore. He jerked the Ace bandage loose and quickly unwound it, letting it drop to the ground. The plastic splint followed. The side of his hand where the bullet had grazed him was slightly swollen and pink around the irregular line of black stitches that extended from the knuckle of his little finger to his wrist. It was sore as hell and weak from disuse, but damn it felt good to be rid of *that* annoyance once and for all.

Anger simmered in her eyes as they bore into his. "What do you think you're doing?"

She needn't think she had a corner on the pissed-off market. Damn if she couldn't push his buttons when she tried. He wasn't only mad at her—he was also irritated with himself because every time he opened his mouth, something other than what he wanted to say came out. He'd told her not to expect anything permanent, and then after he'd made love to her, he hadn't bothered to tell her how she'd blown all his defenses out of the water.

He struggled to rein in his temper, needing to prove to himself that he could. "Getting back to normal. Now, give me the kid."

She stood and stared for a few seconds before he saw the fight go out of her eyes, and she handed Marco over silently. He turned abruptly and started for the house. After a few seconds, he heard her follow across the gravel and onto the lawn behind him.

He stopped inside the front door. The shoppers evidently weren't home yet. The study door was closed. The smell of something Italian hung in the air, but no cooks were in evidence.

Brady met her gaze. "I'll put him down in his room. Then you and I are going to talk."

Mac shook her head. "We've already covered it all, Brady. Unless you've got something new to say to me. I don't expect the world to suddenly change because of what happened this morning, and you're not going to talk me out of going with Nick." She turned toward him and placed her hand on his arm. "Please, let's just leave it at that. I appreciate your friendship, and I don't want to argue with you." She stepped to the stairs and climbed the two flights to her room.

Brady stood still until he heard her door close at the top of the stairs. Then he carried Marco to the room the boy shared with his mother on the second floor, knocked briefly before opening the door, and left him tucked cozily under a thick quilt.

At the stairs again, he gripped the handrail tightly, staring upward to the third floor, where he could just see Mac's closed door. She was right. He should leave it alone. Let things die a natural death while they were still friends—before he did something so fucking wrong that she would hate him forever…if she survived.

As though he had no control over his actions, he put one foot on the stairs leading up, and then another. He didn't want to argue either, but he sure as hell wasn't going to let her head back to Alaska without him to protect her. And going with Nick Taylor was about as far out of the friggin' question as he could imagine. Damn it

TEMPT THE NIGHT 289

to hell. Against every promise he'd ever made to himself, he'd fallen in love with her.

When he took the final step and stood facing her door, he still had no clue what he could say that would make everything all right. She had business to take care of. He had a deep-seated fear of hurting the woman he loved. The best thing he could do for her was to stay away. Anything else was irresponsible. Okay—now that he'd settled that...

He took two more steps and laid his forehead against the door. "Mac?" He rapped softly with his knuckles. No answer from within. No sounds at all. He tried the knob and then knocked again, louder. "Open the door, Mac... unless you want me to tear it off the hinges."

The sound of feet sliding across carpet brought her to the door, and he sensed her leaning on the opposite side, probably unsure just like he was, maybe even apprehensive. Shit. Every time he turned around, he was jerking her emotions all over the board.

"Mac? Let me in. Please? We need to talk."

The lock released with a click, and a couple seconds later, she pulled the door toward her until it was open only far enough for her to stand in the gap, her head leaning sideways against the edge.

She might have been crying, or maybe she was only tired. Her lips pressed together in a thin line, and the hurt in her eyes unmistakably said he'd have to be convincing if he expected her to let him in.

Brady motioned back and forth between them. "I'm an open book to you, Mac. What do you want to know?"

290 DIXIE LEE BROWN

She lifted her head, and a small smile filled him with hope. "Everything," she said, still hesitating before finally stepping back and giving enough room for him to slip inside.

He pushed through the opening and closed the door behind him, then crossed the distance and lifted her off her feet, clasping her in a bear hug. "Sugar, you're the best thing that ever happened to me. I don't want to lose you. Don't ever forget that, okay?"

Mac pressed against him, threading her arms around his neck, a smile making the moisture in her eyes shine. "You're sure about that? You've known me a total of five days."

"I didn't lose count, and I didn't say I was done getting to know you. But I already know quite a bit—your compassion, your brave heart, that ultra-sensitive spot that sends you over the top when we make love, but mostly your honesty." He brought his lips to hers and sipped gently, her sweetness instantly going to his head. He had a vague sense of her stiffening, withdrawing, even as his chest tightened and threatened to burst with the protectiveness that surged through him.

A deep breath later, he met her gaze, his gut telling him that something was wrong. "You need to know me too, so go ahead. Ask me anything."

She squirmed from his arms and stepped back as wariness erased the smile she'd worn seconds before. "I want to, Brady. I'd like to know everything about you, but don't you think we should address the elephant in the room first?" Her hand tightened around his as though she expected him to pull away.

He studied her expressive eyes and wanted to reach out and touch the pulse in her neck that clearly indicated how upset she was. He'd expected her to return to Alaska...just not so soon. Damn Nick Taylor anyway. Brady tamped down an angry outburst that would only serve to drive a wedge between them.

He lifted his hand and traced her collarbone. "Okay, sugar. Let's talk about that. There's something not quite right about Nick. I don't trust him...and you're not going with him."

Mac stiffened and pulled away—his first indication that maybe he hadn't phrased that exactly right. In hindsight, it should have been obvious.

"Nick came through for us on that mountain in Sitka. What does someone have to do to earn your respect?" Mac slapped her hands on her hips.

Shit! The last thing he wanted was to push her into a corner where she thought it was necessary to defend the bastard. "You're right. He's probably an okay guy, but I'm not taking a chance on him in this instance."

"You're *not*. *I* am." She crossed her arms, and her fiery expression dared him to disagree.

So much for control. Anger cut loose and flooded him until he couldn't see for the pounding in his head. He turned his back and took a couple of halting steps toward the door. The image of Nick on the receiving end of his fury gave him a moment of satisfaction.

292 DIXIE LEE BROWN

He balled his hands into fists, welcoming the sharp pain of his wound. Closing his eyes, he breathed in and exhaled, turning to face her. Determination lined her pretty face, but no fear. That might have been an oversight on her part. If he'd never been inclined to toss a woman over his knee and paddle her ass before, this could be a first.

"Are you trying to piss me off?" His throat felt like he'd swallowed ground glass.

Mac had the good sense to glance toward the door. "Aside from you saving my life and bringing me here, I don't see where this is any of your concern. It's not like you took me on to raise. Or did you forget about your whole I-don't-have-much-to-offer speech?"

"Is that what this is about? You're trying to punish me for telling you the truth?"

"*No!* I'd never do that. You were only trying to tell me that I'd be leaving here alone—now or later, it doesn't really matter. That means no one is in charge of making my decisions but me. Not Joe. Not Nick. Not even you. If you can't deal with that, then maybe you better leave." Mac strode to the door and held it open, a slight tremble of her chin the only emotion visible on her face.

Muscles corded in his arms, Brady glanced around for something to punch, then decided to save it for Nick. How in the hell had their conversation gotten so far out of hand? Mac was wound like a top with indignation and purpose, and now was not the time to try to talk her out of anything. Actually, it would have been good if he'd stopped talking a long time ago, because he'd

TEMPT THE NIGHT 293

pretty much talked himself into a black hole. She wasn't liable to give much weight to anything else he said at this point. He could wait, though. She'd cool off, and he'd get another chance to tell her that…damn it…he did get a say in her decisions…because he loved her.

He strode to where she stood at the door and bent to kiss her cheek. She took a step back to avoid his touch, and, for a second, he stared into grief-filled eyes. "Jesus, Mac. It doesn't have to be like this." Brady stepped into the hallway and heard the door close firmly behind him.

Chapter Twenty

MAC WATCHED AS Brady's body language underwent a complete change and his eyes, which had been kind and encouraging, flashed with anger and stubborn pride. Her fault. She should have stuck to her vow to stay away from arrogant, bossy alpha males. They were all the same. Still, Mac hadn't intended for their conversation to end with her telling him to leave, but once she did, she certainly wasn't going to let his warm, wonderful lips touch her on his way out.

She swung the door closed behind him and leaned her forehead against the cool, smooth wood as waves of regret threatened to suffocate her. Man, if there was one thing she knew how to do properly, it was messing up a good thing.

She'd planned on asking Brady to take her home to Alaska so she could see her parents and learn the truth behind Paddy's death. That was the favor she'd tricked

TEMPT THE NIGHT 295

him into agreeing to the morning they'd made love. Although, if she was honest with herself, he'd likely only agreed because he was under the impression the favor would be performed in the bedroom.

Mac had been so hurt and infuriated by Brady's overbearing, pompous commands regarding what she could and couldn't do that she latched on to the first thing she could think of to teach him a lesson, reiterating her decision to go with Nick. She swallowed hard. What mindboggling insanity had forced those words from her lips? She hadn't even asked Brady. Of course, to be fair, he hadn't offered either—to step up and play a bigger role in her life.

But why would he? He'd said he didn't want to lose her, but what time frame was he talking about now? A week? A month? Until he was tired of her?

Mac was a realist. All relationships were short-term in her mind. Still, she'd waited breathlessly for him to explain—hoping there was something more to this. That she'd misunderstood. That he'd misunderstood. His edict had snapped her from that fantasyland…and the rest was history.

She twisted the lock on the knob and turned slowly toward the bed. What she wouldn't give to wake up from this nightmare with Paddy still alive and having never heard of Kalispell, Montana, or Jim Brady.

Heartbreak and loneliness burst over her like a summer hailstorm. Blinded by the tears she couldn't hold back any longer, she stumbled to the bed, curled into a ball, and buried her face in the pillow that—inconveniently—smelled like Brady.

296 DIXIE LEE BROWN

Thirty minutes later, she made herself stand, wash her face, and get on with life. Unfortunately, life had gotten a lot harder this week. First, losing Paddy. Then, falling for a man who couldn't love her back but who had no problem trying to control her. Did these things really come in threes? God, she hoped not.

She straightened the bed so it didn't remind her of their tryst this morning, making a mental note to ask Irene for clean sheets that wouldn't smell like Brady. Perhaps Irene would let her help with dinner. She'd need some chores if she was going to stay for a while, because no chores equaled too much time on her hands to think. Maybe Marco was up from his nap and they could play a game. Or she could throw a ball for the dogs. Her decision was made when she opened her door. Darcy and Cara were just topping the stairs, each loaded down with bags.

"Wait until you see," Cara said. "There are only a couple things you didn't pick out for yourself. Don't worry. If you don't like what we picked, you can always return them."

Mac groaned as the two women swept into her room. Thank goodness she'd made the bed. Darcy and Cara headed straight for it and upended their bags, dumping their day's work in an overwhelming pile. For a split second, Mac considered sinking to her knees on the floor and giving in to the self-pity that welled from her broken heart.

But she straightened instead and plastered on a smile. "You girls have been busy." She could tell by the way both women studied her that her voice had given her away.

TEMPT THE NIGHT 297

"Come on. We'll help you hang these up or fold them and put them in drawers. You don't have to try them on all at once." Concern was etched on Darcy's face as she grabbed some hangers from Mac's closet.

"Is everything all right?" Cara reached for a hanger and hung up a yellow dress.

The knife turned in Mac's chest as she stared at the yellow fabric that would forever remind her of Brady. She was going to be sick. Frantically, her gaze darted toward the bathroom. "Would you mind if we didn't do this right now? I really need to be alone." Her frazzled voice and crazy eyes must have convinced them. They dropped everything and hurried toward the door, mumbling their apologies for disturbing her at a bad time. She didn't argue. Tomorrow, she could make amends.

As soon as they left, her distress passed, but she had to get out of this room before someone else came along and wanted to talk. She glanced toward her bag, debating whether she should take Paddy's gun. Outside, the sun was setting. Dusk would come on fast. Surely there wouldn't be any wild animals in the compound, but she didn't want to leave Paddy's things. Not now. They were all she had left.

With the badge in her pocket and the gun shoved firmly between her waistband and her back, she opened the door a crack to make sure the hallway was clear before she slipped out. Where she was going wasn't open to discussion since she hadn't made up her mind yet, so it would be better if she didn't run into anyone. She skipped down the stairs lightly and had almost made it

298   DIXIE LEE BROWN

to the front door without meeting another person when a sound behind her brought her to a stop.

Maria and Irene were arguing in the kitchen. It could only be about one thing.

Mac rushed to the back of the house, bursting through the door as Maria ripped off her apron and tossed it on the table. "I have to find him," she said.

Mac looked from one to the other. "What's wrong?"

They both started talking at once. Mac held up her hand and looked toward Irene.

"When we called Joe, he said not to worry—that he'd be ready if Hernandez tried anything—but he called again just before Joe got back. I told Maria to put it on speaker so I could listen in."

"We thought Marco was upstairs sleeping." Maria's voice broke, and she covered her mouth.

"Oh God. What did he hear?" Mac looked to Irene again.

"Hernandez said Maria didn't think he was serious enough, so he was coming to get the boy. Went into graphic detail about what he would do to him. Marco was behind us. He heard everything and ran outside." Irene slumped into a chair.

"Any chance he didn't understand? That he just went out to play? You know how kids are." Mac wanted that to be true, but fear was eating away at her insides.

Irene shook her head. "We looked for him, then decided to wait for him to come back. He didn't."

Maria started for the other room again. "I must find my son."

TEMPT THE NIGHT 299

"Wait, Maria. I'll go after him. You and Irene find Joe. Tell him what's going on. Go. Now." Mac raced for the front door without looking back to see if her orders were followed.

She began a systematic search around the house, the kennels, and the outbuildings, but Marco wasn't to be found.

If she let the dogs out, they could no doubt find the boy. On her way back to the kennels, she suddenly stopped and stared toward the northeast. Marco's comment glimmered through her mind. *Do you know why I like the Plateau? No one can sneak up on me there.*

Would he go all the way up there alone with darkness coming on? He was frightened and confused. Of course he would.

It was too dangerous. She had to stop Marco before he got to the Plateau. Mac ran to the shed that housed the Gators, climbed onto the one Brady had driven that morning, and reached for the key.

She jumped as someone slid onto the seat beside her and covered her hand, staying her effort to start the engine. Mac gasped and swung around.

Nick! Why was he here? Had he followed her? Ashamed of her instant distrust of the man, she shoved those thoughts away.

"Hello, Mac. Are you goin' for a ride?"

"I'm looking for Marco. Have you seen him?"

"No. Is he lost?"

"I think he may be on his way to the Plateau."

"Oh, hell." He removed his hand from hers. "We better get goin' then. That walk won't be pleasant in the dark."

Mac stared at him. Even though something about Nick didn't ring quite true, he'd been hired by Joe. Surely that cautious and careful man didn't have people working for him unless he was certain he could trust them. "Really? You'd go with me?"

"Can't let a pretty lady go by herself." A teasing grin hovered on his lips as he settled his cowboy hat firmly on his head.

Mac turned the key, and the Gator roared to life. She backed it out of the shed and set it on the same course Brady had followed earlier. They flew along in the cool of the evening, keeping a constant watch for Marco. When they'd driven as far as they could, there was still no sign of the boy. The sun was setting, and shadows lingered between the trees on the hillside. Marco could be anywhere up there, and they'd never see him.

"It'll be dark in thirty minutes." Nick jerked open the compartment under the dash and rummaged through the contents. He found two flashlights, but the batteries in one were dead. "We'll have to stay together if we can."

Mac swung her feet to the ground. Staying together was definitely okay with her. The whole idea of walking up that slope in the dark freaked her out.

"You go ahead of me." Nick handed her the flashlight. "Save the batteries as much as you can."

Mac nodded and started up the trail.

"So, why'd the kid run off?" Nick fell in behind her.

She hesitated. Nick knew most of the story. He'd saved their bacon in Alaska, thanks to the machine gun

TEMPT THE NIGHT   301

armaments on his helicopter. There was no reason not to tell him.

"Hernandez called the house a little while ago, and Maria answered. He threatened Marco, being quite specific about what he would do to the boy. The phone was on speaker, and Marco overheard the conversation." Poor kid. What must he think about a world that would treat a five-year-old like a pawn in a violent game?

"Hell. That guy's a real asswipe. Pardon my language, Mac, but damn, that gets my hackles up." Nick continued to huff and swear under his breath.

A smile tugged at her lips. Maybe she'd misjudged Nick. He seemed all right.

They walked for another twenty minutes before they needed the flashlight to guide their footsteps. The minute she turned it on, the shadows closed in, coming right to the edge of the beam. The moonlight silhouetted the Plateau up ahead, and when Mac wasn't watching the placement of her feet, she studied that flat expanse of rock.

A sudden movement near the top caught her eye, and she stopped abruptly.

Nick ran into her, sending her forward another step. "What did you see?"

She pointed. "Up there. Toward the top. It looks like...something hanging over the side. There! Did you see it move?"

Nick grabbed the flashlight and shone it off the trail at the hillside that separated them from the rock formation above. "We've found our little guy, but it looks like he's in trouble. He must have tried to take a shortcut."

302 DIXIE LEE BROWN

Nick used the beam of the light to indicate the overgrown slope beside them. "I'll go up this side. You stay on the trail and meet us on top. We better hurry, Mac." He took off at a jog.

With dread churning in her stomach, Mac turned and ran along the trail. She tripped once and fell headlong, wincing as the sharp rocks cut her hands, but scrambled right back up and continued. The closer she got to the Plateau, the fewer trees there were and the more the moon illuminated her path. She scrambled the last few steep steps to the top and stopped to catch her breath. Then she started along the edge, looking for the spot Marco had gone over.

She heard them before she saw anything. Nick's voice droned on as though telling a story, and Marco...*giggled*. It was the most welcome sound she'd ever heard.

Drawing near the edge, she peeked over. "What are you two doing down there?" Nick leaned against the rock wall behind him at an angle that made it appear as though he reclined in his favorite easy chair. Marco sat on Nick's stomach, legs wrapped around his waist. Mac was so grateful for Nick's presence, she could barely speak.

Both of them glanced upward. "Just hangin' out, waitin' for you. Right, Marco?"

"Sí." Marco laughed.

Mac chuckled. "Well, since you two are having so much fun, maybe I should go and come back later."

"No. We're definitely ready to get out of here. As soon as I find a little better footing, I'll lift him up to you. He

TEMPT THE NIGHT 303

weighs about forty pounds. Can you handle him?" Nick met her gaze, all seriousness now.

She nodded. "I've got this."

He nodded, then turned back to Marco. "Ready? Hang on tight."

The boy clung to him like a monkey as Nick rolled to his feet, took a couple of steps to the right, and pivoted to face the cliff. Mac, lying on the flat stone, stretched as far as she could and grabbed Marco's arms as Nick raised him higher.

His weight surprised her, but determination kicked in, and she wasn't about to give up when something so important hung in the balance. Inch by inch, she pulled him toward her until she got a better grip beneath his arms, rolled sideways, and hauled him over the edge to sprawl, full-length, on top of her. Relieved and grateful, she hugged him tightly until he started to squirm.

Marco had tears in his eyes from laughing as Mac ran her hands over him in search of obvious injuries. He twitched and jerked through the procedure as though she'd tried to tickle him on purpose. His antics made her smile, and his childish giggles soothed her fears.

That's how Nick found them, stretched out on the ground, laughing their heads off for no apparent reason. Mac sat up, placing Marco on his feet. She looked Nick over, and he appeared no worse for wear, a happy grin confirming that they'd done well. He sat beside her, and Marco piled into his lap.

"Good job, Marco." He ruffled the boy's hair. "Are you ready to go home now?"

304 DIXIE LEE BROWN

Mac sighed deeply and gazed toward the north where the mountain rose, a darker shadow against the moonlit sky. The perimeter fence was close. Brady had pointed it out to her that afternoon. Suddenly, her breathing stopped. Had she really just seen the end of a cigarette burning red as someone took a drag?

"Nick? There's someone watching us…to the north… on the slope."

Marco left Nick's lap and stood next to Mac's shoulder. Nick shifted around as well. "Are you sure? That would be tough to pull off with as much security equipment as Joe has around here."

She took comfort from his words. Maybe it was only her imagination. Except…there it was again, and this time, Nick saw it too.

"*Shit!*" Nick pushed to his feet. "Get Marco out of here."

Who was it? What was a stranger doing on the perimeter of Joe's compound? She should let him know, but she had no phone. Nick was right—it was time to go. As she stood, she heard men's voices and rowdy laughter, and the sound sent a chill straight to her heart. How many were there?

An alarm suddenly screamed, a warning from the compound to the south. Mac's heart pounded out a wild rhythm as she jumped up and whirled around. Marco cinched his arms around her legs, and she stooped to pick him up. Then she crouched down, suddenly realizing she was visible in the moonlight to the men by the fence.

This was not good. It was her and Nick against God only knew how many intruders. Nobody else knew where

TEMPT THE NIGHT 305

they were. She kicked herself for not letting Brady know where she was going—not that he'd be able to arrive in time to make a difference, especially with alarms going off at the house. He probably had his hands full. If she and Nick were going to get themselves and Marco out of this, they needed a plan.

She turned silently toward Nick, hoping to see the usual level of confidence in his eyes, then swiveled her head in the other direction.

Nick had disappeared without a sound.

Chapter Twenty-One

SPRAWLED ON HIS bed, his uninjured hand wrapped tightly around a wooden slat in his headboard, Brady waged a silent war within himself. Mac's decision to leave with Nick had brought the anger back with the power of a nuclear explosion. He'd committed the unpardonable sin, telling her he wouldn't allow it. *Fucking idiot!* He'd made lots of mistakes in his life, but it seemed as though most of them had been just since he met her. She affected him like no one he'd ever met before. He needed her. She was air and sunshine. If she left, how the hell was he going to live without her?

She hadn't fooled him either, telling him to leave like it was no big deal. He'd seen the pain in her eyes before she turned her gaze away. He had to make sure she stayed here long enough to get over her anger and let him explain the real reason he didn't want her to go. It wasn't only lust for her that churned in his soul. If he was truthful with himself, it was way more than that. She calmed the ache in him. When he was with her, his rage subsided. She was an angel, her calm voice bringing him back from the dark place he'd inhabited for way too long. And part of him wanted to believe he could change for her.

Suddenly the shriek of an alarm shattered the peaceful silence of the compound, followed by the sounds of booted feet running beneath Brady's bedroom window. He leapt off the bed and reached the door in two strides, jerking it open. Carefully controlled voices, laced with adrenaline, carried up the stairs. What the hell?

He started out the door, then stopped and went back for his shoulder holster and handgun. Since the day two weeks ago when forgetting his weapon had saved his best friend Alex's life, he seldom went anywhere without his gun. Ironically, the event had triggered a failsafe within him, making it nearly impossible to prepare for a mission without thinking of Alex…and when he thought of her, he remembered his weapon. Today wouldn't be a good day to fall back into old habits.

When he reached the bottom floor, he saw Joe in the main hall with a small group of men clustered around him. Everyone's eyes held the same question. A few seconds later, the alarm went silent, and Walker appeared from the study.

Joe nodded in Brady's direction as he joined the group. "The perimeter fence has been breached at the northernmost point, on the slope just beyond the Plateau. Looks like our ambassador friend has come calling."

308   DIXIE LEE BROWN

"That's a poor choice for a place to launch an attack." Walker strode farther into the room. "We'll stop him before he even gets close."

"What if it's not an attack? What if it's a diversion?" Brady looked back and forth between the two men. "Now that the alarm is off, odds are they'll be cutting through the fence again any minute…somewhere a hell of a lot closer than the northern section."

Walker grinned. "I hope they *do* think the alarm system is out of commission. They won't know Ty rerouted the signal to cut out the slope. We'll still have coverage on most of the perimeter."

"What about additional manpower?" Brady's gaze swept to Ty.

"We'll have a dozen guys here tomorrow morning, bright and early. That was the best I could do. Sorry, man." Ty obviously felt like hell.

"Getting any of those guys to move in under twenty-four hours takes an act of God. Don't worry about it, Ty. We'll have enough firepower." Joe slapped Ty on the back. "Okay, gear up. Walker, Sanchez, Rayna…you're with me. Logan…you'll cover the house and keep an eye on Cara, Darcy, Irene, and Maria. Ty…you're in charge of the rest. Roust the other team members and those students you think will be helpful, and get every set of eyes on the perimeter fence. Maintain radio silence unless the target is sighted. We're dealing with diplomats here, so fire on my order only. Let's move." Joe stepped away and strapped on his holster while the majority of the team scattered.

TEMPT THE NIGHT   309

Brady didn't miss the fact that Mac wasn't on the list of people to keep an eye on, and dread instantly formed a brick the size of the Empire State Building in his gut. His gaze locked on Joe as the others hurried out to prepare for their assignments. The slight nod Joe gave him confirmed that Brady hadn't been worried for nothing. Something was wrong. He waited until everyone but Joe, Walker, and Ty had cleared out before he stepped closer.

"Where is she?" His hands fisted at his sides.

"Presently unaccounted for…as is Nick Taylor. There was a little problem in the kitchen earlier. Marco overheard Hernandez issuing threats against him on the phone and ran out of here. Mac went after him about twenty minutes ago." Joe donned a cargo vest and pushed two extra clips in one of the pockets.

"We searched the compound. No sign of them." Walker strode to a chair near the door and picked up the black backpack that was sitting there. "We're also missing a Gator. Where do you think she'd go?"

Brady had to concentrate to unclench his jaw, clamped tightly shut by the uneasiness that put his entire body on edge at the mention of Nick Taylor. "Marco loves the Plateau. It's his favorite place. Mac knew that, and if she thought the kid headed there by himself, she'd probably go after him." It suddenly got hard to breathe. If he hadn't been such a shithead, she'd never have gone alone.

"That would be a break for Hernandez—the two people he wants most heading right for him. Seems strange to me that she wouldn't ask for help. Doesn't it, Jim?" Joe's gaze flickered over him.

310 DIXIE LEE BROWN

As usual, Joe's instincts were right on, but there was no way Brady was telling him that he and Mac had argued and that she'd kicked him out of her room. For one thing, if he spoke the words, it would be real, and he suddenly knew beyond a shadow of a doubt that he wasn't ready to lose her. He wanted her in his life permanently, in spite of having no idea how to fix the mess he'd made.

"I'm going with you to the Plateau." He glared at the three men, daring them to object. They exchanged glances in the heavy silence that followed. Brady's tension hitched a notch. If Joe said no, he'd go by himself.

Walker and Ty grinned as Joe stepped toward him and slapped him on the shoulder. "Never expected anything less. Let's get going."

Walker stopped in front of Brady. "Everything okay with you?"

Brady let his breath out slowly and shook his head. "No, but I owe you an apology."

"No you don't. Let's go find her." Walker cuffed him on the arm as he walked by.

Brady turned toward the stairs, needing a few seconds alone to get his head in the game as much as he needed the additional tools of his trade that he kept in his closet. In spite of the situation, he felt more hopeful than he had in years. She was responsible for that, and he wasn't about to let her down now. He'd find Mac, and then he'd convince her he was an idiot, which really shouldn't be that hard, considering. He gave no thought to the alternative, because not finding her wasn't an option.

TEMPT THE NIGHT 311

Grabbing his duffel from the floor of his closet, he dug through it until he found the Beretta in his ankle holster and strapped it on. Next came the partially serrated combat blade he'd never been without on hundreds of missions. He threaded his belt through the scabbard and felt its familiar weight settle onto his hip. The shoulder holster slid into place, and the .357 Magnum fit snugly against his side. He threw a lightweight jacket on, returned to his duffel one more time for his night-vision goggles, and decided to carry his Colt AR-15 rifle too. Who knew how far away these slimeballs would be?

The others were ready when he descended the stairs, and the five of them headed for the shed containing the last two Gators. Joe, Rayna, and Sanchez piled into one and took the lead. Brady and Walker brought up the rear.

Brady welcomed the darkness and the cold breeze that blew steadily in his face. It reminded him of other missions he'd been on with his brothers in the SEALs. Many nights they'd raced across open waters in small rubber rafts with no lights and nothing but night-vision equipment to guide them to shore. Back then, he knew who the enemy was. Tonight, the enemies were yet to be determined, but whoever they were, they weren't going to hurt his woman or Marco.

"What's so funny?" Walker leaned toward him to be heard over the noise of the engine.

"Nothin'." Brady immediately squelched the smile that had pulled at his lips when he thought of her as *his woman*. He was a long way from earning the right to call her that, and he doubted she'd make it easy on him, but it would damn sure be fun convincing her. His lips twitched with humor again.

Walker snorted a laugh. "Yeah, right, bro." He met Brady's gaze and sobered. "Hell yeah, we'll find her."

Brady nodded, grateful for his new brothers, who'd had his back every time he'd needed them.

After a few minutes, they slowed down, and both parked behind the third Gator, abandoned beside the trail. The team scrambled out of the vehicles and scoured the area for anything out of place. Brady pressed his hand to the engine compartment of the four-wheeler Mac had taken from the compound. There was still some warmth. If he had to guess, he'd say the Gator had been parked there for thirty to forty minutes. He hated to contemplate the trouble she and Marco could get into in that much time.

Walker strode up the trail, shining his flashlight on the ground for a few minutes before straightening and returning to where Brady and the others waited. "There are two sets of tracks—both adult sized. No sign of Marco. He might have been carried." With one look at Brady, Walker hurried on. "Or he may be too little to make an impression, or maybe he walked to the side of the trail where's there's more vegetation to cover his tracks."

"If the second set of prints doesn't belong to Marco, who's she with?" Brady scowled, apprehension crawling slowly across his skin as Nick's slimy image took shape in his mind.

"A man, for sure. Weight one-eighty or one-ninety. No sign of a struggle." Walker switched his flashlight off and leaned over the side of the Gator, retrieving his backpack.

Brady reached for his night-vision goggles and rifle, breathing slowly, hoping to dislodge the ache in his stomach. There was no doubt in his mind that Mac was with Nick Taylor. Whether he was a friend or an enemy didn't make much difference to Brady. *Get a grip, man. Find her first, and worry about who she's with later.*

Brady slung his rifle onto his shoulder, slipped his goggles over his head for easy access, and double-timed it up the trail. He sensed more than heard the others fall in behind him. One thing each of the team members did well was cover ground silently.

Halfway to the Plateau, he stopped and maneuvered his goggles into place. Slowly, he scanned the slope ahead, now bathed in a strange iridescent light, paying special attention to the flat expanse of rock that was their destination. Nothing suspicious jumped out at him, but the hair on the back of his neck was standing straight up, and his instincts were seldom wrong.

He slid his night-vision goggles down around his neck again, and his skin tingled as Walker moved alongside him.

The barest wag of Walker's head indicated he'd also seen nothing, and he slipped his goggles into his backpack. "Nice view from here. Be a great spot for someone with a rifle."

314 DIXIE LEE BROWN

"Roger that. Jim, give your rifle to Rayna." Joe appeared beside Brady, his voice low.

Rayna stepped toward Brady, evidently waiting for him to hand off the weapon. He hesitated only a moment. His training and experience had taught him that you better have a good reason for ditching a weapon.

His gaze swept from Joe to Rayna. She studied him, a perceptive grin telling him she knew exactly what he was thinking. Bright and confident, she was the most capable marksman he'd seen in a long time. She'd proved on numerous occasions that she could do what needed to be done. He handed her the rifle.

"I'll take care of her like she was mine." Rayna brought the Colt AR-15 against her, cradling it under her arm. With a mock salute, she left the trail and headed toward the Plateau, probably with her vantage point already picked out.

Joe turned to whisper to Sanchez, who waited, alert and watchful, a few steps away. "Keep an eye on her."

Sanchez nodded and slipped silently into the dense vegetation.

Brady, Walker, and Joe continued on the trail. They'd only gone a hundred feet or so when Joe's phone chirped once, shockingly loud in the silence of the mountain. Joe swore under his breath and dug for the offending device before it could sound off again. Walker and Brady kept moving upward, leaving Joe to catch up after he'd put his phone on silent.

After only a second, Brady heard a hiss from behind him and turned just as Walker did the same. Joe was

TEMPT THE NIGHT 315

striding toward them like he was on a mission, pushing his phone back in his pocket.

Suddenly, a gunshot cracked through the night, echoing off the rocks, followed by another. Brady swung toward the north, his best estimation of where the sounds had originated. It was a .380 short. He'd recognize that report anywhere after hearing it in the alley in Sitka when Mac had defended herself against the trooper gunning for her. Evidently, she was still packing Callahan's state-issued piece…and she was in trouble.

Brady sniffed the air. Was that smoke he smelled? He raced up the trail for about ten yards before he flipped his night-vision goggles into place and jumped off a short ledge to the hard-packed dirt beneath. As soon as he regained his balance, he resumed his dash toward the location where the shots had come from. He heard Joe say something in a low, insistent voice, followed by a whistle from Walker, and then Joe swore. The next instant, the mountain echoed the shrill siren of the alarm from the compound—the second time tonight. The fence had been breached again, but Brady couldn't change his course this time. Mac needed him.

As abruptly as it started, the alarm ceased, but a few seconds later, small weapons fire popped in the distance. He pivoted to stare toward the compound. Ty and the others would make short work of any attack on that end. That was a given. Had Joe and Walker headed back? Rayna and Sanchez? Or were they still behind him somewhere? On any other mission, he'd never have taken off by himself, but this time he'd had no choice.

316   DIXIE LEE BROWN

He skirted the northern edge of the Plateau and stopped, ducking behind cover of the rocks. Up the slope, a hundred yards or better, the brazen bastards had started a bonfire. He counted five of them, talking, laughing, and passing around something they each drank from.

A chill settled in his chest as another man appeared from the far side of the Plateau, clutching Mac's arm and pushing her along toward the group at the fire. Brady froze. The man wore a cowboy hat. *Nick!* How the hell had that man gotten past Joe's safeguards to attack from the inside? Even with his goggles, Brady couldn't make out the man's face, but it had to be that lying, cheating bastard. A black rage made him itch to get his hands on Nick Taylor. This would be the last time he double-crossed someone.

Mac didn't appear to be hurt. She carried Marco in her arms, and he clutched her neck in a desperate hold. As they approached the others, a tall man disengaged from the group and walked toward her. He said something, then reached for Marco. Mac backed away until Nick stopped her. A short conversation ensued, and then he grabbed her arm and pulled her toward the fire, pushing her and Marco down outside the circle of men.

Brady had enough firepower to take them all out, but the chance of Mac or Marco being hurt in the interim was too great. He had to get to them silently, one at a time, until he could interject himself between them and their hostages and finish the job. He settled more comfortably against the rocks and waited for his opportunity.

TEMPT THE NIGHT 317

After a few minutes, one of the men stumbled to his feet, said something in Spanish, and disappeared into the trees at the base of the Plateau with his rifle slung over his shoulder. Brady unsheathed his blade and moved out on an intercepting course.

Chapter Twenty-Two

THE ALARM WENT quiet as suddenly as it had started, leaving an odd ringing in Mac's ears and emptiness in the surrounding forest. The intruders were closer now. They no doubt thought they were being stealthy, but Mac heard their gruff whispers and their clumsy footsteps. *Get Marco out of here.* That's the last thing Nick had said before he disappeared. She couldn't fathom why he had or where he was now, but the one thing she felt certain of was that he held no small amount of affection for the boy and wouldn't want to see him hurt.

The only problem was that by the time she and Marco had reached the point where they could climb down safely from the Plateau to the trail, she would have been delivering them right into the enemy's hands. So she'd backtracked along the rim on the west side of the Plateau until she found a place where they could slide over the side and perch on a small rock outcropping with a sheer

TEMPT THE NIGHT 319

drop below them. As near as she could tell, this would be a one-way trip, unless Nick returned to help them back to the top…but under the circumstances, it seemed the lesser of two evils.

They'd managed to stay hidden for several minutes. The group of men had walked by above them twice already, and Mac was beginning to hope that they would give up and go away. When a man had suddenly dropped down beside her, a rope, fashioned like a harness, tied around him, she'd jumped, losing her balance and almost toppling over the side. The grinning man in camouflage pants had snatched Marco out of her arms, tugged on the rope, and risen quickly up and over the side.

It all happened so quickly, Mac hadn't had time to think, much less fight or protect Marco. She should have been ready—should have known the devils would find them. If something happened to him, she'd never forgive herself.

Now, Marco was whimpering above. A gruff voice cut him off. "Shut up if you ever want to see her again."

"Hey! Leave the kid alone. He's scared enough already. Let's get this done."

Mac's breath left her in a rush, and she sagged against the rock wall. *Nick!* He was up there. He was one of them. *My God!* She'd trusted him, even after he'd run out on them.

She leaned back, and Paddy's gun bit into her soft flesh. As she heard the camo man slipping over the edge of the cliff again, she jerked the weapon free and shoved it in the top of her hiking boot, hoping her pant legs were wide enough to hide the bulge.

320 DIXIE LEE BROWN

The man landed precariously close to the edge, and for a moment, all she could think about was pushing him off. With a little luck, she'd not only get him, but his comrade above who handled the rope. If there really was a God in heaven who controlled the universe, that man would be Nick. But, of course, that wouldn't get her off the side of this cliff. She needed to be up top where Marco was.

Camo man stepped toward her and jerked her against him, his lecherous grin making her nauseous. One of his arms went around her waist, right where the gun had rested seconds ago, and clamped her to his hard form. Then he jerked on the rope again, and in less than a minute, she stood face-to-face with Nick Taylor. His hands rested on Marco's shoulders as the young boy stood in front of him.

"Let him go." She stared at Nick, so disgusted her stomach rolled within her.

He did what she told him, but before he released her gaze, he gave her his easy, laid-back cowboy smile, which served not only to confuse her further, but also made her damn good and angry.

Marco bolted toward her, and she knelt to scoop him up, but the other man, now out of his harness, blocked her and grabbed the boy by his hair. Marco cried out, and Mac drew back her fist, ramming it full-force into camo man's stomach.

It was a wasted effort. The punch had absolutely no effect on the man, unless she counted his right cross that knocked her on her ass and momentarily blackened her world. She fought her way back to full consciousness, a groan the only sound she allowed herself to acknowledge the splitting pain in the side of her head. Marco sat beside her, crying softly, and Nick and camo man were engaged in a serious argument. Neither of them was paying any mind to her.

In an instant, she pulled her pant leg up and freed the handgun, flipping off the safety the way Brady had taught her. Apparently, that was a sound bad guys recognized, because now she had their complete attention.

"You don't want to do that, Mac." Nick raised both hands in a cautious gesture.

Camo man wasn't that smart. With a scornful sneer, he rushed her. She fired once and saw him jerk, but he kept coming so she fired again. He crumpled just short of her feet. She turned the gun on Nick.

He had the good sense not to move. With hands still raised, he had an imploring look in his eyes.

"Don't hurt Nick." Marco's small voice added to her indecision.

"Mac, we've got about two minutes before the rest of those goons come running up here. I know you don't trust me right now, and I don't blame you, but if we're going to get Marco out of this alive, you have to do what I tell you." Nick dropped his hands.

"Really? You're working for Hernandez. Why would I *ever* do anything you told me again?"

"Because this isn't what you think. I don't work for Ambassador Hernandez. I'm a special agent with the DHS...undercover to get enough evidence to clear you

322   DIXIE LEE BROWN

of two murders and get the ambassador shipped home for good."

"I don't believe you. Joe would have known, and he'd have told me." Mac lowered her gun partway, starting to feel the ache in her arm from holding it steady.

"That wasn't part of the deal. Through some of his sources, Joe learned I'd been undercover with the ambassador's entourage for the last two months. When he asked for my help, it was imperative that no one else know. My life depended on it...and I'm kind of partial to my life."

Shouts sounded from below the Plateau. Nick raised his voice to holler back. "Everything's okay. Griff had a little accident."

Turning back to Mac, he said, "For the record, I didn't know Hernandez had planned this tonight. He's reckless and power-happy, and he thinks he can do anything he wants—anytime. I didn't get a heads-up until they were already inside the fence. Hernandez doesn't like to be told he's acting recklessly. As soon as you and I saw them, I sent Joe a text. He knows where we are, so all we have to do is stay alive until he gets here. That's where you doing what I tell you comes in...if you're done holding that Glock on me."

Mac lowered the gun but clenched her fingers tightly around the pistol's grip and pulled her knees up, leaning her forehead against her legs. She was on information overload. Was he telling the truth? His story sounded plausible. She wanted to believe him because the alternative was too ugly. None of the choices available to her were good ones. Either way she was screwed. With a deep sigh, she laid the gun on the ground at her side.

He brushed her arm as he knelt next to her, lifted her gun, and slid the safety on. Then he handed it to her. "Put this back where you got it, just in case." He stood and offered her a hand.

She studied him for a moment. Smart move, giving her the weapon back and lulling her into a false sense of security. But he'd have to do better than that before she trusted him again. "If you're lying to me and if Marco gets hurt because of it, you're going to regret the day you met me."

He helped her to her feet, one corner of his lips lifting in a grin. "Understood." Nick ruffled Marco's hair as Mac took his hand. "That's the whole idea—getting this little guy home safely."

He checked for a pulse on the fallen man and shook his head slightly when she met his gaze. Mac waited for the grief and guilt to hit her, but all she felt was relief. Her lack of remorse didn't seem to bother her as much anymore.

The alarm screeched to life again from the compound to the south, echoing off the rocks all around them. A shiver ran the length of her. Someone turned it off within a minute, almost like they were expecting it to be tripped.

"Hernandez has a second team entering near the house. They're after Maria, but, if Joe's team's reputation is even close to accurate, Hernandez's misfits don't have a prayer." Nick's words were reassuring, but Mac

324 DIXIE LEE BROWN

couldn't help but worry, especially when the distant gunfire reached her ears.

Nick led her and Marco toward the western edge of the Plateau. "Remember, Mac. When we join the others, I'll be one of them. That means I'll say whatever I have to in order to keep us alive. It's important you follow my lead, and try not to piss anybody off." He stopped and slipped his hand around Marco's arm. "You too, buddy. I know it's hard to understand, but you just need to trust me. Okay?"

"I trust you, Nick." Marco looked into his eyes with complete faith.

Nick guided them to a cut in the rock table leading to a steep trail that dropped quickly to the mountain slope below. As they reached fairly level ground, Mac swept Marco into her arms. No way any of those creeps were touching him.

The smell of smoke got her attention, but the men laughing and swearing increased Mac's anxiety level. Were they so sure of themselves that they'd started a fire? As Mac, Marco, and Nick approached the last rock outcropping that shielded them from the enemy's view, Nick gripped her arm. Even knowing why he did it, her first reaction was to jerk away from him.

He must have sensed her tension. "Easy. It'll be over before long."

As the group of men at the bonfire noticed them, they stared, and then their swearing turned into lewd remarks. Mac stumbled, but Nick helped to right her before she lost her footing. One of the men separated himself from the rest and strode toward her.

TEMPT THE NIGHT 325

"Well, Ms. McCallister, we meet again, and you brought my son to me." Hernandez stretched out his arms. "Come, Marco. Let's get reacquainted."

Marco refused to look at him and snuggled tightly into Mac. She backed away until Nick's arm stopped her. Hernandez's hands dropped, and a black fury twisted his face. So much for not pissing anybody off. "Marco needs time to adjust, Ambassador." She hoped her voice was more conciliatory than scornful.

The effort it took for Hernandez to force down his rage was clearly evident on his red face. "Of course. You're right. There'll be time to get to know each other later." He turned toward Nick. "Where's Griff?"

Nick shoved his thumbs in his front pockets. "I told you some of these men were trouble, Ambassador. Griff tried to assault Mac right in front of your son. When I suggested he wait, the bastard tried to draw on me. I had no choice."

The tension was palpable as the two faced each other. Finally, Hernandez nodded and turned toward the fire. "Make Ms. McCallister and my son comfortable for the night."

After he walked away, Mac glanced at Nick. He reached for her arm again, and she set Marco on his feet, gripping his hand firmly. Nick led them to a spot up against a boulder. It was outside the ring of men surrounding the bonfire, but the heat reached them and radiated off the rocks at their backs. Nick strode into the center of the men, took two blankets from their stash, and brought them to Mac and Marco.

326 DIXIE LEE BROWN

"You did good keeping Hernandez from getting angry, Mac. Keep it up." He patted her arm and swiped a finger down Marco's nose, then strode closer to the fire and found a spot to sit.

Mac wrapped a blanket around herself and the other around Marco. Not exactly the way she'd wanted to spend the night, but at least they were warm. Besides, the way she wanted to spend it was no longer open to her, since she'd pushed Brady out of her life. Best to put that brief episode behind her. There were far more pressing things to worry about.

A shiver ran across her shoulders and up her neck. She jerked her gaze toward the east. Nick, Hernandez, and his four men were passing a bottle around while one of them told a story. No one was paying any attention to her or Marco. Yet she had the strangest feeling that someone watched her.

After a while, one of the men stood, picked up his rifle, and entered the stand of timber behind him. The others carried on the conversation for several minutes before his absence was apparently felt.

"Carlos has been gone too long." Nick addressed the observation to Hernandez. "I'll go see what's keeping him."

"No. Philipe, go see what's taking Carlos so long," Hernandez said.

Philipe grumbled, and the rest of the group snickered. After he walked out of sight, the conversation resumed, although quieter and less animated. Everyone was obviously nervous about the first man's delay.

TEMPT THE NIGHT 327

Mac was curious, although any reduction in their numbers was a good thing. Why had Nick volunteered to go check it out? She didn't trust those creeps without him here, and she breathed a sigh of relief when Hernandez sent someone else. Silently counting off the minutes, she waited for the absent men to stumble back into the campsite. Five minutes and they didn't return. After ten, the two remaining hired guns panicked.

They exchanged a glance and then started gathering their gear. One of them kept up a running dialogue. "Something's wrong or they'd be back by now. Didn't sign on to get my throat cut in the dark on some lousy mountain no one's ever heard of. The pay might be good, but not that good. Give me a straight-on fight anytime."

Hernandez stepped into the man and coldcocked him, knocking him down and garnering the undivided attention of both men. "Don't lose your heads. Joe Reynolds is trying to scare us. We have to be smarter than he is." He turned his gaze on Nick, the only person still sitting. "You will find out what has happened to our two amigos."

Nick flashed a confident smile as he got slowly to his feet and pushed his cowboy hat back with his index finger. "Sure thing, Ambassador. I'd love to see what's keeping your men." He tipped his hat to Mac and strode casually into the darkness.

Chapter Twenty-Three

THE HIRED GUNMAN staggered through the brush not fifty feet from the fire's glow. Brady shadowed him, staying out of sight. What was the bastard waiting for? An engraved invitation to take a leak? Finally, he stopped beside a tree, leaned his rifle on the trunk, and unzipped.

Brady was on him in a heartbeat; Joe's warning about them being diplomats and not shooting except on his order wasn't foremost in his mind. In deference to his boss and friend, Brady would do the best he could...but no promises.

One hand slapped over the man's mouth, one arm around his neck, Brady applied pressure until he stopped fighting. He bound the man and hid him in the thick brush, throwing all of his weapons into a hollowed-out tree trunk nearby. It went against every ounce of Brady's training to leave an enemy behind alive, and now he'd

TEMPT THE NIGHT 329

have to move twice as fast to accomplish his mission before the two he'd taken out of the game awoke.

He ducked behind a tree with about thirty seconds to spare before the next lowlife stood from his place by the fire and came looking for his friend. The man walked a zigzag trail, searching the brush and rocks. Brady chose a spot behind a large boulder to put him out of commission. Two down…four to go.

He climbed a tree as close as he dared to the campsite. From there he got a clear view of Mac and Marco, sitting together away from the men. They appeared to be in good shape, so he didn't completely regret not killing the men behind him in the trees.

Four men remained around the fire. Two of the gunmen sat with their backs to him. Hernandez lounged on the other side of the campfire. Brady would know that tall, rangy snake anywhere. Beside him sat cowboy and chopper pilot Nick Taylor, probably feeling pretty proud of himself about now. Brady prayed he'd be the next man to walk into the woods.

Like an answer from heaven, the man stood, pushed his hat back, and turned sideways to say something to Hernandez. Then Nick tipped his hat in Mac's direction and strode into the trees where his two buddies had gone missing. A minute later, he passed under the tree where Brady crouched. When Nick was far enough away, Brady dropped to the ground on silent feet and followed.

Brady unsheathed his knife. *Sorry, Joe.* He was going to enjoy this kill. A traitor in their midst ready to hurt

330 DIXIE LEE BROWN

Mac or Marco on Hernandez's order? He deserved no mercy, and he'd get none from Brady.

Nick veered to the east and picked up the pace. He wasn't going to find his friends like that. Brady kept up with him, planning to hit him on the way back. When Nick finally made the turn toward camp, Brady moved closer, only to have Nick leave the cover of the trees and stride a hundred yards in the open. Either he was really stupid or he wanted to be seen. Brady couldn't think of a single reason for the latter.

Nick covered the last fifty yards at a full-out run, and the camp exploded into action before he even got there. Brady crept close enough to hear.

"What the hell, Nick?" Hernandez waved his arms in the air.

"I found them. Your men are both dead. Throats cut."

What the hell kind of game was Nick playing? If he wanted to panic this crew, he'd sure done that. The two hired guns gathered their gear and lit out of there like goblins were after them.

"That's just great, Nick. Now we've got no one to do the wet work…except you, my friend."

"What wet work?" He suddenly didn't sound so sure of himself.

Hernandez turned to look at Mac, then swung his gaze back to Nick. "If she falls off that plateau, no one will be able to trace it to me. You'll have to leave the country for a while, but I pay men well for that kind of service."

"What did she ever do to you?"

TEMPT THE NIGHT 331

"She was in the wrong place at the wrong time. Once she's dead, there won't be any way to incriminate me in what happened in Sitka."

Brady seethed as Hernandez bragged of his accomplishments.

"What about Maria? Isn't she the one you're really after?" It almost appeared as though Nick was stalling for time.

"I'll be getting the good news from my other team any minute, and then we'll be on our way to the rendezvous point. All of my troubles will be over." Hernandez smiled. "Don't look so concerned, Nick. If you want her dead before you throw her off, I can fix that. One broken neck coming up." Hernandez strode quickly toward Mac.

Brady shot forward, and in his peripheral vision, he saw Nick do the same. Brady yanked his handgun from his holster, but Hernandez was too close to Mac, and he was too far away to guarantee accuracy. He holstered the weapon instead and concentrated on speed.

Mac jumped to her feet and pulled Marco with her. "Run, Marco! Don't stop!"

Marco took off at a dead run toward the Plateau.

Mac faced Hernandez and raised her arm. She clutched the Glock in her shaky hand, but Hernandez only hesitated for a split second. With five feet to spare, she fired. His shoulder jerked back, but he didn't go down. Instantly, she pulled the trigger again. Nothing happened; the gun evidently jammed.

Brady barreled out of the trees at that exact second, sending Nick flying with a swing of his arm. He was

332 DIXIE LEE BROWN

almost on Hernandez as the snake reached for Mac, when a rifle discharged somewhere to the south. Less than a second later, a bullet hit Hernandez in the chest, dropping him instantly.

Rayna! Cutting it pretty close. He'd have a talk with her about that. Brady grabbed Mac and pulled her away from Hernandez's body. He shielded her from the grisly scene as much as he could, and she seemed content to wrap her arms around him and snuggle close. That is, until he heard Nick climbing to his feet.

Brady drew his gun again and turned it on him. "Stay down if you know what's good for you."

"Somebody should find Marco." Nick straightened and put his dirt-covered hat on his head.

"Yeah. Well, it's not going to be you. In fact, if I don't kill you, the only place you're going is jail." Brady set Mac away from him and strode toward Nick.

"Wait, Brady—" Mac tried to push in front of him, but he shoved her into his shadow.

"Wait a minute. I talked to Joe a couple of hours ago and told him what was going down. He was supposed to spread the word. Didn't Joe tell you?" Nick raised his hands as though trying to calm the crowd.

"Tell me what?"

"That I'm one of the good guys. I was undercover to get information that will clear your girlfriend. I'll get it too, now that Hernandez is dead. Some of his men will be only too happy to talk to me in exchange for a plea bargain. She'll be able to go back to Sitka if she wants. Would you tell him, please, Mac?"

TEMPT THE NIGHT   333

Brady glanced over his shoulder, and Mac nodded.

"I didn't believe him at first either, but I think it's true. Joe had to keep it quiet while Nick was undercover so there'd be no chance of it leaking out. But with Hernandez dead, Maria and Marco will be free too." Mac stared into the darkness toward the Plateau. "I'll go find him."

"We'll all go." Brady holstered his weapon, still regarding Nick warily.

"Way ahead of you." Joe's voice came from the shadows, and it was a few seconds before Brady focused on him walking beside Walker with Marco's small form in between. "We followed the sound of the shots up to the top of the Plateau. There was nobody around by the time we got there. Pretty good view from up there though. Looked like Brady had everything almost under control. We were on our way down to lend a hand when Hernandez lost it. I told Rayna to take whatever shot she could get, and Walker and I split up to intercept Marco." Joe's hand rested on the kid's neck while he looked around the group. "Everything okay here?"

"Would have been nice if you'd told Brady I was on your side. The guy was going to shoot me." Nick stood with hands on hips.

"Damn straight. I do my best work on assholes that hurt women and children." Brady smirked, but he wasn't really at a point where it was funny yet.

"Those were *your* orders, Nick. I tried to talk you out of it, if you remember. By the time you called from up on top and gave me the okay to inform my men, Brady had already heard the shots on the Plateau, and he didn't wait

334 DIXIE LEE BROWN

around for further instructions. That's how it is sometimes in our line of work. You took your chances." Joe delivered his opinion matter-of-factly.

"Let's get Mac and Marco back to the house. We can continue this discussion later." Walker squeezed by Mac to check Hernandez for signs of life. He shook his head. "Are there more?" He turned toward Brady.

Brady nodded and led the way into the trees. The two men he'd incapacitated were still out, but by the time he and Walker draped them over their shoulders and carried them roughly back to the campsite, they were starting to come around. Walker checked to make sure their hands were still secured behind their backs and left them kneeling on the ground at the edge of the forest.

The fire had died down, and the men easily kicked the embers apart. Rayna and Sanchez rejoined the group, both grinning from ear to ear. Brady greeted Rayna with a high five for her precision shot that kept Hernandez from touching Mac and shook Sanchez's hand enthusiastically for backing her up. Then they formed a single file for the trek back to the Gators, with the two gunmen stumbling along between Walker and Joe and Brady bringing up the rear. Nick carried Marco most of the way. Mac appeared on the edge of collapse, but she insisted she make it on her own two feet, so Brady fumed each time she tripped.

When they reached the Gators, he didn't ask—just swung her onto the front seat. She frowned halfheartedly, but when he swept Marco up and turned to her

TEMPT THE NIGHT 335

questioningly, she held out her arms to receive the kid. He shoved the prisoners in the back, and Nick climbed into the bed and stood, holding the roll bar. Brady slid into the driver's seat beside Mac, turning the vehicle toward the compound. Joe, Walker, Rayna, and Sanchez filled the second Gator.

Mac fell asleep with her head on his lap halfway there…with Marco asleep on hers. Brady's gaze continually strayed to them; he was thankful beyond measure that he'd gotten there in time, that Rayna was a damn good shot, that Nick had been with them…although that one made the list somewhat grudgingly.

He saw the lights of emergency responders as soon as they broke from the trees. As he drew closer, he could make out three police cruisers, an ambulance, and a coroner's van parked along the drive from the gate to the house. Dread ballooned in his already queasy stomach. Beside him, Mac stirred, and her eyes went wide when she saw the lights.

After they parked the vehicles and unloaded the prisoners, Ty met them in the front yard, and by his clenched jaw and the strain on his face, the news was definitely not good.

Joe stepped close to him. "Who?"

Ty's gaze flickered to the coroner's van, and he exhaled slowly. "Maria." He spoke quietly, but with the expectant hush in the air, his words traveled.

Beside Brady, Mac gasped and gripped his arm. Then her gaze searched for Marco, and she flew to him, picked

336 DIXIE LEE BROWN

him up, and covered the few feet to the door without looking back.

"How'd it happen?" Walker waited until the door closed behind her.

"Irene said she panicked when the alarm went off the second time. She was convinced Marco was outside, and she went out after him. Irene tried to stop her, but Maria was out of her mind with fear. She must have just stepped off the porch when my unit came around the side to push Hernandez's men back outside the gate. They opened fire, and I heard her cry out. By the time I could get to her, she was gone." Pain flooded Ty's face.

"Is Irene okay?" Joe glanced toward the house.

"Physically, she's fine...but she blames herself."

Joe nodded. "Sounds like that's going around. I'll talk to her."

Special Agent Guy Hanford pulled into the driveway, skirted around all the cruisers, and parked near the small group of men. He got out and strode toward them.

Joe brought up the prisoners and handed them over. "You're not going to like this, but Hernandez is dead."

Hanford sighed. "You've just unleashed a shit storm."

"Maybe not." Nick stepped forward. "Hernandez was dirty. We all knew that. Now that he's dead and not able to lord it over his hired hands, I know three, maybe four men—upstanding witness material—who'll jump at the chance to bury him." He handed a notebook to Hanford. "Names and phone numbers." He glanced toward Brady. "I think you'll even find some dirty cops in there who're willing to spill their guts."

TEMPT THE NIGHT 337

Hanford held his palm open to receive the notebook, and a smile slowly appeared. "This is what I've been waiting for. Suddenly it's a damn good night."

Nick scowled. "We lost Maria. Mac and Marco almost became collateral damage. You might want to reconsider your position on what makes a good night."

Okay, maybe Brady would be able to forgive the cowboy...eventually.

Joe turned to the rest of the group. "Ty and I will take care of this. You guys get some rest." His gaze settled on Brady. "Check on Mac. She's had a hell of a night."

The group dispersed, and Brady ran up the stairs to the third floor. He knocked softly on her door. "Mac? Let me in, sugar."

She opened it almost immediately, allowing enough room for him to slip through. He took in the room at a glance. Marco lay on the bed, curled up tightly. He still hiccupped, evidence of how hard he'd cried. Mac's eyes were red and puffy too. Seemed like heartache came in waves for her.

"I...I can't believe she's gone." Her voice broke, and she wiped tears from her face.

"Come here." Brady raised his arm in invitation.

She came to him without hesitation and burrowed into his arms. She was as cold as ice and shook with each fractured breath. He held her like that for a long time, hoping to somehow create a sense of security there in his arms. Finally, he swept her up, carried her to the bathroom, and started the shower. While she undressed and stepped under the water, he went back to the bedroom to

338 DIXIE LEE BROWN

rifle through her new clothes until he found something suitable for her to sleep in—flannel pajama pants and a long-sleeved top. A smile worked at the corners of his mouth. No doubt she'd appreciate him selecting something that damn near covered every inch of her skin.

"Doing okay?" He pushed the bathroom door open tentatively, not sure how she would feel about him seeing her naked after everything he'd said.

"Just about finished." Mac was drying herself behind the shower curtain, so he left the PJs and returned to the bedroom to wait.

When she joined him, she crawled back into his arms, but she seemed exhausted and out of it. He spread the bedcovers open for her, and she lay down next to Marco, pulling him tightly to her.

Brady should have left then, but the need to be there for her was overpowering. After watching her for a few minutes, he took off his shirt and shoes and lay beside her with his arm draped around her, breathing in her familiar scent, so grateful that she was all right.

Toward morning, it occurred to him that he might not be the person she would want to see in her bed when she woke. With disgust, he remembered the pain in her eyes as she'd turned away from him after she'd told him to leave. He'd find a way to fix things between them or die trying, but right now she needed time to deal with yet more grief.

Brady retrieved his T-shirt and shoes, kissed her forehead, and slipped out of her room.

Chapter Twenty-Four

MAC STIRRED AND stretched in her cocoon of warm blankets. Marco slept within her embrace, his cherubic face peaceful in slumber. She smiled and lifted her arm from him carefully, reaching behind her to assure herself of Brady's presence.

Except…he was gone. The covers were tucked around her securely and had managed to lock in the heat from her own body. Had she only dreamed that he'd held her until she fell asleep? Impossible. She'd been on the verge of a meltdown last night. If he hadn't come to her room, taken charge, and let her lean on him, she'd never have slept at all. But apparently, sometime after she'd dropped off, he'd opted for other sleeping arrangements.

Not that she could blame him. She'd been completely exhausted and nearly catatonic when they arrived back at the house. Then they'd gotten the news about Maria, and everything had gone black…until she remembered

340 DIXIE LEE BROWN

Marco. By the time she'd gotten him calmed down and in bed, she was numb, unable to think or even comprehend what came next. Only Brady's arms around her, his body pressed against her back, had grounded her and made her world secure again.

An ache formed in her chest, and tears threatened to spill down her cheeks. Last night she'd thought—hoped—that Brady had wanted her, that the protective way he stayed by her side and anticipated her every need meant he cared about her and didn't want her to leave. She wasn't sure what it said that he'd left her in the middle of the night, but it felt a lot like rejection—like perhaps he'd been nice to her because that's who he was and had nothing to do with who *she* was.

Marco straightened his legs and slowly opened his eyes, so red and swollen they made Mac's own eyes hurt. How unfair for this five-year-old to have suffered so much in his short life.

He scooted around, and his gaze searched her face. One small finger pointed at her. "Your eyes are puffy."

She smiled. "I'm sure they are, just like yours, young man." Mac rubbed his arm through the blanket. "Are you doing okay?"

His brow wrinkled as he gave a one-shouldered shrug. "She said we'd have lots of time. Mama just got here. Why did she have to go already?" His small voice cracked.

Mac blinked frantically to keep her tears at bay as her heart broke. "I don't know, Marco. But I know she didn't want to leave you, and she'll always be with you in your heart and in your memories, watching out for you

TEMPT THE NIGHT 341

always. All you'll have to do is think about her, and she'll be there. You know that, right?"

His little head nodded against the pillow. "I'm going to miss her."

"I know, sweetie." Mac pressed her lips against his head.

"Where will I go now? Who will take care of me?"

Mac's heart shattered the rest of the way. "I'm sure Joe will want you to stay here, at least until they find out if you have any other family. You like it here, don't you?"

"Are you going to stay?" His pleading eyes locked on hers.

"Oh, sweetie. I don't know where I'll be going yet. I'll be here for a few more days, but then I'll have to go back to my life in Alaska." Providing Nick had her problems cleared up by then.

"Can I go with *you*?"

Oh, God. She couldn't make a promise like that. "Tell you what. Let's hold off a few days on making any decisions for either of us. Okay? Things might look different by then."

A frown pulled at his lips for a second, but then his stomach growled loudly and a tiny smile worked its way over his features. "I'm hungry. Do you think I could have breakfast?"

Hungry was good. "Of course you can." Mac was fairly certain *her* appetite had gone AWOL indefinitely, but that wouldn't stop her from making sure Marco was fed. She tossed back the covers. "I'll throw on some clothes, go to your room, and get you some clean things. As soon

342 DIXIE LEE BROWN

as you're dressed and presentable, we'll go down to the kitchen and see what we can find."

Mac flew into her clothes and left Marco with instructions to wash his face and hands while she was gone. One floor down, she entered his room, taking a step back as she sucked in a breath. She'd known that Marco shared a room with his mother, but she wasn't prepared to see Maria's things strewn on the bed, hung in the closet, and littering the bathroom counter. The pain of her death permeated Mac's soul. Was there something she could have done differently to return Marco to her before it was too late? She took a deep breath, adding *that* guilt to what she carried for Paddy.

Blindly choosing pants, shirt, and underwear, she rushed back upstairs like the hounds of hell were after her, hoping she wouldn't run into anyone and have to explain her frantic pace.

A few minutes later, with Marco dressed and his hair combed, they went downstairs together. As they approached the dining area, she heard muffled voices, but when she and Marco stepped in the room, even that ceased. Joe, Ty, and Walker sat at one table. Brady, Logan, Rayna, and Sanchez sat next to them, and they all appeared involved in whatever conversation had been going on. A half dozen of Joe's men, whom she'd seen helping in the aftermath of last night's gun battle but had yet to be introduced to, ate at various tables around the room.

The silence hung conspicuously for a few seconds, and then, as one, everyone stood and came forward to greet

TEMPT THE NIGHT 343

Marco, pat him on the back, or kneel down and give him a few words of encouragement. Tears came unbidden, but Mac smiled through them, her heart nearly bursting with pride for Joe's team as well as for Marco, who accepted their heartfelt attention more gracefully than a five-year-old should.

Finally, Marco took a plate and began to select from the buffet along the sideboard. Mac followed him, clutching a plate in her hands for something to hold on to, but the smell of sausage and southwestern omelets only served to start her stomach roiling. Not even Irene's coffee and blueberry muffins could tempt her today.

Brady came up behind her, so close his shoulder brushed her back and sent a tingle radiating through her. "Holding up okay, sugar?"

Determined not to show how much his disappearing act had hurt and confused her, she turned partway and smiled as she met his concerned gaze. "I'm okay."

"You're not eating? You have to keep your strength up, you know." He raised one eyebrow.

"Maybe I'll come back a little later." She stepped sideways as she followed Marco down the table. Since she wasn't sure what to say to Brady, getting stuck alone with him would be totally awkward. She needn't have worried. Just then, Joe, Walker, and the rest of the team began pushing in their chairs, clearing their dishes, and getting ready to leave.

Brady glanced their way and frowned. "Time to go. Ty got the new recruits stopped in time, so that means the rest of us have a lot of fence to fix." He leaned toward her

344 DIXIE LEE BROWN

and kissed her forehead, his hands never once touching her. "Take care of yourself."

She watched him until he disappeared from sight. *Take care of yourself?* She'd wanted a sign that he felt something—anything—for her that would make her choose to stay, and she'd gotten *take care of yourself.* Not too many ways that could be interpreted. Suddenly she yearned for fresh air—and time alone.

A few minutes later, Darcy and Cara entered the dining area just as Marco was finishing his waffles and sausage. Darcy promised to show him how to build a volcano, and Marco, momentarily at least, forgot his grief and got enthused about the project. Between all of them, maybe they could keep him too busy to think about his mother for the next few days. Then the funeral would come along and knock him down again.

Mac excused herself from the science project the others were animatedly discussing and headed outside for a walk. The scent of pine trees drifted in on the breeze. The temperature was on the chilly side, or maybe the chill came from stepping down off the porch and standing in the same spot where Maria had died. It was wrong for the sun to shine so brilliantly, promising another holdover summer day, when just last night war had been declared on Mac's safe place. If not for the men fixing the fence that had been breached and the hole in Marco's life that could never be mended, she might have believed nothing had changed.

The dogs were loose, and they came barreling toward her as soon as she set foot out of the house. "Sit." Joe's

TEMPT THE NIGHT 345

command came from her left, and Dillon and Ribs immediately dropped to their haunches. "Sorry. They go crazy when they see someone who might play with them."

Mac smiled as she scratched the two well-behaved dogs. "Is this what you call crazy?" She glanced toward Joe and forced her smile to stay in place when she saw Brady walking beside him.

His baggy camo pants and plain black T-shirt looked anything but plain on him. The shirt stretched across his chest and shoulders, tapering nicely to his flat stomach. The sleeves expanded to encompass his biceps as they flexed. When her approving gaze reached his face, a muscle worked in his jaw and a barely noticeable grin touched his lips.

"This is them begging someone to throw the ball. Don't look in their eyes or you'll fall under their spell too." Joe shook his head, crossing his arms over his chest. At that moment, his cell phone rang, and he answered it, stepping away from them to have his conversation.

Brady held up an old, ragged baseball. "If you think you might be game, my arm could use a break." He smiled in that way he had that made her feel special.

But this time it filled her with sadness. She cleared her throat and broke the spell. "Sure. If they want to walk along with me, I'll throw the ball for them."

He handed her the ball. "Walks and playing fetch. Those are their two favorite things—other than food, of course. Which way are you going?"

Mac glanced toward the Plateau to the north. "Anywhere but there."

346 DIXIE LEE BROWN

His eyes flashed with anger, but when he met her gaze again, understanding radiated from him. "There's a nice trail along the lake. If you don't mind me tagging along, maybe we could talk."

Instantly, anxiety left her throat dry. What did he have to say to her that hadn't already been said? Was he going to ask her to leave? It was within his right. This was *his* home. His mixed signals had her all over the place emotionally. In one way, it'd be a relief to finally know. It was one thing, though, to assume how he felt based on his actions and body language, but another entirely to hear the icy cold words of dismissal. Still, the freedom of a walk outside the fence was too good to pass up, and the specter of Maria's death was still too close to feel secure enough to go alone. She pasted a grateful smile in place and started to accept his offer.

"Mac. Phone for you." Joe strode toward her, his face a closed mask, hiding his emotions.

"That's impossible. Who would know to call me on your cell phone?" She snorted skeptically.

Joe's expression turned even more serious. "A friend of yours. Patrick Callahan." He continued to hold the phone out to her.

Pain knifed through her as she searched Joe's eyes for confirmation that he was playing a very bad joke. His gaze never wavered. It took a few seconds to comprehend the meaning behind his words, and when she did, her legs gave out at the same time her heart started pounding like a bass drum. Brady caught her, and he snuggled her up tight against his chest, his arms

TEMPT THE NIGHT 347

wrapped around her stomach. She glanced nervously at Joe's phone.

"Breathe, Mac." Brady's words were authoritative... and kind at the same time. "Joe wouldn't tell you it was Callahan if he didn't have good reason to believe it was him. Right, Joe?"

"I asked Special Agent Hanford to check on the final resting place of your friend." Joe shrugged. "I figured someday you'd want to know. What he found was a surprise to everyone. Callahan was shot five times that night. If he hadn't had a bulletproof vest on, he'd have never made it to the ER. As it was, he was wounded twice—once in the throat and once in the leg. Agents of the State Department, investigating Hernandez's sudden appearance in Alaska, got him to the hospital before he bled out. Hanford couldn't tell anyone that Callahan had survived until Hernandez was no longer a danger—not even me. But this morning he told Callahan where you were and gave him my number."

"But...he was dead...he...so much blood..."

Brady kissed the top of her head. "Sweetheart, was he alive when you escaped the warehouse?"

She trembled violently, grateful for Brady's protective arms around her. "I don't know. He was...and then Simpson shot him point-blank. He couldn't survive that, could he?" Mac leaned her head back and met his eyes.

He heaved a sigh. "In Iraq, I saw people survive who didn't have a chance in hell. It happens, Mac. If it *is* him, don't you want to talk to him? We can give you some privacy whenever you're ready."

348 DIXIE LEE BROWN

Could it really be Paddy? For the first time in her life, she was having trouble coming up with the right words to say to her best friend. That just wasn't right. She'd have to do better than that. She straightened within Brady's arms and dried the tears that had squeezed beneath her eyelids. Brady loosened his grip, but she laid her hand on his arm. "Don't you dare let me go. I need you—both of you. Joe, please put the phone on speaker."

A moment of silence passed.

"Mac?" The voice was a slow, agonizing rasp.

She winced, imagining the pain he must be in from the wound in his throat alone. "Paddy? Is it really you?"

"Doesn't sound like me...I know. You're skeptical. What if I tell you that I worried about you and old man Wagner's dumbwaiter? Knew you'd give those two morons the slip...but those old cables...and with you being so much heavier now." He stopped, obviously waiting for her retort.

It may not have sounded like him, but Paddy was definitely on the other end of that phone connection. She could hear the laughter in his voice, but she wasn't going to rise to the bait—not this time. Her best friend had been given back to her, and there were much more important topics to discuss.

Brady pulled her closer as she wiped at her tears again. "Where are you, Paddy?"

"Hospital in Anchorage. ICU until this morning. Didn't know if you'd made it out...or where you were until about twenty minutes ago. The State Department kept a lid on it until they determined the extent

TEMPT THE NIGHT 349

of corruption within the state troopers. They were after Hernandez, but I understand your friends took care of that little problem."

"Paddy...Maria's dead."

He let his breath out slowly. "I know. I can't deal with that right now. There's something else more important."

She could hear the exhaustion in his voice. "Nothing is more important than your recovery."

"Yes, something is. I'm Marco's father now. Maria and I were married two months ago, and I adopted him. Mac...I don't know anything about being a father."

Joe's eyes registered his surprise, and Brady stood up straighter, holding her steady with a hand on both sides of her waist.

Her smile came without effort. "State Trooper Patrick Callahan...you're going to make a great dad, but you're going to regret the day you decided not to tell me about Maria."

A wispy laugh came over the phone. "Sure. *Now* you start calling me by my proper name and title—now that I'm done with the troopers."

"What do you mean?" The troopers had always been his dream.

"I'm permanently disabled on their roster now, which means I'm useless to them."

Mac didn't miss the bitterness in his voice. "Paddy. I'm so sorry."

"Don't worry about it. I'm not. Maybe I'll find something that lets me use my brain and a computer instead of my brawn."

350   DIXIE LEE BROWN

Joe leaned toward the phone. "Call me back when you're ready, Callahan. I may have something you'll be interested in."

"Thanks, Reynolds. I just might do that, but I've got a lot of recovering to do first. Mac, I'm sorry I kept you in the dark. I thought I could keep you out of Hernandez's sights. You just went in blind instead. Will you forgive me?"

She slapped her hand over her mouth to stop the sob that nearly choked her. It was a few seconds before she trusted her voice again. "I'll think of some way you can make it up to me."

Paddy chuckled. "That's the girl I remember. Listen, I filled in all the blanks with the troopers regarding Simpson and Gallagher, so you don't have to worry. You're a free woman again. One more thing. Will you watch over Marco for me until I can get on my feet?"

"Of course. Don't worry about anything, Paddy."

"I have to go, Mac. Getting dirty looks from a very pretty nurse, and I need to hit her with my charm."

They laughed together. God, she'd missed that.

"I'll call you. Are you staying put for a while?"

"I'll be here for a little while longer, but I'm going to call you every day. You'll be *so* tired of me before I get up there to take care of you." He'd probably laugh if she told him how lost she'd been without him until Brady bulldozed his way into her life.

"No sense coming here yet. My parents and your parents are both here...trying to outdo each other to get on my nerves. Besides, my little nurse won't let me

TEMPT THE NIGHT 351

have visitors. She wants me all to herself. Hey…give me that—"

Paddy was gone, the connection evidently terminated by his pretty little nurse. Mac couldn't wipe the grin off her face. She was so relieved to be out from under the guilt she'd carried since the last time she saw Paddy alive. And knowing she wasn't wanted for murder, that she could return home anytime she wanted or visit her parents was like a fresh breeze in her soul. No doubt she'd still have to sit through her father's grilling because he would likely never understand why his baby girl didn't go to him for help. That was probably the real reason Paddy told her not to come yet, and she loved him all the more for it.

Joe returned her smile as he pocketed his phone and palmed her shoulder. "That's what you call the start of a good day." He whistled, and the dogs jumped up to follow him as he strode toward their kennels.

Brady's hands were still firmly locked around her waist.

She moved to step away from him, but he didn't give an inch. "Thanks for staying with me, Brady. It meant a lot to me, but you can let go. I'm okay now."

"No. Not yet. We need to talk. We can either do it here or upstairs. Those are your choices." Brady leaned close and breathed the last part in her ear.

In an instant, her euphoria at finding Paddy alive was overshadowed by the talk Brady wanted to have. Of course she didn't want to stand there, where everyone could see them and witness her humiliation, but she seemed incapable of making this tiny decision. Her feet might as well have been nailed to the turf.

She refused to look at him, even when he stepped around in front of her. He took her chin between his thumb and forefinger and lifted until she met his gaze. "What's it going to be?"

Mac jerked her head from his grasp and backed away. "I...I can't do this right now." She rushed up the steps and across the porch and pushed through the entrance.

Brady caught the door before it closed, jogged a couple of steps until he was in front of her, and turned, walking backward to stay ahead of her. "What can't you do? Are you trying to tell me you want me to leave you alone?"

That wasn't what *she* wanted. "Isn't that what you want? No strings...nothing permanent?"

Brady stopped suddenly, and Mac collided with a solid wall of muscle. He reached around her, drawing her closer before she could step back. "That's the last thing I want, Mac."

She pushed ineffectively against his chest, frustration seeping into her words. "Really? You gave a very nice speech warning me that you don't have anything other than mind-blowing sex to offer. Isn't that what you said? Oh, let me guess—you want to sleep with me again? You know what? Let's do that, but don't expect me to forget that you're just using me. I'm sorry that I can't be as clinical as you. I really care about you, but you won't ever have feelings for me beyond the bedroom. I get it, so can we just drop this?"

"Mac." His lips pursed disapprovingly.

She glanced around the hallway. "If you don't want all of your friends to hear this, you really should let me go now."

"I don't give a damn who hears us. We're going to talk this out."

She heard the warning in his voice, but she still wasn't prepared when he hoisted her over his shoulder like a sack of potatoes and started up the stairs. She hissed and fumed until she got enough air in her lungs to form sounds. "Put me down, you overgrown Ewok. You have *so* done it now. That sex I suggested? *Off* the table."

His big hand slapped her hard on her bottom. She gasped and pummeled his back with her fists. A door opened and closed, and then he shrugged her off his shoulder, reaching out to catch her around the waist before she crashed in a miserable heap at his feet.

Mac glanced around, ascertained they were in her bedroom, and looked at him. "How dare you! You have no claim on me, remember? That means you have no right to touch me or pick me up…and if you *ever* slap my ass again I'll…I'll make you the sorriest man on earth."

A cocky grin creased Brady's face. With deliberate movements, he snaked his hand along her spine and into her hair, wrapped it once around his fist, and pulled her head back. His other hand moved downward, squeezing her bottom and pulling her into direct contact with the hard ridge in his pants. On a feral growl, his mouth came down on hers with restrained menace.

A twinge of anger ripped through her, and her heart pounded in her ears as she braced her arms against him

354 DIXIE LEE BROWN

and shoved. His kiss became more fervent and demanding, turning her protests into moans. Sure and strong, his mouth devoured hers until she became his to do with as he pleased. Velvet soft lips coaxed hers open. Her body, seriously lacking willpower, responded in kind, heat and desire making it hard to remember why this was a bad idea. Damn him to hell.

Little by little, she gave in and molded her body with his, leaning into his kiss and letting her arms wrap around him. He released his grip on her hair, moving both hands lower to hold her in place while he rocked his hips forward. His erection pressed into her stomach. She let out a moan, lost in the intensity of raw and primitive emotions.

He scraped his stubbled cheek lightly over hers until his lips hovered by her ear. A deep breath sent a shiver through her. "I'm sorry my selfish words hurt you." Another deep breath. "I'm in love with you, Mac."

She drew back and stared, momentarily forgetting to breathe. His eyes sparkled dangerously, desire just beneath the surface. His face, rough and masculine, spoke of honesty, integrity, and peace that she'd never seen there before.

Mac pushed against his arms, and this time he let her go. She took a step back and studied him with helpless fascination, his strength and stature making her feel safe even two feet away.

"Would you please say something?" Brady's tone was deadly calm, and nervous energy danced in his eyes.

TEMPT THE NIGHT 355

"What about all that other stuff? The violence that you seem sure you can't control? Will you want me today and tell me it's over tomorrow? Because I don't really take rejection very well. Not this time—not from you."

"We've got a lot of talking to do…about the nightmare I still wake up in sometimes and the anger that obliterates all my good intentions. You're the only one who's ever been able to reach me and keep the darkness from taking over. I think there's a reason for that. I think we were meant to be together…and that's what I want." Brady squeezed his hands into fists.

"Last night when Hernandez had you, all of my other demons paled in comparison to the possibility of losing you. I know now that I would never hurt you. There's no way in hell that could ever happen. You're the other half of me. The answer to my every need." He raised his hands in surrender. "I'd understand if you were skeptical, though. Stay with me, and we'll take things nice and slow until you're as sure as I am. Or…tell me you don't trust me, and I'll let you go."

With difficulty, Mac held back the joy and excitement that were trying to break free. She searched his face for anything other than the earnestness that made the muscle work in his jaw. All she saw was hope and love. Her smile slowly curved her lips.

His answering grin fueled a gleam of triumph in his eyes.

"I've always known you wouldn't hurt me, from the moment you knocked me down and sat on me that first

356 **DIXIE LEE BROWN**

night." She took a step closer and placed her hand on his arm to convince herself this was really happening. "You're sure? This is not just short-term?"

His arms slid around her, and he kissed her, gently this time. Then he swept her up, strode to the bed, and dropped her in the middle. Immediately, he flopped beside her, pulling her against him for another lingering kiss.

"Stay with me. Move into my room, or maybe I should move into yours. It's a little bigger, and currently, it's the only occupied room on the third floor. Privacy is good for what I have in mind." His gaze burned with fire and intensity. "My plan is to marry you, sugar. That's as permanent as it gets. We'll start looking for a place in town right away."

"What? Wait a minute. Why do you want to move into town?"

"It's great here—don't get me wrong. But there are people everywhere, and everyone knows your business. It's like living in Mayberry. I want you to be comfortable." Brady ran his hand up her side, under her top, and teased the underside of her breast.

"Okay, first of all...stop making decisions for me. And second...are you asking me to marry you?" Brady's grin made her smile as he pulled her close again.

He captured a lock of hair and forced it behind her ear. "Well, yes, but only if you...have strong enough feelings for me." He wrinkled his nose and made a pitiful face.

She laughed, feeling more settled and comfortable than she had her whole life. "Let's see. I had some pretty

TEMPT THE NIGHT 357

strong feelings when you were carrying me up the stairs...
and when you slapped me." Mac narrowed her gaze and
poked her finger at his chest. "I owe you for that, mister."

He massaged the bare skin on her stomach. "I owe
you for the *overgrown Ewok* crack. You might say we're
even." Leaning forward, he lightly nipped her throat,
then licked it until the sting went away. When he looked
at her, the question was still in his eyes.

Mac propped on her elbow and lowered her mouth
next to his ear. "I love you, Brady."

Instantly, he flipped her onto her back and sat astride
her exactly as he had the first night they met. Mac
laughed. "What are you doing?"

"Fulfilling a fantasy that started that night. You were
so soft and vulnerable, and I was so damned hard." He
slid his hand beneath her top, pushing the fabric up as he
moved. When he came to her bra, he stretched it down
and cupped each breast. Then he leaned over, gripping
her tightly with his legs, and took first one breast and
then the other into his mouth and suckled her.

Mac felt the jolt of need in her center, and she arched
her body to bring her throbbing ache into contact with his
engorged manhood.

Brady straightened, love shining in his eyes. "Time for
you to get out of those clothes, Samantha McCallister." In
one motion, he lifted her shirt over her head and tossed it
to the right. Her bra flew to the left.

Mac laughed and pulled him close as he landed beside
her again, one hand jerking open the button and zipper
on her jeans and slipping inside. She bit back a moan

358 DIXIE LEE BROWN

when he found her hub and worked his fingers until she was breathing in rhythm with his strokes.

"What do you say, Mac? Marry me?" He bit her lip and kissed her gently.

Mac was close to climax and lucky she could even speak. "Um...if you're...if you're...*yes!*"

Brady took her mouth, pushing his tongue inside, claiming her very essence in the process. When there was nothing left to hold back, he pushed to his knees and worked her jeans off, leaving only her panties.

He outlined the edges of her bikini underwear with a feather-light touch that tickled and sent her into a heightened state of desire. "What do you want, Mac? Tell me."

She covered his whiskered cheeks with trembling hands. "You, Brady. Only you."

Are you caught up in Dixie Lee Brown's
thrilling Trust No One series?

Don't miss these heart-stopping tales of
love and suspense, available now
from Avon Impulse:

All or Nothing
When I Find You
If You Only Knew
Whatever It Takes

About the Author

DIXIE LEE BROWN lives and writes in Central Oregon, inspired by what she believes is the most gorgeous scenery anywhere. She resides with two dogs and a cat, who make sure she never takes herself too seriously. When she's not writing, she enjoys reading, movies, and trips to the beach.

Discover great authors, exclusive offers, and more at hc.com.

Give in to your impulses . . .
Read on for a sneak peek at seven brand-new
e-book original tales of romance
from HarperCollins.
Available now wherever e-books are sold.

VARIOUS STATES OF UNDRESS: GEORGIA

By Laura Simcox

MAKE IT LAST

A BOWLER UNIVERSITY NOVEL

By Megan Erickson

HERO BY NIGHT

BOOK THREE: INDEPENDENCE FALLS

By Sara Jane Stone

MAYHEM

By Jamie Shaw

SINFUL REWARDS 1
A Billionaires and Bikers Novella
By Cynthia Sax

FORBIDDEN
An Under the Skin Novel
By Charlotte Stein

HER HIGHLAND FLING
A Novella
By Jennifer McQuiston

An Excerpt from

VARIOUS STATES OF UNDRESS: GEORGIA

by Laura Simcox

Laura Simcox concludes her fun, flirty
Various States of Undress series with a
presidential daughter, a hot baseball player,
and a tale of love at the ballgame.

An Excerpt from

VARIOUS STATES OF UNDRESS: GEORGIA

by Laura Simcox

Laura Simcox concludes her fun, flirty
Various States of Undress series with a
presidential daughter, a hot baseball player,
and a fate of love at the ballgame.

"Uh. Hi."

Georgia splayed her hand over the front of her wet blouse and stared. The impossibly tanned guy standing just inside the doorway—wearing a tight T-shirt, jeans, and a smile—was as still as a statue. A statue with fathomless, unblinking chocolate brown eyes. She let her gaze drop from his face to his broad chest. "Oh. Hello. I was expecting someone else."

He didn't comment, but when she lifted her gaze again, past his wide shoulders and carved chin, she watched his smile turn into a grin, revealing way-too-sexy brackets at the corners of his mouth. He walked down the steps and onto the platform where she stood. He had to be at least 6'3", and testosterone poured off him like heat waves on the field below. She shouldn't stare at him, right? Damn. Her gaze flicked from him to the glass wall but moved right back again.

"Scared of heights?" he asked. His voice was a slow, deep Southern drawl. Sexy deep. "Maybe you oughta sit down."

"No, thanks. I was just . . . looking for something."

Looking for something? Like what—a tryst with a stranger in the press box? Her face heated, and she clutched the water bottle, the plastic making a snapping sound under her fingers. "So . . . how did you get past my agents?"

He smiled again. "They know who I am."

"And you are?"

"Brett Knox."

His name sounded familiar. "Okay. I'm Georgia Fulton. It's nice to meet you," she said, putting down her water.

He shook her hand briefly. "You, too. But I just came up here to let you know that I'm declining the interview. Too busy."

Georgia felt herself nodding in agreement, even as she realized *exactly* who Brett Knox was. He was the star catcher—and right in front of her, shooting her down before she'd even had a chance to ask. Such a typical jock.

"I'm busy, too, which is why I'd like to set up a time that's convenient for both of us," she said, even though she hoped it wouldn't be necessary. But she couldn't very well walk into the news station without accomplishing what she'd been tasked with—pinning him down. Georgia was a team player. So was Brett, literally.

"I don't want to disappoint my boss, and I'm betting you feel the same way about yours," she continued.

"Sure. I sign autographs, pose for photos, visit Little League teams. Like I said, I'm busy."

"That's nice." She nodded. "I'm flattered that you found the time to come all the way up to the press box and tell me, in person, that you don't have time for an interview. Thanks."

He smiled a little. "You're welcome." Then he stretched, his broad chest expanding with the movement. He flexed his long fingers, braced a hand high on the post, and grinned at her again. Her heart flipped down into her stomach. Oh, no.

"I get it, you know. I've posed for photos and signed au-

Various States of Undress: Georgia

tographs, too. I've visited hospitals and ribbon cutting ceremonies, and I know it makes people happy. But public appearances can be draining, and it takes time away from work. Right?"

"Right." He gave her a curious look. "We have that in common, though it's not exactly the same. I may be semifamous in Memphis, but I don't have paparazzi following me around, and I like it that way. You interviewing me would turn into a big hassle."

"I won't take much of your time. Just think of me as another reporter." She ventured a warm, inviting smile, and Brett's dark eyes widened. "The paparazzi don't follow me like they do my sisters. I'm the boring one."

"Really?" He folded his arms across his lean middle, and his gaze traveled slowly over her face.

She felt her heart speed up. "Yes, really."

"I beg to differ."

Before she could respond, he gave her another devastating smile and jogged up the steps. It was the best view she'd had all day. When Brett disappeared, she collapsed back against the post. He was right, of course. She wasn't just another reporter; she was the president's brainy daughter—who secretly lusted after athletes. And she'd just met a hell of an athlete.

Talk about a hot mess.

An Excerpt from

MAKE IT LAST
A Bowler University Novel
by Megan Erickson

The last installment in Megan Erickson's daringly sexy Bowler University series finds Cam Ruiz back in his hometown of Paradise, where he comes face-to-face with the only girl he ever loved.

Cam sighed, feeling the weight of responsibility pressing down on his shoulders. But if he didn't help his mom, who would?

He jingled his keys in his pocket and turned to walk toward his truck. It was nice of Max and Lea to visit him on their road trip. College had been some of the best years of his life. Great friends, fun parties, hot girls.

But now it felt like a small blip, like a week vacation instead of three and a half years. And now he was right back where he started.

As he walked by the alley beside the restaurant, something flickered out of the corner of his eye.

He turned and spotted her legs first. One foot bent at the knee and braced on the brick wall, the other flat on the ground. Her head was bent, a curtain of hair blocking her face. But he knew those legs. He knew those hands. And he knew that hair, a light brown that held just a glint of strawberry in the sun. He knew by the end of August it'd be lighter and redder and she'd laugh about that time she put lemon juice in it. It'd backfired and turned her hair orange.

The light flickered again but it was something weird and artificial, not like the menthols she had smoked. Back when he knew her.

As she lowered her hand down to her side, he caught sight of the small white cylinder. It was an electronic cigarette. She'd quit.

She raised her head then, like she knew someone watched her, and he wanted to keep walking, avoid this awkward moment. Avoid those eyes he didn't think he'd ever see again and never thought he'd wanted to see again. But now that his eyes locked on her hazel eyes—the ones he knew began as green on the outside of her iris and darkened to brown by the time they met her pupil—he couldn't look away. His boots wouldn't move.

The small cigarette fell to the ground with a soft click and she straightened, both her feet on the ground.

And that was when he noticed the wedge shoes. And the black apron. What was she doing here?

"Camilo."

Other than his mom, she was the only one who used his full name. He'd heard her say it while laughing. He'd her moan it while he was inside her. He'd heard her sigh it with an eye roll when he made a bad joke. But he'd never heard it the way she said it now, with a little bit of fear and anxiety and . . . longing? He took a deep breath to steady his voice. "Tatum."

He hadn't spoken her name since that night Trevor called him and told him what she did. The night the future that he'd set out for himself and for her completely changed course.

She'd lost some weight in the four years since he'd last seen her. He'd always loved her curves. She had it all—thighs, ass and tits in abundance. Naked, she was a fucking vision.

Damn it, he wasn't going there.

Make It Last

But now her face looked thinner, her clothes hung a little loose and he didn't like this look as much. Not that she probably gave a fuck about his opinion anymore.

She still had her gorgeous hair, pinned up halfway with a bump in front, and a smattering of freckles across the bridge of her nose and on her cheekbones. And she still wore her makeup exactly the same—thickly mascaraed eyelashes, heavy eyeliner that stretched to a point on the outside of her eyes, like a modern-day Audrey Hepburn.

She was still beautiful. And she still took his breath away.

And his heart felt like it was breaking all over again.

And he hated her even more for that.

Her eyes were wide. "What are you doing here?"

Something in him bristled at that. Maybe it was because he didn't feel like he belonged here. But then, she didn't either. She never did. *They* never did.

But there was no longer a *they*.

An Excerpt from

HERO BY NIGHT
Book Three: Independence Falls
by *Sara Jane Stone*

Travel back to Independence Falls in Sara Jane Stone's next thrilling read. Armed with a golden retriever and a concealed weapons permit, Lena Clark is fighting for normal. She served her country, but the experience left her afraid to be touched and estranged from her career-military family. Staying in Independence Falls, and finding a job, seems like the first step to reclaiming her life and preparing for the upcoming medal ceremony— until the town playboy stumbles into her bed . . .

Sometimes beauty knocked a man on his ass, leaving him damn near desperate for a taste, a touch, and hopefully a round or two between the sheets—or tied up in them. The knockout blonde with the large golden retriever at her feet took the word "beautiful" to a new level.

Chad Summers stared at her, unable to look away or dim the smile on his face. He usually masked his interest better, stopping short of looking like he was begging for it before learning a woman's name. But this mysterious beauty had special written all over her.

She stared at him, her gaze open and wanting. For a heartbeat. Then she turned away, her back to the party as she stared out at Eric Moore's pond.

Her hair flowed in long waves down her back. One look left him wishing he could wrap his hand around her shiny locks and pull. His gaze traveled over her back, taking in the outline of gentle curves beneath her flowing, and oh-so-feminine, floor-length dress. The thought of the beauty's long skirt decorating her waist propelled him into motion. Chad headed in her direction, moving away from the easy, quiet conversation about God-knew-what on the patio.

The blonde, a mysterious stranger in a sea of familiar faces, might be the spark this party needed. He was a few feet away

SARA JANE STONE

when the dog abandoned his post at her side and cut Chad off. Either the golden retriever was protecting his owner, or the animal was in cahoots with the familiar voice calling his name.

"Chad Summers!"

The blonde turned at the sound, looking first at him, her blue eyes widening as if surprised at how close he stood, and then at her dog. From the other direction, a familiar face with short black hair—Susan maybe?—marched toward him.

Without a word, Maybe Susan stopped by his side and raised her glass. With a dog in front of him, trees to one side, and an angry woman on his other, there was no escape.

"Hi there." He left off her name just in case he'd guessed wrong, but offered a warm, inviting smile. Most women fell for that grin, but if Maybe Susan had at one time—and seeing her up close, she looked very familiar, though he could swear he'd never slept with her—she wasn't falling for it today.

She poured the cool beer over his head, her mouth set in a firm line. "That was for my sister. Susan Lewis? You spent the night with her six months ago and never called."

Chad nodded, silently grateful he hadn't addressed the pissed-off woman by her sister's name. "My apologies, ma'am."

"You're a dog," Susan's sister announced. The animal at his feet stepped forward as if affronted by the comparison.

"For the past six months, my little sister has talked about you, saving every article about your family's company," the angry woman continued.

Whoa . . . Yes, he'd taken Susan Lewis out once and they'd ended the night back at his place, but he could have sworn they were on the same page. Hell, he'd heard her say the words, *I'm not looking for anything serious*, and he'd believed her. It was

Hero By Night

one freaking night. He didn't think he needed signed documents that spelled out his intentions and hers.

"She's practically built a shrine to you," she added, waving her empty beer cup. "Susan was ready to plan your wedding."

"Again, I'm sorry, but it sounds like there was a miscommunication." Chad withdrew a bandana from his back pocket, one that had belonged to his father, and wiped his brow. "But wedding bells are not in my future. At least not anytime soon."

The angry sister shook her head, spun on her heels, and marched off.

Chad turned to the blonde and offered a grin. She looked curious, but not ready to run for the hills. "I guess I made one helluva first impression."

"Hmm." She glanced down at her dog as if seeking comfort in the fact that he stood between them.

"I'm Chad Summers." He held out his hand—the one part of his body not covered in beer.

"You're Katie's brother." She glanced briefly at his extended hand, but didn't take it.

He lowered his arm, still smiling. "Guilty."

"Lena." She nodded to the dog. "That's Hero."

"Nice to meet you both." He looked up the hill. Country music drifted down from the house. Someone had finally added some life to the party. Couples moved to the beat on the blue stone patio, laughing and drinking under the clear Oregon night sky. In the corner, Liam Trulane tossed logs into a fire pit.

"After I dry off," Chad said, turning back to the blonde, "how about a dance?"

"No."

An Excerpt from

MAYHEM

by Jamie Shaw

**A straitlaced college freshman is drawn
to a sexy and charismatic rock star in this
fabulous debut New Adult novel for fans
of Jamie McGuire and Jay Crownover!**

"I can't believe I let you talk me into this." I tug at the black hem of the stretchy nylon skirt my best friend squeezed me into, but unless I want to show the top of my panties instead of the skin of my thighs, there's nothing I can do. After casting yet another uneasy glance at the long line of people stretched behind me on the sidewalk, I shift my eyes back to the sun-warmed fabric pinched between my fingers and grumble, "The least you could've done was let me wear some leggings."

I look like Dee's closet drank too much and threw up on me. She somehow talked me into wearing this mini-skirt—which skintight doesn't even begin to describe—and a hot-pink top that shows more cleavage than should be legal. The front of it drapes all the way down to just above my navel, and the bottom exposes a pale sliver of skin between the hem of the shirt and the top of my skirt. The fabric matches my killer hot-pink heels.

Literally, killer. Because I know I'm going to fall on my face and die.

I'm fiddling with the skirt again when one of the guys near us in line leans in close, a jackass smile on his lips. "I think you look hot."

"I have a boyfriend," I counter, but Dee just scoffs at me.

JAMIE SHAW

"She means *thank you*," she shoots back, chastising me with her tone until the guy flashes us another arrogant smile—he's stuffed into an appallingly snug graphic-print tee that might as well say "douche bag" in its shiny metallic lettering, and even Dee can't help but make a face before we both turn away.

She and I are the first ones in line for the show tonight, standing by the doors to Mayhem under the red-orange glow of a setting summer sun. She's been looking forward to this night for weeks, but I was more excited about it before my boyfriend of three years had to back out.

"Brady is a jerk," she says, and all I can do is sigh because I wish those two could just get along. Deandra and I have been best friends since preschool, but Brady and I have been dating since my sophomore year of high school and living together for the past two months. "He should be here to appreciate how gorgeous you look tonight, but nooo, it's always work first with him."

"He moved all the way here to be with me, Dee. Cut him some slack, all right?"

She grumbles her frustration until she catches me touching my eyelids for the zillionth time tonight. Yanking my fingers away, she orders, "Stop messing with it. You'll smear."

I stare down at my shadowy fingertips and rub them together. "Tell me the truth," I say, flicking the clumped powder away. "Do I look like a clown?"

"You look smoking hot!" she assures me with a smile.

I finally feel like I'm beginning to loosen up when a guy walks right past us like he's going to cut in line. In dark shades and a baggy black knit cap that droops in the back, he flicks a cigarette to the ground, and my eyes narrow on him.

Mayhem

Dee and I have been waiting for way too long to let some self-entitled jerk cut in front of us, so when he knocks on the door to the club, I force myself to speak up.

"They're not letting people in yet," I say, hoping he takes the hint. Even with my skyscraper heels, I feel dwarfed standing next to him. He has to be at least six-foot-two, maybe taller.

He turns his head toward me and lowers his shades, smirking like something's funny. His wrist is covered with string bracelets and rubber bracelets and a thick leather cuff, and three of his fingernails on each hand are painted black. But his eyes are what steal the words from my lips—a greenish shade of light gray. They're stunning.

When the door opens, he turns back to it and locks hands with the bouncer.

"You're late," the bouncer says, and the guy in the shades laughs and slips inside. Once he disappears, Dee pushes my shoulders.

"Oh my GOD! Do you know who you were just talking to?!"

I shake my head.

"That was *Adam* EVEREST! He's the lead singer of the band we're here to see!"

An Excerpt from

SINFUL REWARDS 1
A Billionaires and Bikers Novella
by Cynthia Sax

Belinda "Bee" Carter is a good girl; at least, that's
what she tells herself. And a good girl deserves
a nice guy—just like the gorgeous and moody
billionaire Nicolas Rainer. Or so she thinks,
until she takes a look through her telescope
and sees a naked, tattooed man on the balcony
across the courtyard. He has been watching
her, and that makes him all the more enticing.
But when a mysterious and anonymous text
message dares her to do something bad, she
must decide if she is really the good girl she has
always claimed to be, or if she's willing to risk
everything for her secret fantasy of being watched.

An Avon Red Impulse Novella

An Excerpt from

SINFUL REWARDS 1
A Billionaire and Biker Novella
by Cynthia Sax

Belinda "Bee" Carter is a good girl, at least, that's what she tells herself. And a good girl doesn't lust after a nice guy—just like the gorgeous and moral billionaire Nicolas Rainer. Or so she thinks, until she takes a look through her telescope and sees a naked, tattooed man on the balcony across the courtyard. He has been watching her, and that makes him all the more unsexy. But when a mysterious and anonymous text message dares her to do something bad, she must decide if she's really the good girl she has always claimed to be, or if she's willing to risk everything for her secret fantasy of lust unlocked.

An Avon Red Impulse Novella.

I'd told Cyndi I'd never use it, that it was an instrument purchased by perverts to spy on their neighbors. She'd laughed and called me a prude, not knowing that I was one of those perverts, that I secretly yearned to watch and be watched, to care and be cared for.

If I'm cautious, and I'm always cautious, she'll never realize I used her telescope this morning. I swing the tube toward the bench and adjust the knob, bringing the mysterious object into focus.

It's a phone. Nicolas's phone. I bounce on the balls of my feet. This is a sign, another declaration from fate that we belong together. I'll return Nicolas's much-needed device to him. As a thank you, he'll invite me to dinner. We'll talk. He'll realize how perfect I am for him, fall in love with me, marry me.

Cyndi will find a fiancé also—everyone loves her—and we'll have a double wedding, as sisters of the heart often do. It'll be the first wedding my family has had in generations.

Everyone will watch us as we walk down the aisle. I'll wear a strapless white Vera Wang mermaid gown with organza and lace details, crystal and pearl embroidery accents, the bodice fitted, and the skirt hemmed for my shorter height. My hair will be swept up. My shoes—

CYNTHIA SAX

Voices murmur outside the condo's door, the sound piercing my delightful daydream. I swing the telescope upward, not wanting to be caught using it. The snippets of conversation drift away.

I don't relax. If the telescope isn't positioned in the same way as it was last night, Cyndi will realize I've been using it. She'll tease me about being a fellow pervert, sharing the story, embellished for dramatic effect, with her stern, serious dad—or, worse, with Angel, that snobby friend of hers.

I'll die. It'll be worse than being the butt of jokes in high school because that ridicule was about my clothes and this will center on the part of my soul I've always kept hidden. It'll also be the truth, and I won't be able to deny it. I am a pervert.

I have to return the telescope to its original position. This is the only acceptable solution. I tap the metal tube.

Last night, my man-crazy roommate was giggling over the new guy in three-eleven north. The previous occupant was a gray-haired, bowtie-wearing tax auditor, his luxurious accommodations supplied by Nicolas. The most exciting thing he ever did was drink his tea on the balcony.

According to Cyndi, the new occupant is a delicious piece of man candy—tattooed, buff, and head-to-toe lickable. He was completing armcurls outside, and she enthusiastically counted his reps, oohing and aahing over his bulging biceps, calling to me to take a look.

I resisted that temptation, focusing on making macaroni and cheese for the two of us, the recipe snagged from the diner my mom works in. After we scarfed down dinner, Cyndi licking her plate clean, she left for the club and hasn't returned.

Three-eleven north is the mirror condo to ours. I

Sinful Rewards 1

straighten the telescope. That position looks about right, but then, the imitation UGGs I bought in my second year of college looked about right also. The first time I wore the boots in the rain, the sheepskin fell apart, leaving me barefoot in Economics 201.

Unwilling to risk Cyndi's friendship on "about right," I gaze through the eyepiece. The view consists of rippling golden planes, almost like . . .

Tanned skin pulled over defined abs.

I blink. It can't be. I take another look. A perfect pearl of perspiration clings to a puckered scar. The drop elongates more and more, stretching, snapping. It trickles downward, navigating the swells and valleys of a man's honed torso.

No. I straighten. This is wrong. I shouldn't watch our sexy neighbor as he stands on his balcony. If anyone catches me . . .

Parts 1 – 7 available now!

An Excerpt from

FORBIDDEN
An Under the Skin Novel
by Charlotte Stein

Killian is on the verge of making his final vows
for the priesthood when he saves Dorothy from a
puritanical and oppressive home. The attraction
between them is swift and undeniable, but every
touch, every glance, every moment of connection
between them is completely forbidden . . .

An Avon Red Impulse Novel

An Excerpt from

FORBIDDEN

An Alabaster Skin Novel

by Elisabeth Staab

An Avon Red Impulse Novel

$\mathbf{W}$e get out of the car at this swanky-looking place called Marriott, with a big promise next to the door about all-day breakfasts and internet and other stuff I've never had in my whole life, all these nice cars in the parking lot gleaming in the dimming light and a dozen windows lit up like some Christmas card, and then it just happens. My excitement suddenly bursts out of my chest, and before I can haul it back in, it runs right down the length of my arm, all the way to my hand.

Which grabs hold of his, so tight it could never be mistaken for anything else.

Course I want it to be mistaken for anything else, as soon as he looks at me. His eyes snap to my face like I poked him in the ribs with a rattler snake, and just in case I'm in any doubt, he glances down at the thing I'm doing. He sees me touching him as though he's not nearly a priest and I'm not under his care, and instead we're just two people having some kind of happy honeymoon.

In a second we're going inside to have all the sex.

That's what it seems like—like a sex thing.

I can't even explain it away as just being friendly, because somehow it doesn't feel friendly at all. My palm has been laced with electricity, and it just shot ten thousand volts into

CHARLOTTE STEIN

him. His whole body has gone tense, and so my body goes tense, but the worst part about it is:

For some ungodly reason he doesn't take his hand away.

Maybe he thinks if he does it will look bad, like admitting to a guilty thing that neither of us has done. Or at least that he hasn't done. He didn't ask to have his hand grabbed. His hand is totally innocent in all of this. My hand is the evil one. It keeps right on grasping him even after I tell it to stop. I don't even care if it makes me look worse—*just let go*, I think at it.

But the hand refuses.

It still has him in its evil clutches when we go inside the motel. My fingers are starting to sweat, and the guy behind the counter is noticing, yet I can't seem to do a single thing about it. Could be we have to spend the rest of our lives like this, out of sheer terror at drawing any attention to the thing I have done.

Unless he's just carrying on because he thinks I'm scared of this place. Maybe he thinks I need comfort, in which case all of this might be okay. I am just a girl with her friendly, good-looking priest, getting a motel room in a real honest and platonic way so I can wash my lank hair and secretly watch television about spaceships.

Nothing is going to happen—a fact that I communicate to the counter guy with my eyes. I don't know why I'm doing it, however. He doesn't know Killian is a priest. He has no clue that I'm some beat-up kid who needs help and protection rather than sordid hand-holding. He probably thinks we're married, just like I thought before, and the only thing that makes that idea kind of off is how I look in comparison.

Forbidden

I could pass for a stripe of beige paint next to him. In here his black hair is like someone took a slice out of the night sky. His cheekbones are so big and manly I could bludgeon the counter guy with them, and I'm liable to do it. He keeps staring, even after Killian says "two rooms please." He's still staring as we go down the carpeted hallway, to the point where I have to ask.

"Why was he looking like that?" I whisper as Killian fits a key that is not really a key but a gosh darn credit card into a room door. So of course I'm looking at that when he answers me, and not at his face.

But I wish I had been. I wish I'd seen his expression when he spoke, because when he did he said the single most startling thing I ever heard in my whole life.

"He was looking because you're lovely."

An Excerpt from

HER HIGHLAND FLING
A Novella
by Jennifer McQuiston

When his little Scottish town is in desperate
straits, William MacKenzie decides to resurrect
the Highland Games in an effort to take
advantage of the new tourism boom and invites
a London newspaper to report on the events.
He's prepared to show off for the sake of the
town, but the one thing William never expects
is for this intrepid reporter to be a she . . .

William scowled. Moraig's future was at stake. The town's economy was hardly prospering, and its weathered residents couldn't depend on fishing and gossip to sustain them forever. They needed a new direction, and as the Earl of Kilmartie's heir, he felt obligated to sort out a solution. He'd spent months organizing the upcoming Highland Games. It was a calculated risk that, if properly orchestrated, would ensure the betterment of every life in town. It had seemed a brilliant opportunity to reach those very tourists they were aiming to attract.

But with the sweat now pooling in places best left unmentioned and the minutes ticking slowly by, that brilliance was beginning to tarnish.

William peered down the road that led into town, imagining he could see a cloud of dust implying the arrival of the afternoon coach. The very *late* afternoon coach. But all he saw was the delicate shimmer of heat reflecting the nature of the devilishly hot day.

"Bugger it all," he muttered. "How late can a coach be? There's only one route from Inverness." He plucked at the damp collar of his shirt, wondering where the coachman could be. "Mr. Jeffers knew the importance of being on time today. We need to make a ripping first impression on this reporter."

James's gaze dropped once more to William's bare legs. "Oh, I don't think there's any doubt of it." He leaned against the posthouse wall and crossed his arms. "If I might ask the question . . . why turn it into such a circus? Why these Games instead of, say, a well-placed rumor of a beastie living in Loch Moraig? You've got the entire town in an uproar preparing for it."

William could allow that James was perhaps a bit distracted by his pretty wife and new baby—and understandably so. But given that his brother was raising his bairns here, shouldn't he want to ensure Moraig's future success more than anyone?

James looked up suddenly, shading his eyes with a hand. "Well, best get those knees polished to a shine. There's your coach now. Half hour late, as per usual."

With a near-groan of relief, William stood at attention on the posthouse steps as the mail coach roared up in a choking cloud of dust and hot wind.

A half hour off schedule. Perhaps it wasn't the tragedy he'd feared. They could skip the initial stroll down Main Street he'd planned and head straight to the inn. He could point out some of the pertinent sights later, when he showed the man the competition field that had been prepared on the east side of town.

"And dinna tell the reporter I'm the heir," William warned as an afterthought. "We want him to think of Moraig as a charming and rustic retreat from London." If the town was to

Her Highland Fling

have a future, it needed to be seen as a welcome escape from titles and peers and such, and he did not want this turning into a circus where he stood at the center of the ring.

As the coach groaned to a stop, James clapped William on the shoulder with mock sympathy. "Don't worry. With those bare legs, I suspect your reporter will have enough to write about without nosing about the details of your inheritance."

The coachman secured the reins and jumped down from his perch. A smile of amusement broke across Mr. Jeffers's broad features. "Wore the plaid today, did we?"

Bloody hell. Not Jeffers, too.

"You're late." William scowled. "Were there any problems fetching the chap from Inverness?" He was anxious to greet the reporter, get the man properly situated in the Blue Gander, and then go home to change into something less . . . *Scottish.* And God knew he could also use a pint or three, though preferably ones not raised at his expense.

Mr. Jeffers pushed the brim of his hat up an inch and scratched his head. "Well, see, here's the thing. I dinna exactly fetch a chap, as it were."

This time William couldn't suppress the growl that erupted from his throat. "Mr. Jeffers, don't tell me you *left* him there!" It would be a nightmare if he had. The entire thing was carefully orchestrated, down to a reservation for the best room the Blue Gander had to offer. The goal had been to install the reporter safely in Moraig and give him a taste of the town's charms *before* the Games commenced on Saturday.

"Well, I . . . that is . . ." Mr. Jeffers's gaze swung between them, and he finally shrugged. "Well, I suppose you'll see well enough for yourself."

He turned the handle, then swung the coach door open.

A gloved hand clasped Mr. Jeffers's palm, and then a high, elegant boot flashed into sight.

"What in the blazes—" William started to say, only to choke on his surprise as a blonde head dipped into view. A body soon followed, stepping down in a froth of blue skirts. She dropped Jeffers's hand and looked around with bright interest.

"Your chap's a lass," explained a bemused Mr. Jeffers.

"A lass?" echoed William stupidly.

And not only a lass . . . a very pretty lass.

She smiled at them, and it was like the sun cresting over the hills that rimmed Loch Moraig, warming all who were fortunate enough to fall in its path. He was suddenly and inexplicably consumed by the desire to recite poetry to the sound of twittering birds. That alone might have been manageable, but as her eyes met his, he was also consumed by an unfortunate jolt of lustful awareness that left no inch of him unscathed—and there were quite a few inches to cover.

"Miss Penelope Tolbertson," she said, extending her gloved hand as though she were a man. "R-reporter for the *London Times*."

He stared at her hand, unsure of whether to shake it or kiss it. Her manners might be bold, but her voice was like butter, flowing over his body until it didn't know which end was up. His tongue seemed wrapped in cotton, muffling even the merest hope of a proper greeting.

Her Highland Fling

The reporter was female?

And not only female . . . a veritable goddess, with eyes the color of a fair Highland sky?

He raised his eyes to meet hers, giving himself up to the sense of falling.

Or perhaps more aptly put, a sense of flailing.

"W-welcome to Moraig, Miss Tolbertson."